CW00381595

KARRAN KINRADE
Volume Two in the continuing story of
the people of
THE ISLAND

Karran was only a child when she came
to live at Ravensdowne – a bastard child
who was used to living rough and
working hard. The luxuries of life as
John Howard's ward at first nearly over-
whelmed her. Her calloused hands and
ragged nails became smooth. She learned
to read and write, to wear clothes like a
lady.

But, as she grew up, it was inevitable that
someone as beautiful, as aloof, as she
was would never be accepted by the
people of the Island. The women
resented her, the men all longed to
possess her. She walked a narrow and
lonely path between the two.

And when she discovered the stranger in
the old stone cottage on the cliff, the
stranger who seemed as much of a misfit
as she was, she fell wildly, hopelessly in
love . . .

Also by Alexandra Manners
ECHOING YESTERDAY
and published by Corgi Books

Karran Kinrade

Volume Two in *The Island* series

ALEXANDRA MANNERS

CORGI BOOKS

KARRAN KINRADE

A CORGI BOOK 0 552 12206 8

First publication in Great Britain

PRINTING HISTORY
Corgi edition published 1983

Copyright © Alexandra Manners 1983

Conditions of sale
1. This book is sold subject to the condition that
it shall not, by way of trade *or otherwise*,
be lent, re-sold, hired out or otherwise
circulated without the publisher's prior consent in
any form of binding or cover other than that in
which it is published *and without a similar condition
including this condition being imposed on the
subsequent purchaser.*
2. This book is sold subject to the Standard Conditions
of Sale of Net Books and may not be re-sold in the UK
below the net price fixed by the publishers for the book.

This book is set in 10/10½ Plantin

Corgi Books are published by
Transworld Publishers Ltd.,
Century House, 61–63 Uxbridge Road,
Ealing, London W5 5SA
Made and printed by Elsnerdruck GmbH, Germany

To Ruby Turberville with love

1

It was surprising how quickly Karran had become part of the Howard household. She had the room next to John's, with long, deep windows overhanging the bay. She could look down on the narrow path with the high, concealing hedge beyond which jutted brown rock where clung a few precarious sea-pinks and tough grass, then there was a deep darkness before the jumble of fallen stones at the cliff foot. The small bay was rough and shingly but the total effect was one of outstanding magnificence. On dull days or in moonlight the whole scene was silver and pewter, out of which the point and the Rock stood black as midnight. She could never tire of the endlessly changing seas and skies or the birds that drifted or swooped close to the glass. Even the rain was a shimmering curtain that pleased her sense of beauty.

When Karran had first come to live with John and Emily she had wondered why they did not share a room. But they were middle-aged and might be more comfortable apart. Emily certainly did not always sleep well and would appear pale, heavy-eyed and inclined to snappishness at breakfast.

It was possible that Emily missed London life more than her husband, for all her obvious interest in country things and her undoubted flair for painting and drawing that complemented his research into the plants and creatures of the island.

John had made his fortune in the East India Company and traces of that connection were visible in every room in the house. Rare carpets and hangings of a quality hardly seen on Man except for the Governor's residence or Fort Anne, the mansion where the notorious Buck Whaley had entertained his gambling friends in a fug of cigar smoke and musk. Brass-topped tables and effigies of Indian gods with more than their share of extended arms. Bolts of exquisite material.

But John had become disillusioned with the mercenary side

7

of his business life and had given in to the growing need for space and isolation. He'd wanted time to observe nature and perhaps Emily, in spite of acquiescing with his proposal to retire into obscurity, resented the ensuing withdrawal from the noise and excitements of the city.

John would be careful not to offend and Karran subconsciously followed his example, then, later in the day, Emily would be more unbending. But it was an undoubted strain never to know what treatment her benefactress required. Karran had always been spontaneous in her relations with others.

Emily's less attractive side had not been in evidence when Karran was a week-end diversion. She always seemed more difficult when Karran showed her fondness for John. At other times, when she had Karran to herself, she would hang over her, stroking and petting her, admiring her dark boyishness until Karran was disquieted. It was not that she disliked affectionate physical contact. It was — contact with Emily.

But Emily was refreshingly intelligent and inclined to an acidity that could be amusing if one was in the right mood. She knew all the secret vices of the local people, their peccadilloes and pretensions, and could mimic them with perfect accuracy and just enough satire.

John Howard was very different, equally intelligent, but his perception took a kinder direction, though he was far from being ineffective. To Karran, the Howards remained far more like brother and sister than anything else. Was this what happened to all couples once middle age was reached? What became of love and intimacy? When did it end and why did it do so? Love should last for ever if it were real.

Released from the grind of necessary chores, she had time to ponder on questions like these. Time, too, to work hard at her lessons and to practise her handwriting. When her family — or all that stood in place of a family to her — had sailed westward to America, John Howard had tried to divert her melancholy at parting with a bribe, a bribe that was also a bet. If she learned to read and write within three months, fifty pounds would be hers. She began with her own signature . . . . As John Howard had said, these two words were the most important. For a woman to be able to sign her own name was practically unheard of, and she was aware of a strong sense of satisfaction at her achievement.

The bet was won but the money paid into the bank at Douglas was not fifty pounds but five hundred. Emily went with her to buy new clothes and saw to it that they were severely, but beautifully, cut to complement Karran's unusual looks. But there was nothing that became her better than the black habit relieved with white. When she wore that, there was only her mouth to give her any touch of colour and there was nothing ascetic or boyish about her lips, which were warm and red and shapely.

Karran was made in the image of Luke Karran, her wild gypsy father, with no trace of her mother, Clemence, who'd been a pale-haired will-o-the-wisp and elusive as a butterfly.

As fascinating as words and letters were figures, and calculations came very easily to Karran once reading and writing were mastered. Initially, she was given an abacus to help her add and subtract, but the instrument was outgrown inside a month and thereafter, all the sums were done in her head, and, as John quickly discovered, very accurately. While riding, her eyes drinking in the beauty of shore and wood, Karran repeated endless tables, so that nature's loveliness was woven into remembrance of multiplication and other intricacies of arithmetic. John's library became a place of wonder and increasing knowledge. She was happy and fulfilled.

Karran's calloused hands and ragged nails became smoother and better-tended, though never soft and useless. (Her mother had married Hugh Conroy, who'd always wanted her, after the death of her lover, Luke, but there had never been money enough to do other than work unceasingly. How wonderful, then, that the Howards had shown an interest in the precocious little step-child with the tragic history!) Riding used Karran's hands and kept them strong and spare, as it retained her body's straight boyishness. Her breasts remained small and firm and set high so that the fashionable French gowns, gathered just under the bosom to fall in elegant folds, suited her above anything else. Disdaining the obligatory corkscrew curls, she swept up her hair into a black swathe that showed off her long and delicate neck to perfection. If her shoulders were too wide and straight for a girl, no one made any criticism.

If Karran ever thought about Croggan and her life before she met John Howard, it was with a feeling of incredulity, that grown people like her step-father should have been so afraid of the influence of the past. They really believed that her mother's death had been caused by the curse of a witch, when it was probably no more than a weak heart. And the misfortunes that followed, the death of the cattle, the failure of the crops, there were plenty of reasons why such things should happen . . . but no, Hugh and Meg believed that the past — the wild desolate love affair between her ill-fated mother and father — was responsible for their present misfortune.

Even her great-aunt in Peel had some mystic aura, though she was only a recluse who owned a cat and gathered seeds and plants to turn into nature's remedies. Karran had visited Deborah once, with her mother, and had fallen under the silver woman's strange, understated spell and the peace of the hidden cottage. But she never believed her capable of super-natural powers.

Ravensdowne was so much more exciting. It was not only the fount of knowledge, but a large house with a big staff. There were constant comings and goings of Man's important people now that the Howards were better known, and the deemsters were pleased that John was compiling a natural history of the island's flora and fauna. Karran was assisting with the making of a glossary and notes, and had, several times, captured moths and butterflies with infinite care and discovered clumps of wild flowers that John had never seen before and welcomed enthusiastically.

It was Emily who drew and painted their finds and outlined them in Indian ink. The sketches were reminiscent of Emily's nature, sharply penetrating and strong in treatment, refreshingly devoid of sentimentality.

The project bore great promise of originality, and time never hung heavily in the Howard household. Gradually, Karran, absorbed and happy, became enmeshed in the atmosphere of creativity and purpose, everything cushioned by the fact that one did not require to light the fires, cook the food, make the four-poster beds or clean anything, not even one's clothing.

The contrast with her previous life could not have been more marked. But it had not been to escape servitude that she'd thrown in her lot with John and his wife. It had been the lure of being taught and becoming better-fitted to cope with a higher level of living, a plane on which one's brain was more important than one's hands and physical strength, that drew her so wholeheartedly. One was not given a mind if one was not intended to use it. There was ample evidence of this in the bible, especially in the parable of the talents.

Emily even allowed her to deal with the household accounts, occasionally at first, then regularly.

Karran was approaching seventeen now and tall for her age,

often being taken for a girl much older. She had her own mare, Floss, now that poor Fiddler was dead. The little horse had come to her as well as her great-uncle Jesse's blue and white plates, the ship in a bottle and the spinning-wheel when the rest of the family went to America. Emily had not considered Fiddler or the spinning-wheel a suitable legacy for their ward but Karran had insisted she keep them. The wheel stood in the corner of Karran's bed-chamber and John always teased her about being careful never to prick her finger on it, in case she were found on her bed in a sleep that might last a hundred years.

'A hundred years! I should be old and ugly, all dried up like a mummy!'

'Old perhaps, but never ugly. Your bone structure would obviate that.'

And then they had talked of the human structure and of medicine, and the hours and the days and weeks had flown to become years.

Today she was not going to saddle Floss as usual, but walk through the wood. She had noticed white ling on her last ride from Port St Mary but it had been too wet to stop and pick some. There could also be fungi in the copses, especially after a spell of rain. Emily had been teaching her to draw and to use water-colour. Karran couldn't wait to try out this new craft on something more than tentative sketches.

Once into the trees, Karran forgot everything but the autumn colours of the vegetation and the pungent spiciness of the disturbed leaves and brown needles underfoot. She had brought a trowel and a basket and was delighted to discover a small 'village' of fly agaric which was particularly suitable for artistic purposes, with its scarlet and white spots and attractive shape.

On the edge of the trees, just where her mind had recorded the fact, was the white ling. Carefully, she knelt and loosened a clump which was all John and Emily would need for descriptive and technical purposes. As she stood up again, she was aware of the scent of woodsmoke and saw the blue drift rise over the wall that marked the boundary of the land surrounding the cottage John deplored.

Karran had not forgotten the long-past day when she had seen the dark young gentleman and the lady from the city. Such a rude, condescending man who had thrown her a shilling and asked if she were selling heather! She had not seen him again, only an occasional light as she looked from her bedroom window in the dark.

There was a crackle and a little shower of sparks ascending. Curiously, she tiptoed to the wall then straightened to look over the top. It was the same man, long and lean in a brown coat, dark breeches and polished brown boots. His hair was tied back with a black ribbon and the only touch of lightness was a fall of white lace cuff and the jabot under his throat. He was feeding garden refuse onto a small and sulky fire. The cottage door stood open and the smell of cooking drifted out. Karran was suddenly hungry. She'd spent longer than she had intended, poking around the tree roots for the fungus. Leaning forward, she dislodged a stone from the wall. It fell noisily. Colour suffused her face.

The dark man swung round, frowning. 'What in the devil?'

'I'm sorry. I saw the smoke.'

'I suppose you're from the big house.'

'Yes.'

He frowned again but now it was not with displeasure. 'I seem to remember seeing you before. Except that you seemed — gypsy-like. I must have been mistaken. Damn this fire! It'll not burn.'

'It's too wet. You should wait until there's been a high wind to dry everything.'

'Why did I take you for a vagrant? Today you seem very much the lady and yet you are wearing the same colour. A muted red. You present a puzzle, Miss — '

'Kinrade.'

'I thought the people at Ravensdowne were called Howard?' He kicked at the smouldering remnants of the fire in disgust.

'They are. They're my guardians.'

'I see.' He came closer and leaned against the wall so that the thin, high-boned face was close to hers. 'But why the disguise when last we met? I seem to recall — '

'That you asked me if I sold heather and threw me a shilling — '

'Which you disdained. I found it later. If I remember rightly, I still have it in a pewter mug on the mantelshelf. Shall we look to see if it's still there, Miss Kinrade?'

Karran laughed unexpectedly. 'I confess I've always been curious about the cottage. More than that, I've found it quite tantalising.'

'Put your foot on that projection, then, and I'll help you over. What a quaint little basketful of country treasure-trove!

I do believe you could be one of the little people. You seem so other-worldly.'

Once on the other side of the wall, Karran was not so sure she should have come. The small plot of land was a wilderness of tough grass and thistles and neglected bushes. But the lure of the tholtan was too great. This open invitation was irresistible. She would have to suffer the threads of her coat being snagged.

'I suppose — you don't have any visitors this time?' Karran asked. 'I seem to picture a fair, ringletted lady — very given to shrieks of laughter.'

'No,' the man said shortly. 'That was a long time ago. I was a fool to allow anyone to come to my refuge, for that's what it is — '

'Then why invite me?'

'Neighbours are different. No man is a complete island, or should be. Elspeth was a mistake and I acknowledge it quite freely. The Queen of Elfland could never become an encumbrance. She'd be so occupied in waiting for handsome young men to capture for seven-year idylls that an ageing roué would be an anti-climax.'

'Ageing? Don't be ridiculous!' Karran's voice was sharper than she intended.

'Do I detect a spirit of championship?'

'On such slight acquaintanceship — no. I'm merely realistic. You don't look more than twenty-five.'

'Thirty, actually.' He opened the door with a flourish. 'Come into my parlour, Miss Kinrade.'

'I don't know your name.'

'Richards. Laurence Richards.'

Laurence. Karran decided that she liked it. It suited him. And in some obscure way she rejoiced in the fact that the golden-haired town lady was now part of the past. Not that it could possibly make any difference. He had made it plain that he wished their relationship to be of an uncomplicated nature. Laurence was probably bored enough with his own company and the inclement weather to welcome any diversion. In any case, as his tastes obviously ran to curvaceous, fair ladies, a lean and stark hermaphrodite was hardly likely to tempt him. Hermaphrodite was a word she had recently learnt from Howard and Emily always told her she was practically a boy, which showed her discernment.

Inside, she gave a sigh of pleasure. The tholtan had not been spoiled. The thick, black roofbeams were still visible and

13

in good repair, there was a dresser with handsome green and white dishes, a spinning-wheel and carved oak chairs. The only refinements were scattered rugs and a dark, polished table in which a candelabrum was reflected, and a crystal flagon filled with wine. A stair to the loft began at the side of the fireplace. There would be a bed of sorts up there, out of sight, as there'd been at Croggan.

'John doesn't like the cottage. He'd like to see it razed to the ground.'

'Oh, I know! His solicitor wrote to me, offering some over-generous sum to me to sell it. But there's something draws me to the place every so often. Don't ask me what it is.'

'Man's like that. I could have gone to America two or three years ago but there seemed some spell that was laid on me.'

Richards drew out a chair. 'Sit there and tell me about it and have a glass of wine.'

She'd have preferred whatever was in the black pot hanging by the chain over the fire. It smelt delicious beyond words. Then she noticed the shotgun fixed to the wall and remembered certain faint banging noises yesterday. Richards had shot hares or rabbits or both.

Karran took the wine he offered. Firelight shone through the ruby liquid. It was like some witch's potion, beautiful but dangerous. If she drank it she'd be committed to some course of action that might harm them both. And only recently she had despised Hugh and Meg Conroy for allowing Aggie Karran to influence them! Dreamily, she drained the glass and set it down.

'Well?' Richards said, a little impatiently. 'I want to know more about this refusal to go to the Americas. And why you were dressed so oddly last time we met.'

'It's complicated.'

'Never mind about that. I've all the time in the world.' He stretched out long elegant legs.

'And I'm a diversion.'

He laughed and looked, for a moment, young and carefree. She wished she had the power to make him stay like that but she didn't know him well enough.

'I suppose it all began when my mother was orphaned and went to live with her Uncle Jesse at Croggan. All was well until he took up with a girl off the Irish boat, in Castletown. Erin Doyle was her name. She cast a spell on him like the island has on me. She was selfish, though, and neglected her home and children after they wed. My mother had to work

14

like a skivvy. She hated Erin and turned away from her uncle. There were only two young men in the vicinity and she had a relationship with both. Hugh Conroy was good but dull but Luke Karran, my father, was wild and exciting — '

'So she took up with him. It's the way of the world,' Richards said and refilled their glasses.

'He wanted her most really, but there was a girl in Castletown with a business that would be hers when her father died.'

'So you were born and the faithful Hugh married her.' He smiled a little cynically.

'There were two Conroy children, but after my mother died, he found the memories too painful and decided to emigrate. Meanwhile John Howard and his wife got to know me and they'd no family, so they prevailed upon Hugh to let me stay with them, as I wished to do. It was Erin's cast-off clothes I was wearing that day because none of us could afford to part with anything. It's odd but now she's quite affluent. She was widowed young and went to work for Barney Kerruish who became as smitten as poor Great-uncle Jesse and took her on with the three children. But she cast out with my mother earlier and never speaks to me.'

'Well! It's the oddest story I ever heard — outside of fairy tales.'

'It's true. Every word.'

'And the faded red jacket and the green kirtle belonged to the now rich wife of Mr Barney Kerruish whose mines are flourishing along with his square sails. I'll not be able to look at the lady and keep my face straight.'

'Please! I told you in confidence None of it was meant to be divulged.'

'I think I should seek out Mistress — Erin, wasn't it? and blackmail her into receiving you — '

'Do no such thing!' Karran rose to her feet, her brain swimming a little from the effects of the wine. 'I'll not speak to you again. Ever!'

'In the face of such a dreadful threat, what can I do? I'll keep quiet, ma'am.' Richards wrung his hands with mock subservience and Karran found herself giggling. In another moment they were both laughing helplessly. He poured more wine.

'I know nothing about you,' Karran said, sobering.

'What's there to know that's of any interest? I'm a fourth son so I wasn't sent to the Army, the Church, or the Law. My father had a factor to look after our estates and doesn't welcome my interference. That's his word for it, not mine. So I am left motiveless and must make my own amusements.'

'And what are they?' The black pot was bubbling enticingly. Karran sipped more wine to distract her mind from food and her protracted absence from home.

'Nothing that makes me proud. Cards and women. The theatre. Wine. I've no redeeming features. The only anchor I seem to have is this place. We bought it years ago from Tom who used to live at Ravensdowne in your Great-uncle Jesse's day, and there's nothing your guardian can do to take it from me. I'll never part with it. Whenever my life palls, I come here to renew myself. I seek my own food, do my own cooking, walk for miles, sometimes entertain, but not often. It seems to spoil the atmosphere. Father, I believe, resented my closeness to Mama.'

'It appears to me that your father's to blame. You'd think he'd be glad you showed interest — '

'We won't discuss him.' Richards' voice hardened. 'The only good thing he did was to allow my mother to buy the tholtan. She had visited Tom in the past, being a distant sort of cousin, and it meant the same to her. A refuge.'

'Does she ever come now?'

'She's dead,' Richards said harshly and got up to stand with his back to Karran. Fireglow edged his figure with red to match the remnants of the wine. He picked up a spoon and poked at the savoury mess in the pot.

'I should go,' Karran said, not wanting to, and the reluctance must have been evident in her tone because Richards turned, the spoon dripping onto the flags.

'Have some stew before you go.'

'I'll be very late.'

'And your guardian won't like you having been here, eh? Why does he have to know?'

'It seems dishonest not to say so.'

'He'd forbid you to come and I'd be sorry about that.'

'Would you?'

'Why should I say so if it isn't true.' He shrugged.

'No reason. It does smell very tempting.'

'Another half an hour won't make any difference. They aren't likely to come looking for you?'

'No.'

'They'll imagine you were carried away by your quest. Well, if you are staying, we'd better eat.' He ladled the meat, gravy and vegetables into wooden bowls and put one in front of her. 'I should take off your coat.'

He helped Karran remove it, his hand brushing her shoulder. She shivered inexplicably. Then he went to poke the fire into a blaze so that she would still be warm enough, and sat down, facing her. It was disconcerting to sit thus, her face illuminated and his in shadow. Karran applied herself to the stew.

'It's delicious.'

'There's wine in it and herbs.'

'More wine! I shall stagger home.'

'Not that much more. What are you doing tomorrow?'

'Why?'

'I wondered if you'd like to walk to Spanish Head.'

'I may be expected to do something else.'

'Can't you make up your own mind?'

'Not altogether. I'm beholden to them.'

'Aren't you of age?'

'Good heavens, no. I'm seventeen.'

'I'll admit to surprise. It's your hair, I suppose. And other things, I may hasten to add. Even in your gypsy garb you looked older — '

'You forgot! The shilling!' Karran cried just as Richards remembered.

He went to the mantelshelf and took down the pewter pot. 'You look.'

Karran took it. The shilling was still there. She laughed as she shook the pot and the coin rattled against the side.

'It's still yours.'

'I won't take it. I'd rather leave it where it is and look at it from time to time.'

'So, you *are* intending to visit me again. How shall I know when if you can't make plans?' Richards replaced the tankard in its accustomed place.

'I can see your window from my bedroom.'

'So you could make a signal of some sort?'

'I could wave a candle very slowly and you could do the same.'

'Make it once for morning and twice for afternoon.'

'Yes.' She stared at him, excited yet consumed with guilt. What harm could it do to talk to someone and eat rabbit from a pot? Who was cheated?

'Very well, Karran. I'll look at your window every night at ten. Which one is it?' He held her coat while she slid her arms into the sleeves.

17

They went to the doorway and she pointed it out, conscious of his hand at her elbow and the scent of woodsmoke that clung to his clothing.

'Goodbye,' she said and turned to look at him once more. It seemed foolish to find his eyelids so irresistible. But they were so deep and smooth and beautifully shaped. Was there anything about herself that appealed to him in the same way? Probably not. She was a diversion and that was what she must remember. She picked up the basket.

'Au revoir,' Richards said softly.

Karran hurried out of the gate, wanting to look back, yet not doing so in case he was no longer there. The trees engulfed her.

Barney Kerruish stared across the room at his wife, his face angry but controlled, and Erin experienced a stab of fright that was quite unlike her normal reaction towards her husband.

But she couldn't have any more children! There was Boyce, son of Sir Dermot O'Neill though she remained the only one who knew it, Sebastian and Elizabeth, Jesse Kinrade's son and daughter, and Barney's own girl, Charlotte. They really should have called her Jane for she was plain as a bun compared with the first three with their white-skinned, red-haired attraction. Erin always turned shrewish at the thought of Charlotte though, oddly, Barney's similiar looks did not detract from her very real feelings for him. Life was such a puzzle.

The fact remained that Boyce was practically a man, training to be a soldier down there in Sandhurst and Sebastian, at boarding-school, would probably arrive on his next holiday with a moustache. Elizabeth, between her two brothers and quite annoyingly beautiful, was ripe for marriage. How could Barney expect her to produce more puling infants with perpetual wants and dribbling so inconveniently at both ends!

What a fool she'd been to let slip that clue to her deception.

Some chance remark had made Barney aware that she visited Mistress Payne in Lilac Lane, Port St Mary, fairly frequently.

'There are two things she trades in,' Barney pronounced. 'Love philtres, and you can't have needed those. I've never looked at another woman. And abortion.'

The ugly word lay between them like a cloud.

'Whichever it is, I'd prefer that you didn't go again. Do you understand me, Erin? It's bothered me for years that nothing happened after Charlotte. You must have known I'd welcome any child of yours — '

'Like you welcomed Boyce and Sebastian?' The words were

out before Erin could choke them back, born out of guilt and a desperate need for self-justification.

'I kept those lads for years before their attitudes made me see they'd never welcome *me*, ever. I'm someone who stole you from them, someone not fit to kiss your boots, never mind — '

The images of what they were to one another danced in Erin's mind like a dragonfly by the river. Since that day when he tossed the champagne bottle down the shaft of the mine he'd called after her, she had realised what his love was worth, and how little she deserved it. It had been the strangest, most unexpected lesson of her egotistical life. And now he had presented her with this ultimatum. How long had he brooded over her continuing childlessness? What a fool she had been to waste the last ten years. Now she was in her forties and childbirth would hold dangers she dared not risk.

'I won't go again.'

'I can't think why you felt you must.' All of his hurt was plain in his tone. His unaccustomed pallor touched her. She could almost hate him for stripping away the layers of indifference and callousness. For that was what she had been. That obtuseness had cost poor Jesse his life and she was sorry for it now. Daily proximity with the kindest man she was ever likely to know had eroded that earlier hardness. Not even Dermot's father, who had made it so cruelly obvious that she was trash under his feet, should have made her so oblivious to the feelings of others. But she had been so young — Liar! It was only a small part of the truth.

There was nothing she could say to Barney's accusation and he had gone away, remembering her guilty silence, leaving her in torment. There were two alternatives ahead of her. Either acceding to her husband's wishes or losing his goodwill and what had recently grown between them, something she could not contemplate giving up. True, her mother had borne children up to her mid-forties, but there had been no decade in between while her bones and muscles grew stiff and unused. Not that she hadn't died in the end —

Erin was afraid of death and too many women died forcing children from their bodies, often against their will. She could never again go to Lilac Lane herself, but there was no reason why she could not send someone else. A stricture to keep silent and a remuneration to enforce it, then she need not lie to Barney should he bring up the subject again. She could swear before God that she'd not set eyes on Mistress Payne.

Of course, Barney wasn't *really* angry with her, just worried about the Englishman, Clive, who had acquired that land he'd wanted, high on the moor, giving the newcomer possession of the old Donaghue mine on which he'd set his sights and his heart. Still Erin worried about Barney's unaccustomed coldness, in spite of her certainty of her own power over him.

In the meantime, there was this business of young Mr Wheatley Clive. It might be better to have him as a friend rather than an enemy, and if he should tire of his purchase or of the limitations of living on an island, he'd think kindly of Kerruish and his family. What a pity there was no lever, no overwhelming attraction.

'Mama!' Elizabeth said crossly. 'Have you gone deaf! I asked if we might go to Douglas.'

Elizabeth. Erin was suddenly hopeful that Clive might become a regular visitor at the house in Castletown. It was time her daughter was settled and Barney had a preference for living at peace with his fellows. What better solution than that they had some sort of merger with the Englishman? If he made as much money as Barney had predicted on Nat Gelling's research it would be sensible to have some share in it.

Barney had found Nat, a talented engineer, over two years ago, on a trip to Liverpool, and he'd worked wonders for the Erin and the Charlotte mines. Barney did little without Nat's advice and had made him manager of the Charlotte, leaving Norton to cope with the Erin, an arrangement that suited the older man who had no pretensions to seeking overmuch power. They said that Gelling, for all his youth and quiet ways, would welcome it.

'Douglas?'

'Yes, Mama! What *is* the matter with you?'

'Nothing, my dear.' Where was it that Clive took his luncheon? Was it the Schooner? She could easily find out from Norton who was due to deliver his report to Barney tomorrow. 'What a good idea. I feel that we'd both benefit from the change.'

'Charlotte won't need to come, will she?'

'Of course not, Elizabeth. Now leave me for the present, will you? I have some business to put off hand before it slips my mind.'

'Very well, Mama.' Elizabeth took herself off in a rustle of turquoise-blue silk that became her infuriatingly well. Erin was not unaware that she was becoming overshadowed by the girl's dramatic looks and freshness. More and more, Erin sought refuge in candleglow and diffused light. Another reason why she could not risk losing her figure to a belated pregnancy. And she could just imagine the reactions of the boys, should she conceive.

Slowly, she crossed the room and tugged at the bell-pull. Nellie knew her place. She'd be willing to go to Lilac Lane.

The new carriage took Erin and Elizabeth in reasonable comfort in spite of some evidence of rock falls on the road that was eroded by the weather. It seemed iniquitous that there were only three such highways on Man and none in better condition.

Erin listened to Elizabeth prattle about having seen Elinor Neece's husband, James Drinkwater, who was to be invested Mayor of Liverpool, and the hero John Quilliam who had saved the *Victory* for Lord Nelson when her wheel was shot away at Trafalgar.

'Quilliam has a fiancée, Miss Stevenson, at Balladoole,' Elizabeth said.

'I wonder what she'll think of that miserable house of his on the Parade?'

'I admit it's a dingy place but it'll be different once he takes her there. It must be fun to furnish a home to one's own taste. I like the balcony.'

Erin was at last roused from dark thoughts about Barney's reaction to finding out about her treachery. But Nellie would be close as an oyster. He'd never know about the girl's secret journeys, and Nellie had a family dependent on her contribution to the household. The extra money would ensure her silence.

'So you think you'd like a home of your own?' Erin asked with just the right note of indifference as she adjusted the angle of the green bonnet with its curled feather.

'Every girl wants that, Mama.'

'I suppose so. Even if your Papa has a perfectly adequate one you share?'

'That's not the same, is it. I'm bound to have one, anyway, when I marry.'

'You'd like to be married, would you?' Erin took the small mirror from her reticule and studied the new slant of her headgear.

'Mama! Stop being so self-centred! I don't believe you've heard a word I've said.'

'Oh, I have,' Erin told her. It would never do to let Elizabeth feel she was being pressured into marriage. That would only

21

make her dig in her heels.

'It's not so much fun without the boys. I do miss Boyce.'

They had always been inseparable when they were younger. How much did Elizabeth remember about Croggan days? Did she recall Luke Karran who had made those crude wooden peg dolls all those years ago? Luke who had fallen down the Chasm. Jesse. Poor Jesse. Erin was horrified to find herself suddenly vulnerable to the memory of her first husband. She saw, in the mirror, that her eyes were huge and sparkling with unshed tears.

'I miss them too,' she said, staring out of the window in case Elizabeth should notice. 'But Boyce says he's happy at the Junior College and should be passing out soon.'

'Sebastian isn't. I saw his last letter. He was crying when it was written.'

'He must learn to grow up,' Erin said remotely.

'Oh, Mama! You always sound so much more interested in the boys,' Elizabeth protested, even if it wasn't quite true at this moment.

'You can look after yourself,' Erin told her. 'They are different.'

Elizabeth tossed her head and stared out of her own window. It *was* dull with Mama's mind always somewhere else and Charlotte so mousy and quiet. And Barney interested only in Erin and that unprepossessing half-sister of hers. She began to compose a rhyming couplet concerning Charlotte but the only word that would rhyme with that name was harlot. The thought made Elizabeth giggle and she arrived in Douglas in great good humour.

For some reason, Mama had decided to have luncheon at the Schooner. The dining-room was rather dark with sturdy beams as black as tar, but the chairs were comfortable and the food was good. Elizabeth was fond of eating and so far that greed did not show in her figure, which was slim and shapely. Perhaps it never would. Mama was wearing well and she loved her meals, though she did pick at her food today for some reason.

There were four gentlemen at the next table and from the beginning it was obvious that they were not unaware of Elizabeth and her mother. They did not bother to lower their voices and the name that predominated was Clive.

Elizabeth recognised the name as that of Kerruish's late antagonist. It was not difficult to decide which was Mr Wheatley Clive since the other three deferred to him with lamentable frequency. There was nothing dramatic about him. His face was pleasant enough most of the time, but every now and again there was a flash of something that came near to exciting her. The grey eyes would narrow and turn almost translucent, the thin well-shaped lips compress themselves into a hard line she could almost feel.

It was a stupid reaction, Elizabeth acknowledged silently, suddenly aware of those grey eyes studying her from neck to waist and the thin, attractive mouth curling up a little at the corners as if he found her amusing. She became intensely conscious of the kingfisher gown Mama had insisted she put on. It was a fraction tight and showed off every line and curve of her body most explicitly. She saw Clive lean towards the man on his right and whisper something in his ear. Two pairs of eyes surveyed her briefly. Another whisper and another faint infuriating smile. Elizabeth could have struck both of them. Ostentatiously, she turned her back and went on with the meal that had unexpectedly lost its savour.

There was a great scraping of chairs some time later on and a thud of boots across the floorboards. Venturing a quick glance that was, annoyingly, intercepted by young Mr Clive, who now sat alone, nursing a glass of brandy, Elizabeth flushed and looked away. 'Can't we go now, Mama?'

Erin, shorn of excuses to remain, rose regretfully, but allowed her reticule to slide from her arm. It fell to the polished floor, dislodging an assortment of coins and small objects, some of which rolled under the next table.

Quick as a flash, Mr Wheatley Clive had gone down on bended knee, his strong, square fingers retrieving the scattered objects, the steel mirror that reflected the guttering candlelight.

'Thank you,' Erin breathed gratefully, every inch the grand dame, 'how good of you, Mr — ?'

'Clive.'

'Clive? I seem to think I've heard that name?'

'Naturally, you have, Mrs Kerruish.'

'You know who I am?' The green eyes changed from artlessness to shrewdness, remaining beautiful.

'Who doesn't know you, ma'am.' He bowed expertly.

It was a clever answer, Elizabeth acknowledged, and Mama made the most of the gallantry while recognising that astute Mr Wheatley Clive had successfully left it to her to continue the war into his camp.

'My husband's mentioned you.' Erin decided on honesty. 'It seems — you were rivals and he did not win.'

23

'There's always a loser, ma'am. Unfortunately.' But he could not look contrite, for all his efforts, Elizabeth noted. Clive would be an arrogant winner but a bad loser. Not that that detracted in any way from his undoubted aura. Elizabeth never enjoyed losing either.

'I'm afraid so,' Erin murmured. 'But there's no reason why we should not applaud a victor. That would be mean-spirited, and, to tell the truth, Barney has so many irons in the fire, that, had he been successful, I might never have seen him at all. So you've done one Kerruish a service, sir.'

'You are magnanimous, Mrs Kerruish.'

'Oh, I've not introduced my daughter. This is Elizabeth.'

'Charmed,' Mr Clive said softly, and bent over Elizabeth's hand. The touch of his lips on her skin made her stomach muscles contract in a way that was not totally unpleasant.

'Perhaps we may meet again, Mr Clive.'

Clive straightened. 'Do you think your husband would be so open-minded?'

'I think he might, once I've pointed out the futility of feuds. They are the curse of an insular society, Mr Clive.'

Elizabeth had a desire to giggle again. Mama had certainly observed the behaviour of those of Barney's acquaintances who came from a superior background. The Bascombes perhaps. The way she aped their speech and manners! One really had to admire her. She hid a smile.

'They are indeed.' The grey eyes narrowed again to luminous slits and Elizabeth was forced to admit her own interest.

'Like you,' Wheatley Clive said to Erin, following up his advantage, 'I hope we may meet again in the not too distant future.' He bowed again, then walked away with hard, metallic footfalls that impressed themselves onto Elizabeth's consciousness like mallet blows. Not that she'd ever admit the fact.

'That young man will go far,' Erin predicted, almost casually, and replaced the well-filled bag on her arm with an air of satisfaction.

Elizabeth, lost in her own thoughts, said nothing.

Karran's heart beat fast and irregularly as if she had run a long way. But she hadn't. Deliberately, she'd walked away from the house, conscious of Emily watching from the window almost as though she knew that Karran was deceiving her. John, the proud possessor of a hedgehog from Cronk-y-dooiney, one of only a few of these creatures to arrive on the island via a wrecked passenger ship some years ago, noticed nothing different about his ward.

As usual, Karran carried the basket that was her alibi. Richards had shown her where two fungi were growing, an agaric of a copper-green shade and a yellow, flattish fungus he said was called Death Cap. The Howards were not to know that she'd not spent hours looking for them, but the deception still disturbed her after their kindness towards her.

The sun shone today and the late autumn colours were hectically brilliant. There were pools of purple shadow, bronze leaves and the darkness of late heather, bracken that was drying and turning orange. The air was as cold and crisp as winey apples.

They were to walk to Spanish Head again and so Karran had told John and Emily she meant to make the most of the weather and would return just before dark. 'It'll be winter soon,' she amplified, 'and then I'll have to stay indoors whether I want to or not.' She would miss the excursions with Richards.

'We were hardly over the door last year until March,' John agreed, and went back to his hedgehog. Emily had said little. What was she thinking?

The sight of the blue twist above the chimney set Karran running at last. The gate swung, creaking, and the door opened immediately. Richards had obviously been watching for her. He took the basket and set it on the table.

Karran waited expectantly while he put on a thick cape and took an ash-stick out of the corner. The pockets of the cape bulged but he did not tell her what was in them. He looked at the fowling-piece and she willed him to leave it behind. It would spoil the whole expedition to see something killed. It would remind her of the wren, murdered to provide the trappings of an escapist ceremony.

'I'm ready, then,' Richards said, with a last glance round the room. 'Lead on, Macduff.'

'Macduff?' The name made her laugh. 'Who's that?'

As they crossed the steepness of the glen, he told her about Shakespeare's play and the tragedy of Macbeth. The fact that there had been witches in the story and that a future King of Scotland could take them seriously, made it seem real to Karran with her images of Johanne and Aggie. To think that they were her aunt and grandmother!

By the time the gory tale was unravelled, they were climbing the sharp bend towards the Chasms and the wind was blowing in their faces and whipping up the folds of cape and cloak. When Karran touched her cheek it was deliciously cold. 'Oh, I love it!' she cried, staring across the dangerous waste land that sloped to the high cliff edge.

She had obviously forgotten that her father had died not many yards from here, Richards thought. But she had only been an infant and could not possibly remember him. Happy people had no sense of haunting and this afternoon she was transported with delight. Her pleasure touched him.

After the Chasms, the track wound closer to the edge and it was possible to stare down into the stony crescent of Bay Stacka and on the dark outcropping of the Sugar Loaf. The tide was high and the sea flung itself in showers of milky spray on rock and shore. Mud rendered the narrow track so slippery now that Richards had to put an arm around Karran to guide her past the worst.

His foot slipped once and Karran screamed and clutched at the sprawling heather roots, her stomach seeming not to belong to her. Her eyes closed, she was aware of nothing but a vertiginous fear and the hard pressure of his body as he forced himself back from the slimed rim to plant his feet on safer soil, dragging her with him.

They said nothing for a minute and then she laughed shakily.

'How fortunate we were together. I had you to hold on to and you had me.' She hoped it would always be so.

'You have mud all over your skirts.'

'So I have. But I don't care. It was exhilarating being only one step from disaster. I had no idea it could be so exciting to cheat the Fates.'

'Were you afraid?' Richards asked, steering her onto the heather that clung to their ankles.

'Terribly. It was as if my inside had fallen and left just the shell of me, like an empty chrysalis. And my voice, as you may have noticed. I'm ashamed of myself for crying out like that.'

'You needn't be. You behaved very well. But on the return journey we'll skirt that section. The moor will be safer. Now, how far is it to Spanish Head? I forget.'

'Not far. Where those huge rocks are. We can sit up there and shelter from the breeze and look down on the Calf and Chicken Rock.'

Richards lengthened his stride as if he could not wait to reach the height and Karran was forced to hurry after him, half of her mind on the strange shapes of broken roots that lay detached in the hollow of the track. There was one like a snake, another like a prehistoric bird, all curled and twisted. She picked up the bird skeleton and thought how John would like it.

Laurence Richards had reached the big stones now and threw his cape to the ground below. 'Come, Karran!'

Another few feet and she could look down into the narrow channel between Man and the Calf. The sea was boiling and the water a pale green swirled with loops of whiteness that tumbled and shifted ceaselessly. The rocks shut off the wind and the attendant sounds. Gulls swooped, clustering on the small island below the Head.

Karran felt safe and protected in the stony haven. While she positioned her back against the rock face, Richards knelt and removed the parcels from his pockets. There was a silver flask and a tempting-looking pie, two rabbit legs wrapped in damask napkins and two pears from the old tree behind the tholtan.

'The pie's a little squashed at one side but I'll have the broken piece. It was damaged when I slipped.'

'I don't mind having that bit.'

'Who says you're having any of it?' he teased.

'You wouldn't be so mean!'

Richards produced a pearl-handled pen-knife and cut the pie. It was filled with cubes of meat and jelly.

'Please,' Karran begged, curling her feet under her muddied skirt.

Laughing, he handed her a piece and watched her bite into it.

'Did you make it?'

'No. I bought it in Port St Mary. I cooked the rabbit, though.'

They sat close together, watching the view as they ate, then wiped the pear juice off on the napkins. Karran sighed with purest satisfaction.

'Have some brandy.'

Richards uncapped the flask and held it out. Karran put it to her lips and tipped her head back. The spirit ran down her throat like fire. She spluttered and he laughed. 'Is it your first time?'

Karran nodded, watching as he drank. She was consumed by warmth and a vast sensation of well-being and something else for which she had no name. She wanted to keep the sensuous pleasure for ever.

Richards pocketed the flask then put his arm around her. Her head dropped to his shoulder. She had never been so close to a man before and she hadn't known there could be such feelings of sweetness and companionship. And that other sensation that made her put her arm slowly around his neck while she turned her head to look into his face. His mouth came down on hers almost fiercely, bruising her lips, making her move in his embrace, not knowing what she should do next, yet instinctively choosing what was right.

He released her so suddenly that she fell back, hurting her shoulder on the corner of the stone. His pallor made her afraid.

'Why are you angry?' She was distressed.

'That's what I never meant to do. I wanted your company, yes. But it's a mistake to be so free with a man you hardly know. Perhaps it was my fault for not warning you about brandy. One has to treat it with respect. Do you always kiss a man first?'

'I never did it before. I — never wanted to.'

'Then don't do it again, not on such short acquaintance.'

'Didn't you like it? I seem to remember you kissed that girl behind the cottage.' Karran was confused.

'That was different. I can't say I ever respected Elspeth.'

'And you — respect me?'

'Yes, damn you. And now we'd better go, otherwise we'll both be in trouble.'

Richards was thrusting on the cape and seizing the stick as if he hated the sight of her and couldn't get away quickly enough.

She scrambled to her feet, reaching out for his hand, but he seemed not to notice. Separated by several feet, they descended from the rocky crest and began the journey back. Totally miserable, she could not think what she had done wrong. If being esteemed could also make one feel rejected, she'd rather have been Elspeth. She had been unable to prevent herself from responding to his proximity and her forwardness had spoiled their relationship. She must be bad, like her father who had shirked his responsibilities and somehow roused Clemence's undying hatred. Perhaps Richards hated her now. She ran towards him, closing that unhappy gap.

'You don't hate me? Say you don't!'

He turned towards her and caught her to him roughly. 'I don't hate you. I just want us to go back to where we were last time.'

Where had they been last time? Caught up in her new, dangerous feelings, Karran no longer remembered. All she saw was that he did not want her love, or whatever her emotions amounted to, that he was distressed and embarrassed and that she wanted to go somewhere very quiet and isolated and cry. She could not recall when last she had cried.

'Then you forgive me for what I've done?'

'Forgive you? What's there to forgive? I wanted — ' He released her slowly and stood back from her as though he wished to examine her from head to foot. A tear hung on her eyelashes and her expression was tormented.

'All I wanted was friendship,' he told her in a withdrawn fashion that hurt her inexpressibly. It was like having all the warmth and relaxation in her body turned into a hard little cannon-ball and fired back in her face.

Conscious of an almost physical hurt, she began to run away from him blindly, heedless of the twigs and roots that caught out at her legs and tore at her cloak.

'Karran! Karran?'

She ignored his voice as she did the scratches and spiteful thorns. She was humiliated and ashamed. Karran tried to tell herself it was the fault of the brandy but that was only a small part of the reason for her behaviour. Clemence had always said she was wanton. Like Luke. And the spectre that had been missing when she and Richards had begun their momentous journey was with her now, following hard on her heels and laughing at her pain, remaining as she gained the back stair at Ravensdowne and rushed to the sanctuary of her room.

Even when she had locked the door and was lying on the bed, she could feel Luke's presence. The shadow on the darkened window-pane was his.

She would never be free of him.

Barney said little when Erin told him of the meeting with Wheatley Clive. 'He's much younger than I imagined. I have a feeling Elizabeth was rather taken with him.'

'Have you?' Barney rustled the news-sheet a little brusquely.

'If he'd not been who he is,' Erin ventured, 'he might have been a most suitable husband for her.'

'But he is who he is.'

'My dear, that sounds so complicated!'

'No more so than your machinations.' He did not look up

from his perusal of the paper.

'Are you — reproving me?' She could not hide her chagrin. He worshipped the ground she walked on! Or he had until knowledge of Mrs Payne had caused a division between them.

'Norton told me, in all innocence, you'd enquired where Clive ate his luncheon as a rule.'

'Oh.'

'I wish you were not so devious. I've come to feel I can never really trust you. And it's a bad thing when there's mistrust between husband and wife.' He did not look at her.

Fear struck at Erin. What if he turned against her? She was forty-five though she pretended she was younger. She'd felt so safe. And she did depend on him. But she would *not* admit to loving him while he was so cool. Then she could not help herself. 'I know I'm not perfect,' she said, going to Barney and kneeling on the carpet at his feet, 'but there's more between us than my machinations, as you call them. They are games I've always played and habit dies hard. Only, you must have noticed recently that I'm more than fond of you.' Her fingers touched his thigh as though by accident. He could not help but be aware of her new scent and the fact that her hair was soft and newly-washed.

He did not respond immediately and the fear dug deeper.

'Barney! I love you.'

'Do you, Erin? That's what I've always wanted to hear and now that I do, I cannot believe it. I find myself searching for a reason for that declaration, some situation that can only be resolved by my acquiescence. That's how it has always been, hasn't it, my dear.'

'Barney — '

'Don't make matters worse by denying it.' He got up and pushed past her crouched figure.

Erin watched him go with a sensation of dread. If he could be so unkind about a small subterfuge like the one concerning Clive, how would he act if he knew about Nellie's errands? He wouldn't find out, of course. The maids and household staff were her concern just as the pit and the boatyard were his. As Wheatley Clive was; and she had meddled in that, arousing Elizabeth's interest, for the best of reasons, but antagonising her husband.

For a moment, she almost hated Barney. Not that one could keep on detesting a saint, though even a saint must have drawbacks like the rest of humanity.

She would bathe and put on her best gown for dinner. Be

meek as a lamb and hope for the best. How Jesse would be laughing now if he could see her! But he, unlike her, had never underestimated Barney Kerruish.

Karran had told a lie about having put down and lost her basket containing the two new kinds of fungus. But she had described them accurately enough at supper, over food she scarcely touched. The wild elation induced by the brandy had long since worn off, leaving her spirits flat and her heart heavy.

Tomorrow she would go back for the basket and Richards would have forgotten her error of judgement. He, himself, had said that the brandy was to blame. But she could not forget his unexpected anger and rejection of her need for him. When he put his arm around her shoulders he had released pent-up feelings she had never, previously, known to exist.

At least he could have shared the blame. It might be very awkward seeing him but he had had a whole night to mull over the incident and could easily have decided to forget the matter, rather than allow it to spoil their friendship.

Emily looked at her in a way that set Karran's heart beating guiltily. She couldn't know of those snatched visits? Of course not. John was so natural, so full of his research into the hedgehog and the thollog faiyr, as the Manx folk called the pigmy shrew. Emily had made her usual, forceful drawings and Karran could not help but admire them. The light and shade was so right and there was that lack of insipidness that marred most of the work of artists they knew. Islands seemed to beckon the creative, the misfits and the solitaries.

Richards was a lone wolf. Karran had known that from the beginning, on his own admission. He was a gambler, a womaniser, a hunter, and he hated his father. He made no bones about any of these things. And yet he could turn against her because of one injudicious kiss. It seemed to make no sense. Surely there was more between them?

She pleaded fatigue after the meal and went to her room, but though she waited at the window, the rough noise of the waves pounding against her ears, there was no signal from the tholtan.

She slept only intermittently, and was glad when it was light enough to rise and put on her clothes by the fire that was already lit in her bedchamber. Mary must have been up at five or six to attend to that. Karran felt suddenly useless and parasitic. At Croggan, she had been necessary with her contribution to the running of the modest household and still had callouses to prove it. Now she rode and made much of a newly discovered intellect, was waited upon – and sensed that no one was worthy of having another person rise in the chilly dark so that they could dress in comfort. Yet how else were the poor to earn their keep?

Neither John nor Emily rose early so Karran ate her breakfast quickly and absent-mindedly, then put on her cloak and went out, leaving a note that she intended to search for the basket.

The strong, sad smell of late autumn pervaded the air and there was a choking damp that misted over the bay and the trees. It inspired the fancy that she wandered in some goblin landscape that might fall apart, showing her what lay beneath her feet and inside the soaring trunks, not all of it pleasant.

She hurried past the rhododendron bushes that would look so spectacular in spring and the fuchsia that brightened the summer, the long spiteful trails of the bramble. The rosebay willow herb was pale and wispy in death.

Karran could not bear the atmosphere of things gone and lost for ever. She began to run, stumbling over tree-roots and stones but hardly noticing, intent only on reaching the cottage and putting matters right with Richards. She acknowledged now what she had not done before, that she loved him. It was stupid, considering what she knew about him, as foolish as her mother crumbling before Luke Karran's advances, but just as inevitable. Love was never measured by rationality. There was that hard-headed businessman Kerruish who was besotted with Jesse Kinrade's widow. Mama had always called Erin a cold bitch.

The wall of the tholtan rose before her but there was no welcoming smoke from the low chimney. Richards, like herself, had slept badly and was not up yet, she decided.

Karran hurried towards the gate. Another minute and he'd open the door, yawning and unshaven. Apologetic.

She leaned against the gate, her body suddenly weak, the scent of autumn's dying stronger. The gate creaked as she opened it and walked warily towards the door, knocking gently. The black lion's head grinned back at her.

Disturbed, she knocked again. No one came. The acrid silence became oppressive.

'Richards? Laurence? Laurence!'

The copse threw back the echoes of her voice.

She lifted the latch but the door would not give.

It was barred against her.

'Laurence — '

A wood-pigeon cooed softly and bit off its crooning in mid-song. Too late, it seemed to say. Too late —

She saw something she had previously missed. The basket stood to one side of the laurel bush that crowded close to the small window. He had gathered the fungi and placed them inside with great care. And there was a sheet of paper —

Karran's mind became blank. There was nothing in the world but that piece of folded whiteness.

Very slowly, she took it from the basket and opened it out.

'Karran', he'd written, 'I have to go and it could be some time before I come back. You must live your life without me complicating matters. Howard must have plans for you and it's not for me to undo them. It would be unfair. I've enjoyed the last week or two. Always your friend. Laurence.'

The world rocked on its axis. She beat on the door, knowing that he would not answer. Karran had never been lonelier.

2

They met Clive again by accident. Barney and Erin had been invited to dinner by the George Bascombes and Muriel Bascombe had said, 'Bring that young beauty of yours. Elizabeth, isn't it?'

Erin had agreed. Barney had still not thrown off his bad mood and they had not slept together for the best part of a month. She had tried everything, quietness, seduction, consideration and eventually anger. She threatened to leave him and he had not argued against it.

Boyce had decided not to come for Christmas. He was going to London with a fellow officer, Stephen Grant, to stay with Stephen's uncle in the city, and Sebastian's school was so far away that he could rarely come home, even when the weather was fine.

Elizabeth, who was bored, dressed herself in white velvet against the frost and snow, and trimmed it with a dark green sash, and her lovely hair with matching ribbon. Wrapped in a green cloak lined with red, she seemed the spirit of Christmas.

Erin, for all her problems, was proud of her daughter, and Barney had unbent sufficiently to wear the waistcoat she had given him as a present. They set off in a better humour, carrying parcels wrapped in gold paper and tied with silver ribbons.

The Bascombes had a tall house behind the harbour, with two huge trees as sentinels. Barney had often said they would make splendid masts. They were one of the sights of Castletown. Yellow light and sapphire darknesses lay over the snow and ragged children sang carols with piercing sweetness before the garlanded doorways.

Barney, touched by the scarecrow look of the youngsters in the thin lantern light, handed out a fistful of coins for distribution. A small girl, dirty and neglected-looking, stared inside

34

the carriage, her eyes widening incredulously at the appearance of Erin and Elizabeth, resplendent in their finery. They were a more splendid sight than the beribboned wren in the handsome casket she had seen lately and coveted.

The horses' breath steamed out into the icy air as they clashed impatient hooves against the rimed cobbles. Then the door opened onto warmth and pleasantness and was closed behind them, shutting out cold and want.

Barney was taken off by a red-faced George and the women to a chamber to spread their cloaks on the high, comfortable bed. The number of similar garments told Erin that the Bascombes had more guests than they'd anticipated. But Muriel enjoyed large parties and was rather a scalp-gatherer, so the evening could prove to be interesting beyond anticipation.

Holly and mistletoe garnished the pictures and door lintels and from somewhere Muriel had obtained Christmas roses, now arranged in green and white vases of Chinese origin. Supper was to be taken in the huge room with the refectory table and the fireplace of Poyllvaaish marble that Erin secretly envied. She hoped there would not be too much talk of red herrings and smoking kilns, or lime-burning and clay-pits, nor of the continuing clamour against the smoke from Charles Small's smelter. This last had been a thorn in the flesh for well over a decade, though critics would soon retract should the place be closed and men thrown upon the goodwill of the parish.

The glittering parcels disposed of, Erin was pleased to see Barney talking almost amicably to William Shanks about the progress of the mine cottages. A pity they must revert to the Duke of Atholl if the ore ran out, but that mineral was hearteningly in evidence at present and Nat Gelling was worth every farthing of the salary Barney gave him.

Her reflections were abruptly disturbed by a familiar face near the windows overlooking the harbour. All the repressed memories of Croggan came flooding back. Herself and Jesse in the stable with Fiddler, the warmth of the straw and the pricking against her bare skin. Laughter that must be choked down if Clemence were there with her blue, condemning eyes and possessive jealousy. Those gipsy Karrans and the Conroys, all smugness and cleanliness.

Erin would hardly have known Karran Kinrade if it had not been that Luke was imprinted all over her features. That long, lovely neck, the black, high-piled hair, those slightly slanting eyes. And the gown that was so simple and yet so elegant with its French Empress look and restrained magnolia shade, unadorned and needing no touch of colour to set it off but Karran's naturally red lips.

Elizabeth was suddenly garish and obvious and Erin felt overpowering in her gold-trimmed dress. Clemence had possessed that same knack of making others look showy and common. Briefly, Erin was furious with Muriel's mischievous sense of humour. It had amused her to confront Erin with her past.

That distinguished-looking older man and the odd, spinsterish woman with Karran would be Mr and Mrs Howard. They must have had more money than sense, adopting that girl with the Karrans in her blood. But hadn't Barney taken on *her* children, the offspring — all but Boyce — of a condemned smuggler? Everyone here would know and memories were long on an island. It had been very difficult for a time after Jesse was hanged, but Barney had never allowed any of the gossip to permeate his household. 'They'll forget in time. And those who keep casting it up are no friends of ours so we'll lose nothing', he'd say, never deviating from his intention to make her his wife and those gallows' orphans his own family.

Erin swallowed sherry quickly and made her way through the thickening throng to reach Barney's side. She slipped her hand into his, aware of Shanks' gaze on her, knowing that he had always fancied his chances with her. Captain Jayce had always maintained that Erin Doyle was a whore and it was surprising how many quite respectable men had been influenced by that malicious campaign. She still detested the Captain.

Elizabeth, abandoned, did not want to join her parents.

Nat Gelling came up to her, to Elizabeth's surprise. He'd always been reserved and quiet in her presence. Perhaps the glass he held had contained the key that had previously locked his tongue.

'Good evening, Miss Elizabeth.'

'Why not — Elizabeth?'

'You've never suggested it before.'

'Haven't I? Perhaps you're right. Kerruish didn't say you were coming.'

'Why do you always call him that?'

'It's his name, isn't it?'

'It's not very warm, though. Not very daughterly.' Nat

seized another glass from a passing flunkey. 'And one for —
Elizabeth.'

'I'm not his daughter!' She disdained the proffered wine.

'Such passion!' Nat laughed a little loudly.

'I do believe you are the worse for drink,' Elizabeth told
him, intrigued by this so unexpected facet of Gelling's
character.

'Am I? I'm not used to these routs. To tell the truth I was so
nervous an hour ago that all I could think of was to rouse my
bravery and I'd been told that liquor does that faster than
anything.'

'But not so much so quickly. You look very pale. No, green,
I should say. Nat!'

Gelling removed himself in a greater hurry than he'd joined
her and after a moment's rueful pity for Barney's henchman,
Elizabeth allowed her gaze to wander. She noticed Karran;
who could fail to be impressed? It had never seemed quite real
that her dark, rough little cousin should be taken into a household even more comfortable than Kerruish's and treated as a
daughter. She wondered vaguely what had become of the
Conroys. Erin had always insisted that Clemence had been
responsible for the severance of family relations and that nothing would induce her to try to heal the breach. One did not
always find gold in America —

She forgot the Conroys and Karran and her thought-
provoking change of fortunes. Wheatley Clive had just
entered the room, surveying the gathering through those pen-
etratingly slitted eyes that roused an odd little tattoo in her
mind and senses. The slate-blue coat was well-cut and the
thigh-hugging breeches matched the cream silk waistcoat
with its self-coloured embroidery. He looked calm and as
usual, faintly amused.

Elizabeth was suddenly over-warm in the velvet and the
green spencer Erin had made her bring in case the rooms were
draughty. All these candles made the place like a hot-house
and the fire would roast an ox. She took off the spencer and the
movement focused Clive's attention onto herself. The raised
brows and conspiratorial smile quite obviously meant, 'Shall I
join you?'

She nodded almost imperceptibly, not wanting Barney to
complain about any forwardness on her part. He'd been so
different lately, sour and morose and not even unbending
where her mother was concerned. Elizabeth wanted very
much to find out the reason for the coolness, and wished

matters would revert to their former felicity. The old Barney was infinitely preferable, even if she had despised him.

Watching Clive come towards her, she saw, with a prick of anger, that the grey, narrowed eyes lingered on Karran Kinrade for longer than was necessary. She had never envisaged being jealous of that dark, boyish child, but she was. Everyone was aware of this new Karran. Few of them would recognise the girl who sold butter and cheese at the market, dressed in cast-off clothing and with a mane of hair like a pony's. She'd like to remind people, only they could turn on her and recall that her own father died outside Castletown gaol. She'd not be shown in a good light. Any tactics she might employ against Miss Kinrade must be subtle enough to have no repercussions.

A pity the Bascombes had thought fit to invite the girl, but if they wanted to know the Howards better they could not leave her out.

'Good evening,' Clive said. 'I thought I'd have seen you before this?'

'Good gracious, why? Because you picked up my mother's small change?'

'My, my, I see you came provided with claws.' The steely note in his voice warned her. Clive was young, interesting, wealthy and successful. There would be no lack of girls wanting to be introduced. Erin's methods were usually well-received. Perhaps she should start again and emulate her mother. She mustn't spoil things.

'I'm sorry.' The green eyes softened. 'It was Kerruish who put his foot down. Mama would have invited you to dinner but he's so seldom balked, business-wise, that he's been like a bear with a sore head. It makes things difficult at home.'

'I'm sorry he should take his defeat so badly. But the Duke was against having another monopoly at this time. He maintains that the sett is a better method of getting the most from his mineral rights. Several men with money behind them must be more satisfactory than one major, and probably ignorant, leaseholder. And mining's a gamble, isn't it, like putting your wealth on a horse's nose.'

'It might fall at the first fence. Doesn't that frighten you?'

'My dear Miss Kerruish, a fine gallant I'd seem if I confessed to faint-heartedness. I was lucky. My father had an excellent head for business and an inborn flair for sensing disaster. I hope I've inherited it. Here, my good fellow!' He stopped a passing flunkey and took two glasses of wine.

It was pale gold and very dry. Elizabeth did not like it at first but it grew on her as Clive was doing. And he was no longer looking at the other guests. All his attention was concentrated, very satisfactorily, upon herself.

Elizabeth became aware of Barney's frowning scrutiny just as Bascombe said in his loud, jovial voice, 'Please to take up your positions at table! You'll find a card with your name on it. Muriel's idea to keep husbands and wives separate. There's not much fun in staying together all evening, and it is Christmas. You're all mixed up like the currants in a pudding, or the parcels in a treasure barrel. And may there be as many surprises.'

'How annoying,' Clive said. Sincerely?

'It's a stupid idea. I may find myself beside someone most uncongenial.'

'Like that stout gentleman with the ear-trumpet? A difficult partner, I'd hazard.'

'Oh, no! I should want to crawl under the table.'

'Perhaps they'll sit him beside that rather deaf little woman in puce, then, under cover of their exchanges, we can all say what we will and remain unheard.'

She laughed. Everyone was pushing and jostling good-humouredly. Elizabeth caught sight of the Howard man with his arm protectively around Karran. Again she experienced that thrust of jealousy. They were the only two very young women in the company and for the first time in her life, Elizabeth was not the cynosure of all eyes. The Bascombes would be sure to put Karran next to Wheatley Clive, knowing Barney's view of him.

Elizabeth could not bear the thought. She turned away, wishing she had not come. She had nothing to say to old men and pompous women. Life wasn't the same without Boyce. Even snivelling Sebastian had been better than nothing. At least they all had their dramatic colouring to draw them together. She did not even think of Charlotte. No one but Barney ever did.

Nat had come back into the room, pale and dark-eyed. He went to the table a little unsteadily and for a moment his eyes and Elizabeth's met. She had the terrible feeling that they'd be seated together and that Nat would create some sort of disturbance. Be sick, perhaps, at the sight of some rich food. The crumbs of sympathy he'd warranted earlier were all used up. She smiled perfunctorily but he moved on. Nat would be at the other end of the table — below the salt.

She read the flamboyant cards one by one. Erin was sitting next to Shanks who looked delighted. Barney was beside Muriel. Her own card stared up at her, festooned with Christmas roses to match the ones in the Chinese vases. Unwillingly, she sat down and stared in front of her. John Howard took the seat opposite, returning her defiance with a well-bred curiosity. Flushing, she turned her head, detesting the Bascombes for putting her in this false position. There was no help to be had to her left. The gentleman with the ear-trumpet was there. Half hysterically, she ventured a glance to her right.

'You must be psychic,' Clive murmured mischievously. 'When do you intend to get under the table?' It was obvious he was extremely entertained.

She could not resist a smile. The evening took on a new dimension. It was not that she wanted Clive especially. It was just that she must have what everyone else desired. A swift look towards Erin told her all she wanted to know. Mama had informed Muriel Bascombe of their predicament and she had played fairy godmother. There was no question now of losing face to Luke Karran's bastard. Clive would not make matters more difficult for himself by entertaining thoughts of a liaison in that dubious direction, however attractive he thought the girl. Men might want Karran but they wouldn't marry her.

Still smiling with self-satisfaction, Elizabeth allowed her gaze to stray along the animated board. Karran was some seats away, her black eyes curiously empty. It was like walking into an unlit cellar, Elizabeth thought, with a touch of superstition. Karran was of uncertain stock. It might be better not to antagonise her. Not that she believed in witchcraft —

'You're the prettiest girl in the room,' Wheatley Clive said.

But she knew she was not the most striking, and the knowledge soured her. The Magnificent Trio was what she, Boyce and Sebastian had always been called. There was a great gulf between prettiness and beauty and that was what Karran now possessed in abundance. Jealously, Elizabeth flirted with Clive and assiduously ignored the Howards. After all, wasn't that what Erin had always told her to do?

Clive had spent a satisfactory day. He'd dressed like a miner and climbed down the ladder to the first levels, then progressed to the lower, the candle-flame on his hat illuminating the strange troglodyte world below the surface.

The mine appeared dry enough and the sound of the engine

throbbed, sending its fluctuating heart-beat along the echoing levels. The props seemed adequate although they should be examined more fully in the distant tunnels. He had glimpses of sweat-filmed shoulders, muscles rippling under the coating of pale dust, brawny backs and legs braced to move the sluggish trucks that were helped on their way by crouched boys, and, in one case, a woman. He promised himself he would investigate the case of the woman. True, she had seemed of prodigious size and strength, and even had facial hair, but Clive was inclined to be fastidious over employing women and children. There were men enough on Man requiring work. If the woman turned out to be a widow she'd be better off washing the ore. He'd be the last man to deprive orphans of their keep. That wouldn't make for good relations.

The new shaft looked promising and the uncovered lode had so far not narrowed. In fact, he'd swear it was widening a fraction, and the quality of the ore seemed good, though only time and further tests would make that certainty.

Hammers and mallets made an encouraging cacophony of sound that drove any doubts from his mind. All mining was a gamble but the island had not, so far, too many predators. His speculation had been timely.

Emerging into daylight, he saw the shadow of the engine-house fall across the adjacent moor. Little grey tracks bisected the heather. The miners had made their own small roads, some leading to the row of cottages, others to the cart tracks to the nearest villages. He did not notice the wild beauty of the area around the mines. Not that he was impervious to all beauty. In Karran Kinrade he had seen something so rare that he could not wait to put into operation his plan to know her better. And that Kerruish minx had something out of the ordinary. Her hair seemed to have a separate life and she was the first girl he'd encountered who had truly green eyes.

While he washed and tidied up, Clive asked Bob Harrison, his overseer, about the woman in the mine.

'Aye, she's widowed and does her man's work. She's better than he was.' Bob laughed drily.

'Children, has she?'

'Nine. And up and about the same day after bearing them by all accounts.'

'I'd prefer she washed ore. She'd rather that than not work at all?'

'She was taken on before my time. When Fergie was here. He knew her situation.'

41

'Tell her there's a farmer's son I want in her place. Strong lads they are on farms, I've always noticed. I don't intend to send women below. And I was going to ask you about the new hostler. He's satisfactory, is he?' Cliver buttoned his clean shirt and flicked out the cuffs.

'He'll do. Maybe not as quick as Dick, but he'll manage that with practice.'

'He'd better! And I seem to recall a wagoner broke his arm.'

'He's replaced. By one of Wright's boys. That's three from Wright's farm.'

'I'd as soon have them as some fishing smack.' Most farm boys turned to fishing in the autumn.

'Will you be back again this week, Mr Clive?'

'No, I don't think so. You seem to be managing quite well. That's all, Harrison. Ask Jack if he'll bring my horse round. I must not be too late. I'm dining over at the Howards and I've overstayed my visit.'

Once mounted, Clive rode quickly, aware of the hills only as inconvenient obstacles in his way. Though he did think the house in the trees rather handsome. It was fairly close to the mine without overlooking the engine-house and adjacent buildings. Those beeches and elms made a fine barrier. If there were ever any chance of owning it, he'd have no second thoughts. It was convenient to have rooms in Douglas, but there was an impersonality he was beginning to find irksome. Time he had a wife and he'd quite a fancy for the Howards' ward. It was odd that there was a connection between the girl and Kerruish's adopted family. No one would have suspected it.

It was dusky when he went through Port St Mary and took the cliff path for greater speed. The sea was dashing against the rocky shore and the moon was thin as a wafer, reflected in the gunmetal depths. He pulled against the rein at Kallow Point for there the cliff face was sheer, and his mount wearying. Across the most beautiful little bay in Man, he could see the dark silhouette of the Chasms and a fraction of Black Head. The Calf was tucked away, just out of sight.

There were lights on in Ravensdowne and he pressed forward, eager, now that he was within reach, to be part of the welcome within.

Once inside, he saw that he was not the only guest. There were two men of about his own age, one fair, one dark, and two girls, equally nondescript. He never remembered their names or faces. They were only a small Greek chorus attendant on Karran who seemed made of moonlight and pitchy shadows, and quite unreachable. The flight into poesy startled him. Intrigued, he settled down to contribute his measure to the conversation and the uneasy banter. It had been simpler to cope with Elizabeth Kerruish who was selfishly uncomplicated.

But studying Karran was a delight. The dark eyes set in haunting shadow and the charmingly concave cheeks below the high slope of bone gave her a quality he had seen in no one else, and he'd had as much experience of women as anyone of his age and station. Even her low-pitched voice was a constant pleasure.

He got on well with Howard but was inclined to be wary of Mrs Emily who, very occasionally, seemed to survey the company with just a fleeting glimpse of dislike that set him on his guard. The reason for the gathering was fairly obvious. Karran was to be brought to the notice of the right people and the two plain young ladies were so much camouflage, there to set off the uncommon good looks of the Howards' pearl.

She, herself, seemed unaware that she was to display her accomplishments. She listened without hearing, looked without seeing; the only clue to her inner concentration, the hands that were clasped so tightly that the knucklebones showed plainly. Wherever Miss Kinrade was, it was not here and it was nowhere pleasant.

Later, at table, Clive was pleased to find himself seated next to her. She looked startled when he spoke to her and did not relapse again into that abstraction that had seemed so sombre, but though she answered courteously, she ignored any attempt at gentle flirtation almost as if she did not recognise the stratagem. She was the most perplexing person he had ever met, real yet unreal. Tantalising. But he would try to get her to himself sometime soon. She might behave differently then. He was already aware that Karran was allowed enviable freedom. It was a matter of common knowledge that Emily Howard had advanced ideas about feminine equality.

'Would you go riding with me?' Clive asked when they had fenced sufficiently and Karran seemed less withdrawn. 'To Spanish Head, perhaps?'

She changed before his eyes from someone alive to a being without depth, like some intricately beautiful shell.

'We needn't go there,' he said quickly, sensing that the location must be the cause of her inner disturbance. It was unusual for him to be so perceptive. Normally, in his dealings

43

with women, Clive was the aggressor rather than the wooer, but this time it was as if he pursued a hind who could hide herself in a moment. He must not frighten her into permanent concealment.

Howard must have been listening for he said, 'It would do her good to have company. She's been mopish lately. You can't go back to Douglas tonight. Sam says your mount is wearied enough, but it was our intention to have you stay the night in any case. Stay as long as you will, unless your business will not allow. I know what a jailer that can be. Hence my change of purpose. Nature is infinitely less demanding.'

'I should be fascinated to see your compendium when it's finished,' Clive said politely, though flowers and toadstools, birds and frogs would undoubtedly fail to excite him greatly.

'Then that's settled,' Howard told him. 'Karran will show you some of the terrain close to Perwick and if your horse is still unwilling, there are walks in plenty. Mind you, she's an early riser.'

'And so am I. The breakfast-room at eight, then, Miss Kinrade?'

'Yes. If you wish.'

He might have welcomed a greater show of anticipation, he reflected, then caught sight of Emily's expression. She was staring at Howard with what could almost be construed as hatred, then seeing Clive's interest, she at once veiled her eyes and returned, composedly, to finishing the wine in her glass. Why did she resent Howard's attempts at match-making? Did she have some other partner in mind for Karran? She had certainly seemed sour all evening.

Clive forgot Emily's disapproval in a glimpse of Karran's profile, pale and remote as some high Himalayan peak just before the mist descended.

The other-worldliness had gone next morning. She seemed curt and businesslike over the elaborate breakfast, eating little, her hair not so immaculately coiffed and her habit concealing the perfection of the body he had noted so lustfully the previous evening. Over eggs and slices of ham he fantasised over images of Karran in little but diaphanous draperies. She had purposely roughened her speech into Croggan dialect, eating little but drinking copiously of black coffee for which she appeared to have a passion. There were bruises around her eyes he longed to touch. And all the time she was putting up thorny barriers he could not fail to observe.

His horse seemed sufficiently rested so they decided to ride,

44

then walk later on their return. She turned her mare's head away from the Chasms route and took Clive over the moor path that bordered Glen Chass, and on to Port Erin. It was a fine morning and light bathed the long, lovely sands. They followed the cliffs by Rowany and Bradda until they looked down on the tiny islet of Creg Harlot. From Bradda Hill they saw Fleshwick Bay as far as the Stacks and right on to the blue distance that was Niarbyl.

It was very quiet. Karran sat the mare silently, her eyes fixed on a horizon that Clive could not see. He disliked being shut out by invisible ramparts and longed to challenge that mute inviolability. Why not? He might free her from those painful bonds in which she seemed imprisoned.

'Come down,' he said. 'We could see better from that stone.'

She dismounted, still in her state of abstraction, and they walked as far as the big boulder. The light breeze carried the lingering traces of some perfume she wore. A strand of her black hair blew across his neck and the small intimacy worked on his senses. He seized her and crushed his mouth on hers. For a moment she was still, as though quiescent to his rough embrace, and then she struck his arms away from her and retreated a yard or so to stare at him angrily. His forearms must surely be bruised. Her strength astonished him.

'I do not blame you as much as John and Emily. I know perfectly well what they are up to, not that they've any idea how useless it all is — '

'Why? Have you no use for men? Is that it?' Only a very violent antipathy could cause such a brutal reaction. She was as strong as a horse.

Her expression changed at his question and her eyes were drowned in pain. A tear gathered on the black fan of her eyelashes and stayed there. Her lips were compressed.

'I see. There is already a man.' He could hardly get out the words for grudging disappointment. 'That's certainly awkward. Shouldn't you tell them?'

She shook her head and the tear flew out to fall upon the breast of her habit.

'I see,' he said again. 'They wouldn't approve.'

Karran turned and began to hurry back towards her mare. Just for a moment, he had the strongest desire to stop her and throw her down in the heather. But he'd feel a fool if she got the better of him. His arms still tingled. There was little else to do but admit defeat. His mouth was full of the dry taste of

45

regret. Women like Karran never changed. He envied the man who held the key to her affections.

Several feet apart, they began the journey back.

'It was not an affair I envisaged,' he said tentatively, unable to let her go without a fight. 'My intentions are perfectly honourable.'

'I have no intention of marrying anyone.' Her words fell like stones into the well of his chagrin.

'But — it is not that you find me disagreeable in some way?'

'You are not disagreeable,' she conceded coolly.

It was as if he were a dog to be patted on the head and put in its place. For Karran he had no reality. He was merely something inconvenient to be kept at a distance. He should dislike her for diminishing him in his own eyes, but somehow he could not.

Karran saw the drift of smoke and could not believe at first that it really existed. She had been watching the cormorants in the bay, and making notes, when the bluish haze had shown in the direction of Richards' tholtan.

He was back! She forgot the eternity between today and his departure last autumn. She pushed aside the remembrance of the interest other men had shown in her. Wheatley Clive had made no bones about his disappointment in her lack of enthusiasm. Howard had been endlessly patient in his efforts to bring Karran to the notice of the right people. It was easier for girls to stay in the public eye in places like Liverpool and Carlisle, harder on an island with its limitations and lack of fresh blood and faces. Clive had gone in search of other prey and Karran had relapsed into a kind of self-hypnosis in which she told herself, repeatedly, that Richards meant nothing to her.

Now, seeing the tell-tale traces of occupancy, her senses clamoured their denial of this assertion. She was still under his thrall. All that he'd told her was dust to brush under the carpet. Impossible to believe that he drank himself insensible, took numerous women to his bed, and gambled away his substance. It was against his nature, whatever he told her.

Suddenly alive, Karran left the notes that had become meaningless, flung on her jacket and went out by the servants' stair where she would not encounter John or Emily. She saw nobody and the feeling of freedom was intoxicating.

Hastening through the rhododendron bushes and past the budding fuchsias, she remembered nothing that appertained towards her past. It was as though a shutter had come down in her mind. All she saw was the dresser with the green and white plates, the deep window recess and the inglenook under the smoked beams, the pink firelight.

The gate creaked under her trembling fingers. She lifted the lion's head knocker and let it fall. Eternities passed.

Unexpectedly, the door opened and Richards was looking out at her.

'Karran?'

'Do you take me for a ghost?' Her whole body trembled. He must notice.

'Karran. How did you know I was here? Oh, I see. The fire gave me away.'

She held out her arms and he was close to her. Close enough to see his unshaven chin and reddened eyelids. Something was wrong. Her heart beat faster.

'I'm sorry,' he said. 'Sorry I went away so precipitately — '

'It doesn't matter.' She held him tighter.

'But, you don't know — '

'Know what, my darling? I love you. Let me come in. I've been outside, so long.'

The door closed behind them and they were alone with the rosy fireglow, the shadow-striated ceiling.

'I love you,' Karran whispered. 'Don't leave me again.'

The soft roaring of the fire became a part of her pulse and of the wanting between them.

'You shouldn't love me,' Richards told her without conviction, his fingers plucking at the small buttons on her bodice. She could not have opened them herself, bound as she was in a debilitating weakness that was as much mental as physical. He must choose for her what they did. With anyone else, it would have been unthinkable to have her breasts exposed in this fashion, to have her gown and petticoats discarded, to stand naked in the roseate light from the inglenook.

'That's why I went away, in the first place,' Richards said unevenly. 'I knew it would end like this and it did not seem fair to you. I'm taking an advantage I swore I'd never allow. You're a child — '

'I'm not!' Karran was roused at last from her delicious apathy. 'I've loved you from the beginning. Right from the Elspeth days. I envied her. Don't ask me why. I hated her for having you. I wanted both you and the cottage, though I wouldn't admit it. Either seems incomplete without the other. It's the most desirable dwelling-place in the world as far as I'm concerned, and I've never thought any different from the first glimpse of you. Wouldn't I have changed if I'd been too young to have properly formulated ideas? Try to think of me as a woman, for that's what I've become — '

'Don't say any more.' Richards picked her up in arms that were both strong and gentle. 'I warned you and you've disregarded the warning. But it's mutual, that indifference to what the outside world thinks. You fill the horizon. I see nothing else.'

He deposited her onto the bed. The recess was dark and cool like a pool in a thicket, somehow safe and comfortable. A few rustles later, Richards leaned over her, his own body unclothed, his chest very smooth and brown so that she longed to stroke it, to slide her arms around it and caress the back that was well-muscled and warm to the touch. She pressed her mouth to the column of his neck and felt his body thrust against her own.

'I've hurt you,' he said a little later. 'I didn't mean to.'

'I don't care. I'd die for you if I had to.'

His fingers caught at her loosened hair. 'Do you mean that? Foolish child.'

She nodded and burrowed her head against his chest.

'I should have told you first — '

'What? What should you have told me? Not that it would matter. Not to me.'

He was silent then, his body loose and relaxed. A kind of peace encompassed them and time meant nothing. He would tell her in his own time.

She was reluctant to go.

'You must. I have to be sure that you still have a haven — Howard will provide that.'

'Why must I? Why should I need that?'

'Not today, Karran.' He slid from the bed and wrapped a robe about him, then came to the recess to stare down at her. Was it shameless of her to exult in that long and somehow painful scrutiny?

'You are the one good thing in my life,' he said at last.

'I'm nothing. Nobody — '

'You're everything. I was selfish to take you.'

'I'll never regret it.' She leaned towards him, took hold of his hand and kissed it. 'Thank you. I do thank you, Laurence.'

'For God's sake, don't make too much of it! I've already said it was wrong under the circumstances, but I couldn't help myself. Pitiable, isn't it. If I'd been more of a man I'd have sent you packing again. And now, here I am bleating that I was too weak to behave decently. Although, I must give you this accolade, you're the first person ever to make me feel shabby.' He pulled himself away from her detaining grasp and went to the window, his back turned towards her.

Disturbed and apprehensive, she got off the bed and began to put on her clothes, remembering the roughness of his chin and his red-rimmed eyes. Richards was fastidious and whatever it was that had caused his self-neglect must be taken seriously. The cottage, too, showed signs of indifference and there was none of the usual aroma of cooking.

Karran saw things she had not previously noticed. The half-empty decanter and the used glasses beside it. The fowling-piece standing in the corner beside the door. He never left it there as a rule. It was almost as though he expected some enemy.

'Have you eaten today?' she made herself ask as she finished fastening the hooks on her dress and restored her hair to some sort of order.

'Eaten?' He did not move from the half-shrouded window.

'Breakfast? Luncheon?'

'Don't sound like a wife!'

So that was his dreadful secret. He was married and disenchanted with his state. A tightness gripped her stomach muscles.

'I wasn't aware that I sounded like anything other than my usual self. You don't look well and there's no sign of any meal.'

'Just go, Karran. I've no wish for Howard to find you here.'

'But you do want me to come back tomorrow?'

He left the window impatiently and took up her jacket, slipping it around her shoulders. Their eyes met and neither could look away. He touched her cheek and let his fingers travel downwards to her throat and breast. She shivered.

'Yes, damn you. Come tomorrow.' His voice was rough. 'But on your own head be it! I've tried to keep you away. Remember that when things go wrong.'

He sounded as though it were inevitable they should.

Again Karran was seized with that spasm of foreboding. But she smiled at him and leaned forward to kiss him. 'I love you, Laurence. That won't change. And I still thank you, however you choose to throw my thanks back in my face.'

He became very white and his lips were pinched. 'You'd

better take yourself off or I might abduct you and hide you from the rest of the world. Make you my prisoner.'

'I mightn't object.'

'I could behave badly. I can be cruel.'

'You make yourself sound a monster.'

'Just the word I was looking for.' His tone was bitter.

'Please take care of yourself.' She hesitated at the doorway, overcome with a sadness for his patent unhappiness. She could almost hate his wife for causing him such pain. He'd been so different in the beginning. But she could not regret any facet of her relationship with him. However stormy it proved to be, it was her chosen path in life. No one lived on roses, or expected to —

She looked back as she closed the gate but the door was already shut and she heard the rattle of the bolt. The pallid distortion of his face showed at the window and she waved as gaily as she could.

All the way through the glen and the wood she retained the memory of the afternoon.

Throughout the evening meal she wondered if the day's momentous changes showed in her face. She supposed she should feel shame but she could not. Both mind and senses grappled with the knowledge of her new maturity. Later, in bed, she was swamped with the need for Richards to possess her. But there was no light in the tholtan and he would be asleep. In any case, she dared not stay out all night. The servants would very quickly find out and Emily would be informed. John would know and she must try not to hurt him. Would he understand? She decided not. He disapproved of the cottage already and wished to see it gone. She could not expect him to approve of her taking any married man as a lover, especially Richards.

Emily was up earlier next morning, almost as if she had sensed Karran's new responsibility towards Laurence. But no one could know. Consciences could be uncomfortable soulmates.

'I heard that second cousin of yours was to wed quite soon,' Emily said, her grey eyes more penetrating than usual. She nibbled at a finger of toast.

Karran frowned. She hadn't been listening but did not care to admit the fact. 'Who?'

'Elizabeth Kerruish. The whole of Castletown's gossiping about the affair.'

'Who is she marrying?'

'Clive.'

Karran's interest was now genuine. He'd not wasted much time since her refusal to become serious about him. 'Really! I'd never have thought — '

'You missed your chance, there.'

Had Emily been too casual with that last remark? But who could ever penetrate that steely reserve?

'I never believe in encouraging people to think I am about to embark on some great liaison. What's the point?'

'I'm glad you aren't a scalp-hunter. You'd have had a beltful by now. You aren't interested in men, are you. I've watched for the signs.'

'Not men en masse,' Karran replied carefully. 'If there was someone special — '

'But there isn't.'

Karran shrugged. It seemed the safest thing to do until her future was secured.

'They are to go to London on their honeymoon. Then later, when the mine allows, to the Continent.'

'Oh! I should have liked that.' Karran's reaction was spontaneous.

'Really, Karran?'

'Of course. France, Germany, Italy. The Grand Tour. But you and John must have visited all these places.' Howard was financially successful. They must have travelled.

'We have. But there's no reason why we shouldn't do it again.'

'Not on my account!' Karran was alarmed at the thought of being separated from the new, pitiable and hag-ridden Laurence. She must be here to sustain him and give him comfort. Love demanded that.

'Why not? To all intents and purposes, you are part of our family.' Emily got up and came to Karran, ruffling her hair and pressing her hands against her shoulders. Karran did not as a rule care to be touched and could never reconcile herself to the feel of Emily's fingers on her body, fingers that were strong and somehow — predatory.

'I'm only someone you wanted to help — '

'No, Karran. We look on you as ours. Ours. Our own.'

'But you mustn't! I'll disappoint you — ' Karran twisted in Emily's hold and stared at her. 'Don't put too much store on my being the sort of child you might have had.'

'It was John who wanted children. I'm happy enough without.'

'Then — why?'

'Friendship with another woman. That's much better. A special friendship,' Emily said softly in a way that made Karran afraid though she could not have rationalised that fear.

'That's what we are, isn't it? Friends? What's changed?'

'Nothing.' Emily let go of her and Karran felt reprieved. 'But friendships can deepen.'

'I'm going to look for things for the book.'

'Shall I come with you?'

'I'll manage perfectly well alone. I — like to be alone. I always have. You know that.'

'Very well, my dear. You aren't disappointed that Clive has transferred his affections to that spoiled cousin, are you?'

'Good heavens, no! They are welcome to one another. As you say, I had my chance.'

'That's all right, then. I did wonder — '

'You needn't worry about me. I shall know when a relationship seems right.'

'That's what I thought, my dear. Take your time. We can wait, John and I.'

'Thank you. And you don't mind — ?' Karran made for the door purposefully.

'Not at all. You'll make the right decision. Eventually — '

But Emily would most definitely not agree that Richards had been the right decision.

I don't care, Karran told herself. He needs me and I love him. And the memory of the episode in Richards' wall-bed came back to reinforce her determination to see him again as often as they both should wish. Not that it was entirely a passion of the body.

Today, she did not notice the sea or the cormorants or the smoky depths of the glen.

Richards let her into the tholtan which was dim except for the firelight.

Wordlessly, she allowed him to remove her garments and take her to the bed.

Boyce found London thrilling beyond words. The Grant house was in a big square surrounded by cream-coloured houses. Trees nodded gently in the centre, a green oasis. Stephen's relations were unlike his own. David Grant was a soldier and a gentleman and his wife Adelaide charming. He liked their son, Peter. Perhaps the only disquieting note was Nina, their daughter. Small and dark, she nevertheless made her presence felt almost too forcibly.

At times, he almost forgot Castletown and the house that was owned by Barney. To think that such an upstart would have relatives who could pull strings enabling him to be taken into the Army without question! Boyce would have preferred that he had not owed his lieutenancy to Kerruish. The Army captivated him completely. The uniforms, the clubs, the sense of power he experienced on the parade ground, the inevitable women dazzled by red coats and gilt braid. The horses. Companionship of splendid young men, most with a sense of humour that turned service into a pleasure. The older men with their tales of the French wars and Bonaparte, of Trafalgar and Waterloo. David Grant had fought under Wellington and been commended.

Stephen and Boyce had driven over London to inspect Nash's Regent Street, then the beauties of Tavistock Square and Sloane's Pitzhanger House. He'd seen the Elgin Marbles with their memories of Greece, the British Museum, Walpole's Strawberry Hill, the pagoda at Kew, Newgate, Somerset House, and, on a delightful week-end, the increasing splendours of the Brighton Pavilion which might not be completed for another decade. The Prince's plaything —

They had mulled over Scott's *Romantic Poems* and Sheraton's *Dictionary*, visited the Dulwich Picture Gallery and ridden down Rotten Row and round the Ring with most of London's fashionable society. Nina, in an eye-catching habit, rode like a centaur. She'd been much admired.

Over dinner they'd discussed the Charlotte Dundas and Trevethick steam carriage and railway locomotive, the up-and-coming George Stephenson's 'catch-me-who-can'. It was a new world made even more stimulating by the sharply stinging comments of Stephen's cousin, who was a tiny dynamo of taut nerves and uncommon beauty of the variable kind. Nina was so unlike the predictable Elizabeth and the oft-times shrewish Erin with her peasant origins. Boyce would never forgive his mother her capitulation to Kerruish after years of amused tolerance, just as he would always hate Barney for his intimate relations with Erin. Not that those relations seemed to be in operation at present, according to Elizabeth who was full of self-importance about her forth-coming nuptials and Wheatley Clive.

Boyce, who had raged inwardly over Barney's privileges in marriage, was delighted with news of a termination of the same, while wondering about the cause of the unexpected rift. Long might the estrangement continue: he'd raise his glass to that any day. Perhaps Elizabeth would be able to elucidate when she arrived on her wedding tour next month.

Boyce turned his attentions to present company.

'I've a mind to ride in the Row tomorrow,' Nina said challengingly. She seemed, always, to be tilting at windmills, strangely aggressive, yet so small and perfectly formed, like expensive porcelain.

'Shall I come with you?' Boyce asked.

'Why do you think I mentioned it?' She laughed insinuatingly and the sound excited him.

That should have warned him that he was being stalked, but, immersed as he was with his mother's affairs, he missed the implication.

'When do you intend to start out?'

'As early as possible,' Nina told him with a secret smile. 'Nine o'clock? Eight?'

'Eight, then. I seem to wake early in town.'

'London's not so sleepy as your island.'

'Obviously not. I'll look forward to it.' There was something about her narrow body in a frogged coat that fascinated him. She could have been Chinese with her slanting smile and inscrutability, that oriental darkness.

'Eight of the clock, then.' Her words hung in the air like a promise.

Sebastian awoke as soon as the first glimmer of dawn touched the window. His primary thought was always of his mother. She was so beautiful. It hurt to dwell on her beauty. Far off there was a recollection of his real father, brown and bearded, white-toothed, not at all like his stepfather. As always, the resentment built up over the unwilling rise from bed, the cold bath and the frugal breakfast. Shivering, he went from one classroom to another. Latin, History, Mathematics, Sciences. Greek — and all Kerruish's fault.

He loathed mathematics with a deadly hatred born of inadequacy and desperation. It was only history he liked because he had the facility of responding to old stones and buildings.

Sebastian had never been comfortable with the other pupils. The older boys demanded subservience and the young ones were either unattractively self-assured and with older brothers as bulwarks, or soft and snivelling, made to become fags for the seniors.

He, himself, had been allocated to a senior in his house, but because he had a curious affinity with Richard Bailey there was nothing distasteful about the relationship. From the moment he had come under Bailey's ironic scrutiny, he had been conscious of a relieved thankfulness that he was in such undemanding hands. Besides that, Bailey possessed the blonde good looks of one of the carved angels in the chapel and Sebastian had always responded to beauty as well as ancient buildings. Bailey was sympathetic yet tough enough to repel any older boys who might have tried to torment Sebastian as they did most new pupils.

Gratefully, Sebastian performed those chores that Bailey demanded as his right, one of which was providing tea for Richard and his close friend Giles Jordan. There was nothing onerous about seeing to the afternoon tea as Jordan and Bailey were always eager to be left alone as quickly as possible. Sebastian sometimes wondered what they did.

The odd thing was that Giles had red hair. It seemed that Richard favoured that colouring.

Lessons over and with a spell before preparation, Sebastian devoured his mother's last letter. She missed him but always thought of him. Not that she had when Kerruish banished him from home! But Erin would not have had any real say in that. She was under that man's influence. Her letter said as much. Elizabeth would be able to give him all the news when she travelled south with Wheatley Clive. The fact that Clive owned a mine excited Sebastian. He had once prevailed upon Norton to take him down into the Charlotte and the lamplit tunnels and alcoves had worked strongly on his imagination. The candle-flames and the shadowed wood props left pictures in his mind that would not be erased. Surely his new brother-in-law would allow him a similar privilege? He'd have liked to have been at the wedding, but he only went back to Castletown once a year and Elizabeth had not wished to hold back the ceremony until then. She was plainly in love.

'What's wrong?' Clive whispered in the darkness.
  'Nothing.'
  'Then — why? Why not?'
  'One doesn't always feel inclined.'
  'That's no answer. I'm your husband. You're not ill.'

'You hurt me.'

'I was careful — '

'But not careful enough.' Elizabeth moved across the big bed, accentuating the gap between them. She had enjoyed the wedding ceremony, all the dressing up and pretty trappings, but she had hated Wheatley's advances and the disagreeable business of becoming a woman. She was not sure what she had expected, but she had not envisaged being spread-eagled so humiliatingly on the bed and forced to accept what Clive had done to her with so little regard for her feelings. In spite of her struggles, which appeared to excite him, he had gone on with his painful intrusion until he was satisfied.

Clive moved across the intervening space and pulled her towards him. 'I'm your husband now and I want you.'

'No,' Elizabeth repeated. 'Another time — '

'Next month, I suppose, or next year? No, my dear. Now.' He tugged at the white night-gown. 'Come on, Elizabeth. Don't be a fool. You're my wife and I have the right.'

'Wheatley — '

He took no notice of her protestations, or of her hands pushing against his chest. She did not like the male smell of his sweat or the damp bareness of his body against her. He put his leg across her thighs and lowered himself into position.

'Please,' Elizabeth entreated. She had never begged before in her entire life. And this was supposed to be a kind of heaven which all brides longed to attain!

'It hurt.'

'That was last night,' Wheatley said, 'and I don't think it unusual for a husband to want his wife more than once during the first week of marriage. I'd be a fool to let you become master this early.'

This was the man she had schemed to ensnare because he was wealthy and, she had imagined, attractive and a gentleman! Elizabeth did not know why she had bothered. He meant to do this every day and she loathed the operation as she had never detested anything else.

'Don't — '

'Oh, my God,' Clive said with barely repressed anger, 'I can't imagine your cousin behaving like a vestal virgin. I regret more than ever that she refused me.'

Dumbfounded, Elizabeth stopped her ineffectual strivings. 'Cousin?' she whispered.

'Don't pretend Karran Kinrade isn't your relative. I know better.'

'You — asked her, before me? To marry you?'

'Since you are so anxious to know, yes. Well, as good as — '

'How dared you!'

'It's all in the past,' Clive told her, 'and now, my dear, for those privileges of which I intend to avail myself, with or without your co-operation.'

She was no match for his strength and determination. Painfully, she learnt the lesson that everything must be paid for in full. But greater than her present hatred of her husband was her antipathy towards Karran. Let Miss Kinrade look out in the future.

'There,' Clive murmured, 'that wasn't so terrible. Was it?' and rolled onto his side, his back towards her. 'Go to sleep, puss. You'll feel different tomorrow.'

Elizabeth, still and wide-awake, did not answer. She never meant to speak to him again. It was bad luck that she had picked on the only person who would refuse to be influenced by her wiles. And to think that he had preferred Karran! She was only second best.

She bit into the lace-trimmed pillow and a few small white feathers drifted away in the darkness like the ghosts of yesterday.

They left the Douglas Hotel next morning to catch the Liverpool boat. The crossing was so rough that Elizabeth was genuinely ill and Clive left her, green and moaning, to gamble in the saloon with a quartet of businessmen returning after showing off their new pumping-engine, the Simpson, named after the designer.

Clive, as well as a number of other Manx businessmen, had visited the exhibition in Douglas where the model of the pumping-engine was on display and induced to work by anyone interested. Gelling had been there on Barney's behalf, and Barney himself had made it his business to see the engine for himself after he'd heard his young manager's report. There'd been talk at the wedding. The businessmen brought also a plan for a modern and supposedly efficient smelter, judging by the letters of recommendation he was shown. They had thought to sell him lime as well, but the perquisites were obtainable from the Duke's commons, and free to him on Man.

However, mellowed by brandy and success at cards, Clive ordered the Simpson and promised to study the smelter plan. He intended to build it but it would never do to sound too keen at this stage. The news that Barney Kerruish was investing in both jolted him a little but since he'd taken the precaution of snapping up Elizabeth, it was not the same as being in conflict with a rival. The old smelter was of the bellows type and quite out of date.

Clive, returning to the cabin where he'd left his bride, found her still pale and inclined to retch, and not even his appetite was fanned by the faint, sour smell of stale vomit that lingered still after a rigorous cleaning of the small place. Her mother, he reflected, would have made a more satisfactory bed-mate and a more courageous sailor. Indeed, he had imagined Elizabeth to be a carbon copy of Erin and that had been a serious mistake, probably the worst he could have made, considering a wife was a lifetime speculation.

If he had not been so needled by his rebuff by the Kinrade girl — he had never taken kindly to failure — he might have spent more time finding out about Elizabeth. But it saved his face to be seen with a pretty girl on his arm, and Elizabeth was eminently personable for all her distressing frigidity. A man should be allowed a bite of the cherry before marriage, to see if it were sweet enough, but all he was permitted was a succession of whores. True, they broadened a man's outlook but to know a prospective wife, one must first sleep with her, and girls like Elizabeth were too scrupulously chaperoned. Of course, their true value was supposed to be their virginity.

But Karran Kinrade was different. She was in a kind of no-man's land, not the Howard's blood-kin and allowed an enviable freedom since Mrs Howard, amazingly, did not believe in inequality between the sexes. Yet Karran had been remote and untouchable, while working strongly enough at his senses to send him mad with impotent desire and raging at her indifference.

Fortunately Liverpool was, by this time, a smudge on the horizon that grew darker and more definite by the minute, and Elizabeth would cheer up once her feet were on dry land. Thoughts of Karran made him want a woman, and one's wife was always available however short she fell of perfection. He'd stand for none of this nonsense about lack of inclination. Elizabeth was spoiled enough already and must be taught her place if she were to fit properly into his scheme of things. She was too ready to sulk and glower when balked, neither of these traits much in evidence during their brief courtship. It had not occurred to him how young she was, how sheltered. Karran Kinrade was far more of a woman.

All the time he watched Liverpool grow and come closer, Clive wondered how it would be to know Karran intimately. Someone, somewhere, was going to find out the answer. It was surprising how much he envied that unknown man.

Later, bathed and changed and ready to face a light meal in their suite in Liverpool's best hotel, Elizabeth recovered some of her looks and spirits. The suite was very grand, the sofas and chairs covered in oyster velvet and the curtains the forest green that became her most. She was grateful for the cessation of her sickness and Wheatley looked at his best in the cream satin with the blue coat. He seemed his pre-marriage self over belated supper — she'd not had the stomach for it earlier — smiling and attentive.

There was the journey to London to look forward to and surely Clive would dip into his pocket when they were in that magical city? All bridegrooms bought tokens of their pleasure in their partners, and Clive was by no means poor. Erin had taken good care to find out his financial position before allowing the engagement.

But the shadows of last night were not so easily exorcised. Surely Clive had only told her of his interest in Karran to enrage her during his frustration over her coolness?

He had not hurt her as much as she made out. The fault must be hers for finding no enjoyment in his behaviour as a husband. It would never do to be compelled to admit her failure as a wife. Old maids were a source of jokes and unkindness and so would women be who could not hold their men. She must pretend that the two previous nights had not existed, whatever the cost.

'Shall we retire, my dear?' Clive asked smoothly, and much too early.

'I think so. It's been a long day.' Elizabeth forebore to say how tiring. She got up from the table, conscious that the white, beruffled robe set off her positive attraction and that her hair had not really suffered during that abominable voyage. She must not allow her brothers to sense her disillusionment. And it would only be sensible to keep Wheatley's interest, for fear he might take a mistress and make her look a fool. She had learnt her second lesson.

They were in bed and Clive advanced on her like one of his mine machines. There must be more than this? Panic overtook her attempts at common sense. Her body became rigid.

'For God's sake,' Clive growled. 'It's like making love to a

59

fish. Like expecting to taste a strawberry and finding you've bitten into a crab-apple. What's wrong with you?'

'I don't know.' He hadn't hurt her. She hadn't felt anything. Except distaste —

'You'd better liven yourself up, hadn't you?'

'You should know how. Men always know more than women. I've had — no experience.'

'That's lamentably obvious.'

Tears stung her eyes. How cruel he was. But hadn't he a right to expect fulfilment? Just as much as she did? Perhaps it was his fault, or partly his, not that she could, at the moment, bring herself to suggest it. Maybe there were things a man did with a mistress that were not proper with the woman one married, yet more enjoyable. It could be to her advantage to find out. Boyce would know. She had never had secrets from her elder brother, not since they'd played in the Croggan woods with the peg dolls Luke Karran made for them. Tonight she recalled Luke most clearly. He was Karran in breeches and a sweaty shirt, his hair dragged back with a string. She hated both of them.

Clive had no reason to be pleased with himself tonight. There had been no satisfaction. At least she had learnt enough to know that hers was not the only deficiency. They were, both of them, lying on their backs, staring at the ceiling, all thoughts of sleep gone.

He got up later and went out of the room, not returning for over an hour. Perhaps he'd found a chambermaid who'd managed the whole thing more professionally than she was ever likely to. The fact that he turned over towards the opposite wall and fell into a slumber quite quickly seemed to point to the probability.

If only she'd known how difficult the role of wife was, but she'd never looked beyond the flowers and the dresses, the food and the jollification. She could not even remember what vows she had promised in church. They had been meaninglessly repetitious, quickly forgotten. Was one supposed to listen?

Dawn was long in coming.

London seemed at the end of the earth. There was the long, stuffy, odorous coach journey by day, then a concerted rush for supper at a table congested with unattractive and predatory fellow travellers. If the soup were too hot and one was slow there was little left for the second course. And the beds were soft, yet lumpy, and there were always fleas.

Once Clive had brought a bottle of brandy to their room and made her drink some of that. But, if it made her less difficult in bed, it also made her sleepy and she was not awake long enough to decide if that made it more bearable. All she knew was that the faint, burgeoning pleasure that came like the tentative touch of a paint brush on a pale water-colour, never reached its promise, yet nagged at her next day. Its sensuous insistence was thwarted, since Clive went out the following nights and did not return until morning. He said that he could never sleep in strange beds and knew that she'd not regret his absence too greatly. This with a note of sarcasm she could not fail to recognise and resent. What a truly horrid thing this married situation could be!

But once London was attained and they had journeyed past the dreadful outskirts with their dirt and poverty that made one want to puke, the city improved beyond recognition. There were still glimpses of disagreeableness down the pokey side streets, but the main thoroughfares were impossibly grand. They were choc-a-bloc with sedan-chairs and carriages of all sorts and sizes depositing splendid personages on lofty doorsteps or outside magnificent shops.

Elizabeth, immediately entranced, noted the fashionable gowns and pelisses, the Paisley shawls that were like nothing she had so far encountered. There was a sheath gown that took her breath away, for the flimsy material seemed to have been damped and it was obvious that the woman who wore it had little or nothing on below it.

Clive had noticed it too, for he leaned out of the carriage window quite openly, admiring all he could see, his lips pursed in a way she had learnt to recognise.

'There's a gown you should copy,' he told her. 'Then I'd stay at home of nights.'

Elizabeth resolved to have nothing so provocative. More demure were the high waistlines and long, tight sleeves, and very fashionable were the sabre taches, fashioned after a cavalry uniform bag and bearing bold designs. There was still a lingering Spanish influence but the French was much more in evidence. One had a most satisfactory choice, except that none of the clothes she had brought were in the least bit *right*! Fascination turned to despondency. Clive was already so out of patience with her that he'd never allow her the run of the dressmakers.

They were delighted to see the last of the coaches and be

61

taken up to rooms where their boxes awaited them. Elizabeth ordered hot water and took a bath in her own chamber, then put on the only gown that could compare with the array she'd seen that afternoon, a pale eau-de-nil with a matching feather spray that sat in her curls like a quiescent bird. She was pale from the journey and her eyes looked dark against the pallor, but the coils of her hair were magnificent and drew the eyes of most of the people in the huge dining-room. Some of her inadequacy began to leave her. It was not everyone who failed to appreciate her.

She fluttered the blue-green fan against the heat of the chandeliers and thought about Boyce. She'd written to him, telling him they were coming, and in no time he would present himself. There would be two, at least, of the Magnificent Trio. How far off Castletown seemed. It was only a pin-prick on the map. And so provincial!

The maitre d'hotel drew near to the table. 'I beg pardon, sir. There's a young gentleman to see you. A Mr Kerruish.'

Elizabeth stood up in her excitement, all of her weariness and disappointment dropping away like discarded clothing. 'Boyce! Oh, Boyce!' Forgetting Clive, forgetting everything, she began to run between the tables like a dryad. There was not one soul who was not aware of her.

Wheatley Clive watched her progress with a kind of detached bitterness. She had never looked like that for him and never would. She was alive for the first time since he'd met her, pulsating with a magnetism that matched Erin's and might even surpass it. Yet, towards himself, she might as well be dead.

She and her brother came back, arm in arm, Boyce in a dark green that complemented Elizabeth's gown, everyone's attention on the picture they made.

Clive could imagine the effect if the other brother had been with them. Sebastian had been judged the handsomest by more than one of the Castletown worthies. Together with their mother, they'd be unbelievable.

Elizabeth effected the introductions with sufficient warmth to hide her true feelings. She wasn't ready yet to have what could be an embarrassing heart-to-heart with her soldier brother, but she could never broach the subject with Erin and there was no other woman in whom she could confide.

Boyce talked more than the Clives put together, as though he sensed some awkwardness between them. Regimental facing colours, army buttons, gorgets, sashes, culottes, crossbelts, the frog for his sword, all were described in such detail that Elizabeth could see Boyce in his uniform, his boots glittering and his horse groomed.

He told them about the Grants, which led him to David's part at Waterloo and roused Clive to pronounce his own views on the battle that had changed the course of war, and those concerning the statesmen who had helped or hindered the cause.

Elizabeth, in spite of her present lack of affinity with Clive, was, for the first time, proud of him. He was so far removed from their hated stepfather with his clogging common sense and self-satisfied shrewdness. Although Clive's parents were dead, they'd been of finer stock than Barney. Wheatley was their only child and the few relatives he possessed, too old and disinclined to make the arduous journey to see him wed. He was in no hurry to visit them so she might never meet any of the Clives or Wheatleys, after whom he'd been baptised. Elizabeth was relieved, rather than disappointed. She found the old tiresome and depressing. She sometimes told herself that she would like to die when she reached thirty, for after that there could be nothing to live for.

Meeting her husband's pale, slitted gaze, Elizabeth recalled how exciting and novel she had once found it. Now she recognised it to be the outward manifestation of his nature. He was master and that must never be forgotten, whether it was concerned with his work or his private life.

'How is *he*?' Boyce asked in the tone of voice he reserved for Barney.

'Just as usual.'

'I thought you mentioned — some — difference?' Boyce went on more carefully.

'I may have imagined a coolness.' Elizabeth was unwilling to discuss her mother while Clive sat there, smiling enigmatically.

'I must fetch some cigars,' Clive said, unexpectedly considerate. Of course, it could only be because he wanted badly to smoke. He was not a man to subdue his more urgent needs.

As soon as he had gone, Boyce said, 'I want to know!'

'They were in separate rooms for a time. Mama said it was because she could not sleep and wished not to disturb him. Then, after the Bascombes' party, she returned to his and they seemed easier with one another, but, just before the wedding, the maid, Nellie Dare, fell in the street and cut her hand very badly on a bottle she was carrying. It was Kerruish who was

63

told by a friend of his from Port St Mary. He questioned the girl in her sick bed and she began to cry and said the mistress had told her to say nothing about her errands and they were performed in her own time, she'd not cheated her master. Unfortunately, I was not able to stay behind the door any longer for I was called away. Some business about the wedding that could not wait. But the upshot of it all was that Mama was very pale and quiet at the ceremony and afterwards, and Kerruish as white and silent with her. It does seem odd, considering how he's always doted on her. I had too much to think about at the time, but now, I do feel uneasy. But I did overhear cook say something outside the church. She said "Mistress Payne of Lilac Lane had much to answer for". What do you suppose that means?'

'Nothing, I can think of. Couldn't you find out when you go back?'

'I'll try.' Elizabeth was reluctant to think about her return. Clive had insisted they leased a house at Foxdale so that he could be close to his precious mine, and it would be very quiet out there. Only that big house set in the trees and the miners' row a mile away. Nothing else. Before the wedding it had seemed romantic. With her new knowledge, she dared not dwell on the prospect. Every evening, only herself and Clive.

'Have you seen Sebastian?' she asked, pushing away the future as though she would bury it twelve feet deep.

'Twice.'

'And? How is he? Does he still cry?'

'He's changed. I thought he'd be a victim of the boarding-school disease — '

'What's that?'

'Bullying. He seemed such a likely candidate. But I found him self-assured and very content with his master, young Mr Bailey, whose tastes run to red-headed acolytes. It seemed there was another before Sebastian and he has a bosom friend with the same colouring. Strange, when most shy away from us. Remember the day we dared you to go down to Port St Mary at dawn and not one of the fishing fleet would put out? If you'd also had crossed eyes they'd have run screaming.'

She began to laugh and Boyce joined in. More than ever, they were watched greedily by those around them, unused to such a pleasing surfeit of colour and gaiety, and youth.

'And you, Boyce? Isn't there anyone in your life? A girl?'

Boyce frowned. It should have been easy to say that he found Nina Grant quite the most fascinating woman he'd ever met. Only there was something beyond the attraction, some quality that kept him from venturing too close.

Elizabeth understood that look, just as she recognised Wheatley's arrogance and need to subdue everything to his will. 'So there is!'

'I didn't say so.'

'You didn't need to.'

And then Clive was back, his cigar already lit, and Elizabeth's heart was hammering. In another hour or so *it* would begin.

Her husband and brother took up the threads of their conversation but she did not hear a word.

They all went down to Sebastian's school, Elizabeth in a new gown Clive had chosen. He naturally wanted a wife he could show off whatever he thought of her in private, Elizabeth realised. How would he have been with Karran in those intimacies she herself so disliked? She'd be whorish like her mother. Elizabeth dismissed the Kinrades angrily and contemplated the long, narrow sleeves of palest mauve. Lilac was not a colour she would have chosen but Clive was more enterprising. Lilac. Of what did that remind her? Something to do with her mother and stepfather —

But the day was too glorious to spend on discordant thoughts. The sun shone on all the green-ness of the countryside. She looked her best and Boyce was beside her, excitingly broadened into a quite Adonis-like man. Any girl would want him. Beside him, Clive was strangely colourless but that was because his lids drooped over his eyes, concealing all of that forceful magnetism. How she had disappointed him. She hated to feel so lacking. He had spent two nights with her since they were installed in the comfortable hotel suite, but since then, he had gone out, to play cards he said, but she knew London was full of brothels . . . . Now she felt even less inclined to allow him the freedom of her body in case he'd contracted some unpleasant disease. It was Boyce who had told her that such things existed. He called it the clap, never imagining the story could strike home. Wasn't she on her honeymoon? And somehow, she'd never been able to put her inadequacy into words, not even to him. No one must know.

Discord! Discord. Elizabeth made herself smile quite radiantly, and concentrated on the blue-green shadows cast by the chestnut trees and the nodding borders of Queen Anne's Lace that decorated the ditches with creamy whorls.

The school building was like something out of a dream, long and pillared, with virginia creeper covering half of it, the sun turning the red leaves to flame and gilding the hundreds of windows. Sebastian, released from his mathematics class, was doubly happy to see his brother and sister. They were together again, the bond made stronger now that they were cast onto a world that was full of pitfalls. United, they were invincible and Sebastian, now that he no longer sought refuge in tears and was growing so tall and beautiful — that was not too strong a word for his fabulous looks — was a worthy member of that select band.

He showed them some drawings that Elizabeth could hardly believe were his. They were more draughtsmanship than imagination, and some were unmistakably the school and its several gazebos, the lodge, the chapel and great hall. They were fine, strong and yet delicate. She began to remember the sketches he'd done as a child and the promise they had shown. Promise they had all forgotten.

'What's this one?' she asked. It was like the interior of a church, the windows very beautiful and the pillars and arches like rainbows in stone.

'It's nowhere. Nowhere real. I — made it up.'

'Did you, by jove,' Clive murmured and reached out for the etching. 'It's good. Excellent, in fact. What does your tutor say?'

'Nothing. I do them in my spare time.'

'Could I have one to frame for my own room?' Elizabeth asked.

'Which?'

'The Greek temple,' she suggested, selecting the best of the gazebos.

Sebastian seemed well-pleased that she wanted the trophy. He was touchingly diffident about his work. Only Boyce remained unimpressed.

They met Bailey and his friend Giles as they left the building and Sebastian introduced his family. Richard, as usual, looked on with that irony that seemed the basis of his nature, bowing very suavely to Elizabeth as he wished her happiness in her marriage, but the words did not ring true. She was obscurely uncomfortable.

Then they went out into the heat of the afternoon, Sebastian intent upon showing them everything, and she forgot Bailey and his secret amusement.

Sebastian took them along the river bank that was a

paradise of bees, butterflies and kingfishers. There were marsh marigolds and briar-roses, sweeping larch boughs and oaks, fish jumping after flies, viridian patches under the trees and hedges, a glimpse of deer, a kestrel hovering, the white scuts of rabbits.

Elizabeth, Boyce and Sebastian, brilliant as jewels in a crown, disported themselves like the Greek deities. They returned, flushed with the heat and tired with recounting tales of their togetherness, to eat poached salmon and strawberry sorbet and drink the wine of Greece. How fitting, Clive thought wryly, as he allowed that slitted glance to pass over Adonis and Narcissus. . . . And his wife? Was there a Greek name for emptiness? He supposed there must be.

3

Karran put away the long letter from Hugh. He had not written it himself but dictated it to a clerk he was by now well able to pay for the service. The Conroys had not had an auspicious start to their new life. New York teemed with immigrants, all wanting work to keep their families, and Howard's generosity would only keep them for so long. Each precious guinea must be conserved as though it were the last. And then it was the last, and Karran could picture Hugh's despair.

Then, at this lowest point in his fortunes, everything changed. He had gone out after dark to walk the streets and decide on his next move, when he had seen three men attack another emerging from a hotel. It was late and there was no one else about and the victim of the attack, though strong, was outmatched. Violence had always angered Hugh, rousing him from his normal kindness to an unnatural passion.

Seeing a pit-prop lying in the street — it had obviously fallen from a cart — he'd picked it up and run towards the unsavoury affray, in which feet as well as fists were being freely used. The man, his head bloodied, was lying in the gutter, curled into a foetal position. Hugh shouted and began to lay about him with the post until a crashing blow from behind sent him flying sideways. The human jackals were by now rummaging in the man's pockets. He saw the glint of a watch and heard the clink of coins. Immediately, he rushed back in spite of his aching head and swung the piece of wood again and again, this time with his back to the wall, and his increased anger for fuel. The booty fell into the dirt and other citizens, alerted by Hugh's cries, were pounding towards them. The thieves fled, and the injured man looked up in the weak glow of the flares and whispered, 'What's your name, friend?'

He was, as it turned out, an associate of the John Jacob Astor who was the biggest fur trader in New York. Astor had started life as the son of a German butcher from the town of Waldorf. A town was named after him, Astoria, on the Columbia River, and now Astor was to found a series of trading posts along the banks, using canoes to connect the enterprise.

Schmidt, Astor's associate, was touchingly grateful merely to be alive, but also to retain the legacy of his father's watch and the money in his pockets. His gratitude knew no bounds. Quickly, he'd found out Hugh's present position and told him there would be a place for him in one of Astor's posts, provided he did not mind the isolation and the necessity to pit himself against the weather, predatory beasts and Indians who might not be as friendly as one could wish.

Hugh had decided the life would have no worse hazards than living at Croggan, and would be infinitely better paid. The children were thrilled at the thought of the journey which would be undertaken by a boat taking stores to the new posts.

He would write again when they were settled in their new home and hoped she was still as well-pleased with her own life. Meg and Jim sent their regards and looked forward to the snowy North. His mother doted on Joseph and Dinah and would be the tower of strength she'd always been. Their star was rising.

There was no mention of Clemence. It was as if her mother had never existed. Karran went immediately to the garden and picked some roses. Then she saddled the mare and rode to the tiny cemetery where Clemence was buried. Some dirty, gypsy-like children played among the gravestones. It was quite sacrilegious. All the time Karran knelt, arranging the flowers under the tiny marker stone that was all Hugh could afford, she was aware of their shouts and the flutter of their ragged garments. Poor Mama. She had no peace, not even in death.

It was as she was leaving that she recognised the eldest of the unruly tribe as Aggie's son. These were her cousins. Karran burned to tell them that graves were not playgrounds, but instinct told her that these were the wrong tactics. In any case, Mama was so far removed from this walled plot with its lichened stones and tablets that it could no longer matter to her. But Karran's heart burned as she went away, knowing that the flowers would be stolen or despoiled as soon as she was out of sight. She must come more often.

The shadows of the past still spilled as darkly as those tree patterns across the track. But not for everyone. Hugh's letter was filled with hope and pleasure in the unknown future and she rejoiced with him. Boyce Kerruish had achieved his ambition to become a soldier and Elizabeth had made a good marriage. Erin prospered. It was impossible to believe that she'd once begged on the quayside before Jesse married her. Their star too was in the ascendant.

Karran pushed aside the memories of Jesse and Clemence. Richards was uppermost in her thoughts. He'd expected her an hour ago but he'd understand her sudden need to show her love for her mother. For a time, that had been in abeyance, but she had come to understand how adversity changed people and that they did not always mean what they said. She wondered how Richards would accept the news she had for him.

The Howards had no claim on her today. She had finished the accounts last night, proud of the neat columns and tidy handwriting. Emily's was spiderish and John's often indecipherable. They could be justly pleased with their pupil in that respect at least.

Her heart beat faster as she skirted the glen. The knowledge that Laurence was only a quarter of a mile away always caused this disturbance in her blood and bones. She wondered if she would still have loved him without this physical response. But a mere bodily need would not transport her beyond herself and into that state in which she was part of the night, the earth, the whole of the universe. She remembered that iridescent bubble that shattered almost every time they were together. There had been one or two occasions when it had not and she had wondered then if it was gone for good, but the next time it had been especially wonderful. Even without it she had wanted to stay with him and hold him in her arms for as long as he would allow.

'Doesn't that woman ever suspect?' Richards had growled more than once.

'I don't know,' Karran had replied. Certainly Emily was sometimes abrupt, and she never commented that Richards seemed to be in residence, as one might have expected after John's efforts to buy him out. Perhaps it was because they had decided to wash their hands of the matter after Laurence's last irritable letter to their solicitor. When Karran mentioned this explanation Richards seemed to accept it as fact. She herself was never sure. And now there was this uncomfortable situation. He'd be angry.

She heard him at the back of the cottage when she dismounted and tethered the mare. The sound of axe-blows rang out in regular rhythm. As she rounded the corner of the cottage, she saw him, his white shirt-sleeves rolled up to the elbows, his body braced against each down swing. The black bow that tied his hair was a little askew and she felt a little stab of tenderness for the small imperfection.

'Laurence?'

He stopped immediately and laid the axe against the fence. 'You're late.'

She began to tell him of Hugh and his auspicious start in America, of Clemence's absence from the letter and her own impulse. Anything but what was most important.

'Well, you don't expect me to take you to task, do you?'

'No. But you started to cut logs because you thought I wasn't coming.'

'My dear, it's tiresome to become such an open book.'

It was one of his difficult days. Karran's spirits flagged a little. She hated to tread on eggshells. 'Isn't it good to — understand the person you love?'

'Perhaps it is,' he replied, more brusquely than she liked. He almost insinuated he didn't love her sufficiently to know the answer. No, she mustn't imagine things. That was the sure road to spoiled relationships.

They entered the cottage, not really in accord. It was tidier than usual, almost as if he were preparing to go. White-faced, she turned to him. 'You aren't leaving, are you? Are you, Laurence?'

He did not answer immediately and she was conscious of a swift panic.

'I may have to,' he said at last, his voice harsh as broken stones.

'Well at least you waited to say goodbye this time.'

'That was cowardly of me, but I imagined I'd apologised.'

'As you will next time you return, I suppose.' It was all going wrong. So wrong!

'I — may not be back.'

Her eyes flew wide open. 'Why? Why won't you?'

'I had a letter — '

'Oh. From your wife, I suppose. I wondered when you'd bring yourself to mention her.' Where had all that bitterness been? Lying in wait for this moment?

71

'Wife?' He looked genuinely surprised.

'You said there was something you'd tell me in your own time. It was the worst thing I could think of.'

Richards laughed. The sound shocked her. She stepped forward and slapped his face with all of her strength. One moment his face was white, the next his cheek was imprinted with the shape of her hand. The scarlet mark was like a brand..

He lifted his own hand and covered the violent redness. 'Well, you do surprise me.'

'How do you expect me to feel when you say you may never be back?'

'I tried to warn you. At the beginning — '

'Why, then?' She was suddenly tired and defeated. Faint. Karran put out an arm to support herself while she pulled a chair towards her. Her head felt light and swimmy and she had a sensation of falling. A long way off, Richards' voice sounded sharp and anxious, then died away into nothing.

She was not sure for how long she lost consciousness. A long beam of light from the little window bathed the bed recess where she lay. Richards was a black silhouette between the window and the bed. Karran wanted to reach out, to pull him close to her but she had not the strength.

'You mustn't go,' she told him. 'I need you. Need you in a special way — '

'What sort of way?'

'I'm having a child. I won't know what to do if you aren't here.'

'God,' he said violently. 'Oh, God! I knew I shouldn't have let you in with your wheedling and tantalising. Your damned insistence — '

'You aren't sorry?' She almost screamed the words. 'Not altogether? Tell me you meant some of it. You aren't sorry? Are you?'

'Yes, but not in the way you seem to think. Only because I've spoiled your life as well as my own. Dragged you down quite needlessly. All I had to do was to keep you out of my bed but I was too weak to do it. Please forgive me.'

'Laurence, if you haven't a wife, why is it impossible for us to put matters right? Why, Laurence?' Her voice was high and strained as if she already knew the answer.

'Why must you go? I think I deserve to know.'

'Because — while I was away — I injured a man, very terribly, and now that man has died and if I stay, I'll be apprehended sooner or later and — ' He shrugged.

She could not make out his face. He was nothing but a man-shaped blackness. Some of that darkness was finding its way inside her, wrapping itself round the new life he had implanted there. She was crying soundlessly, her fingers tearing at the bed-clothes. She saw — gallows. The cry escaped of its own volition.

'Karran. Don't — I never meant to harm him. We were playing cards and we'd drunk too freely. He said I cheated. We fought and I flung him away from me in a blind anger. He hit his head on the mantel. A very handsome mantel if I remember rightly. Carved. There was blood on the carving. There were witnesses. I had to leave in a hurry. My friend said he'd let me know what happened. Now he has done so.'

She sat up. 'We can go together — '

'No. Even if you were not pregnant, I'd have refused. That was why I had to be sure you'd have someone. Howard. He won't throw you out, even with matters as they stand, will he?'

'If he knows it's you, that could make a difference.' She was calm now and terribly empty. Laurence had to go and she was to stay. Never to see him again. And she'd bear a child nobody wanted but herself. The responsibility weighed her down like a millstone.

'You could let me know where you are later. When it's all forgotten — '

'No, Karran. It will never be — all forgotten.'

'Your friend will say you didn't mean it.'

'And there will be three of *his* who will swear that I did.'

Perhaps, Karran thought numbly, that was why she had gone to Croggan to put roses on her mother's grave. Because, subconsciously, she had needed Clemence more than she'd ever anticipated.

'When will you have to go?'

'Very soon.'

'Shall I see you again?'

'I don't think anyone is likely to come for me quite so soon. But I must book a passage. Decide where I am to go. Ireland? Liverpool?' He shrugged again.

'Is Liverpool very large?'

'Big enough. And I can go anywhere in the world from there. Almost anywhere.'

Suddenly, she was trembling and could not stop.

Richards went for the brandy and forced some between

her lips, then held her hands until she recovered herself.

'Stay with me,' she said, 'only near me. I won't be a nuisance — '

'I'm a murderer,' he told her. 'Doesn't that make me — a sort of leper?'

'Not to me. The only thing that would really hurt me is if you told me all the things we've done together were only — expediency. That there was no love involved.'

'Oh, but there was,' he whispered. 'There was! Don't you realise I'd have gone weeks ago but for you. I never meant to stay more than a few days. Only you kept me — '

He did not attempt to make love to her and she did not want him to. It was enough to be close to him and stroke his sun-warmed shoulder. Listen to his breathing and pretend she would always hear it.

'You aren't listening,' Emily said a little sharply.

'I'm sorry. What did you say?' Karran's cup clattered into the saucer. There was a mist over the sea and Shag Rock was a shadowy blur. Beyond the grey-green nebulosity there was nothing to remind anyone that the mainland existed. Richards' enemies would never find him here. He'd done nothing. It had been an accident.

'There you go again,' Emily pointed out. 'It's disconcerting to address a deaf mute.'

'I'm tired, I suppose.'

'You do look very pale and you've eaten nothing. Are you sure you should go out?'

'I need the fresh air.'

'It's damp and if you are sickening for something — '

'Please, don't fuss. It's nothing.'

'I have the impression you aren't happy. Why is that, Karran?'

Emily's directness should not have surprised her but Karran was still aware of a sense of shock. Lies and deceit did not come easily and she had hoped for no such confrontation.

'You could not be kinder, either of you.'

'That is no real answer, is it. You know my views on free speech.'

'I am just — tired.'

'Then I ought to insist that you go to bed. One can abuse the nervous system as well as the body.'

'I hate being idle.'

'You need not lie doing nothing. We have plenty of books. Rest and quiet — '

'No, thank you. I'd rather walk and rid myself of whatever ails me.' Karran wished she had not said that. Part of her did not want to be rid of the child, even if she did feel that the difficulties that faced her were enormous. She could do nothing that would harm it. Yet, knowing in advance the Howards' disillusionment, she would not have been human had she not envisaged some spontaneous termination of her pregnancy. Later, when the child had developed, she sensed that there would be no countenancing its loss.

'You haven't had second thoughts?'

'Second thoughts?' What did Emily mean?

'About young Clive. They say he returns this week-end.'

'I have no regrets.'

'I'm glad. It seemed to me that your indisposition began when I told you he was to marry Elizabeth Kerruish. Have you noticed that island names all seem to begin with Ks or Qs? I wonder why? We could try to find out.'

'Yes, we could.' Karran was glad of the diversion. 'It's interesting.'

She rose. 'I'll go to the garden room for my cloak and basket. I'll look for samphire.'

'The accounts might be more restful.'

'They're done.'

'You do fling yourself into things so whole-heartedly, my dear,' Emily said. 'However, I'll not forbid you. It would be against all I've taught you. If we cannot have trust — '

'Thank you,' Karran interposed. The matter of trust was a sore point. She should insist upon going away with Richards. A ship's captain would marry them. There must be somewhere they could live undisturbed. Except that never again would they find peace, or indeed, be entitled to expect it.

She hurried from the room. It was a week since Laurence had told her about that man's death. She didn't even know his name, nor wanted to. A name would give him an unwelcome identity. It was understandable that Laurence must react angrily to an imputation of dishonesty. But to kill someone! She made herself face the fact without emotion, but her feeling for Richards broke through the false calm. She could be indifferent to nothing that concerned him. They were both part of him, herself and the child. If she went away, the Howards would forget her in time. She

75

would be a bad investment they had made towards the future. She would miss John very much, and Karran minded hurting him a great deal more than she would regret Emily's disappointment.

The garden room was cool and green-shadowed. Branches hung across the dusty glass against which a spider's web was stretched, two or three silk-swaddled victims caught in the sticky mesh. A chill crept out of the flagstones and Karran shivered. The room was full of echoes. Jugs and buckets stood about the fringes of the place and her cloak swayed gently in the draught from the open door. She reached for the cloak, then was distracted by the sound of boots crunching on the gravel outside. John's voice, a little annoyed, said 'I'm not surprised by your news. I've had a long-standing feud with Richards for years. Apparently the cottage was well-kept in his mother's day, but he did nothing for some time after her death and the garden ran wild very quickly. My predecessor did not particularly care but I found the tholtan a thorn in the flesh. My factor met with a hostile reception when I sent him with a request that he either take the place in hand or relinquish it. He brandished a fowling-piece at poor Brand.

'After that I approached him through the offices of my solicitor but got little but boorish refusals, then nothing at all but one last sarcastic reminder that a man can do as he likes on his own piece of land so long as he harms no one else.'

The two men had come to a halt just outside the window, almost obscuring the small pane. John's was the tall, spare shadow. She could see little of the second man but a dark, square bulk and the suggestion of a large nose.

Karran was visited by a dread that set her shaking.

'So you'd say he was quick-tempered and not above enjoying doing someone a mischief.'

'I'd not condemn a man for what I have not seen for myself.' Howard became cautious.

'Quite so, Mr Howard. But, on the other hand, you personally found him antagonistic.'

'Yes.'

'Did you never find it strange that a young man should lead such an isolated existence?'

'I heard he originally brought female company. Then, recently, I was told he had a local mistress though no one seemed to know her name. Brand, my factor, saw them together but they were too far off for him to see who she was.'

The big head with its large, questing nose was suddenly

uplifted. 'She'll be the reason he came back here and stayed. None of the family told me of the existence of the cottage. According to all Richards' brothers, they'd never heard from him since he left Carlisle. But one of my men, on my instructions, took up with a chambermaid at the Richards' house and she saw a letter that made it plain he was on Man and not too far from Port St Mary. A fine estate you have, Mr Howard.'

'I am pleased with it.' Howard's coolness told Karran he disliked the subterfuge of the private correspondence.

'And you say there's a path across the glen that comes out at Richards' back garden?'

'There is.'

'We've got him, then!'

'It begins just there.' John pointed out the beginning of the track through the trees. 'You can't mistake it. It's well-trodden. But you'd do well to remember he's armed. It could be difficult to dislodge him if he sees you or hears your approach. The walls must be four feet thick.'

'But the roof's of straw. It'd burn.'

'Surely, you'd not set fire — ' John could not hide his disapproval.

'As you pointed out, we'd have little chance of winkling him out should he bar himself inside. His would be the advantage. My men would be at risk, and he has killed before. True, his victim lingered for a time but it was his hand struck the blow. We may have little choice.' The stranger did not sound daunted by the prospect.

'I'll not say I'm entirely happy, Mr Molesworth,' John said. 'Anyway, I have shown you the way you are most likely to surprise him, and I hope, without blood-letting. After all, he is still to be proved guilty. You must remember that.'

'There are several witnesses who will all swear to the same story.'

'And is there no one for him?'

'One only, and his word suspect since they have been lifelong friends. Counsel will no doubt make mincemeat of such a witness. No, I fear he *is* a rogue and that we may have trouble apprehending him.' Karran hated the unctuous satisfaction in the man's voice.

'You'll perhaps take a glass of canary first? The man's been there for some weeks now, and unlikely to expect imminent arrest since his brothers were sworn to silence. Ten minutes can make little difference.'

77

It seemed to Karran, through the veil of horror and despair, that John was repenting of having assisted the abominable Molesworth to hunt down another human being and wished to delay the man's departure.

'Well. As you say, another ten minutes is of little significance. We may leave our horses with you? They'd make too much noise.'

'Of course.' John moved away somewhat unwillingly. He was surely regretting his complicity, Karran thought numbly, with a picture before her of the tholtan in flames and Richards screaming.

Molesworth's heavy tread sickened her. Everything about him was ponderous and chillingly relentless for all the note of joviality. There was a lightening of the garden room. The hand that still clutched at the cloak on the peg was washed with an eerie green.

Relaxing her hold, Karran went to the doorway and watched the two so widely differing figures walk past the larger windows of the morning-room. Molesworth's back was wide as a door. He wore his own sandy hair tied back with brown ribbon. His legs were sturdy and his arms powerful as an ape's.

She stepped back as they reached the corner in case either looked back. When she peered out, they had gone. With no more thought of the cloak, she ran to the entrance to the wood and plunged into umbrageous depths.

She ran until her breath sawed in her ribs and the tree-tops swung above her in a dizzying canopy. Molesworth must have finished his glass of wine and would be assembling the men he had brought. But they would not be able to hurry as she did. Her flying feet disturbed leaf-mould and cracked ancient twigs. Her skirts caught on projections and were torn. Branches scraped at her face and hands as she sought for the shortest route.

Karran, dishevelled, smarting and breathless, toiled up the bank on the opposite side of the glen and staggered towards the cottage. 'Laurence! Laurence?' Her voice, cracked and husky, broke the dreaming silence. There was not even the sound of a bird.

She flung open the door and cried his name but there was no response. The long, dim room echoed with emptiness as the garden room had done earlier. This was something Karran had not foreseen. He could not be far away for he'd left the place unlocked, knowing she would come. But Molesworth must have started off by now.

78

Outside, she called again for Richards but dared not do so too loudly. A hot, tight anxiety took possession of her. She dared not go off in search of him in case he returned by some other path and fell into Molesworth's trap. The inspector was sure to hide himself and his companions around the tholtan to wait. The fire burned and it was obvious Richards meant to come back.

'Laurence,' she whispered. 'Why don't you hurry?' What had taken him away? Perhaps he'd thought to please her by producing some plant or fruit or shell for the compendium. He'd left no note and there was something simmering in the big black pot.

The anxiety turned to impotence. Perhaps she could fire a warning shot? She'd never used a firearm but the mechanism seemed simple enough. Karran went back inside the building, but a swift survey of the corners showed her that Richards had taken the fowling-piece. Yet she must let him know of the danger that awaited.

Ashen-faced, she went round to the back of the tholtan. There was tar in the little outhouse and a pile of thick, dried roots. She stuck one of these into the tar barrel and darted back towards the cottage, the tar dripping onto her clothes and the clay floor. Poking it into the fire she was rewarded by a burst of flame. The root burned brightly.

She hurried away from the cottage so that she would not, inadvertently, set fire to Richards' home. The pale flames licked at the passing trunks and branches but she could not bring herself to damage a living tree. It took her several minutes to find the lightning-struck elm she sought. Karran poked the fiery brand into the hollow heart and waited, in an agony of suspense, for it to ignite.

Presently, she was rewarded by a dry, spitting sound and a shower of sparks that fell into her hair and over her bodice. Her lips stung suddenly and she let out a stifled scream. Then the rotten centre caught properly and the trunk was filled with a roaring sound. Smoke and flame shot upwards in a dancing pillar.

There were voices in the distance, scattered shouts and a crack of feet on old wood. Dropping the torch, she launched herself towards the nearest gap in the birches and twisted between the slender spikes where grown men would be unable to follow. There was a squat, hydra-like oak some yards off – she could sit in the branches and watch what happened. In spite of her exertion, her hands and her spine were cold and her throat

79

filled with dryness. She found that she was whispering disjointed sentences, all of them entreaties or prayers for Laurence's safety.

He must have seen her beacon by now. The whole district would be aware of it.

From the platform of the oak, Karran could see the cottage through the screen of birch. Though hazed by smoke, she made out the square figure of Molesworth. He was coming out of the house and she saw his face for the first time. It was a wide, large-featured visage, everything disproportionately big but for his eyes that were small and not deeply set, and gave the impression of pale beads stuck into dough. He reminded her of a picture she had seen of King Henry the Eighth, in one of Howard's books.

Her stomach muscles clamped together. She had forgotten Howard completely. Nothing had mattered but Laurence's safety. John would see the burning tree and think it was Richards' roof. It was inevitable that he must find out her part in all this.

Molesworth looked grim. Dourly, he directed most of the anonymous figures to spread out in the adjacent woodland. He naturally thought that Laurence had escaped, leaving the fired elm as a diversion. Two others were sent down to the stream with buckets to fetch water to put out the blaze.

Karran dragged her skirts further up the branch in case they were seen by the fire-fighters. Laurence could not be far away. Apprehension swelled up in her and she had a sensation of being trapped. Sooner or later one of Molesworth's men must come this way and he would look everywhere, even above his head, if he did his job properly.

'Karran.'

She thought at first that she had imagined the soft whisper, but it came again, just to her right. Peering down, she made out the dim shape of Richards, crouched behind a bush, a game-bag by his side.

'Thanks for creating the diversion.'

She nodded and made to scramble down but he stopped her. 'They'll see you.'

'Have you been there long?'

'A few minutes. I should go now. They are fanning out and I can't stay. I just wanted to say — goodbye. And thank you, Karran. For everything.'

A wild tempest of feeling raced through her body. 'I want to come.'

'Don't be a fool.' His soft rejoinder was purposefully curt.

'I'd ask no one to share what's ahead. How did they know?'

'Prying into your brother's correspondence after making up to one of the maids. I heard them tell John.'

'Charming. I suppose they have their job to do.' His mouth twisted.

'It's not a way I'd want to earn my living.'

Part of her wanted to keep him there. The rest was torn with anxiety. 'Don't let them catch you.' Her lips were stiff. She thought she would never smile again. One of Molesworth's recruits swung a bucket powerfully and the jet of water hissed against the blackened trunk. It still burned but not so fiercely. Sparks spiralled.

Karran looked back to where Richards had been, but in that moment of inattention he had slipped away soundlessly. The world became shockingly empty. What was she doing here? She forgot that there were men close by. She had not said good-bye and it was important that she should.

Someone shouted as she slid to the ground. Her ankle struck a projection and pain shot through it.

'Over there! No, there, you numskull.'

For a moment she was frozen with immobility. Her brain would not function any more than her body. Then life came surging back and with it, the instinct for survival. The two men had thrown down the buckets and were splashing through the stream.

Hobbling, she ducked under a spread of branches and into a narrow aisle between thin spears of birch. Ahead of her she thought she glimpsed a flicker of movement. She began to run awkwardly, casting a backward look over her shoulder. The noise of splashing and of boots on stone grew louder.

Halfway down the aisle Karran realised she was taking her pursuers towards Richards. She'd never catch up with him now and the knowledge scored at her senses like a knife. As well as the pain in her ankle, she discovered, now that Laurence had out-distanced her, that she was deathly tired. She slumped to the mossy ground.

'It's a tinker's wench,' a man said in disgust and seized her by the shoulder.

'Leave me alone! I'm doing no harm.' Karran cried out as his fingers dug into her flesh.

'Where's he then, that fancy man of yours? He is your fancy man, isn't he?'

'Who? I don't know who you mean.' Her eyes were wide and black as night.

'Young Mr Richards.' Her captor grinned and showed broken teeth. 'Not that I blame him for coming back to you. What do you say, Jake?'

Jake, who had arrived, breathless and bad-tempered, said sourly, 'Dirty, gypsy trash! Tell us which way he went, or it'll be the worse for you.'

She compressed her lips and drew back from him. His hand flew out suddenly and sent her crashing against the nearest birch trunk. Her ears sang with the force of the blow.

'Get away from her!' Richards' voice rang out. He had stepped out of the undergrowth and the fowling-piece was pointed in a business-like fashion at the man called Jake. 'Come here, Karran. The first man to follow dies. I've nothing to lose.'

'Laurence — 'She started towards him, steadier now as the worst of the pain died from her foot, leaving a dull ache. But her face and back hurt quite badly. Only God knew how it all would end. At least she'd be able to say goodbye.

'You shouldn't have stopped,' she said when she was close to him. 'I can't run any more. What happens to me doesn't matter.'

Richards' arm was around her shoulder briefly. 'She had nothing to do with all this,' he said loudly enough for Jake and his companion to hear. 'Karran knows nothing of what I've done and I should be very careful how you treat her after I've gone. She's Howard's ward and he'll want an account of how she received these bruises. I should put a round of shot through your backside except that it would bring your friends.' His eyes returned to Karran's face. 'Goodbye again, my love. A pity I've not been better for you. Don't call the child after me. I've always disliked my name.'

The softness of his voice was totally disarming. He bent and kissed her very gently.

She shook her head blindly, the tears obscuring the sight of him. Her hands groped for him and encountered nothing. Somewhere behind there were voices. Jake and the man who had caught her were coming down the track. Brushing away the tears, she saw them very close, then they thrust her aside to plunge into the wood's shadows.

A shot rang out. Karran waited, disbelievingly, for the next. But there was only a silence that seemed to burn her like fire. All sounds of movement had ceased. The hot unease consumed her. She pushed aside the foliage and followed the marks of crushed twigs and displaced beech-mast. There were several figures some distance away, where a gap in the wood created a small basin of light. They were all strangers, all staring at something that lay on the uneven ground.

The trees moved, shot upwards towards the sky like a flight of arrows. It was dark.

Clive and Elizabeth had arrived back from the honeymoon trip. Both were glad but for differing reasons. Clive was anxious to get back to the Donaghue with all its fascinating problems. The Simpson was due to arrive from Liverpool and he wanted to inspect the available ground to decide upon the best position for the projected smelter. He had the advantage over the rest of the mine-holders, for the Donaghue was the most isolated of the Foxdale shafts and the house he and Elizabeth were to occupy was the only building for miles and protected within its thicket of trees. There'd be no one to complain about the atmosphere.

Elizabeth needed the stabilising influence of her mother's home after her traumatic experiences and before she was expected to take up her new role as Mistress of Mingay. She was first out of the carriage, almost running up the steps, her hand clutching at the new bonnet that threatened to blow away as far as the quayside where Qualtrough the boat-builder's *Peggy* lay at anchor. Barney had admired the *Peggy*. He was certain she would still be in use in another hundred years, so strong and sturdy a craft was she.

Charlotte was in the parlour when Elizabeth burst in, eager to greet her mother. How insignificant she was, the new Mrs Clive thought scornfully. That anyone so mousy could deliberately accentuate her dowdiness by wearing brown! Green would have been better with hazel eyes. Charlotte's eyes were her only redeeming feature and had little unexpected glints of gold and olive when they were caught in sunlight.

The girl put a defensive hand over the book she was reading. 'You'll wear out your sight in this poor light,' Elizabeth could not forbear pointing out. 'Where's Mama?'

'At the dressmakers. She won't be long. Did you — enjoy yourself?'

Was there a flicker of knowledge at the back of her sister's eyes, Elizabeth wondered. But how could there be? She had told nobody of her lack in marriage. Clive had insisted the fault lay with herself. Other women gave themselves naturally and generously. And then he had said that once she was in their own home matters might become better. They had done little but travel and tire themselves since the ceremony. He looked forward to some improvement when they were at Mingay. What was wrong with her? She had not found him unpleasing before they were married. The deficiency must lie with her, and she detested the knowledge.

Clive had come into the room and Elizabeth made a pretence of affection. She slipped her arm through his and smiled up into his face. 'She wants to know if we enjoyed ourselves. A silly question to a newly-wed pair, isn't it! Isn't it, my dear?'

'As you say,' he replied and went to the table where a decanter stood half-full, to pour himself a glass of wine. 'Where's your father, Charlotte?'

'In his study with Mr Gelling.'

'Oh, Nat. Is he here?' Elizabeth had not seen the overseer for some time. She remembered the evening at the Bascombes.

'Some business in connection with the Erin. A new engine. Installation problems.'

'So he's got it already!' Clive was chagrined. While he'd been wasting his time in London with a cold wife and none too compatible brothers-in-law, Kerruish had stolen a march on him. Not that they were really opponents, not with Elizabeth to cement their relationship, but it was not good policy to lag behind a rival. It was a pity he had not gone straight to Foxdale after putting Elizabeth into the carriage. But she would have protracted her stay in Castletown, and he was determined she'd carry out her side of the bargain. He must be master. There'd be none of the sort of nonsense Kerruish put up with from Elizabeth's mother.

'And what's been happening in this backwater?' Elizabeth asked, tossing her bonnet onto the sofa then relapsing, yawning, into a velvet armchair.

Charlotte sat up. 'You missed all the excitement!'

'Why? What happened? Shipwreck? Pit disaster? Fire?'

'A man was killed last week. Some friend of Karran Kinrade's. He'd a cottage near the Chasms. The authorities were seeking this Richards for murder.'

'Murder?' Elizabeth broke in. 'There's been a murder on the island?'

'No, Carlisle. Richards was accused of cheating and struck the man who accused him. Too hard it seems. But he came to live at the cottage near the Howards. They say Karran was assisting him to escape — '

'Indeed!' Elizabeth said, her voice hard with remembered humiliation. 'So she did have other fish to fry! Do you hear that, Wheatley?'

'The girl's in trouble!' Clive reminded her sharply. 'It's

no time for spite.'

'How do you expect me to feel! After those disclosures — '

They had both forgotten Charlotte's presence. Deliberately, she allowed her book to fall to the floor. Such naked antagonism was disagreeable and frightening.

'I'm sorry,' Clive said. 'Our manners are atrocious, aren't they. You didn't finish your tale.'

'No one seems to know very much more. The servants let it out. One can never keep anything from them.'

'And Miss Kinrade? What of her?'

'She's ill and cannot be seen. They say she collapsed at the sight of the man's body in the wood. He was armed and Molesworth, the man in charge of his capture, said it was either his life or Richards'. He'd threatened someone just before they met. Another minute though and he'd have slipped through the net. The difference a minute can make. . . . '

'What unfortunate irony,' Clive murmured.

'He'd committed a crime!' his wife expostulated.

'What do we know of it all, Elizabeth? Charlotte says the story came via the servants and they might have been biased, or had it themselves at second or third hand.'

'We are in danger of becoming notorious,' Charlotte said. 'It's not the first time we've had — shall we say — disgrace in the family?'

'What do you know about that!' Elizabeth cried. It would be Barney's work, stirring up the past. Erin would certainly not rake up Jesse's death, especially not for Charlotte.

'What's this?' Barney was coming into the room and behind him the tall, dark figure of Gelling. 'I hadn't expected to see you. Did you write?'

'I did, though I couldn't say which day we'd arrive. Didn't Mama tell you?'

Barney turned towards the decanter. 'She may have done,' he answered after a pause, 'I disremember. Wine, Elizabeth? I see Wheatley has some already. And you, Nat? Tell me about those brothers of yours.' He never referred to them as his sons. They were apart.

'Well. Boyce is quite dashing and I suspect he's no longer heart-free.'

'Oh? Who is the wench?'

'Some general's daughter, I believe, though we never met. And Sebastian has changed out of recognition. You remember his drawings? Well, I should say he has the makings of a considerable draughtsman.'

'H'm!' Barney grunted, unimpressed.

'She's right,' Clive told him. 'I was surprised at their quality.'

Gelling had moved towards the window and Elizabeth followed him. The dark green gown emphasised the whiteness of her skin and the prodigality of her fiery hair.

'Well, Nat? How are you?' She was aware, most unexpectedly, of his stalwart masculinity.

He stared at her and she saw, suddenly what she had not previously recognised. There came into men's eyes at certain times a particular look and it was alive now in Nat Gelling's. He glanced down at the carpet but it was too late. How flattering it was when one knew that nothing could come of it, Elizabeth thought. All this time and Nat Gelling had wanted her. She found herself wondering if his technique would be the same as Clive's. But it was a dangerous reflection and it would be foolish to seek for an answer. She could not even pleasure her own husband, and she was not a second Karran.

Nat's shoulders moved uncomfortably under the plain dark coat. He said he was well and that he'd like to take this opportunity of wishing her well. He'd not been able to get near her at the wedding breakfast.

'It was far too crowded,' Elizabeth agreed. 'And the mine. How goes it?'

'We repaired a derrick while you were away.' His eyes encountered hers again and, for a moment, the look was quite naked. But it was not quite like Wheatley's lusting arrogance. There was something else she did not recognise, except to experience the strangest compulsion to discover what it meant. He continued to talk of horse gins and windlasses and the new Simpson which would do the work of two previous engines, but Elizabeth heard only the inflections of his voice, saw the forced impersonality of his expression and felt a curious triumph that she had been allowed beyond that veil, however transiently.

They heard Erin's arrival, the clop of the horses' hooves and the grinding halt behind Clive's carriage. The quick tap of her feet on the steps. 'Elizabeth? My darling!' Gusts of musky scent and Elizabeth's conviction that her mother had begun to touch up her hair with henna. The colour was not quite right around her forehead and temples.

Disengaging herself, Elizabeth was forced to reply to the spate of jerky questions. Erin's occasional laughter sounded forced and her eyes were not happy. She had lost weight. And, Elizabeth could not help noticing, Barney did not come to his wife as he used to do, with unfailing affection. They were still estranged. It had to do with a woman in Port St Mary. Violet Lane? It was something like that. A flowery name —

'Are you happy, my dear?'

It was the question Elizabeth had dreaded. Erin knew her too well. She would give herself away, whatever she said. 'Oh, Charlotte told us about the happenings at Ravensdowne. You always said the Kinrades were a bad lot. It seems you were right.'

'Oh, that.' Erin picked up the glass Barney had set down beside her. 'I heard more in the dressmakers. It seems the factor Brand had seen a woman going to the cottage quite frequently and recognised Karran, though naturally he could not tell Howard that. He pretended the distance made it impossible to see her face. Of course, the Howards know the whole story now. They must regret ever having befriended her. It was touch and go whether she was arrested but this Richards said, in front of witnesses, that she knew nothing of what he'd done. A likely story!'

'He could have been telling the truth,' Barney said coldly. 'One's own yardstick need not necessarily apply to everyone else.'

There was a pause in which one could have heard a pin drop, then Nat Gelling said, 'I must go now. When will you visit the Erin, Mr Kerruish?'

The two men moved away, Nat's tall darkness in total contrast to Barney's short, pear-shaped figure and bowed shoulders. Kerruish looked old, devoid of his former warmth. Erin had dealt him some hard blow and Elizabeth longed to know what it had been. They would pass through Port St Mary, herself and Clive, on their way to Mingay, and she would look out for the lane. It wasn't Violet but a word quite smiliar. Lilac! Mrs Payne of Lilac Lane. Any local woman would know who she was and what she did.

She became aware that Charlotte was slipping quietly out of the room, the book clutched in one thin hand. Clive had gone with the others.

'Is everything all right, Mama?'

Erin's lips moved in a shockingly white face, their painted redness obscene. The travesty of a smile touched Elizabeth more than she would have thought possible. 'What would be wrong with us?' Erin asked and laughed shakily. 'You know Barney. The kindest man on earth. And now, tell me about the boys.' She refilled her glass and they sat down together. But though they chatted energetically enough about Boyce and Sebastian and Elizabeth's impressions of London, their thoughts were of two other people.

Karran jerked into wakefulness. The curtains were drawn and the bed-chamber was cast into a cerulean gloom. The canopy pressed down claustrophobically and remembrance rushed upon her in a murky tide. Nothing would bring him back. Molesworth had killed him and there was no witness to show whether Laurence had threatened him or not.

Her mind recoiled from Emily's reception of the news that she had been Richards' mistress. Karran could never forget her expression. 'I loved him,' Karran had said. 'I know it was wrong to keep it from you but you'd have stopped me. John disapproved of him so much. Yet there was really very little harm in him. Or in our relationship.'

'Little harm! He kills a man and you say — '

'It was not the blow that killed him, but his fall — '

'And he'd not have fallen if he had not been struck.'

'It is not pleasant to be called a cheat.'

'How do you know he was not?'

As if she had not asked herself the same question! Over and over again.

Emily's face had been hard as limestone and her voice would have cut glass. It was obvious to Karran that she could no longer stay here but where could she go?

Karran got out of bed. She felt very weak and a little dizzy. Somehow she could not bring herself to summon a maid to help her to dress. The servants must know the whole story. But her head swam as she bent to pull on her stockings and slowly put on her clothes. Even to brush her hair seemed to take more effort than she could cope with today.

Someone knocked, then opened the door.

'John — ' She stared at him through a raven mesh, the brush clattering onto the chest top.

'You shouldn't be up yet. The surgeon said — '

'I have to get back my strength. And I'll never do it lying here.'

'Give yourself more time.'

'Emily wants me to go.'

'It's not Emily's decision.'

'I couldn't stay, knowing how she feels. Think of the atmosphere. It wouldn't do and I'm sure you know it as well as I. She's your wife and I'm — of no account. I'd have gone away

88

with him if he'd let me. Not that I'd have enjoyed hurting you.'

'Oh, Karran — ' His face was tormented.

'It's my own fault. I knew what could go wrong but it seemed to make no difference. I can't even mourn at his graveside. His brothers insisted he be taken to Carlisle. There's nothing left of him here but the cottage. What will happen to that?'

'Revert to the family unless he decided otherwise.'

'They won't come.' She went to the window and looked out at the autumn garden. The leaves were too bright. All that flaunting orange and yellow. 'They'll let it go to wrack and ruin, or pull it down. You'd like that but I wouldn't.'

'It's not for me to decide. The back of your gown isn't fastened. Let me do it for you.'

She waited obediently while his firm, not too steady fingers fastened the hooks one by one, very slowly almost as though he savoured the task. Perhaps it was just as well that she meant to go. His hands brushed her shoulders and she stiffened her body into resistance.

'Karran — '

'You know I must go. Please don't make it harder for me.'

'That's the last thing I want to do.'

'There is one thing. That money you paid into the bank — '

'Will still be there,' John said almost angrily. 'You earned it.'

'You should take it back. I've disappointed you. You gave it when it seemed I'd be here always. I don't expect — '

'It will be there,' John repeated. He was pale now and beads of perspiration lay on his brow. 'And if you should need more, you have only to ask.'

'You are truly kind. I wish — '

'Wish what?'

'That I'd been what you expected.'

He said nothing and they stood for a space, quite immobile, until he turned and went away. The impress of his presence remained.

'I'll go tomorrow,' she thought. 'Tomorrow.' Then she sat at the window and watched the trees in the glen. It was not possible to see more of the cottage than the gable and the window from which Richards used to make his signal. There would be no more lovers' beacons.

The letter came next day, heavily sealed, closely written.

89

It was from Richards' solicitor. Laurence had left the cottage to Karran, and everything that was in it. She had not cried until that moment. Now the tears came thick and heavy. He had arranged it after the fatal blow was struck, just before he started on his way to Ravenglass. It was almost as if he had known he must make some arrangement for her.

She went to John's study when she was composed and showed him the document and the deed made out in her name. He was silent for a minute, then he said, 'I'll send someone round to tidy the garden and fill the woodshed. If there's any furniture you need — '

'Thank you. I always seem to be thanking you for something. I'll only take the things that belonged to Jesse.'

'And your mare. The men will put up a stable. You'll be quite independent.'

'You will come sometimes?'

'Of course.' He pushed aside the plants he had been examining under the microscope.

'And if I should need to find some sort of work, someone will keep a look-out — '

'My dear child. Why ask? Take that for granted. I am not asking you to go.'

'I'm sorry I upset Emily.'

'Doubtless we will both survive. It's not as if you were leaving the island.'

'I have not much to pack. Personal things — '

'You know, of course, that there may be some local feeling against you? One can never educate a certain element. They could be harsh in their judgement of you.'

'I do see that, but do you really think anyone is going to come so far, just for the pleasure of calling me a harlot?'

'You might be surprised. Lock the door at night. I'll give you a firearm and ask Brand to keep a permanent look-out.'

'You're very good.'

John swept the plants away with one sharp movement that also tipped over the microscope. Flowers and slides were scattered on the floor in a broken mess.

'They're spoiled,' she said, knowing that the act had been symbolic. Karran knelt down and began to gather the battered flora, the segments of glass that pierced her fingertips so that she drew in her breath with pain.

'Leave them alone,' he said harshly. 'I have servants to do that sort of thing. You've cut yourself.' He took out his kerchief and dabbed at the beads of blood.

'It's nothing.' She rose reluctantly.

'You will be all right? You're strong enough?'

'I think so.'

'Take the mare now and go by the top path. I'll send your things.'

She hesitated, not wanting to say goodbye, remembering how she had not said farewell to Laurence. But she mustn't think of that. There was the future to think of and to plan for, the child that was her secret.

It had been painful at first to live full time in the cottage. Secret visits of short duration, most of them flavoured with the excitement of being welcomed and made love to by a man with whom she had a compulsive affinity, were not at all like the reality of her solitary occupation. Karran would wake to loneliness, be reminded immediately of what she had lost when her eyes encountered the so familiar confines of the bed. It seemed incredible that she would never again see the outline of Richards' shoulder and the tangle of his hair on the pillow. She infinitely preferred the smell and reality of him to the sterile emptiness of the newly-laundered sheets with the fragrance of lavender.

She would dress quickly and go immediately to the new stable and speak to Floss who would snicker in reply and toss her handsome head. She would groom, feed and water her, then usually hear the sound of Howard's factor on his round. It had occurred to her that it might be pleasant to go out and speak to Brand occasionally, but her approach could be misconstrued, and for Howard's sake she'd not add the sin of over-familiarity to those already held against her. There would be plenty of gossip later when it became obvious she was pregnant.

The days passed more quickly than she had expected. There was the fire to clean and light, the bed to air and make, and, once a week, to change and sheets to wash. The clean laundry was kept in the handsome oak chest Laurence had left her, carved with oak leaves and acorns and almost black in colour. An oak press sent over by Howard held her not too extensive wardrobe and boots and shoes.

She learnt afresh how to clean the floor and to polish. There had been no need to do these tasks at Ravensdowne. There was weeding and cultivation to see to, the provision of fuel, not that that entailed more than the carrying of it into the house. Howard, ever sensitive to her needs, had provided a desk, ink, quills and paper, and two shelves of books. She went to Port St Mary to watch the candle-maker, then gathered reeds for making tapers and candles of her own.

Always, in the evening, she would take out the shilling Laurence had once thrown at her and stare at it until she knew every scratch and blemish on its carved surface. It would grow warm in her hand and she disliked putting it away. Then she conceived the idea of having a small hole pierced through it at the forge and wore it on a chain so that the token was always next to her skin, a bond with the past.

It was almost winter when Karran rode to the cemetery to visit Clemence's resting-place. She had taken flowers sent from John and found the grave neglected and sad. There were no unruly children today. It was dark and quiet with a mist between the stones. She pulled away the dead grass and the blown leaves and arranged the yellow flowers in a fan. They were the one bright note of colour in a nebulous waste.

Not far away was the wooden cross that marked Luke Karran's grave. The painted lettering was almost obscured by the high brown grass and some impulse made her drag it away so that the cross and text could be better seen. The same dictate made her fetch one of the shaggy blooms and place it on the hump of ground that covered her father's bones.

As she rode off, she fancied she saw a fleeting figure in the distance, a huge humped man on a mount too small for him, but it was no sooner seen than lost. In a mist like this, one could mistake even a dog for something much larger.

She knew she should not be riding in the early stages of her pregnancy but Floss seemed the only real pleasure left to her. Emily, she had not seen since that last bitter encounter. She'd want nothing to do with Richards' child. And John, what would be his reaction? With a nagging disquiet Karran approached the beginning of the track that led to the tholtan. Twice lately she had heard sounds after dark and Floss had neighed. John had told her she should have a dog. Perhaps he was right. Women who had lost their reputation could not expect to escape totally unscathed.

She entered the dusky sea-green of the ride with its fluctuating shadows and punctuations of light, feeling safer now that she was enclosed. No one could see her until she emerged quite close to the cottage. Floss's hooves drummed on the track, drowning the other noises until it was too late. Out of the side path she had forgotten, a man suddenly appeared, only yards ahead. Floss reared in fright and Karran had to fight to regain control. By the time she was straight in the saddle and had her knees dug into the mare's flanks, the man had dismounted and reached her. He grabbed hold of the bridle roughly and grinned up at Karran, showing the dark stumps of his teeth.

'Ain't yer got a kiss for yer cousin, eh?'

With a sensation of shock, she recognised Aggie Karran's common-law husband, Jem Boswell.

'Let go,' she said sharply to cover the creeping fear. 'I'll have the constable on you if you don't. Not to mention your master! He won't employ someone who intimidates a defenceless woman.'

'Master thinks what everyone else does, Miss Kinrade. That you're an upstart too free with your favours, and that anyone who beds with a murderer deserves all she gets.'

She tried to kick out at him but could not free her boot from the stirrup. His huge hand grabbed at her knee. Strong fingers dug into her thigh.

'Let go!' she protested furiously and kicked at Floss's flanks, but the mare was held too close by that large, relentless hand. Jem let go of the horse and took hold of Karran's waist. Terrified, she struck out at his face, dragging her nails down the dirty cheeks so that he shouted with the pain. He was lifting her down, one thick arm holding her prisoner, the other pulling up the skirt of her habit.

Karran screamed and kicked out strongly. Jem smelt of unwashed flesh and clothing. She could not bear his proximity or the thought of what he meant to do. He lowered his head and pressed his mouth over hers but she wrenched it free and screamed again and again.

The ground seemed to move under her feet.

Jem raised his shaggy head and stared, then released her suddenly, muttering something under his breath. She fell against a tree trunk, her body limp with relief. Her attacker ran to the rough-coated Manx pony that waited patiently, and was off again up the side track in great haste, while a well-dressed gentleman on a roan horse made his way urgently towards her.

'Are you all right?' Clive asked, dismouting.

She could hardly speak for the disturbance of her heart. Nodding, she strove to control herself. She gasped and swallowed, felt her breathing begin to steady.

'I'm — glad you were there.' Now that the shock was over,

she wondered why he had been.

'I had some business in the Port and I came up to the cottage to see if you were managing by yourself.' In the half-dimness, his slitted eyes were caught in grey light.

'I was — until just now. That will teach me to keep away from unfrequented places.' She turned away, ostensibly to dust down her disarrayed clothing, not wanting him to see her distress too plainly.

'Who was he?' Clive sounded furious. 'I've seen him — somewhere.'

'I don't know. Some half-witted farm hand who doesn't know his own strength. He wouldn't have done more than snatch a kiss.' The sickness had begun to ebb away. Miraculously, she was safe.

'You make too light of it. From what I saw — '

'What else do you expect me to do? I've no defences. No reputation. You shouldn't be seen with me. You realise your name could be destroyed — ?'

'Come. I'll take you home,' he broke in brusquely. 'You're talking nonsense.'

She allowed him to help her to mount, to push her feet into the stirrups. 'What do you suppose your wife is going to say, should she find out?' Karran asked wryly.

'Why should she?'

'There'll be others, besides — ' She had been going to say Jem. 'Others besides my bucolic attacker. Although Laurence and I thought we were unnoticed, it wasn't so. And you are recently married. Any bride would be insulted, however innocent the visit. I take it, it was meant to be so?'

Exasperated, Clive guided the mare towards his own horse, then swung himself up lightly into the saddle. The sight of Karran had afflicted him with the same feelings of mingled pleasure and desire. Even the initial glimpse of her struggling in another man's arms was a kind of aphrodisiac. Now, her averted profile and the haunting hollow of her cheek, the lock of black hair that escaped from the rest, all worked upon his senses.

'I meant only to reassure myself that you were able to cope,' he lied.

'Everything was well until ten minutes ago.'

'It seems it will be dangerous for you to remain alone until recent events have been forgotten, or decently blunted in folks' minds.'

'I have nowhere else to go.' She shrugged. There was a

smudge of green on one cheek, where she had touched the bark of a tree. 'They'll forget in time.' She nudged Floss into movement and he followed closely.

'At least, invite someone to stay with you.'

'There's no one. But — I may not always be alone.'

Damn her, Clive thought. She practically admitted that she'd not spend the rest of her days in sack-cloth and ashes. It seemed insensitive so soon after Richards' death. Perhaps she had hoped to rid herself of his unwelcome presence by the remark, sensing, no doubt, his unchanged interest in her person.

The cottage was in sight and Karran drew rein. 'It would be better if you left me here. Howard's factor comes by each day, morning and evening. Brand is not close-mouthed, as I have reason to know.' She was pale now, all the darkness of eyes and hair accentuated into a chiaroscuro. Clive wanted to touch the little patch of green dust on her face, to smooth it from the velvet texture of her skin with his fore-finger. He could not understand the ache inside him.

'Please go now,' she said quietly. 'I will never be able to thank you enough just for being in the vicinity. It was good of you to worry on my behalf. But it would be a mistake to repeat the visit. Your Elizabeth would think little of that and if the boot were on the other foot, I'd feel the same.'

'But you'd not object to me speaking to you if we met somewhere else, by accident?'

'No. I just think that assignations are out of place, if that was what you had in mind.'

'Very well. I would like you to make me a promise, however.'

'What promise?'

'That if you are ever in trouble, you would let me know.'

'I'm not your responsibility — '

'We are friends. At least, I think so.'

'I'll keep it in mind. Though I cannot see how it would ever be possible.'

'Promise?'

'What harm can it do?' She smiled at him.

'Be sure to bar your door.'

'I will. Good day to you.' Karran lifted her hand, pressed her knees into Floss's flanks. She rode astride these days in case she fell from the mare. She had never felt so safe side-saddle.

He watched her all the way to the gate, right until she led

the mare round the little dwelling to put her into the stable. She would never ask him for help, but he had offered it.

Slowly, Clive turned his horse's head and set off the way he had come. He had remembered now where he had seen the big, rough-looking man who had dared lay hand on his betters. He'd kept a dirty stall at Castletown and sold Croggan cheese. It would be an easy matter to find him and teach him a lesson he'd never forget.

Clive's fingers fastened tightly over the riding-crop he carried.

4

The winter wind howled around the windows of Mingay. Elizabeth hated the sound. The high keening was as desolate as a wolf's cry and drowned even the ever-throbbing heart of the Donaghue. She hated the mine as much as the sobbing of the wind that rattled every casement and blew the smoke back down the chimneys. Because Clive was so bound up in his work, they would be here for ever and she did not think she could bear it.

Thick flakes of snow came out of the storm-torn void, driving past the glass panes like irregularly-shaped pieces of paper. Desperately, Elizabeth turned her back on the February afternoon and returned to the fire. If it had been fine she would have ridden onto the moor as she so often did, to the large rock from which she could overlook her husband's real love, the Donaghue that smoked and made ugly the surrounding country. Further off were the mine cottages and further still the row that belonged to Kerruish and the steaming chimneys of the Erin and the Charlotte.

Occasionally Elizabeth rode from the Fox Stone to Foxdale, past the cottages with their little smoky roofs and drab women, the clusters of sparsely dressed children who clutched, large-eyed, at their mothers' skirts.

There was no other big house, nowhere she could be received into pleasant or civilised surroundings where she might be appreciated or admired. The Nortons would not presume to invite her and even if they did, she considered them as dull as ditch-water, with their homely pride in Norton's rise and their lack of social graces.

Erin and Barney came infrequently and there was little comfort to be had from those strained appearances. Elizabeth knew now the reason for their estrangement. Barney had obviously wanted another child and her mother had resorted to

Mrs Payne's ergot and camomile to prevent a birth. And now Erin was too old and Kerruish could not forgive her. The woman to whom he'd given everything had denied him the one thing he'd ever asked of her.

Elizabeth became aware of a banging that was not that of the rattling window-frames. She frowned, unable to imagine who might come calling on such a day. Quickly, she ran to the mirror and scrutinised the green velvet turban with its curling feathers and the square neckline of the matching gown. Only a few curls escaped from under the turban, their redness exciting against the white skin. She had dressed up to amuse herself and now she was glad.

'If you please, ma'am,' the maid said nervously from the doorway, 'it's Mr Gelling called to see you.'

Elizabeth, her boredom vanished, said that she'd be pleased to receive Mr Gelling and would Bessie bring some tea and muffins and plenty of butter. Cook was unexpectedly good with tea things.

Nat seemed to fill the doorway. Clive was all narrow elegance but her visitor was broad and well-muscled, a real man under the dark, plain clothes he always affected. He might not be conventionally handsome, though there was an undoubted attraction about the emphatic nose and brows and the well-shaped mouth. But it was his eyes that were most remarkable, a smoky grey that could have indicated a touch of Irish in his ancestry. Yes, Elizabeth decided. It was an Irish face and there was always something about a man from the land of the shamrock. Liverpool was full of such men and that was Nat's birthplace.

'What a surprise!' There was still snow in his hair. It dripped onto the shoulders of the neat black coat. She laughed suddenly with a curious, amused happiness.

'I've not disturbed anything of importance?' He grinned crookedly.

'Of course not. Come over to the fire.'

He obeyed, holding out large, reddened hands to the blaze.

'It must have been difficult getting here.' She sat down and indicated the opposite chair. It seemed too small to contain him.

'I confess I cursed the wind and now that the snow's added to it — ' He shrugged.

'Why did you come? Has something happened?'

'I was over in Castletown and your mother asked me to bring your brothers' last letters.'

'How was she?' Elizabeth accepted the missives and put them down on the pie-crust table.

'Much as usual. She sent her love but will not be able to visit for some time owing to the difficulties of the journey now that the weather's so bad.'

Elizabeth rose to her feet and paced the room. 'As if this place were not a morgue already! Only her visits have kept me from a decline!'

'I should have thought,' Nat said carefully, looking anywhere but at her, 'that you would have had everything to keep you happy. This beautiful house — '

'It's a prison!' she cried passionately.

'And a new marriage.' He went on as if she had not spoken. 'You lack for nothing. You had an exciting journey after a wedding one could only call lavish. Yet you call your home a gaol. I fail to understand you.'

Nettled, Elizabeth sought refuge in rudeness. 'It's not your place to preach to or understand me. You are presumptuous, just because my stepfather finds you indispensable. What did he take you from? Some Liverpool slum?'

A spark of anger showed in his face. 'No slum, Mrs Clive. A decent home if not too moneyed, not that we suffered by the lack. And there was love in it.'

Bessie came back with the tray which looked much too heavy for her. Nat was on his feet in a moment to relieve her of the burden while the girl stared in astonishment and gratitude.

"Don't stand there gawping!' Elizabeth said sharply. 'Go back to your work.' Bessie slunk from the room, chastened.

'A gentleman isn't supposed to notice servants. How do you suppose I could keep order if Wheatley were to run about doing their chores? Giving them airs — '

Nat continued to watch her without speaking and Elizabeth was suddenly and inexplicably ashamed. She sought to justify herself. 'The stupid ninny should have brought two trays. Shall I pour you some tea? That is, if you are staying? Or am I too unworthy of such a paragon?'

'I merely think that nothing is ever lost by consideration. Surely you have always been surrounded by kindness? Your stepfather — '

'Do you wish milk? Sugar?' she snapped.

'Tea only, if you please.'

She handed the delicate cup, noting out of the corner of her eye that the snow still swirled past the windows like white butterflies seeking haven. Why were they having this strange conversation? Out of the deep well of her disillusion came the need for honesty.

'You say I was always wanted. It's not true. Kerruish has no real love for us — Boyce, Sebastian and me — because we are not his. It was Mama he coveted and because of her he'd have taken on a regiment. Only Charlotte has his love. Not even Mama now, it seems.'

'But there's still Clive,' Nat pursued doggedly.

'No,' she said, the word drawn by some strange compulsion. 'I have not said this to another soul. It has all been a terrible mistake. I'm not happy — '

'Perhaps you think too much of yourself. Of *your* comfort and peace of mind.'

Angrily, the tears crowding her lashes, she said, 'I wish I had not told you. Now you will have that confidence to pass on where you will — '

'I have never betrayed a confidence,' he said coldly. 'I'd sooner cut off my right hand.'

'I don't know why I said those things. I have felt so enclosed. So alone. I seem to have no real friend and that is why I made such a fool of myself. Forget what I said. I see I have given you the impression of being selfish and unfeeling and you have only contempt for me!'

'You are quite wrong. There's something under the self-ishness — I'm certain.'

'Buried very deep,' she said and laughed a little wildly. 'I only know I must do something quite radical! Anything that will change my life.'

She got up again and walked to the window. The snow was beginning to pile up on the sill and the moor had vanished. 'If it stays like this you will not be able to leave.'

He followed, staring out into the dizzying whiteness. 'Clive will be lucky to find his way here.'

'He won't care. The mine is all he cares about lately. He'll be glad of an excuse not to come home. It's my fault, you see. I'm not a proper wife to him, nor ever will be, it seems, to anyone. Some essential ingredient is missing. There!' She swung round, her huge green eyes glittering with unshed tears. 'You could dine all over the Isle of Man on that story. What a windfall!'

'Don't talk nonsense!' he answered roughly. 'I have already said I'll be close as an oyster. Unburden yourself to me if it helps. I'm a good listener. And, as you say, I could hardly ride back in that blizzard.'

'The muffins are growing cold.'

'I'm not hungry.'

'But we'd better both eat at least one or it will look odd. Don't you think? Now they are ordered.'

'Perhaps we could sacrifice two to the flames. Pretend they are to the household gods. The lares and penates I believe they were called.' He laughed.

'Whatever language is that?'

'Latin.'

'You don't learn that in a slum. I'm sorry I said that.'

'And I'm sorry if I appeared over-condemnatory.'

'Let us,' she suggested, leading the way back to the hearth, 'pretend you have just been announced. Why did you come, Mr Gelling?'

'You've always called me Nat.'

'If you are to be my confessor I must keep some distance between us. Mustn't I?'

'I brought news of your brothers, Mrs Clive.'

'And you used to call me Elizabeth. I'd forgotten the letters. What do they say?' She bent her head over the crackling papers so that all Nat could see was the velvet turban and the curling feathers, the curve of her neck.

He watched while she read then told him, 'Boyce has been to view the Pavilion at Brighton again. He says it is all onion domes and minarets. Moorish arches — like finding some Eastern city by an English shore. They say that inside it is all to be silver and scarlet and filled with dragons. It sounds very exaggerated. He had a girl with him. I wish I'd met her. And there are steamships on the Thames. Boyce wants a taste of battle but Mama would not like that. Boyce is her favourite. Her attitude to him has always been different. As if he were — special.

'And now for Sebastian. He seems to have conceived a passion for his friend Richard Bailey. He speaks of no one else. I did not care for him.'

Elizabeth put down the letters as a louder than ever blast struck the window.

'It seems that you'll have to stay, after all. I'll ring for Mrs Quinn and have her put a warming-pan in the guest-room bed. We'll dine together.'

'What if Clive does not return. Cannot return?'

'It will not be our fault. Country folk must look after stranded travellers. It's their code. You'd not subject your mount to the moor tonight?'

'No.'

'And you do not find me too uncongenial?'

He shook his head. The teacup looked small and fragile between his fingers.

Some colour came back into Elizabeth's face. 'You must tell me about yourself. You do know something about me. And if we are to be friends — I can't think why it has taken me so long to realise — ' Her voice had dropped to a whisper.

'What?' Nat asked. 'What have you realised?'

'That we could have been friends long ago. If I hadn't been so blind. And so stupid.'

'I wish we had.'

'Yes,' she said quietly. 'But it isn't too late.'

'Not for friendship.'

'That's all I'm offering. All I have to offer. And don't imagine you've seen the last of that side of me you so dislike. Leopards are notoriously faithful to their habits. Tomorrow could see me just as full of spleen and awkwardness. I do know my faults.'

'Try to stay as you are at this moment. It seems I was wrong in my assumption that you had no cause for — '

'My bad behaviour?' she suggested astringently.

'I was searching for kinder words.'

'Don't bother. It seems plain speaking agrees with me. Although, it works exactly opposite when Wheatley — '

'When Wheatley,' Nat prompted.

'When he speaks plainly,' Elizabeth said defiantly. 'He never minces *his* words. It's been obvious from the beginning that I fall very far short of his expectations. Of course it would have been quite different if I'd been — '

'Who?'

She stared at Nat in amazement. 'How did I come to be telling you all this? When in the past we've never exchanged anything but trivialities? How?'

'Because we are now friends. Because we are snowed in and trapped in a little pocket of isolation and you are feeling confidential. Because something has made you vulnerable. I wonder what that something could be? There's vulnerability of the mind and the body. Either could fashion an insecurity.'

'Thank you, Doctor Gelling! For your diagnosis. But my body is perfectly healthy.'

'And just who is this woman who threatens your marriage?' he asked again. 'It is a woman?'

She could never bring herself to tell him or anyone, for then the last frail rags of her pride would be shredded beyond repair.

'You want to know too much,' she said harshly and bent to pour herself another cup of tea in a silence that was suddenly filled with something she could no longer recognise. But she had never felt more alive.

John Howard had battled his way to the cottage to see Karran. He thought she looked beautiful sitting in the firelight. When she moved, he saw what he had not known earlier.

Her eyes met his. 'Do you hate me now?'

He shook his head. 'You've made a hard rod for your back. Come back to Ravensdowne?'

'You know I can't do that, especially now. Emily made little secret of her dislike of children in general. There were certain remarks she made. And I, the exception to her rule, dealt the decisive blow by defecting.'

'Did Brand leave the hare and the ham? And the eggs?'

'He did, thank you. You are far too good to me.'

'Have you come to terms with — your loss?'

'Not altogether. We were much closer than anyone could imagine. At least there will be something of him left.'

'Are you ever afraid the child may inherit — the violence?'

'Circumstances form all our characters. And Laurence did little more than most men who are unexpectedly enraged. I have heard since that some human skulls are more delicate than others. That man's could have been one of these. Do you remember the talks we had about the human structure and medicines? All those other things.'

'I do remember. I don't think I will ever forget.'

'And the natural history. How is it progressing? It's some time since you came.'

'Well enough, I suppose. It was always slower to take shape in winter, even more so now without your enthusiasm.'

'If I should find anything of further interest, I'll send it with Brand.'

'You'd — never come yourself?'

'Not so long as Emily is there.'

'I see.' John thought about this for a minute. 'Well, you know your own mind. But since I now know your secret I must hark back to my suggestion that you have someone here, until your child is born at least. Suppose you had some accident, or if a tramp or a thief should pester you?'

Karran shivered and bent to throw a log onto the fire. She had not forgotten Jem Boswell. There were still prowlers but she always barred the door at dusk. It was time she had company but she was unwilling to allow a stranger into the peace she had so hardly won.

'There's always that aunt of your mother's at Peel,' he suggested.

'Yes. Yes, there is Deborah. If she will tear herself away, and in this cold weather. She could not come anyway until the thaw.'

'I'll send someone over to fetch her as soon as it's possible. You'll be all right until then?'

'The weather makes prisoners of us all. Who would seek me out when they are liable to vanish into a drift?'

'People talk and are self-righteous — '

'Except for you.' She smiled and looked beautiful. 'You see that I have fuel, food, books, paper, even my mare. And a cat has taken up residence in the stable, a wild, brindled creature who will take care of the mice and shrews and be company when it gets to know me.'

'I have taken the liberty of putting some more money into your bank account. If you must cut yourself off, you'd better have an allowance. I am still legally responsible for you, after all.'

'Even if you had not been, things would be no different. I wish you were not so good. I am made to feel so — shabby. Inadequate — '

'You needn't. What dreadful thing did you do but fall in love? It's Richards who was shabby, to encourage you, to leave you — as you are.'

'You're wrong! It was I who wouldn't leave him alone — '

'There's no need to elaborate.' John's face had stiffened into the mask he always wore when Laurence was mentioned, an expression so alien to his nature that Karran never failed to marvel at its bitterness. 'I must go now, before fresh snow fills in the tracks I've made. If I were truthful I'd say, Brand's tracks. I merely made use of them. Bar the door when I've gone and expect to see Deborah Quine before long. And if there is any emergency, remember to fire the pistol. Everyone's been told to listen for it.'

Everyone but Emily, Karran thought and remembered Emily's possessive touch. She was better off here in her own home and she'd take care to use as little of John's money as was possible. Later, she'd try to earn her own livelihood. It would not be fair to Howard to burden him for ever.

Going to the door, she saw the holes in the snow gaping greyly and John fitting his boots into each one. He turned and waved before he disappeared among the trees. The cottage would be lonely without his tall presence.

Flinging on her cloak, Karran made her way to the stable. In the light of the horn lantern, she made out the gleam of the cat's eyes in the straw. Pushing aside the saddle and harness that hung on the wall, she went to the creature, crooning and whispering to it until it suffered her to lift it in her arms where it felt warm and soft.

It would be something to which she could talk.

Clive had not shown particular interest when Nat Gelling was forced to spend the night at Mingay after delivering the letters Erin had sent. He, himself, had spent the entire time of the prolonged blizzard at the Donaghue. The great moving parts of the pump and the engine fascinated him and he spent several hours of the enforced occupation in studying the relevant papers and familiarising himself with their workings. He had decided that the smelter be as near the farthest boundary as possible, where it would discommode his household least. Although it would undoubtedly affect the miners' rows, they were already used to spoliation of the atmosphere from Kerruish's chimneys. They'd not quarrel with bread and butter.

There was also a deep satisfaction in the fact that he had decided to follow Barney's example: other irons in the fire were prudent, particularly on an island, so far, not overly rich in any one particular sphere. Though he'd said nothing to anyone else, Clive had tied up a portion of his capital in part share of a schooner which would trade between Liverpool and any other country that required the goods his partner obtained, and from which Britain's requirements could be profitably supplemented. His partner was a university friend. Robert Owen had been Clive's first choice as groomsman at his wedding only, unfortunately, he'd been on an extended voyage to Brazil for coffee and hides. When Clive had written to Owen later about his married state, Owen had put forward his proposition.

Underlying the sense of achievement, Clive felt the faintest twist of unease. The new Simpson engine was costing him more than he cared to confess, added to the escalating price of the smelter, and he had been unable to rent Mingay as was his first intention. The only way he could get the house which he coveted and was so well-placed for him as a mine-owner who wished to be near his property, was by buying it outright.

Elizabeth had dreamed of a Grand Tour but she would have to wait. Perhaps if he had felt that she was worth it, a mortgage — temporary, of course — would have taken care of the journey, but Elizabeth was not. She would sicken on the boat, refuse to accommodate him in the bed-chamber or lie like a corpse if he insisted. He had had enough of that last summer. Clive decided he would plead busyness and hope that the schooner, the *Helen*, would soon pay him back in profits. He buried deeply the thought that those profits might not be forthcoming as quickly as he wished.

Whenever Nat was in Castletown, he would call at the Kerruish household, and Erin had adopted the habit of giving him her sons' letters to convey to Elizabeth, and receiving one from her daughter in return. This meant that Nat Gelling was able to call at Mingay, if not frequently, at least regularly. Even if Elizabeth were shrewish at his arrival, she showed her better side before he left with the sealed letter for her mother. The paper would always smell of Elizabeth's scent, evoking her presence until it left his possession.

The arrangement suited everybody. Clive saw no reason to look beyond the delivery of the letters which were real enough and left out for his perusal, and Gelling's visits were welcome in that they kept Elizabeth from moping around the house and gave her an excuse for putting on a pretty dress now and again. Clive grew to like Nat himself.

Realising Elizabeth's lack of company, Clive suggested that she invite Charlotte over regularly, but his wife's almost hysterical refusal made him see that the old jealously still simmered despite the lengthy separation from her half-sister.

'Why do you dislike her so much?'

'Because she's cunning! Not like us — '

'Because Kerruish spoils her, eh? Why shouldn't he? Charlotte's the only flesh and blood he has. Anyone who has anything to leave wants his own to leave it to.'

Elizabeth was careful not to show her shock at his words. Clive had obviously thought of children in relation to his own achievements, and her own fear of becoming pregnant had been accentuated lately by her growing pleasure in Nat's company. Brusque and outspoken as he could be over her shortcomings — and she could now see them quite plainly — she valued his interest, but the sight of her body, clumsy and

106

swollen with another man's child, would surely terminate their flowering friendship and that would hurt.

Experiencing a second jolt, she confessed to herself that it was no longer merely rapport she felt for the big, dark man who had opened her eyes to the worst of her imperfections, and on whom she now, unashamedly, leaned.

Unfortunately, the pains she had taken to make herself as attractive as possible in case Nat rode up to the door had the effect of renewing Clive's flagging interest in herself. Now, when he mounted one of his cavalry charges in bed, a sense of betrayal was added to her usual reluctance. If it were not so sad, one could laugh at the idea of considering the husband the interloper.

And then, the thing she dreaded had come to pass. The date for her flux came and went. Surely it was a transitory condition brought on by her divided emotions? Stress could hold back one's normal courses. But the desired bleeding did not come on the second month and Elizabeth took no pleasure in the budding flowers of spring and the sun that warmed the wastes of Foxdale and the garden of Mingay.

Riding was considered effective in dislodging an encumbrance, she remembered, and rode until she was tired, with no effect. Neither did hot baths bring on the longed-for menstruation, nor the secret quaffing of Dutch gin. Her gowns became difficult to fasten and her stomach grew delicate. She could not hope to conceal her condition any longer. Perhaps it would die at birth or soon after? It happened all too often, however comfortable the parents' circumstances. Perhaps she *herself*?

Worst of all, the weather became so good that there was no longer any reason to make Gelling postmaster.

When Erin came for her first spring visit she knew immediately. Both she and Clive made such a fuss and Clive brought his wife a gift that, only a few months ago, would have filled her with acquisitive delight.

Elizabeth turned the emerald ring on her finger and thought of grey Irish eyes and broad, comforting shoulders.

It was better that he didn't come. But, oh, how she missed him.

Deborah had come with the snowdrops that were late this year. John had stayed away since he had discovered Karran's condition, although Brand came unfailingly with Howard's offerings and instructed the keepers to fill the wood-box and deliver the peat and the hay for Floss.

Karran had not needed to spend any of the guineas lodged with Messrs Dunn, Kelly and Scatchard, but soon she would have to lay in a stock of clothes for the baby. Deborah said she could sew and knit and Karran was willing to learn. The cat, Finn, named after the hero who was supposed to have thrown the great piece of earth that originally formed Man into the Irish sea, was the greatest company for both women. Deborah, who had been forced to leave her own cat at Peel with friendly neighbours, took to Finn immediately.

They took turns at the spinning-wheel that had belonged to Jesse's mother and for the first time in years, Karran was able to talk of Clemence. A picture was built up in her mind of the fair, pretty girl who had set off for St John's to meet Luke Karran on that fateful summer so long ago.

But remembering Clemence meant recalling Aggie and Jem Boswell and the incident in the forest ride. Now that the snow and ice had gone and Croggan was not far away, it was not impossible that darkness would bring danger.

Deborah, watching the ritual barring of the cottage door and seeing the primed pistol on the mantel, asked her great-niece why she was so careful. There was nothing to do but tell her the whole story.

'I'll go to Port St Mary for the materials for the child,' Deborah said. 'It won't take long if I ride on the mare. You'd trust me with her?'

'Of course I would.'

So it was settled. Deborah was by now an arresting figure. Her long hair was silvery white, escaping in long tendrils however carefully she tried to confine it. With her water-pale eyes and grey clothing, she was like an attenuated ghost, and children shrank back from her in fright while adults experienced frissons of unease as she stood at corners or walked the narrow streets in search of Karran's requirements, oblivious of their reactions.

'They are for my niece, Karran Kinrade,' she said more than once in the hearing of church elders and tradesmen, thinking that this would break some ice. It was an adventure to come so far from home and she was not ashamed of her connections. But the haberdasher's wife had come from Peel and was also acquainted with the recent scandal over Richards. The gossip about Deborah's presence spread like wildfire.

A youth threw a stone as she rode out of the village but she did not connect it with more than prejudice against an eccentric stranger. She could not know that the old scandal of Jesse and Luke was revived.

The cut had dried before she reached the tholtan and she had almost forgotten the cause. Karran was sure to be pleased with the materials and threads, the narrow ribbons that were Deborah's extravagance. She would knit a shawl for the infant. There was a spider-web pattern of her own devising —

'The nights are stretching out,' Deborah said as they opened the parcels once Floss was made comfortable and Finn had slunk in to flop in front of the hearth. There was a fine smell of hare and herbs, and pink shadows flickered against the ceiling, beautifying the roofbeams. There was a fishing-pole strapped there alongside the dried fish. She would use it in the stream tomorrow. A catch would vary the diet.

'How did you come to cut your cheek?' Karran asked as she ladled the stew.

'A branch that overhung.' She must not worry the girl, Deborah decided.

'It looks sore.'

'I'd forgotten it.'

Karran bathed the wound and rubbed some salve into it. Something about the cut made her uneasy. Surely a branch would have made a scratch? This obviously was not.

Brand was walking past the cottage, whistling as he always did now that the sun had returned. What could happen when they were so well protected?

Forgetting her fears, Karran sat down to her supper while Finn stared up at her from the hearth, his eyes lambent, his paws curled with expectation. She must not disappoint him.

Emily would not pass the cottage on the way to the Chasms. She had no wish to encounter the little whore who had so skilfully wormed her way into John's affections. It pained her to reflect that Karran had found the cracks in her own armour. She pushed back the recollection of the girl in the black habit and white linen, her thick hair swathed upwards to show the long, lovely line of her neck. To think that she'd preferred the attentions of a wastrel and murderer, and to live like a peasant in that tumbledown shack! But, of course, it was not so decrepit now that John had spent his money on its improvement.

And now Karran's slim, boyish body would be stretched and distorted with that seducer's seed. Emily did not want to see such despoliation.

John did not insist, but he had been very quiet as they left their horses tethered and began to skirt the notorious clefts down which Karran's father had fallen, or been thrust, to his death. The greatest horror of the Chasms lay in their invisibility.

Emily was well aware that John felt Karran's ostracism had lasted long enough. Insidiously, he worked on her sensibilities by remarking that the account books had suffered since Karran's day, that the house seemed empty of late, and that they had not found anything worthy of the history for months. It stagnated.

Ignoring the references to the ledgers and the silence that reigned over Ravensdowne, she replied tartly that there was nothing to prevent them going in search of specimens them-selves, and John had suggested an excursion to Spanish Head. When Emily had ridden the longer route to avoid the tholtan, he had followed unwillingly, acknowledging defeat.

'He'll *not* force me to accept her,' she insisted silently and the spore of hatred fed on the force of her repudiation until it became a monster in possession of her mind and heart. Karran would never be reinstated.

Karran had been like Kate, rejecting the love Emily would have showered on her. An unconventional love perhaps, but none the less real for that. Pretty, fair Kate and dark, hob-bledehoy Karran. Both shying away from what she had to offer. Both going off with wastrels.

Sometimes she thought she could not bear their defection.

Once on foot, the warm wind blowing at their capes and scarves, they laboured along the path that had turned to mud under the unaccustomed sun. John's tall shadow and Emily's short one flickered side by side, though their thoughts were separated. There seemed nothing that they would ever again be able to say to one another.

The quaggy mess under their feet became more difficult to negotiate and now that the Chasms were left behind the path skimmed the cliffs that encircled Bay Stacka. More than once they slithered and clutched at the moor's edge.

Emily had a good head for heights and was not unduly disturbed. Then she became aware of a figure coming towards them and was struck by its spectral quality. It was tall and grey, reflecting the weak sunlight like an inferior metal. She concentrated on its strangeness and the suggestion of flut-tering rags and skeletal frame. For the first time, the depths to her left assumed their real danger. The mud sucked at her boots like voracious lips so that she lost the fine edge of balance and swayed.

'I have seen death,' she whispered and half-turned to seek John's aid. 'Death comes for me.'

His arm shot out to help her, or that was what she imagined. Instead, the expected grip was somehow turned into a push and for a moment Emily's body undulated, floundered. Her vision seemed filled by the approach of the tall silvery figure that appeared to have blind discs for eyes. Round, gleaming emptinesses —

Emily screamed and her arms flailed futilely. 'John — ? John!' And then she had plunged over the edge. Her body struck a protuberance and was flung off like a doll filled with sawdust. For a moment her arms and legs stretched out in a starfish shape, then she hit the rocks below. Little runnels of blood stained the cold, sea-worn surfaces and slid into the water of the encroaching tide.

She remained perfectly still but for her hair which moved gently with the incoming waves.

'Why did she fall?' Deborah asked, aghast, drawing abreast of John Howard.

Dazedly, he gestured towards the path. There were still the scores of her feet as they slid.

'You tried to save her. I saw you.'

John said nothing, only stared at the sprawled shape below like a man in a dream, seeming not to notice the bony fingers that were clasped around his arm, pulling him up onto the damp wiriness of the dead heather.

'Did — I?' he whispered at last. 'Did — I?'

And then the tears slid down his face.

'You're sure?' Captain Jayce said much later. 'You are positive that her last words were, "I have seen death. Death comes for me"?'

'Perfectly sure,' John agreed tonelessly. 'Of course, what she really saw was the woman, Deborah Quine, my ward's great-aunt.'

'Ah, yes,' the Captain said softly. 'The person you sent for to look after Miss Kinrade when she decided to live in that lonely cottage. But, didn't Mrs Howard recognise the woman? Surely she must? If you brought her from Peel.'

'No. She refused to meet Miss Quine or to visit Karran.'

'Because of the Richards' business.' It was a statement, not a question.

'As you say, because of that. I did not hold it against Karran. I should have been glad for the girl to return to Ravensdowne. But Emily — ' He shrugged.

'Felt different?' Again, it was not an enquiry but an assertion.

'Yes.'

'And the reason for your walk — perhaps a foolhardy one in the circumstances — was to procure local plants for a natural history volume you have been compiling over the years you have lived here?'

'That is so.'

'May I see what you have done so far?'

'Of course.'

John led the way to the study and brought out the laboriously written sheets and the corresponding pages of illustrations. The sharp sunlight accentuated all the fluency and truth of Emily's handiwork, the subtlety of the colours.

'She was very talented,' Jayce said. 'I should imagine you'd find it very difficult to get anyone else to finish what she had started. You could not employ anyone whose style differed too greatly. The transition must not be too obvious.'

'No.'

'And the book, evidently, means much to you,' the captain mused.

'It means everything. Years have been spent on it. I had great expectations — '

'Naturally, you did,' Jayce said soothingly. 'And now it may never be completed.'

'No. It would be almost impossible to find someone with — with Emily's technique. She was ahead of her time, as you must see. I have studied other artists who have settled here in pursuit of their work but they are mostly distressingly anaemic.'

Captain Jayce bit back the remark about killing the goose that laid the golden eggs.

'Your wife was not afflicted in any degree with vertigo?'

'The opposite. I was the one who was not happy with heights. Emily had no such problems. She was an extremely decisive person.'

'So, really, you'd say it was completely out of character for your wife to lose her footing?'

'Absolutely. And she sounded so strange — not like herself at all.'

'Tell me, again, what she said.'

'I have seen death. Death comes for me.'

'Yet, all she saw was the woman from Peel?'

'There was nobody else in sight.'

'Very well, I'll keep you no longer from your work.' The Captain's eyes lingered reflectively over the open manuscript and the flowing drawings. 'I suppose you'll look for someone else to illustrate this?'

'There's no point in my continuing unless I first have someone to carry on Emily's excellent, and, I fear, irreplaceable work.'

'Your ward — Miss Karran — would not be able to — fill the gap?'

In spite of his confusion, John saw the trap. 'Karran, in spite of attempts at painting and drawing, could hardly draw a box. Her talents ran to writing and accounting. We left all the accounts to her latterly. Before Molesworth came to arrest Richards,' he ended bitterly, 'and Karran went.'

'Yes. It has all been very shocking. The fabric of your life torn — '

'That is all, is it?' John asked directly, not wishing to dwell on the turn of events that had left him widowed. He still did not know if he had tried to hold on to Emily, or if —

'I'll take myself away from your natural grief, then,' Captain Jayce said smoothly. His eyes seemed to notice everything, even that involuntary shudder of repudiation.

And then he was gone. John sat unmoving, his gaze fixed on the strong, sweeping lines of Emily's imagery, the subtle vignettes. Slowly, they were superimposed by the likeness of Karran, all black and white as moonlight and shadow. At least he was free now, after so many years of rebelling against a life-style grown increasingly unsatisfactory. He had not appreciated how much until he had retired from business and was thrown absolutely into his wife's company. Not that she had been a wife in the accepted sense for longer than he could remember.

'It's wrong to think so,' his mind told him tiredly. 'And I am still not sure you tried to save her.'

'I did! I did!' his thoughts insisted, panic-stricken.

But the inner anger was not convincing. He would never be certain, however long he lived.

Karran and Deborah had been silent over the simple meal. Sunshine slanted through the small, thickset window and through the open doorway, laying puddles of green-gold on the fresh rushes. There was a snowy cloth on the table. The room was as clean as hard work would make it, but Karran was aware of the deepest unease.

Deborah's story of the meeting with the Howards and Emily's subsequent fall did not correspond with what Karran knew about John and Emily. Yet, against her doubts, Karran could not help thinking of the day she and Laurence had experienced the same conditions. He had covered her with his body and dragged them both to safety. She had mud all over her skirts and boots. It *could* have been the same with Emily and her husband. But the maggot of disquiet persisted. Emily was too strong.

Captain Jayce and his sergeant had spent some time on Friday with Deborah who was the only witness to the tragedy. Over and over, he had made her tell her story.

'Did you hear Mrs Howard's words?'

'No, I did not. I was not close enough and the wind was blowing in any case.'

'Do you know what she said?'

'No. I have said so already, many times.'

The captain repeated Emily's last remarks before she cried out to her husband for help.

'Do you not think they were very strange?'

'I do not pretend to understand them,' Deborah agreed, frowning. 'Perhaps she felt unwell.'

'But you saw Mr Howard try to catch hold of her?'

'Yes. He stretched out his arm but she had already begun to swing away. He touched her shoulder but seemed not to get a proper grip.'

'But in your opinion, he intended to grab at her upper arm?'

'Of course. What else would he do? I've told you all I know.'

Captain Jayce had not answered and they were left in a tingling silence for longer than was comfortable.

Deborah was glad she had omitted to repeat John's agonised question. 'Did — I?' It haunted her after the two men had gone. Her eyesight was not so keen nowadays and she was thankful she had not been asked to swear that John meant to clutch at his endangered wife. Only he must have, mustn't he? Why should he do otherwise?

Now she and Karran picked at their supper while Finn waited patiently for scraps.

They listened as always for Brand to pass by and when he did, just as Deborah rose to clear away the dishes, Karran went automatically to bar the door. She had not seen John as yet, though she had sent a message of condolence with the factor. Howard would come when he was ready but she could not understand why he had not done so already. Of course there were all kinds of things one must do after a bereavement. Officialdom must be served. Thoughts of the authorities evoked Captain Jayce with his penetrating questions and cold eyes. Clemence had hated him.

The sun dipped low, reddening the rim of the sea.

Deborah fetched fat candles and lit them from the fire. They flared and trickled hot wax onto the pewter stands. The two women sat close to the yellow light to continue making the baby garments they had begun after Deborah's shopping foray into Port St Mary.

Karran could not say exactly when she felt the first prick of unease. It was probably when Finn raised his head and stared into space with eyes that were mostly pupil. Then he licked his lips as he did when he was uncertain.

It was some time before a pinkish glow showed through the surrounding trees and there were vague sounds of distant voices and the faint thud of boots against exposed roots and stones.

Karran put down the piece of sewing. Fear rose to her throat and lodged there.

Deborah sat perfectly still, remembering the stone that had struck her cheekbone. She was not a fool. Other voices had been raised against her in the past. There had been unpleasantness. But at Peel she had friends as well as enemies and the good outnumbered the bad. She had not, knowingly, hurt another living person. Here, she was a stranger living with a girl who had consorted with a murderer and carried his child. That there were extenuating circumstances in Richards' unpremeditated act meant nothing, since gossip paints every incident as darkly as possible. Karran's lover was, to the scandal-mongers, a crude killer who had beaten a man to death and was killed as one would shoot a rabid dog, and his harlot must, of necessity, be as black as he.

Rabble-raisers had the power to make themselves believed and Karran was damned because of the company she'd kept in the past. Deborah herself had, only days ago, been involved in that cliff-top accident in which strange and damaging words had been spoken by the dead, and respected, woman.

'Witch!' someone shouted and the torch-light grew closer.

'Harlot! Witch. Devil's whore!' A stone clattered against the barred door.

'Oh, God,' Karran whispered. 'What shall we do? There seem so many of them.'

'The pistol,' Deborah said through dry lips. 'You must fire that as Mr Howard said you should. Then I'll pinch out the candles so that they won't see us.'

'Yes! Yes.' Karran got up so suddenly that the stool rolled away across the floor. Her body felt heavy and useless though she was not gross. Stumbling, she reached the hearth and slid her hand along the mantel.

Deborah brought a candle nearer and the girl knelt in front of the fire and directed the muzzle of the weapon towards the flue. The shot reverberated in the chimney and brought down a torrent of soot to smother the peats.

Finn sprang on top of the dresser, his hair standing on end, his eyes a weird green in the candlelight.

Karran sank to her knees while Deborah pinched at the candle-flames. Light filtered in from the glow of the torches, outlining their bearers' silhouettes.

'Witches, both of you! Fire's good for the likes of you. Or drowning. Which'll it be?' Someone laughed. 'Choose! Bitches!'

Deborah gasped as the flames of the candles burnt her fingertips. 'Come away from the window, Karran. I'll put something heavy against it. The peat-box would do. No! You mustn't try to lift anything.'

Karran saw her attenuated body against the outside glow, then, surprisingly easily for a woman so slim and not young, Deborah had swung the solid box in front of the window recess and pushed it as far onto the sill as possible. Into it, she began to cram as many heavy objects as she could.

'Take my books,' Karran said when there were no more fire-dogs and iron pots.

'Your books!' Deborah was aghast.

'My baby's life means more to me.' Karran did not voice her conviction that only their deaths would satisfy the growing crowd outside. There must be many people who had walked all the way from Port St Mary. She was reminded of the day she had heard Molesworth say he'd set fire to the thatch if there was no other way of getting Richards to leave.

Distracted, she pushed back her loosened hair with fingers that smelt of soot. They had done all they could. The pistol had been fired, the window made as safe as was possible. Deborah was cramming the heaviest of the books into the sturdy receptacle, and the window-frame would preclude any disturbing of the now almost immovable barrier once all the glass was broken.

Not satisfied, Deborah was pushing the tallboy across the window space, crushing it against the peat-box. The door was firmly barred and as thick as a man's arm. Blows resounded against it and Karran recognised Aggie's voice, shrill and hysterical, shouting, 'You'll be sorry you sent your other fancy man to whip my Jem! Mother said you was not to be cursed but I'm doing that now because of what he did to my man. I curse you Karran Kinrade, you and your bastard child, for there was no cause to beat Jem who never harmed you. Beat 'im sore that Clive did so that 'e couldn't move for a 'ole fortnight and near lost 'is job into the bargain. 'Ad to go an' do 'is work myself, I did, an' never a word o' thanks. And your precious Clive'll 'ave to answer for it one o' these days, mark my words. 'E's not the same man, Jem Boswell, since your whore-master scourged the skin off 'im. Open the door, you bitch, and see 'ow it feels!'

'What does she mean?' Deborah whispered and seized hold of the broom in case the door gave way under the thrusting and kicking that followed Aggie's outburst.

'I have no idea. I didn't send Clive. Unless he guessed! That's what must have happened. Boswell attacked me once and Clive came upon us but I refused to name him — '

'Witch Quine! You put the eye on Mrs Howard, didn't you, because she bore a grudge against your niece. You knew she'd not be allowed back to Ravensdowne so long as Mrs Howard was alive, so you overlooked her so she'd fall to her death. The two of you's murderesses! And you deserve to pay for it. We'd be better off wi'out the likes of you. Come on, lads. We can get this door down, can't we?'

The cat whined desolately from his perch on top of the dresser. He must have shifted as the first thuds from the renewed onslaught shuddered against the door, because plates crashed to the floor, adding to the general terror and confusion.

The two women moved together, Deborah grasping Karran's wrist.

'Burn the thatch!'

They were the words Karran had dreaded. 'I'm sorry I asked you to come. You'd have been safe at Peel. I wish I hadn't listened to John.'

'Your Mr Howard will come.' The thin fingers tightened on the girl's wrist.

'What can he do against so many?'

'There may not be so many as we think. Empty vessels, you know?' Deborah attempted a joke.

'Why do they hate us so?'

'Ignorance. Fear of anyone different. Superstition.'

'Aunt Deborah, I'm afraid. I'm ashamed — If there was something I could do, I wouldn't be, but, waiting in the dark! Like a trapped animal — '

It was not so dark and there was a spiteful crackling from the corner of the ceiling. Plaster began to fall into the room and smoke and flame gushed through the hole.

The smoke increased and they were driven, coughing and retching, towards the door. Karran saw that the end of the roofbeam had caught fire. A crumbling redness was spreading through the thick darkness of it and a flurry of wind through the gap was both fanning the blaze and driving more smoke towards them.

Finn screamed.

'I must unbar the door,' Karran said desperately, her eyes blinded. 'Surely they've done enough to us?'

'You will have to.' Deborah peered into the fiery haze in search of the terrified cat. Outside Floss stamped and neighed in her stall, kicking the timbers.

The bar grated as Karran lifted it from the socket and pushed at the door. A wave of cold air and flickering light greeted her. She fell to the ground, her lungs almost bursting with the pain of the smoke. 'Deborah?' she gasped. 'Where are you?'

'Finn?' Deborah said from inside the cottage. 'I must find Finn, poor beast.'

'No!' Karran screamed. 'Don't go! He'll find his way — '

Karran was remembering something Clemence had once said. That every person she truly loved was doomed to die unpleasantly. Luke had. Jesse — only Deborah remained. Deborah mustn't waste her life. To be burnt to death was obscene —

Shadows surrounded her.

Someone laughed. 'There she is! Richards' harlot. Clive's strumpet. And who else has been her lover? Howard, do you think? I wouldn't put it past her.'

Karran raised herself painfully and stared towards the

118

room she had just left. The fire in the roof had a great hold now and a rain of sparks burst out of the loosening thatch to fall inside. Deborah cried out, then there was a silence.

'Deborah?'

The girl struggled to her feet disbelievingly and was seized in cruel hands that dragged her from the doorway. Fingers pulled at her hair but she hardly noticed. 'Deborah!' she said again.

Weeping, she was conscious of blows struck, of her head being jerked back savagely so that she screamed. She was pushed against a tree and there was another sound. The sharp crack of a whip. Pain struck her shoulders and gathered there, accentuated by a rain of further blows that half-drowned the crackling blaze of the cottage roof and the silence inside it.

There was another report that was not the lash of the whip. It echoed in the wood like the sound of judgement and all the shouting and laughter ended as if a tap was turned off and the water had dwindled to a trickle. Then there was nothing more.

Karran awoke to pain. The room was dark and low down in her stomach, cramp tortured her. Gasping, she doubled over, drawing her knees towards her chest.

The spasm passed slowly and, for a moment, she wondered where she was. Then she remembered. Perhaps she had dreamed that terrible evening? But her throat hurt and her body was bruised and lacerated. The dreadful thing had happened. She still bore the searing of the smoke and the mishandling by Aggie and Boswell and the village folk who came with torches and hatred. She pressed her hand to her mouth to stifle her torment.

Laurence's house was gone, and deep inside her lay the knowledge that Finn and Deborah too were beyond rescue.

The cramps came again, making her groan and clench her teeth, then welcome the comparative ease when the pain became muted and finally died. She had twisted some nerve, or had caught a chill when she was dragged away from the house.

Either the sounds she had made, or her movements, had brought someone to the door. It opened softly, letting in a panel of widening lamplight.

'Karran?' The soft whisper was sexless.

'Who — is it?'

'John.'

'I thought I must be at Ravensdowne. Deborah. Is she — ? She's dead, isn't she.'

'I'm sorry. We were too late. The smoke overcame her.'

'And Finn?' She watched his face change.

'Finn? There was someone else with you?' His voice sharpened.

'My cat. He was so afraid.'

'He must have run out when the door was opened. Or — we have not yet got rid of the debris. But he could have freed himself. Floss wasn't harmed. She's here now.'

'Deborah could never bear to see anything suffer. Even in the short time she stayed, I knew that. She hated me to use those books as ballast. Even books had souls.'

'Those people were animals! No, that's too kind a word. Beasts have their own codes. What's wrong? Karran?'

The griping torment had come again and she writhed upon the bed. It was hard to tell which hurt most, her back or the abdominal cramps that left her weak and breathless.

'I've twisted something.' She tried to smile but the effort was too great.

For a moment she read murder in John's eyes but it was not directed towards herself.

'You got my note? About Emily.'

'I did. Thank you.'

'I'm sorry. You'll miss her.'

'Yes,' he answered mechanically as though he had said it many times.

'They blamed Deborah. Those people — '

'I wish we'd caught one of them! But there were only three of us and they scattered as soon as we fired over their heads. You must have seen some of them?'

Her body jack-knifed. 'Oh!' she gasped. 'It's back again. I think — I begin to fear it must be the child coming before its time.'

John sprang to his feet, his face ashen. 'I'll wake the surgeon. I prevailed on him to stay, to sleep while I sat in the dressing-room. I must fetch him at once.' He almost ran from the bed-chamber.

Karran had been spared the necessity of answering his question. What would it accomplish to accuse the Boswells? She had seen no one else and could recognise only Aggie's voice out of the many she had heard. There was no way in which last night's events could be undone, and what good would it do to have Boswell and Aggie tossed into gaol and their children thrown onto the parish which would probably turn them into criminals? She was not vengeful, only sick and hurt, grieved that the home Richards had left her must only be charred walls.

Doctor Gough came bustling into the room just as the next contraction came, and all other thoughts were banished as she tried to come to terms with what was so surely happening.

The quiet house was filled with scurrying and whispers. Doctor Gough's highly-coloured face came close to hers, directing, abjuring, exhorting. A woman who had been brought from the village on his instructions gave her a stick to bite on and kept her forehead cool with wet cloths. None of John's staff had any experience of childbirth, and they were of no practical help.

How strange it would be, Karran thought, if the woman, who gave nothing of comfort, were one of the mob who had surrounded the tholtan! She could not have refused to attend for that would have directed unwelcome attention upon herself, and Captain Jayce was to be feared.

But she would never know if her suspicions were justified, Karran decided, then was torn with anxiety in case she was right and the woman might somehow harm the baby as it was born, thinking it devil's spawn.

'Don't leave me,' she pleaded and held Doctor Gough's arm. 'Promise me you'll take care of the child.'

'That's what I'm here for,' he replied testily and sent the woman for hot water and clean linen. Before she returned, the room was filled with the weak cry of a premature infant, determined to survive.

'Give it to me,' Karran insisted. 'It can be washed later. Please — ' In her arms it would be safe. Staring into the small, now quiet face she saw little trace of Laurence.

5

Elizabeth's confinement took place some weeks later. Erin had installed herself before the date, partly to escape Barney's prolonged coldness, and also because she realised how Elizabeth needed her at this particular time. Erin had borne her babies easily, but her daughter was a different kettle of fish. Right from the beginning she'd gauged the tensions that existed between the girl and her husband. Imagine Erin Doyle getting herself a frigid daughter! It would make a cat laugh. Easy, too, to read Clive's growing restiveness, and who could blame him if he journeyed to Douglas to taste the dubious joys of a back street whore-house, or went gambling at Fort Anne, the beautiful house built last century by Buck Whaley of notorious reputation.

Once, when he had drunk too much, Clive had told Erin that his finances were temporarily over-stretched and that was why Elizabeth had still not had her tour of the Continent. 'But she will,' he had said in the way that meant, 'not if I can help it.'

Why was Elizabeth so different? She had that touch of the puritan that had afflicted Jesse, in spite of his sensuality. It was Jesse's bequest to his daughter. There would be none of that nonsense with Boyce. Boyce would be like the O'Neills, as strong as his grandfather and as sybaritic as his father, as hedonistic. Sebastian? Erin had always shut her mind against what would become of her younger son. It was dangerous to cling so to one's mother. She was not sure why, but her intuition had never failed her yet. Boyce would accept that beagles hunted hares. Sebastian would have a missish nicety about the fact. He might be — womanish. That was the worst adjective she could apply to a man.

And now that she had lost Barney, she must at least have her own flesh and blood to cling to; that was the way in

122

Ireland. She was never certain why she'd left her homeland so decisively. It must have been because of the way Dermot had obeyed his father. That had hurt, that and the fact that her father'd have knocked the daylights out of her for becoming pregnant. Perhaps she would tell Boyce one day, if ever he returned to Castletown in his fine, flashy uniform and recognising his mother's feet of clay. How could he fail to see them and he spending all his time with the real gentry?

Erin pushed aside the growing conviction that as soon as Elizabeth discovered that she could produce babies without her mother's presence being essential, she would become redundant to all her children, and decided to make the most of the present. Charlotte had not crossed her mind since she left her in charge of the housekeeper at Castletown.

She wondered, without really believing it, about that rumour that Clive was somehow involved with Karran Kinrade? They said he'd horse-whipped some tenant-farmer, Croggan way, because of the girl. It couldn't be true, of course. Clive had always been set on Elizabeth and the foolish girl had not known how to hang onto her luck. Everyone said he was bound for success in spite of his reservations about his present monetary position. There were always set-backs in business. Even Barney experienced those.

It was at this juncture that Elizabeth had screamed and Erin found her crouched against the wall in her bed-chamber. The pains had come on as she studied her silhouette in the mirror, hating what she saw.

'Vanity,' Erin reproved as she helped Elizabeth undress and put her into a clean night-gown. She looked very beautiful in spite of the terror in her eyes. Erin had a sudden picture of her as a child. Castletown had grown dull without the Magnificent Trio.

Erin did not send for Clive. Instead she summoned the surgeon-doctor and midwife just in case she had lost her skill, instructed the kitchen staff as to her requirements and stayed in the bed-chamber throughout every twinge, grunt and gasp. Even when they turned to screams, she remained.

The child came hours later with Clive still at the Donaghue and Elizabeth black-eyed with exhaustion.

'It's a boy.'

'I wanted a girl,' Elizabeth said fretfully and turned uneasily in the disordered bed. 'What should I do with a boy?'

Quarter of an hour later she had her wish.

'Twins?' Clive muttered. 'God —'

'Aren't you pleased?'

'Not particularly. I'd rather have news of the *Helen*.'

'The *Helen*?'

The whole story came out in Clive's cups. He had drunk freely since he came in the door.

'You allowed the ship to sail uninsured?'

'The cargo was perishable and Robert careless. He's the one on the spot, after all.'

Erin helped herself to a liberal goblet of wine. 'Wheatley!' Her hand shook.

'I know. It never occurred to me that Rob would be such a fool. Now the mine is all I have and if it fails —'

'It won't. Could it?'

'No mine is a certainty.'

'All that expensive equipment — ?'

'Means nothing. It's fine if the lode progresses. If it doesn't, all the engines, pumps and smelters in the world can't manufacture ore.'

Erin could think of nothing to say. Was there anything in that whisper about Karran?

'I heard that Karran Kinrade has a son.'

The slitted eyes opened wide. 'I haven't been to Port St Mary lately.'

'You've met her, of course?'

'At the Bascombes. When you and Elizabeth ignored her. Remember?' he taunted.

'The — quarrel was with her mother. Before your time.'

'One suffers, it seems, for loyalty. I've not heard one kind word about the girl since she had the misfortune to become over-fond of a criminal.'

'Surely she must have known?'

'I don't think so. Her feelings were obviously real. He'd no money to speak of, nothing to compare with what Howard is worth. And what did it get her?'

'She's back at Howard's house. Now that Mrs Howard is — so conveniently? — out of the way.'

Clive rose to his feet unsteadily. 'I think I'll go into Douglas. I — I've a notion to go to the Royal Theatre. Some — of my friends will be there.'

'Do you think — ?' Erin began delicately.

'You knew you'd upset me, didn't you! Well, since you're

124

so concerned, I once asked Karran to be my wife. Before I turned to your precious, unsatisfactory daughter. And I am naturally sorry that I didn't wait to find out if Karran might change her mind. It's comforting to know that I now have an unwilling wife, two squalling brats, an overdraft, and a lode that seems to grow narrower daily. Oh, and half of a ship that is probably, by this time, on the sea-bed. Felicitations, mother-in-law.' Clive raised his glass derisively, then drank deeply. 'See you — sometime.'

'And Elizabeth?'

'Damn her.' Clive turned away and stalked carefully from the room.

Erin could not decide whether she was intrigued or shocked by his frankness. Elizabeth would not be pleased that she knew of the marital difficulties.

Thoughtfully, Erin went upstairs to look at her first grandchildren.

Clive was sober by the time he reached Douglas. The sea was high, rushing up on the long bare sands, the gulls screeching overhead. There were schooners anchored and he was reminded, disturbingly, of the *Helen*.

Stabling the lathered horse he went to his club and found three of his cronies. All were in favour of going to the theatre, the majority bent on seeing Mrs Siddons at the New Theatre in Atholl Street. That decided, they made an early supper of oysters and beef with libations of claret.

'Your wife's in pup, ain't she?' Henderson asked when conversation flagged.

'Not now,' Clive told him.

'You mean, she's had it?'

'Them. Twins.'

'You see before you,' Henderson said, mock-admiring, 'a man who must always do everything better than anyone else. I suppose you even managed to have one of either sex?'

'Naturally. And the boy came first.' Clive was beginning to feel a belated sense of achievement. If Elizabeth had had her way there never would have been a child. He now had a son.

'You've named them?'

'We — couldn't decide.'

'Best to keep in with Kerruish, old man.'

'I prefer to break new ground.'

The table exploded with laughter and crude suggestions as to how Clive should carry out the suggestion. The babies' heads were wet and later there was the stumbling and noisy entry to the theatre, where a positive dragon glared at them from the stage until they were reasonably quiet.

Clive, lost in nostalgic restrospect over Karran and the son he would have liked to have fathered, still managed to appreciate the Siddons' magnetism and artistry. Anything would have been an anti-climax to that electrifying performance, and after brandy at Henderson's Clive fell asleep on the settee and was left there under a goosefeather quilt till morning.

He did not want to go home, or even to the Donaghue, which was highly unusual, but he could not allow the occasion of the children's births to pass unmarked. So after a sketchy breakfast he went to the town centre and purchased three silver christening mugs. Two he asked to be engraved with the initials C. He hesitated over the third for some time, then decided that K was the only possible solution.

While he waited for the engraving to be done, he pondered over a gift for his wife. She had, after all, done double duty, however unwillingly. There might have to be an overdraft or a mortgage on Mingay, but Elizabeth need not know.

Clive visited his bank and then purchased a brooch to match the ring he'd previously given her. He must go home now and make his peace. The presents for Elizabeth and the twins would smooth the path.

He left instructions for the third mug to be sent to Karran at Ravensdowne, together with a sealed note from himself. It was the most he could do.

Karran, up and about again and still not quite convinced that her child really existed, went often to look at the sleeping infant. He was not yet as strong as a full-term baby and she had a horror of losing him to some germ against which he might have no resistance. It was this fact that kept her at Ravensdowne, though she had not forgotten the slanderous statements made by the St Mary folk about her possible relationship with the new-widowed John Howard or with Wheatley Clive.

The receipt of the christening mug had sent the hot colour flooding her face and neck. The short message was innocent enough if one had no knowledge of her last meeting with Clive. His continued interest was dangerous, yet she was still touched by his token of friendship after the traumatic experience of unwittingly incurring the ill-will of the neighbourhood. She could think of no one else but himself and John who'd want to continue intimacy after all the damaging gossip.

She had nothing to fear now, in a physical sense, since Deborah's death in the smoke-filled cottage. Karran had not been able to bring herself to look at the little dwelling but she supposed she must, sooner or later, or brand herself a coward.

In the meantime, she had a haven and her small, precious son. His name had presented problems for Laurence had been so determined that the boy should not take his, but Richards' father was Bartholemew and Karran had come to think that this would do as well as any. Even an illegitimate child had the right to a grandfather's name.

John had a visitor. Karran had heard the sound of hooves some time ago, but she had not wished to intrude. He'd been so good to her that she could never repay him by a deliberate flaunting of herself in his drawing-room.

There was a knock and the housekeeper, Mrs Percival, presented herself, her expression, as always, just masking disapproval. 'Mr Howard would like you to go to the drawing-room, Miss Kinrade.'

'Thank you.'

Karran waited for the indignant frou-frou of the woman's skirts to recede before she went to join Howard. Through the hall window, she could see the light glittering on the sea around Shag Rock. A cormorant flapped black wings.

Through the open door she could glimpse John's visitor. He was young and very fair. The eyes that were turned enquiringly in her direction were a clear blue. His clothes were a little shabby but retained traces of former quality and his boots were dusty, as if he had walked as well as ridden to reach the house.

'This is Mr Abel Costain, my dear,' John said. 'Miss Kinrade.'

'How do you do.' The young voice was pleasant enough though Karran thought it permeated with undertones. Some papers protruded from the portfolio that lay on the table beside him, and Karran received an impression of swirling colour and the same kind of assurance that was reflected in Emily's work.

'Mr Costain has brought some of his handiwork for me to see. Captain Jayce mentioned the fact that I needed another illustrator.'

Karran smiled at the visitor. 'May I look? Properly.'

Costain stood aside with a charming bow, his hands indicating pleased acquiescence.

As she crossed the room, Karran knew that she was being assessed. Young Mr Costain knew how to make the fullest use of his God-given attributes. She picked up the top-most sketch, realising that he also had his fair share of talent. While his technique was not quite Emily's, it was close enough not to quarrel with the original style of the history. Studying the strong lines and subtleties of shade, Karran thought Costain was a degree cleverer than Emily. Some of the off-beat tints of olive and aubergine, the muted browns, were exceptionally appealing. She'd never liked the obvious.

Her black eyes met the sky-blue gaze. There was a momentary glimpse of something knowing and vaguely unpleasant that disturbed her. He must have been told about the odd relationship between herself and John Howard, and the fact that Howard had taken her back with her illegitimate child after a series of traumatic disasters.

The new limpidness of Costain's regard seemed almost worse than the fleeting shadow of knowledge. Here stood a highly dangerous person, Karran decided, and one who would leave his mark on the neighbourhood. But his work was what John needed and he'd never find anyone more suited to that requirement.

She picked up the rest of the sketches and took her time over her perusal, aware that Costain's smile had become fixed, noticing how white the teeth were against the warm brown of his skin, and how fair his hair in contrast. He had obviously expected her to rush into an instant and girlish rapture over his efforts and her prolonged silence had disconcerted him. It would do him good to wait.

'Yes, John,' she said at last, with just the right intonation of distant approbation. 'Mr Costain would, I imagine, be able to fill the gap.'

'I thought them excellent,' John replied, a fraction put out.

'You are the person most concerned and must decide. I have agreed the style is the most appropriate you are likely to find unless you go to the mainland, but I must leave the final choice to you.'

'There's no one else.'

'Then it will have to be Mr Costain.' Karran rejoiced in the brief flicker of dislike that appeared in those otherwise unclouded eyes. It occurred to her that Costain might expect

128

to live in as part of his wages and the thought was not pleasant. Ravensdowne could cease to be the oasis John had intended if this attractive stranger were allowed to undermine the present peace. Howard was so good that he'd never notice the small signs which indicated to Karran that Abel Costain was just the opposite.

'But you liked the sketches, surely?' John asked anxiously.

'I liked the sketches.' But I needn't like the author of them, Karran told herself, and hoped that Costain had noticed the slight emphasis she'd placed on the last word.

'Very well, Mr Costain. The post is yours.'

'I take it you have adequate lodging in Port St Mary?' Karran asked quickly, before Howard gave out any invitation.

Costain smiled very sweetly. 'I do have a room but the landlady is not over-friendly. She finds it an irritation to have my painting accoutrements about the chamber. I fear I must look elsewhere. Not that there is much choice in so small a place, but I would not wish to be far from Ravensdowne —'

'Say no more,' Howard interposed. 'There is more than room enough here.'

'I had not intended —'

'Of course you hadn't. But what could be more convenient?'

'What, indeed?' Karran hoped John would miss the brittle inflection. The whole arrangement filled her with unaccustomed foreboding.

'After all, we will have to work closely together and it will do Karran good to have some other young person in the house.'

'Are you sure my presence will not inconvenience you?'

'Perfectly.'

'I'll fetch my things, then, such as they are, and come — tomorrow?'

'I'll have a room made ready.'

'How can I thank you?' Costain asked with agreeable humility.

'My dear fellow, you've done me a favour,' Howard insisted. 'I'd almost given up hope of continuing —'

'There's a baby crying,' the young man said. 'Miss Kinrade —'

'I hear him.' Karran hated the knowing smile. 'It's my child, as you are probably already aware, if you lodge in the

·village. I'd best go and quiet him.'

'Till tomorrow, then.' The fair head was inclined courteously.

'Tomorrow.'

All the way to Bartholemew's room, Karran saw the derisive twist of the well-shaped lips. She should not have made an enemy of him so quickly, but she had not been able to help herself. John would be hurt a second time. It was a pity he had such a compulsion to fill his so comfortable nest with cuckoos.

Elizabeth was so taken with the babies' christening mugs that she decided to have porringers and serviette rings in the same design. Clive had told her they were bought at Reid's which was close to the harbour in Douglas.

A wet-nurse had been hired to help with the twins, who, disappointingly, had not inherited the Doyle looks, but Clive's. So far Elizabeth had felt scant affection for the mousy little creatures who had been named Timothy and Virginia after Clive's parents. Clive had suggested Barnabas, tentatively, but Elizabeth had been dead set against the link with Barney. Almost the only benefit from her marriage was in the change of name from the hated Kerruish to Clive.

She did not mention that she was going to Reid's. Clive was busier than ever these days, yet in spite of his constant presence at the Donaghue he was tired and on edge, almost as if his work only brought him worry instead of achievement. It puzzled her.

The nurse preferred taking complete charge of the twins so Elizabeth felt more free than for many months. She had her mare saddled and wore her new and becoming riding-habit. The winter had been so long and lonely and she had suffered cruelly giving birth to Clive's babies; today was to be a kind of reward. She would not admit even to herself that she'd overheard that Nat was usually to be found in Douglas on Thursday afternoons at the iron-master's office, and that she meant to be somewhere in the vicinity. That wouldn't be difficult, as Reid's back window overlooked Clay's yard and the door through which Nat Gelling would enter.

Warmth suffused her entire body. She shouldn't think so constantly of Nat. No good could come of it. But she couldn't help herself. Only with Gelling could she be her better self. He was a rock and a comfort and she was sure he loved her, not with Clive's kind of desire — not that that was much in evidence at present — but with a selfless wish to see her happy and fulfilled. He understood that she did not at present want the physical side of any relationship with a man. Perhaps she would change? Others were happy in that way. Her sense of incompleteness still had the power to wound. Clive, quite openly, called her abnormal, a freak who should have been shown at a fair like the fat lady or the inevitable mermaid eating her raw fish like a seal. She roused the worst in him.

The track by Eairy and Braaid was beautiful once the mine machinery was left behind. Because it was so fine, she cut across to Braddan, looking down on Spring Valley and across to the outskirts of the town where the sea stretched beyond the smoking chimneys that sloped towards the bay. Now she could see the sands and St Mary's Rock with the Tower of Refuge pointing skywards like a blunt finger. Derby Castle and Onchan Head. Douglas Head. The bushes high and leafy and wild flowers shining against the banks. There were dog-roses. A vast cloud-blown heaven criss-crossed with gulls' flight.

She could not recall ever having noticed so much detail. It was as if the world had been washed and burnished, so clean and bright that one couldn't repress the burgeoning of joy.

Elizabeth rode down the steep bank to the sea road, invigorated and released from the past. It seemed she was a being as new as the day. The glitter of the sea dazzled her. She forgot Clive and the fact that she was a mother. It was almost the first time she had been entirely herself.

The light shone on Reid's window. Elizabeth tied the mare to a hitching-post and entered the shop. Old Mr Reid was alone, seated at the long table and inspecting some articles of jewellery. He sprang from the chair at the sight of Elizabeth, so tall and lovely in her green habit, her hair clustered under the hard hat.

'Mrs Clive! If I may say so, my dear, you make me think that summer is the loveliest season of the year.' His worn eyes reflected admiration.

'That's prettily said,' she replied, ridiculously pleased by the compliment. It seemed so long since she'd been approved. Her good humour was accentuated by the fact that she was close to the window from which she hoped to glimpse Nat. It had been weeks since he'd called and she was hungry for the sight of his broad, dependable figure.

'I hear I have to congratulate you on two fine babies. Lucky children!'

She became aware that Mr Reid had been pursuing his gallantry unheard, but had reached the stage where curiosity as to the purpose of her visit had taken over.

He brought a chair, seeing that she made no move to leave the window, and bustled off to fetch her a glass of sherry while she settled the green folds about her knees.

'And now, dear lady? How can I be of service?'

'It concerns the twins, Mr Reid. Those christening mugs —'

'Nothing wrong with them, I hope?' The old man looked agitated. 'Fine craftmanship —'

'Just the opposite. I admire them so much I wanted porringers and serviette rings to match. I liked the engraving particularly, that ivy leaf design. And the initials, you'll remember, were C but now the babies are named, they should perhaps be V.C. and T.C. That would be more personal.'

'It would indeed. And what of the third? Do you want the additional items to match that also?'

'Third?' Mr Reid now had all of Elizabeth's erstwhile wandering attention.

'Yes, my dear. The third mug Mr Clive ordered. The one with the initial — now what was it? I remember. K. That was it! K. The same design as the twins' —'

His voice receded into a grey fog as Elizabeth was consumed with a rage that exorcised all the pleasure of the day. How dared he! How dared Clive! So he *had* been serious about his feelings for Karran Kinrade. He could even be the father of that boy she had. Why else would he give her anything so intimate? All the time Karran had been whoring with that murderer from Cumberland she must also have entertained Elizabeth's husband. Mixed with the sick fury was a queer envy for Karran's ability, not only to attract men, but to hold them physically. There had been whispers lately about her relationship with John Howard, and about Mrs Howard's death.

'You look quite pale, Mrs Clive,' Reid was murmuring solicitously. 'Perhaps you should have waited before riding so far, and your infants so young.'

'You are probably right.' Elizabeth spoke with an effort.

'I'll fetch some water. Or would brandy be better?'

'Brandy,' she whispered and shivered with a creeping

coldness that threatened to engulf her. 'Please —'

After he had hurried into the back regions of the shop, she turned to the window. The light hit her eyes like a sword but at the same moment she was conscious of the dark-suited figure of Gelling, crossing the glistening cobbles without haste.

Impulsively, she raised her hand and knocked on the pane with so much urgency that Nat stopped, staring in surprise. Something in her intense pallor and strained features brought welcome concern to his eyes. She beckoned to him, only dimly aware of her indiscretion, thankful that he was now making his way, purposefully, towards the shop where she waited, trembling.

Mr Reid had not returned when Nat forced his large frame through the narrow doorway and planted himself in front of her shuddering body.

'What's wrong, Elizabeth? You look ill.'

'I can't tell you. Mr Reid will be back in a minute. Can we go somewhere to talk?'

'The hotel?' He exuded strength and deliverance. She responded to the timbre of his voice and the bulk of him, wanting to touch him as if for reassurance, yet unexpectedly conscious that touching might lead to other things with which she might not be able to cope.

'Have you eaten today?' Nat pursued.

'I — only coffee at breakfast.'

'Then you ride all the way to Douglas! And so soon —' His voice died away.

Elizabeth realised that he could not bring himself to acknowledge the presence of her babies. It was as if they represented an insuperable obstacle between herself and Nat.

'It was not that made me unwell. There's another matter —'

'I'm sorry to have taken so long,' Mr Reid said apologetically, 'but I couldn't lay hands on — Oh, I didn't see you, Mr Gelling. Can I do something for you?'

'I saw Mrs Clive at the window. She looked ill so I came to see if she needed help.'

'There you are, my dear.'

The brandy glass was pushed into her hand. Elizabeth saw the curiosity that Mr Reid could not hide. He must have heard her frantic rapping on the glass and sensed Nat's disquiet. She hoped he would not think back to the turn of

133

conversation that had led to her exhausting emotional collapse.

'We — have not seen you for so long,' Elizabeth said in a voice washed bare of feeling. 'When was it that you brought the last letters from my mother?'

'I can't recall.' Nat's face was almost as pale as her own in the gloom of the little shop. Mr Reid hovered silently like a ghost in the background, his little shrunken face sharp with the inquisitiveness of the old caught up in a titillating situation, anxious to draw from it every scrap of life-giving gratification.

'You've been very kind,' Elizabeth told him, handing back the glass. A little colour had returned to her cheeks, but the glorious well-being had not been regained.

'I must go,' Nat said. 'The iron-master —'

'Don't let me keep you. I'll be all right now. I'll tell Wheatley I saw you. He was saying only yesterday that you must come to supper.'

'I'll see you — soon.' Nat pressed her hand and she was suddenly alive again. He'd go to the hotel once his business with Clay was finished.

The shop seemed lighter and very empty once he had gone.

'The porringers.' Mr Reid returned to business now that Mrs Clive was looking more herself. 'We were discussing if there were to be two or three.'

'Two,' Elizabeth replied with false calm. 'The third — the other was for a relative. She'd not expect —'

'No,' Mr Reid put in quickly. He must not seem too anxious for business. 'I'll send you a message, shall I, when they are ready?'

'Thank you.' Elizabeth smiled. Mr Reid thought there was sadness behind it. What was the meaning of this morning's little drama? A relative, she'd said. The initial K. It shouldn't be too difficult to find out. His assistant might have had instructions to post it to a local address. And to think that the quiet Mr Nathaniel Gelling could be such a knight errant! He'd give anything to be a fly on the wall when next Nat and Mrs Clive met.

'I came as quickly as I could,' Nat said, lowering himself into a chair next to Elizabeth.

He'd found her sipping at a cup of China tea behind a large potted plant. She still looked pale and tired and the sunlight accentuated the darkness around her eyes. She had taken off her hat and the red abundance of her hair enchanted him afresh. He wanted to run his hands through it, see it hanging around her shoulders and down her back.

'Thank you.'

'Why didn't you order chocolate? It would have been more sustaining.'

'You mentioned food. I thought we might eat together.'

'Do you want to be seen with me? Give rise to gossip?'

'I don't care any more.' The furious bitterness had returned.

'There are oak settles with high backs at the Swan. We could choose a dark corner.'

'Everyone knows you are Kerruish's man. Why worry so?'

'Everyone knows you're Clive's wife. The mother of his children.'

'That's what you'll never forgive, isn't it! Do you imagine I invited him to my bed the night they were conceived? Begged him to take me?' Her voice had risen. 'You know better.'

'You'll draw attention to yourself,' Nat said quietly. 'Don't do it, please?'

'I don't know why I wanted to see you. Talk to you.'

'Because you knew I'd listen.'

'We'll dine here. I'm not afraid of being seen with you. Unless you mind?'

'Of course I don't. What have I to lose?'

They were sitting at a table with a very white cloth and a steak and kidney pudding smouldering in front of them, flanked by carrots and floury potatoes.

In spite of herself, Elizabeth felt the onset of a real hunger. She waited until they both were satisfied, then she told him of this morning's discovery.

'Are you sure you haven't got hold of the wrong end of the stick?'

'How could I? Wheatley tells me nothing of a third christening mug and I'd have seen it if it were in the house. It was for a child with the initial K. I can think of no other child born recently who might fit that description, can you?'

Nat shook his head. 'He might have been sorry for the girl. Contrasting his own fortune with that of your cousin. I remember, at the Bascombes, he spent some time with her.'

'Oh, he spent time with her!' There were two hard spots of colour in Elizabeth's face. 'I know, for he told me so. Told

135

me the night after our wedding that he'd practically asked her to wed him! That she'd have been so much more bedworthy —'

'So it was Karran Kinrade who threatened your marriage. You never did say. That was cruel of Clive. Unless you forced him to — You refused him, perhaps?'

'What if I did?'

'I know how I'd have felt had it been me.' His strong, craggy face was stamped with a rueful understanding. 'But it still was cruel —'

'I hate him.'

Shock flickered in Nat's eyes. 'You shouldn't say that. Not to me.'

'You're the only person I can say it to.'

'On the contrary, I'm the only person you should keep it from. That knowledge makes me even more sorry you aren't free and never will be —'

'Nat. Oh, Nat —' Her eyes glittered with unshed tears.

'Please don't look at me like that,' he told her harshly. 'It's not calculated to make my lot any easier.'

'You do love me, then? It's not just — friendship?'

'No, it's not merely friendship. But you have a husband and now children. If I'd realised there were to be babies I'd not have allowed myself — No, that's untrue. I loved you before that. Only now we must both forget that unhappy fact. If you'll take my advice, don't let Clive know that you've found out about the gift to your cousin. It can't have been more than a gesture of pity. I find myself almost applauding him for not adopting the general attitude of censure. And worse. Have you forgotten the events that led to the child's premature birth?'

'No. But she must be wanton —'

'Why must she? Because she refuses a man in comfortable circumstances to have an affair with another who could only leave her a wretched cottage after he'd been shot down like a dog, his last words exonerating her from any complicity in what he'd done, probably accidentally? Turning her bene-factress against her in the process? She was as good as a daughter to the Howards. She must have known what she was losing.'

Elizabeth laughed unmusically. 'That's not what local people say! Not now.'

'Gossip. Malicious rumour.'

'Why, you're as bad as he is! My precious husband!

Taking up the cudgels on behalf of that — harlot!' She could not bear Nat's championship of that woman.

'I don't think I like you very much in this mood,' Nat said remotely.

'A fine lover you'd be!'

'That's something you must put out of your mind. You've just made it perfectly plain how you feel about women who bestow themselves over-freely. What's sauce for the goose?'

'How hateful you can be.' To think that she had considered today an oasis, a special day she wanted to treasure. It had started so well. And now she'd made Nat hate her.

'And you —'

'Don't let me keep you. Go away! Go away, Nat.' Her voice rose again.

'Very well. I'm sorry I was indiscreet enough to say things that would have been better untold.'

'And I that I actually believed them!'

'Goodbye, then, Elizabeth. Perhaps you should re-assess your life and what you have?'

She did not answer. Could not —

Nat was walking away, opening the door, letting it bang behind him.

The floods of sunlight that washed the table with its litter of used crocks were part of a nightmare. A feeling of desperation overcame her. Now there was nobody. The emptiness frightened her. Nat couldn't expect her to turn into his kind of person overnight. Leopards didn't change. He should have known that.

He'd be sorry by now and come back, contrite.

Elizabeth sat watching the door but it didn't open.

She went down to the beach when she knew at last that Gelling would not return. Mixed with her sensation of bitter loss was hatred for Karran. She had not really hated her before. Disliked, envied perhaps, but never this black bitterness that now consumed her. She wanted to hurt her rival. Injure her, beyond recovery.

Elizabeth, head bent, stared unseeingly at the bare sand. Her boots crunched the fine shingle and the sound merged with that of the sea. She was jerked out of her self-pity by hearing Charlotte saying, 'Elizabeth? I hadn't expected —'

Elizabeth found herself facing her half-sister and a young man she'd never before seen. A fair, rather beautiful young man of poetic appearance. But there was a shadow in the china-blue eyes that gave the lie to any softness in his nature.

'Where's Mother?' Elizabeth asked. 'And who's this you're with?'

Charlotte reacted uncharacteristically by blushing. 'This is Mr Costain. He's employed by Mr Howard. To paint the illustrations for the book. Now that Mrs Howard —'

'Now that Mrs Howard is dead,' Elizabeth finished for her, brutally.

'And Mama is at the dressmakers,' Charlotte said quickly, aware of her sister's suspicions. 'I was bored and she told me to amuse myself —'

'So you amuse yourself with a total stranger. You should know better, Mr Costain, than Charlotte, that reputations can be lost by such behaviour? Why encourage familiarity?'

'My apologies. We meant no harm. The only two persons on the shore and we are expected to pass one another without a glance?'

'Which you would have done if you weren't aware that Charlotte is Kerruish's daughter,' Elizabeth challenged.

Costain turned pale but it was not possible to tell if it were with anger or dislike of being censured.

'How dare you!' Charlotte almost screamed. A gull flew up at the sound. Elizabeth had never seen the girl so positive. The slender body was taut as a bow and her hazel eyes were wide and bright with a fury Elizabeth had never believed her sister could possess.

'It seems I have compromised you, Miss Charlotte,' Costain said very softly. 'But I really had no such base intention as your sister implies. I did not know who you were: we were passing ships who signalled to one another in disinterested friendship. We have spoken a dozen sentences at most, yet now I am made to feel a fortune-hunter —' Costain shrugged ruefully.

'And how do you know that Kerruish has a fortune?'

Costain's eyes met Elizabeth's and held them in a blue, expressionless stare. 'You made it so obvious. But I swear I meant no harm. And Mr Howard can vouch for my bona fides if you care to enquire at Ravensdowne. I came to Douglas today to purchase paints and other requisites for my work. As I did this more quickly than anticipated, I decided to stretch my legs before returning. Miss Charlotte and I passed the time of day and were just returning to our separate destinations. I cannot express, sufficiently, my

138

distress if I have made trouble for your sister —'

'There is no question of trouble,' Charlotte interposed harshly. 'Elizabeth has succeeded in spoiling another small pleasure. It's something she has always enjoyed. But my father would not feel as she does, Mr Costain. Rest assured of that. And now, excuse me while I go to find Mama.' Close to tears, Charlotte hurried away towards the embankment.

'Well! Well!' Costain said even more gently. 'What a storm in a teacup.'

'I have to look after my family. Protect them from themselves,' Elizabeth insisted.

'Of course. But you were wrong.'

'I don't think there's anything else to say. Charlotte's father is not such a fool as she makes out. He'll be very careful about her friendships.'

'How hard you are for someone so — attractive.'

'My looks are none of your concern.'

'They are everyone's concern. One sees. One is — uplifted?'

'Don't think to flatter your way out of your error, Mr Costain.' He must know Karran. Hatred seeped back through the temporary forgetfulness. 'I do know John Howard, of course. We've attended various affairs together. There's a young woman at the house. You must have met —'

'Miss Kinrade? Yes. We've met.' His tone was now cool.

'You sound — as if you dislike her.'

'For the mother of a bastard, she does give herself airs.' For a moment there was a spark of something quite ugly at the back of those baby-blue eyes.

Elizabeth saw that there might be advantages to be gained from currying Costain's favour. What, after all, had he done that was so dreadful? Exchanged a few words? Knowing Charlotte's negativeness, they'd be of little account. It was possible Costain knew nothing of Charlotte's expectations but had only pitied the child her plainness and obvious loneliness.

'I'm sorry if I jumped to the wrong conclusion. But, if you had had wrong intentions, it was my duty —'

'Of course it was.' Costain pushed back a lock of primrose-coloured hair in what Elizabeth could not fail to recognise as a carefully-rehearsed gesture. He was so unlike Nat, so superficially effeminate. Yet somehow, at the core of him, basically ruthless. She did not know how she gauged him so clearly in that one fleeting second. Or had she just imagined that brief look into his soul? There was no sign of it now, that cruelty. If ever it had existed.

Nat was so different. So tough externally, yet good inside. A goodness that was a strength instead of a softness. And she had driven him away.

Costain had noted her own brief weakness. Elizabeth could see it in his slow smile.

'I must go,' she said abruptly. 'Catch my mother before she leaves. Good day.'

The echo of his voice followed her. 'Perhaps we'll meet again?'

Not if I can help it, she thought, then remembered his proximity to her enemy.

Perhaps, then. If it is necessary.

And, of course, it would be.

6

Elizabeth had not, after all, mentioned the discovery of Clive's misplaced generosity. Instead, she nursed the bitter resentment until it became an almost physical effort not to reveal her feelings to her husband.

Their conversation became more brittle and Clive's absences more frequent. They had not slept together since the twins' birth and Clive had finally pleaded insomnia as an excuse to use a separate bed-chamber. They ate their meals in a near silence, the hot sun flooding the table and turning Elizabeth's hair to golden-orange. Once or twice, the colour of that hair made Clive briefly desirous but the pale, tight-lipped face below destroyed the urge. The summer faded and the autumn and winter rushed upon them.

Elizabeth had not seen Nat, except at a distance, since the meeting at Douglas. The thought of the lost friendship tormented her. It had been more, far more than camaraderie. He had said as much, while condemning her for her lack of charity. It amazed her that she could be attracted by goodness. She'd laughed at the quality as a girl, wanting only to rebel against a set of values. She'd wanted excitement and Wheatley Clive, and now she had him and it seemed an empty victory. The growing babies resembled him more than ever and she had no patience with the small clutching hands and the permanent dribbling over her pretty gowns.

'You aren't natural,' Clive had been driven to expostulate when he saw how she often pushed the twins away, frowning.

All of Elizabeth's instincts had told her to cry, 'And Karran Kinrade is, I suppose! I can't think why you haven't run to her! She'd not turn you away. It's anything in breeches for her. Everyone knows that.' But she bit back the impulse as she hid so many other things over the long, silent winter. This year, unlike last, there were no sanity-saving visits from Nat.

He had moved out of his lodgings so as to be nearer the Erin and there could be no excuse to deliver her mother's letters. Clive had noticed his absence, of course. 'Gelling must be wenching,' he said with the knowing smile Elizabeth had learnt to hate. 'Who'd have thought of it? Still waters run deep.'

'Don't they!' she snapped viciously, then turned away, aware of Clive's look of amused perception. Not that he could know of the strength of her feelings for Nat. He'd put her annoyance down to pique.

She modified her tone sufficiently to ask him for money for a spring pelisse but Clive had turned moody, saying, 'You've garments enough. The press won't shut if you have more.'

'I've little fashionable —'

'Who cares if you're not modish up here on the moor or in Douglas for that matter?'

'Would you have my mother smarter than myself?'

She can afford to be with a successful husband, Clive thought resentfully. Everything Barney touched seemed to prosper. As the lode in the Donaghue slowly diminished, the Erin flourished. Kerruish was sinking a fresh level, following the will-o'-wisp of fortune that attended each venture.

'Wait a while,' Clive told his wife. 'Just a little longer —'

'Why must I?'

'Because I ask you to,' he replied coldly.

Elizabeth burned to ask him what gifts he'd bestowed on Miss Kinrade recently but could never quite bring herself to do so. When Clive slitted his eyes so that they were pale, glittering scratches she knew it would be a mistake to try his patience so far. He'd be sure to cast up her inadequacies as an excuse and do it so loudly that the entire household would be informed.

She dreamed, one night, of Nat approaching her as a lover but before they could come together she had been awakened by the cries of the babies from the nursery and had lain in futile longing, listening to the nurse's soothing tones, and the dawn chorus from the trees that separated the house from the mines across the moor. How could she hate her own children?

The arrival of Boyce and Sebastian that spring created a welcome diversion. Boyce had been instructed to bring his brother while he was on leave and the Clives were invited over to Castletown for a celebration supper. Erin had made a great fuss over the event: the Bascombes were there and several of the boys' young friends. Erin still called Sebastian and Boyce, the boys.

It had been a long time since the Kerruish household had

been so animated and Erin took on a new beauty. Her face was often pale and tired in repose nowadays, but the advent of her sons and the excitement of presiding over a full table had brought colour to the hollowed cheeks. The thinness of her face gave her a refinement she had so far lacked.

Barney was quieter than previously but only Erin noticed. Elizabeth and her brothers had drawn together into their former closeness, excluding everyone else. Elizabeth felt like a child again, clinging first to Boyce and then Sebastian, a touch of hysteria in her outbursts of laughter.

Clive's sensuality was revived by this altered girl, so dramatically charged with life and colour. Perhaps some of that hectic excitement would last until bedtime. They were to spend the night at Barney's and, naturally, share the same room.

'We must do something special while the boys are here,' Erin said.

'Mama! We've grown up. Remember?' Boyce grinned disarmingly. How attractive he was!

'So you have, my darlings. My handsome young men.'

Barney's eyes met Erin's with an accusation that still had the power to cut her to the heart. There was a ghost in the room, the shadow of the child who might have been. And it was too late. Far too late — She'd seen to that.

Sebastian was not so happy as he made out. He merely followed the high-spirited abandon of his brother and sister with a semblance of their almost frantic enjoyment in one another's company. Over and over he saw Richard Bailey's face grown strange and intent. Heard Richard's voice whispering, 'Giles Jordan's leaving. We must become better friends, Sebastian, mustn't we.' His own voice agreeing. A room filled with firelight and shadows.

'You aren't listening!' Elizabeth practically shrieked in his ear.

He stared at her almost blankly. 'What — what were you saying?'

'The something special we must do while we are all together. We thought — the theatre? And supper afterwards.'

'Why not?' Sebastian agreed, but all the time his heart thudded like a piston at the thought of Bailey and that darkened room, wondering how their expressions would all change should he tell them what had happened there. Kerruish. What would he say or do? Sebastian's stomach muscles contracted. He could picture Barney's face. It would be filled with disgust but no surprise. He'd always expected Sebastian to turn out

143

perverted. But it was Bailey's fault. Wasn't it? Sebastian sat silent, a fixed smile hiding his inward emotions.

'We'll go on Friday night,' Elizabeth planned happily, 'and have the week-end to recover. Surely I can have the pelisse for that?' She challenged Clive, knowing he'd hate refusing her in front of the family.

Clive scowled. He'd told no one of the eventual loss of the *Helen*. Weeks and weeks of intermingled hope and despair, then Bob Owen's letter verifying the fact that the vessel and her cargo had foundered and sunk in a gale off Cap Gris Nez. Wreckage had floated ashore. The carved and painted figure-head was recognised.

'Can't I?' she persisted hardily.

He shrugged. 'If you must.' It was one tiny nail in a coffin that was suddenly and horrifyingly oppressive. Like being totally lost in his unproductive mine. He'd have to close it soon and that widow-woman who laboured in the ore-washing room to keep her nine children would be left destitute. She seemed, unexpectedly, more important than his own wife and infants. Elizabeth was like a cat. She'd always land on her feet. And Erin showed signs of enjoying the prospect of becoming a matriarch. If only Elizabeth had really been like her mother. If only the Donaghue had come up to initial expectations —

'Good. I've seen the very thing.' What did it matter that Elizabeth had no one for whom to wear the garment? It was a diversion. Increasingly, she needed distractions. They were a protection.

'What will we see at the theatre?' Charlotte asked practically. The sound of her voice was startling. No one had remembered she was there. But she seemed to have changed in the last few months and developed a figure that was not unattractive in its understated way. The voice was no longer a child's. The dark green dress complemented the hazel eyes that seemed larger and less myopic.

'It's a Shakespearean company. And on Friday they are performing *Macbeth*.'

'*Macbeth*!' Charlotte sat bolt upright. 'That's extremely gory. My tutor knew some of the plays.'

'*Macbeth*?' Erin said. 'What is it?'

'*Who* is it, Mama!' Charlotte was reproving. 'He was a Scots king. A murderer.'

'Oh. And I'd planned a pleasant evening.' Erin was crestfallen.

'We'll probably love it. It's therapeutic to rid oneself of

spleen via an intermediary,' Boyce drawled lazily. 'So much better than hitting out oneself at an adversary.'

Barney released a bark of laughter. 'Quite the gentleman since you became an officer, ain't you.'

'Wasn't that the desired effect?' Boyce asked, dangerously cool.

'Didn't expect you to come back a Macaroni.'

'Damn you!' Boyce said in a soft, savage whisper. 'You haven't changed. The eternal boor. And a decade or two out of date. As always.'

'Boyce! Remember it was Barney who arranged for you to do what you so enjoy,' Erin protested, seeing her much wished-for reunion about to lie in ruins around her feet.

'I do remember. But I can't spend the rest of my life grovelling. Can I?'

Sebastian wondered, a little sickly, what Barney's reaction would be if he were to get up and tell them what he himself now was. Kerruish would prefer a Macaroni to Sebastian's new designation. Sebastian felt sick. His skin assumed a greenish tinge.

'Then that's all settled,' Erin said quickly and too brightly. 'We go to *Macbeth*.'

Boyce got up and left the room and after a pause Elizabeth followed him. It was hard to fill the silence that remained.

Abel slid the sheet of paper across the table. Karran could see the outline of the butterfly from her seat at the window, and the wallflower colourings of the wings.

'It's good,' John said. 'Look, Karran,' and raised the painting.

Bart stirred in her arms as she appraised it and her senses responded to the warm squirming life she held. She kissed the top of his dark little head and was immediately aware of the flicker of distaste in Abel's pale blue eyes. It did not surprise her. Karran had known for some time that Costain disliked the child. Perhaps she should ignore his creativity in the way he despised hers but honesty made her say, 'It's the best thing you've done so far.'

It was quite beautiful, the velvety texture of the tortoise-shell wings against the dark shiny greens of rhododendron leaves. In the time that Costain had lived at Ravensdowne his work had improved, becoming even more subtle and atmospheric, surpassing Emily's at its best. One could not be grudging about genius. People talked about artistic hands, in the sense that they must be slender and graceful, but Abel Costain's were square and capable just as Emily's had been. Without his hands, Abel would be nothing. The realisation was somehow frightening.

Costain's lips thinned into a smile. Most people's faces seemed to fill out when they smiled but his became thinner and hungrier, Karran reflected uneasily.

'Bart's waking,' Karran said. 'I must feed him.'

John set down the picture. 'We can't starve *him*, can we?' His tone was fond. 'Let me see him. Hold him up. He gets more beautiful every day. More like you.'

Karran caught the blue flash of Abel's furious glance. He was jealous and could never quite hide the fact. Several times Karran had intended to leave John's house, and always Bart's helplessness had kept her there. But there was not room for both herself and Costain and he was never going to relinquish his favoured position. As cunningly as he painted, he worked on John's good nature, making himself as indispensable a companion as a craftsman.

There was the money that lay in the bank, accruing interest. With it she could purchase a small house but she also needed an income to keep herself and Bart. It was not right that John must always be responsible for them. Yet she shrank from bringing up the subject for fear of hurting him. She could not give the true reason for her need to defect and he would only invent others, to the detriment of his peace of mind. And he had suffered enough over Emily's untimely end. Karran had heard him pace the floor of his bed-chamber for months afterwards and had gone in once to find him pale and sweating with the memory of her death. Just as she herself remembered Laurence and Deborah and poor Finn. There had never been any trace of the cat around the burnt wreck of the tholtan and she knew he could not have escaped. No cat would have gone away once the bond was forged.

She rose, lifting the child against her shoulder.

How beautiful she was, John thought, with a sense of mingled pain and wonder. His life would be so empty now without her and lacking Abel's presence. Two handsome young people whose lives were interwoven with his own. It would have been so natural for Abel to fall in love with Karran. John had expected it. But there had been no sign of any strong emotion between them, nor, oddly enough, of any brother-sister closeness that might have ensued from their proximity in his house. Yet wouldn't it have hurt him beyond measure if they had become lovers? Even before Emily's death, before the discovery that Karran was so deeply involved with Richards, John

146

knew he was irrevocably attached to the girl he'd made his ward. He could not imagine life without her.

And sometimes, as at this moment, when she stood tall and lovely, flushed with the fire's warmth and the brimming-over of her affection for her child, he wanted her with a passion he had never previously known. But he mustn't spoil their relationship by frightening her off in an unguarded moment, divulging what must never be revealed by a look or gesture. He was too old for her and he must never make her feel that she owed it to him to love him for his care of her and Bart, at least, not the kind of love he now so urgently wanted. He must just think how lucky he was that she was there and that he had the bonus of Abel's so rewarding companionship. If it had not been for the boy's incredibly fortuitous appearance just when he was most needed, the history of flora and fauna would never have been completed.

Captain Jayce had called one day to see how it progressed and had been amazed at John's good fortune in replacing Emily. As if he had *wanted* to reinstate Emily, who had grown progressively more strange and aloof and who had come to look at him with what was surely — hatred?

John was suddenly cold and unsure. 'Let's do something!' he said almost too loudly, making Karran turn just before she reached the doorway, and Abel look up with a sharp blue gaze that warned him that he must return to normality or arouse their suspicions.

'Do what?' Abel asked, his square fingertips thudding on the table-top like warning drums.

'Something — special. The theatre. We could spend the night in Douglas. Have supper.'

'What about Bart?'

'He could be left with Mrs Quinn for one night, surely?' Mrs Quinn had been engaged to help in the nursery.

'I've never left him before.' Karran rubbed the child's head with her chin, lovingly.

'She'd adore an excuse to have him to herself. And what harm could come to him?'

'None, I suppose. What do you want to see?'

'It said in the last news-sheet that there was a visiting Shakespearean company. I don't know which play would be on, or, indeed, the quality of the players.'

'It doesn't really matter, does it!' Karran was infected with an unexpected need for new places and events. It had been more of a strain living in the shadow of Costain's dislike than she had

147

confessed, even to herself.

'I'll send young Brand to reserve a box. And you must dress up. There's the gown I gave you for your birthday. I've not seen it as yet.'

'Only because it's too fine for a mother of a small boy. I wonder if he'll behave?'

'Of course he will.'

'You don't think — ?' Karran hesitated.

'Think what?'

'That I'd still be — condemned? It's not for myself — it's for you that I mind.'

'It's been a long time. And the persons who went to the cottage that night are not the same as those who'd frequent the theatres. Not to listen to Shakespeare, anyway.'

'I suppose not. Only, I've not forgotten —' She shivered, her face paling.

'How could you? But you'd have us as champions. Abel and me.'

'So I would. Oh, it would be rather splendid!'

'Then, that's settled.' John was delighted. Impulsively, he kissed her on the brow and ruffled Bart's hair. The baby chuckled and held out his hands to clutch at John's embroidered waistcoat. A button flew to the floor.

'I'll sew it on later,' Karran said, intercepting Abel's faint sneer. It was odd that however disagreeable his expression, he never looked anything but personable. She felt sorry for any girl who lost her head over him. It would be like losing oneself in a desert.

'We'll go on Friday,' John told her, gently disengaging Bart's grasping fingers. 'I always like Fridays. There's a feeling of expectation. Or there is for me.'

'I like Fridays too,' Karran answered, shifting the baby to a more comfortable position. A lock of hair had fallen over one eye and John had an overwhelming desire to put it back.

'And you, Abel?' he asked, resisting the temptation.

'Me? Oh, I will just have to like Fridays too, it seems.' Abel laughed and looked like an angel.

Life's good, John thought. I have all three of them. All — The incredible fortune.

Karran read the playbills under the erratic light of a swinging lantern. People were streaming into the building, young men in cravats and long-tailed coats, girls in their best gowns, old men with paunches and florid complexions, middle-aged

148

women, some powdered and rouged. Everywhere wigs and ribbons, shawls and cloaks, the rustle of silk and the slither of satin, the clatter of French heels and boot soles, the tap of sticks. Scent and the sound of voices, all those disjointed conversations that could never be put together. Good-natured voices, vinegary comments, disagreeable tones, giggles, laughter, odd snatches of sentences. Bubbling excitement. An old woman selling flowers —

'Here,' John said, indicating some red roses. 'I'll have those.'

'Not all of them?' Karran asked.

'Why not? They're the same colour as your dress.'

'Won't it look rather — flamboyant?'

'They'll all look at you anyway, won't they, Abel.'

'They'd be blind not to,' Abel agreed politely.

The slight petulance was lost on John who paid for the flowers and thrust them into Karran's hands. Carriages were drawing up, lamps flaring.

'Thank you. You really are the most generous man. But I can't always be taking from you. Only — I've nothing to give.'

'Oh, you have. The pleasure of your company. Don't take that away. Please?'

She stared at the roses, aware of Costain's black and silent repudiation. Why did he hate her so? More to the point, why was she so set against him? He was bad. She felt it in every bone, suddenly glad that he was with them now. If he had been at home she would have worried constantly, fearing for Bart's safety just as she had mistrusted that St Mary woman brought in to assist at his birth. A woman's intuition. But she *was* right.

'If that's what you want.' The naked admiration in John's glance was a balm.

'It's what I've always wanted. Ever since I ran you down in that rainstorm.'

Her laughter was a fraction high-pitched. 'What a way to meet!'

'Wasn't it! Your advent, Abel, was much less spectacular.'

'Are you, by any chance, insinuating that I'm an exhibitionist?' Karran demanded, mock-angrily, setting John off laughing with her. They were inside the smoky, paint-smelling building now, candle-flames flickering and a scent of stale orange peel. Heads turned at the pleasant sounds of their amusement. Only Abel was silent.

Candlelight suited Karran. It emphasised the pearly pallor of her skin and the blackness of hair and eyes and level brows. Only she could have carried off the crimson gown so that it escaped the flamboyance she had suspected, assuming impeccable taste.

A stout man with sturdy calves hurried before them up the creaking stair that led them to the curtained doorway of their box. There was a strong scent of patchouli.

Karran went forward, staring, fascinated, into the waxen-smelling dimness that was punctuated with circles of lamplight. The orange-seller waited by the door, a waif-like girl in a shabbily smart gown that was too loose for the childish body. She called her wares in a husky, common voice with Liverpudlian inflections. A Manx girl would not have been allowed to push her way along the aisles, fumbled by drunken spectators. Peel was already strewn around the seats, some dry, some fresh and looking like marigold flowers. Great pitchy shadows bloomed and diminished in the erratic lighting. Whispers, sniggering, a few hoarse chuckles, smiles, full-blooded grins, the occasional roar of laughter from one of the well-padded merchants or their buxom wives and sons. John and Abel seemed immeasurably far away, lost in shadows and dimness. And silence.

The box was an isolated ante-room. There were glints of dull gilt and the plushy sensation of velvet hung in folds. A small candelabrum edged the backs of the gilded chairs with fugitive gold. Dust pricked at Karran's nose and made her sneeze.

Sounds emerged from behind the red curtain screening the stage. Furtive footfalls, smothered giggles, knocking and rapping, stifled admonitions. Sighs —

'Oranges? Nice juicy oranges!'

'Why not?' John said and gestured grandly from the carved edge of the box. 'We'll take six, child. Six!' He flung a coin into the proscenium and the thin girl snatched it up and tested it between her teeth. A scrawny boy brought the fruit up in a little basket.

Karran's gaze was drawn to the large box opposite. Ten chairs were arranged in the enclosed space as though a large party were expected.

A man the worse for drink waved his arms and shouted up to her as she leaned against the intricacies of the painted configuration. 'Hey, missy! Come down! Like the cut of your jib, by jove, I do.'

'Come away,' Abel urged with exaggerated calm. 'We'll have the bumpkin up here if we aren't careful.'

'Seamen work hard and play hard,' John commented. 'There'll be no harm in him. But come and sit down, Karran.

150

You can see all you wish through these opera glasses.'

Karran saw enough to keep her interested. Mark Cosnahan of the Santon Broadstone family sat smoking a thick green cigar. George Drinkwater, son of Liverpool's Mayor, was with a party of young bucks, and William Leece Drinkwater. William Thomas Radcliffe, Sir John Stanley, the Nelsons with their precocious daughter Esther, Quayle, the shipbuilder, Deemster Crellin with a family party, Thomas Gawne of Ramsey, a party of troopers in blue tunics cuffed with scarlet and buff breeches tucked inside their black boots, all carrying their bearskin-trimmed helmets for fear of obscuring someone else's view; it was entrancing. She forgot the long, withdrawn months when she had seen no one but John, Abel and Mrs Quinn, the occasional maid or gamekeeper. The theatre seethed with life and untold tales. Young faces and old, sad, happy, thoughtful faces —

The curtains parted in the opposite box. Karran, riveted to the delicate chair, watched the Kerruish dynasty file into their seats like a regiment of lost Tudors. All that white skin and blood-red hair, all that exaggerated splendour! She wondered what most of the audience would say if they could have seen Erin in her Kinrade days, the cottage neglected and the children grimed with dirt, Sebastian snivelling. How handsome they were. A hush had fallen on the theatre. Karran almost expected Erin and Elizabeth to acknowledge the interest of the auditorium like queens greeting their subjects. The fancy made her laugh softly.

Clive was there, and that dark overseer of Barney's. He looked nicer than any of them, Karran decided, still amused by the airs the women of the party gave themselves. Apart from Charlotte, of course. Charlotte always seemed to be enclosed in a tight little glass-covered world where nothing could touch her. Yet, even she was different this evening. She wore a green gown instead of her usual brown or grey, and her hair was dressed more imaginatively than usual. There was a string of expensive-looking beads around her slim young neck, gold round her thin wrist and slender fingers. Childhood had been pushed, decisively, away.

Erin, in peacock trappings and Elizabeth in shades of lilac and lavender – surprisingly effective on a woman with such outlandish colouring – the gleam of emeralds. Boyce and Sebastian, the gap in their ages subtly closed, provided the necessary foil of white shirts and dark coats.

They must see us, Karran thought. They know me. All Erin

had to do was to lift her white-gloved hand and nod her head. But she didn't. The large green eyes were everywhere except straight ahead. Elizabeth showed a cold profile. Only Clive smiled and Nat Gelling, sitting uncomfortably in the further-most corner, inclined his head courteously. Barney Kerruish was wrapped in his own apparently joyless thoughts. Karran was aware of a deep pity for the man. It was a long time since he had looked at all happy, yet, at the beginning, both he and Erin had seemed content. Tonight they sat at opposite sides of the box, Elizabeth next to her mother and Charlotte beside Barney. The brothers and Clive made a kind of bulwark in the middle, with Nat seated some distance behind Erin. There was a palpable suggestion of only half-buried discord.

But were they any better, she, John and Abel? Karran had to be honest. John had something on his mind and was not so close as he had been. Abel wanted to come first with his benefactor and co-writer. As illustrator, he'd be assured of half of the rights of the natural history volume. John could hardly offer him less. But Abel also saw the advantages of having an emotional hold over Howard, who had been disappointed in his relationship with his wife and who'd been denied children. Their problems were equal to any the Kerruishes might have.

A man in a tartan plaid and buskins came in front of the curtains. His thatch of gingery hair was obviously unreal and went ill with his black brows and blue-skinned chin. He announced the play in what Karran surmised to be broad Scots. It certainly sent the older members of the audience knocking at their ear-trumpets and frowning at their inability to make sense of what was said. Those with perfect hearing were little the wiser. Wives nudged husbands and the young tittered at the splendid unintelligibility of the proceedings.

The prologue ended with little understood but the words Macbeth and Duncan, the man retreating to the wings. With much creaking and many hesitations, the curtains parted to show a blackcloth of tortured trees and grey heather roots, in front of which crouched three ragged women round a black pot. Some trick of the light bathed their faces while leaving the rest in dimness. To Karran, the women were three she had known too well. The thin one with the long silvery hair was Deborah and the two dark gypsy-like creatures could have been Johanne and Aggie. They grimaced and cackled, twisting their half-seen bodies.

'Fair is foul and foul is fair'

The words seemed oddly familiar to Karran. The hunched

figures disappeared as a flash of blue lit up the stage, heralding the appearance of a king with his lords and a soldier gory and white-faced, staggering realistically to cheers from the pit, from which a strong whiff of oranges now rose.

The dialogue was strong and bloodthirsty.

'Till he unseamed him from the nave to the chaps and fixed his head upon our battlements.'

Karran glanced across to the Kerruish box to see how they withstood the torrent of drama and fatality and surprised Charlotte staring fixedly into the shadows beside herself. How had the girl come to know Abel Costain? It was certainly the artist who interested Barney's daughter. She never took her eyes away from him.

Venturing a quick sideways look, Karran saw that Abel was perfectly aware of Charlotte's intent regard. A faint smile played about his well-shaped lips and he had the tips of his fingers pressed together, as always when he was planning something of importance.

The stage darkened, creaked, then was vaguely lit to show the same desolate heath. Deborah, Johanne and Aggie — she could not think of them in any other way — returned to caper and report disastrous happenings, make direr predictions, while a drum rolled softly behind the scenes. Rat, tat. Rat, tat, tat —

A huge red-haired man strode on stage, almost eclipsing scenery and witches. Foul and fair fitted him as it did the lines of the play in which the words were doomed to repetition. Macbeth, fearsome yet compelling, quietened the wags in the audience and captured wandering attention until the curtains rattled together with much arthritic complaining.

As scene-shifting was unmistakably in progress, oranges were eaten and cigars lit. Ladies took comfits from their reticules and quizzed the company through their glasses. Much attention was devoted to both boxes, but the quality of the interest in Howard's was markedly more hostile than that afforded to the shipbuilder's. Barney had always been popular.

Karran heard the tale-end of whispers of Mrs Howard, Deborah Quine and Laurence Richards float upwards out of the dimness of the pit. Pain gripped at her, locking her stomach muscles. What did they know of any of them? It still hurt to hear Laurence and Deborah reviled. They had been decent enough people who had been caught up in situations beyond their control. Neither had been wicked. No one had harmed Emily.

John had also overheard the condemning susurration. He turned pale and there was a gleam of sweat along his brow. She caught at his hand and pressed it. 'Do you want to go? They've upset you.'

He shook his head. 'Only if you want to.'

'I don't! I've nothing to be ashamed of and I don't see why one should be afraid when one hasn't acted wrongly. Indiscreetly perhaps, even stupidly, but never wickedly.'

'Perhaps, not you —'

'Do you mean you — ? Oh, John, no one could believe that. It's me they snipe at.'

'Maybe we should go. They are hurting you.'

'I have decided I won't let them,' she replied, far more calmly than she felt. 'Honi soit qui mal y pense, after all. How many shabby secrets do *they* have!'

'How brave you are.'

'I love you,' she whispered, touched by his vulnerability.

'Do you?' His pale stare seemed to burn through the dimness and Karran was suddenly disturbed by its intensity. Surely he knew what she meant? It was a daughter's love she offered, but his reception of the declaration was anything but fatherly. He took hold of her hand in a hot urgency that dismayed her. Abel could not have helped seeing and hearing everything and would doubtless draw his own erroneous conclusions.

To Karran's unspeakable relief, the scene was at last changed and the limping curtains revealed, foot by foot, a rich apartment that set the condemning stares back to the play. An outburst of handclapping swelled at the advent of the King. But she wished the play did not harp on so of death, treachery and murder.

'Stars, hide your fires!
Let not light see my black and deep desires'

The words struck at her like knife-blows. Laurence had quoted passages from the play and in them there was so much of her feeling for him. The desire remained but he — he was surely a collection of bones no more at rest than herself. If only she had stayed with Bart. The initial magic and anticipation of the evening was gall and wormwood. Her 'crimes' would never be forgotten.

Macbeth returned to dominate the stage until his wife appeared, a thin and hungry shape with a face so stretched and hollowed that her skull showed plainly. She spewed out the wicked, seductive words to terrifying effect. No one

154

moved or spoke. Breathed —

When the break came, Karran could not sit still to be verbally dissected and disembowelled a second time.

'I need some air. No! Please don't come with me. I really prefer to go alone.'

She left before John could protest and pushed her way past a group of townsfolk with the same idea. Quickly, she hurried down the stairs and out of the door, past the stout keeper with the strong calves who had shown them to their places, and who looked after her with admiring curiosity and more than a tinge of lust.

It was cool now and she had left behind her warm cape. She shivered a little and sniffed at the clean, salt-laden air. The sound of the sea beckoned and she longed, uselessly, to go down to the wide sands and walk herself into a state of peace. In a few minutes she must go back. Back to the battery of accusing eyes and malicious faces. They probably thought she shared her favours between John and Abel. As if she could ever let Costain touch her in that way! Couldn't Charlotte Kerruish see for herself that inner badness? But why should she when it seemed to escape John Howard, who was far more sophisticated?

A hand touched her shoulder. She recoiled, thinking it might be Abel sent, unwillingly, after her. Clive's voice said, 'Are you all right? I saw you leave. Heard those insensitive oafs.'

'Oh, it's you. Why should you be bothering about me? Won't she mind?'

'Elizabeth? If she does it's for the wrong reasons. She doesn't really want me. But I daresay she'd very quickly object in a dog-in-the-mangerish fashion. It's all appearances with her. If there's anything amiss, the servants and family must be deceived into imagining ours is the greatest romance since Romeo and Juliet.' He laughed humourlessly.

'You know your Shakespeare.' She tried to divert him.

'Yes.'

'But you shouldn't be telling me your most intimate secrets. What wife could forgive that? However much truth might lie in the confidences. We are all but strangers —'

'She's not a woman. She's not warm. Not — approachable.'

'I don't know enough about her. She continues to ignore my existence.'

'She hates you.'

Karran perceived that Clive had been drinking, and quite heavily, to indulge in these rather embarrassing confidences. Several other people had been tempted out into the fresh air after the heavy staleness of the theatre and she and Clive must be plainly seen.

'You mustn't tell me these things.'

'I must tell someone. There's no one else I can talk to.' Clive had forgotten Erin and his original disclosure when the twins were born.

'I'm the last person you should tell. There's enough bad feeling between your wife and me, though not of my making. I always wanted things different. The bible does say, though, that the sins of the parents are visited upon the children and it seems that's true. People are watching us. Please leave me for your own sake. I've no reputation left, it seems.'

'What if I don't want to go? Oh, God, how I wish things *had* been different. Dear Jesus! Here's Elizabeth. I think I'm past caring.' Clive shrugged.

Elizabeth stormed out of the doorway towards them.

'You Jezebel! I suppose you just had to crook your finger and he came! Haven't enough men had their will of you? To think one can't go to the theatre without a whore plying her trade under the noses of the management.' Elizabeth's face was alabaster pale. 'I shall complain, of course, of respectable citizens being opportuned in this flagrant fashion but in the meantime, Miss Kinrade, take that!' A strong white hand landed painfully across Karran's face, making her stagger back against the wall.

'Bitch! You impotent, frigid, cesspool-minded bitch!' Clive said with a soft, cold hatred that still carried on the quiet air, and struck Elizabeth in her turn.

For a long, ghastly moment, the three figures turned to a tableau under the gratified gaze of Douglas's chief gossips, and, more unfortunately, the horrified regard of two senior members of the Tynwald who knew Wheatley Clive and his relatives very well. Deemster Crellin looked at Deemster Barr and turned on his heel. Barr followed.

'I shall leave you,' Elizabeth said in a voice breathless with passion.

'Good,' Clive rejoined, deliberately careless, and laughed woundingly.

Karran thought of several things she would have liked to have done. Drowned herself for instance, or thrown herself under a carriage and four. But she did none of them. Instead, she held a handkerchief over the burning mark on her face and went back inside. Her footsteps rang out hollowly on the stairs. Men stared and smiled insinuatingly.

Regaining the box, she sat down trembling. John would not

find out yet about the dreadful scene, and it would be difficult for the few bystanders to speak freely about what they had seen and heard above the broad accents and loud declamations of the troupe who entertained them with such a noisy hotch-potch of melodrama.

'Wash this filthy witness from your hand,' Lady Macbeth was saying with spine-chilling relish. 'The sleeping and the dead are but as pictures: 'tis the eye of childhood that fears a painted devil.'

The sleeping and the dead. The phrase evoked pictures of Laurence in the shadows of the bed they had shared, of Clemence in the windblown graveyard where the Boswell children shrieked and cavorted over the grassy mounds. Karran was enmeshed in sadness.

Bart, she thought suddenly. Both of them lived on in her son. She had the best possible motive for going on with her life. But hot tears still trickled onto the crumpled linen that hid the burgeoning bruise.

Sebastian had been caught up in the dark atmosphere of the play. Little by little, the images of Bailey had receded, like some monstrous thing overswept by the tide and safely covered for the time being. The spectre could wait until later. In the meantime, he could feast his eyes on the spectacle before him.

Vaguely, he wondered why Elizabeth had left the box so suddenly and returned so belatedly as though she hugged the dimness like a friend. Clive must be bored for he had not come back at all. Because of her lateness, Elizabeth sat down in the shadows, not far from Nat Gelling. They were like statues, neither moving.

But the play was far more compelling. The great, ruddy figure of Macbeth held him in thrall. Sebastian found himself thinking that he would not have minded that great, eye-catching man doing what Bailey had done. A hot flood of shame followed the admission. It was as if it were not the act but the instigator who repelled him. It was true then. He loved men. There had never been a girl who raised any flicker of interest or emotion. But there had been people like this huge actor with his blazing personality and virility who touched something in his nature. Something unspeakable. Forbidden. He had been like Adam and Eve and the Serpent, eating of the Tree of Knowledge. The archaic language seemed suddenly ridiculous and extravagant, arousing a sour amusement. He shouldn't have come when Boyce appeared at the school and begged a fortnight's release.

He'd stay in his room tomorrow and his excuse would be the work he'd promised to take back in return for the privilege. In the meantime, since there was no escape, he could watch Macbeth without guilt or shame. They would never meet.

He stared at the wide shoulders and pelt of lion-coloured hair, oblivious of all else.

He was too beautiful for words, Charlotte decided, intoxicated. For hours, it seemed, she and Abel Costain had played silent games across the crowded theatre. She knew the play already and the actors were a crude, barbaric lot, though maybe the Scots were like that. The cruelty and gore passed over her like a forgotten nightmare. Only the still, gilt-edged figure opposite had any reality. He had smiled three times and raised a hand, very briefly, once. But all through the performance and the interminable intervals she had been intensely aware of him, remembering that day on the Douglas sands. How hostile Elizabeth had been! Charlotte had disliked her more than ever after that inquisition and dictatorial dismissal.

The winter had seemed never-ending and there had been no sight or sound of Costain, only insidious rumours of his relationship with Howard and Karran Kinrade. Every ounce of jealousy in Charlotte's thin body had been directed towards Howard's ward with her bastard baby. Once a girl fell, she had no inhibitions. Why should she? What was lost could never be regained and it would not have been taken in the first place unless the girl was loose. She had hated Karran with a terrible violence. Hadn't her mother been just the same, giving herself to the abominable Luke? All families had skeletons in the cupboard and Clemence and Karran were theirs, beyond the pale forever.

But overlying the distaste was a delicious, almost salacious curiosity. What did such girls do? All Charlotte knew was that they anticipated marriage and broke laws of behaviour. Children could not be born without some kind of gestation, like plants. But how, and where? A hot, not altogether disagreeable sensation swept her body, centring on an area that she had been taught to ignore. Not there! But the exquisite hankering that ensued pointed out the fact that she could well be right.

Light slanted into Costain's blue eyes, accentuating the mouth that curved so pleasantly on her behalf. He was like a god, one of the Greek heroes in the legends she loved.

She would ask her father if she might invite him home. Perhaps Barney hadn't heard the snippets of gossip that circulated about the goings-on at Ravensdowne. She didn't believe them.

Costain looked too fastidious to share any woman's bed with another man. And why should he bother with herself unless he were interested? He must already be comfortable enough with Howard, who was reputed to treat him as a son.

He hadn't looked at Karran once since Charlotte had entered her box. That wasn't strictly true. But they didn't even seem to like one another. All those gossips were quite wrong. Abel Costain hadn't forgotten Charlotte and it was many long months since that meeting.

Her gaze centred on the strong, square-tipped hands that gripped the edge of the opposite box. With a terrifying violence she had imagined totally alien to her own nature Charlotte wanted to feel those hands about her body, touching her bare flesh.

She shivered and Barney whispered, 'Cold, dearest?' Charlotte shook her head. 'Just — excited.'

'Don't know why,' her father whispered. 'Can hardly make out a word.'

'It's like going to an opera. You let your eyes do most of the work.'

'Well, it stands to reason. Always in Italian, operas, aren't they. See what you mean. She's good,' Barney agreed grudgingly as Lady Macbeth portrayed growing madness. 'Like a cat I once had, that killed everything it set eyes on. Took a half-grown duckling from a brood once and I can still hear that duck flying round and round the house, calling to her lost offspring. And to make matters worse that cat didn't even eat the little thing. Just beheaded it and left head and body lying neatly together. Eventually the mother gave up her anguished flight and the cat went on guarding the corpse and watching her out of wide green eyes.'

'It wasn't Manny, was it?' He'd been named after Mannanan, the giant of Rushen.

'No. Long before his time. But it was a lesson in cruelty I'll not forget. It should have warned me off big green eyes.'

'Mine are green.'

'Not that sort. Yours are like mine.'

He meant Mama's and Elizabeth's. He no longer cared for Erin, only for herself. It shouldn't be too difficult to let him understand how important Abel was. How essential —

Charlotte pulled her chair closer to her father's. Costain smiled secretly.

Boyce watched the machinations of the murderous lord with fascination. This was how war used to be, this blood-stained

159

mixture of brutality and guile — before the strange custom of deciding hours in advance, the where and when of a battle, and even the minute of the first shot. A time-wasting, mechanical, cold-blooded business, against which thinking officers should long ago have protested. Only it was a soldier's place to obey orders, however stupid or potentially dangerous they were. If he were to change anything he must make it his business to keep his nose clean and become a general as fast as he could.

He had hidden his ambition very cleverly from his family. Elizabeth and Wheatley had imagined him totally engrossed in the empty splendours of uniforms and sword, the vapid pleasures of clubs and gambling. Instead of these, Boyce burned for the taste of some real-life engagement in which he could shine. Blood did not upset him.

For the rapidly disintegrating Macbeth he felt a kind of superior scorn. It was his wife who, though crumbling in her turn, was a far stronger and more admirable character. A man who could defer so to a woman deserved his end, whereas one could feel for his lady. She had so nearly succeeded.

'The way to dusty death'. He liked the phrase as much as the image of the wood that walked. Stealth and secrecy were far better tactics than drawing up one's army on a plain and blasting away with cannon. A movable forest. That was genius.

Something in Lady Macbeth reminded him of Nina, not so much in looks, although there was the suggestion of the tigress in them both, but in her original, implacable spirit. The difference between them was that Nina was likely to be indestructible.

One day he would be forced into the position of finding out.

Every now and again, a member of the clan turned anxiously to glance at Elizabeth. She had started off very gay and at her imperious best, offsetting Clive's moroseness. It was obvious they had engaged in some spat during that second interval.

Gradually, curiosity died as each became wrapped in his or her own private thoughts. The largely imcomprehensible but compelling saga unfolding on the creaky stage was of more immediate interest. Afterwards, they would doubtless find out what the trouble was and be forced to take sides.

Ignored, Elizabeth felt her passion and misery seep away into a limbo. The switch from pain and anger to a chill resignation drained her for a time. Then she began to feel a resurgence of strength and emotion. More than ever, she hated Clive. It had been no idle threat when she screamed out that she meant to leave him. Now she must think how she could achieve that end.

The twins didn't need her any more than she required them. They were totally alien, unwanted, at least by herself; they could have dropped from one of the stars in the sky or been the progeny of a Hottentot tribe or a Chinese Tong.

The only person that she loved, apart from her brothers, who had their own lives to lead, was Nat Gelling. Initially, she had sat at the back of the box in order to conceal the mark of Clive's hand. Karran Kinrade had no such scruples. She had returned to her original seat between John Howard and that artist who had tried to latch onto Charlotte, ignoring the censorious whispers that still circulated. The trouble was that the Kerruishes and Howards had captured the general imagination and would always be a focus for attention. And Karran was notorious.

Slowly, her proximity to Nat worked on Elizabeth's starved senses. They couldn't keep up the coolness forever and she did need him so badly. She wouldn't tell him that the quarrel had concerned her infamous cousin. Another reason could be invented. Something that would show her in a better light. Perhaps she could say that Clive had resented the fact that she'd asked for money. That wouldn't be a lie. Then, when she'd persisted, Clive had attacked her. The bruise on her cheek would bear out her story. She'd say it hadn't been the first time her husband had struck her. Nat wouldn't like that.

The play excited and bored her in turn. Some of it was so naive, yet this was offset by the brute force of the rest. All the way through, the Scots character proclaimed itself, first uncouth, then strongly aggressive, occasionally touching as when Macduff could not quite believe that his wife and children were dead. She could never react like that. Was it true what Clive had said so bitterly? That she was unnatural? Because of Nat the notion seemed abhorrent.

It was on Lady Macbeth's dying scream that Elizabeth could bear Nat's silence no longer. There seemed so little left that was worth looking forward to but him. Barney would not welcome her return to Castletown. He had always feared the influence of Erin's children by Jesse. She knew what he'd say. 'You made your own bed, lass, and you mun lie on it.' Everything was black or white to Kerruish, and he had no opinion of her and the boys. They were extravagant weaklings at best, hostile beings at worst. Of course, he was right. That's what they were to their stepfather. For the first time she agreed with him.

'Nat?'

'What is it?' He leaned towards her, his dependable, irregular, captivating face showing a great deal more than polite enquiry. Why did she yearn towards him? Perhaps because he represented both a haven and a nameless, exciting territory she had yet to explore.

'I'm — lonely and hurt.'

'Hurt?'

She uncovered the darkening area of her cheek and listened to his indrawn breath.

'He did that?'

'I asked him for money. He's been very parsimonious lately. You'd imagine a mine-owner would be able to afford a pelisse —'

'And?' Nat leaned towards her, his finger gently touching the painful, aching mark.

'He said no. Then, when I asked why, he completely lost his temper —'

'There must be more to it than that. Your personal relationship — ?'

'Is non-existent,' Elizabeth said sharply.

'That could explain the violence. But he still should not have done it. We are given self-control.' Nat pushed his chair closer. 'I'm sorry I was so condemning that day in Douglas.'

'It was as much my fault,' Elizabeth whispered. 'More —'

'What are you going to do?'

'I — I shall leave Clive.'

'And — the children?'

'Them too. They love their nurse better than they do me. I'm a shadow on the edge of their safe little lives.'

'Isn't that being — cowardly?'

'Only realistic. They are too much like him. And I've hated him almost from the beginning.'

'There's no chance you'll feel differently?'

'None.'

'What, then, do you intend?'

'I'm not sure. I only know that Kerruish would not listen. There's no one close. No one sympathetic. Only —'

'Elizabeth!'

'Only you.'

'How could I?' His grey eyes were tortured. 'Interfere — ?'

'If you don't take care of me, I'll — I'll die. I can't go back to Mingay. Don't you understand? I can't.' The tears coursed down her face unheeded.

'Not even tonight?'

'I'll go back to the hotel with Mama this evening. Meet me tomorrow.'

'Where?'

'There's a little coffee-shop. Past the brewery. The Prince Regent.'

'What time?'

'Eleven o'clock?'

'It won't be easy but I'll find some urgent need to stay in the town. Rest assured.'

'You've forgiven me? For my lack of charity?'

'Yes.'

'Very well. Tomorrow. At eleven.'

'Producing forth the cruel ministers of this dead butcher and his fiend-like queen,' the actor who played Malcolm was declaiming, 'Who, as 'tis thought, by self and violent hands took off her life —'

For Elizabeth, the rest was drowned in a flood of self-congratulation. Shakespeare could not have dissembled better, she thought triumphantly, her gaze encompassing Nat's dark, reassuring bulk. She had won him back, with lies, it was true, but she had him at last and she'd not let him go, whatever came.

7

The letter came in the afternoon. Abel had been painting in the garden that morning and little Bart had toddled up to him, away from Mrs Quinn. She had taken him out for a short time while Karran did the accounts for John, who detested figures. Bart had upset some water over Abel's picture which had run in all directions and sent Costain springing to his feet in a white rage.

Mrs Quinn picked up the chuckling baby and carried him off prudently while Abel tried, uselessly, to repair the damage.

'You can't blame a little tot like that,' Mrs Quinn told Karran. 'The way Mr Costain went on!'

'To a painter, his picture *is* a child of sorts,' Karran replied, 'and water-colours can't really be rescued. How unfortunate. It's as if Bart had killed something.'

'What nonsense! If you ask me, there's something wrong with that young man. A face like a devil, he had, Miss Karran. If he wants to be left alone he should shut himself in his room, that's what I say. Why should little Bartholemew be denied the use of the garden?' Mrs Quinn was allowed enviable freedom of speech.

'Abel does live here too and he says he prefers to paint on the spot. It gives him better results. I should go to him and apologise.'

'I shouldn't yet, not for a time.' Mrs Quinn took Bart away to change him into dry rompers and doubtless to give him a gingerbread man warm from the oven.

Bart was very easy to love, Karran thought without sentiment. His sloe-black eyes were always alive with vitality and amusement and his well-shaped head thickly covered with equally dark hair, contrasting with golden skin. But there was nothing of Laurence to hold on to, none of his detachment and

164

wryness, that lone-wolf quality that had so touched her and bound her to him. Bart was demanding, yet giving, interested in everybody. How strange to think that Richards had fathered such a son. The beginnings of panic seized her as she thought of her responsibilities. What if anything happened to her? Or to John? Who would care for Bart who was Luke's reincarnation?

Soberly, she pushed aside the account books and went outside to make her peace with Costain. He was still at the scene of the catastrophe, his face rather pale and his hands unsteady as he mopped at the thick paper.

Karran saw at once that his efforts were doomed to failure. The outline of the plant was quite blurred and there were thick, ugly ridges on the dried background. It would have been good. Very good.

'I can't say how sorry I am,' she ventured.

To her surprise, he smiled crookedly but without the malice she had feared. He shrugged almost philosophically. 'I admit I could have wrung his neck for a moment. But it's not as if I couldn't do another.'

'That's very generous of you. If I had been with him I'd have kept him at the other side of the house. I know he's prone to these sudden lunges.'

'Don't lose sleep over it.' He smiled again with more warmth and Karran was attacked by doubt. Had she been wrong about him? The Abel she thought she knew would have been furiously angry. Bitter and spiteful. Unforgiving.

'Thank you,' she said with spontaneous warmth and reached out to touch his arm.

'I feel I've been unjust,' he said, still smiling and his eyes like bits of sunlit sky. 'But I can see my own unfairness. Shall we bury the hatchet?'

'Yes. Of course.' Some of the load of pressure was easing and a tide of relief lapped about her, making her doubly attractive. 'I'll admit I was apprehensive. Mrs Quinn seemed to think —'

'Mrs Quinn exaggerated. There's nothing that can't be put right. In more ways than one. I've been a stiff-necked fool. Forgive me?'

'I don't think it's a question of there being anything to forgive —'

'It is.' He scooped up the spilt brushes and spoiled painting with those capable hands and stuffed them into the box he used for transporting his materials. 'I think a cup of tea might reduce everything to proper proportion.'

'Fine. I'll fetch it,' Karran told him and wondered, suddenly, if she were dreaming. But the sunlit grass and the gently swaying shrubs were still there, and the mackerel sky and Costain with his transformed face and generosity. She must accept the unexpected olive branch, especially after the morning's disaster.

Abel was amiable enough over the peace cup and then took himself off to his own quarters. John came back from Port St Mary, hot and a little dusty for there had been no rain for days. There had been a letter lying just inside the door though none of the servants had seen who had brought it. No one had rung the bell.

It was addressed to Karran in queer, twisted writing that filled her with an obscure distaste, as though the author of the epistle had written it under the stress of an unbearable hatred. John, it seemed, had entertained similar suspicions, for he had tried to find out its origin before bringing it to Karran. Naturally, he could not open it first.

'Aren't you going to look at it?' he asked, sipping at his own tea and crossing his dusty-booted legs comfortably. There was something womanish about the tangled script.

'Later. I'd rather hear what you've been doing.'

'I ordered a rocking-horse for Bart. He'll be big enough to sit one shortly.'

She wanted to protest but he'd take no notice. He was happy to do things for her and he'd accepted Bart as readily as he'd taken her into his care all those years ago. But just lately she had the sensation of being put under restraint, and the restriction irked her in spite of her tenderness towards him. She should be firmly on her own feet, striving to stay on them, whatever came.

'You're kind. He'll love that. Perhaps it may keep him out of mischief.' She told John about the spoiled painting and Costain's forbearance.

'It's what I'd expect of Abel,' John said, setting down the cup.

'He'd have been justified in taking quite another attitude,' she admitted.

'To a child of Bart's age?'

'I'm grateful, anyway. And what gossip have you heard in the port?' Karran had vivid recollections of last week's theatre visit. She still flinched from the realisation of the hostility she'd aroused in the neighbourhood. Hadn't any of those

166

hard-faced women known what it was to be young and in love? There had been no one but Laurence, yet one would imagine she'd had a host of paramours.

'Something that will interest you.'

'Oh?'

'Elizabeth has left Clive.'

'Oh!' She coloured hotly.

'You don't seem surprised.'

'Didn't anyone say it was my fault? I'd have expected that.'

'Why?'

'I wasn't going to say anything, but now I must be honest.' The story of the encounter with Clive and her cousin seemed even more sordid and damaging with the telling.

'I shouldn't worry about Deemster Crellin. He's a strait-laced old bigot.'

'But he could be influenced if I were ever in any kind of trouble that required the attention of the Tynwald.'

'Surely he'd be more set against Elizabeth?'

'No. For all his distaste of her language he'd decide she had right on her side. He'd believe I'd entice any man away from his wife or sweetheart.'

'They say, though, that Elizabeth was seen with Nat Gelling the day after, very discreetly tucked away in the darkest corner of the Prince Regent. Then leaving with him in a carriage that was almost certainly Kerruish's.'

'He's Kerruish's manager.'

'The carriage was not travelling towards Castletown or Foxdale.'

'Where, then?'

'The harbour.'

'Gelling often goes there. The mines need coal and wood and iron. Ropes —'

'It came back empty but for the coachman.'

'They could have walked back later.'

'Mrs Erin was heard soon after, asking if anyone had seen her daughter. It seems she expected her to return to the Kerruish household hours before.'

'And — Clive?'

'Got very drunk after *Macbeth* and closeted himself in the Donaghue from which he hasn't yet emerged. He's spent most of the time in the lower levels.'

'The babies! What about them?'

'They're perfectly adequately cared for by a wet-nurse whose sole task is their welfare.'

'I could understand her leaving him. But her own children!'

'At least while people malign them, you may be left alone. Which brings me back to the letter you've been toying with ever since I gave it to you.'

'I should read it in case it's urgent. But if so, why didn't they wait for an answer?'

'Would you like me — ?'

'No. It would be foolish to allow myself to be intimidated by the sight of a letter.' Karran broke the indecipherable seal and unfolded the sheet. The words danced in front of her eyes like little black devils. A cry broke from her lips.

'What is it?'

'It's — horrible. I wish I'd burnt it. It's — disgusting.'

'Let me see.' John almost snatched the letter away.

Karran was trembling. All of that terrible night when Deborah died returned to haunt her. She was hated and reviled and because of that John was touched with the same taint. Clemence had once told Hugh that she herself destroyed everyone she truly loved. Even after she was dead, Deborah had met the fate of the others. It seemed that the curse had come upon herself, Karran thought. She was hurting John. Laurence had died so shabbily after knowing her.

'Oh, God,' John whispered, grey-faced. 'We mustn't let Abel see this. It's bad enough that we know, but for him to see it —'

'No! I'd be so ashamed, and just when he seems to like me better. It can't be from anyone who knows us or they'd never have suggested —' She seized the scurrilous sheet and threw it on top of the dancing flames. 'No one else can possibly read it now. I'd not have rested if I'd known it still existed. Oh, John. Who can detest me so?'

'Not the Boswells. They're illiterate. For all the misspelling there was a kind of rhythm to the sentences. Someone not too low or too high. A clerk or shopkeeper. A cleric. Schoolmaster —'

'You don't believe — ?'

'About you and Clive?' John was suddenly withdrawn. 'Abel?'

'You think I might have seduced him? As I did Laurence? I did make it impossible for Laurence to ignore me, it's true. I made no secret of it, but only him.'

'Let's — not rake up the past.' He watched the blackened paper shift and curl against the grate, then leaned across to lift the heavy poker and bring it down time and time again on the charred remains. The violence was out of character.

A sickness settled over Karran. The horrific details of her supposed ravishment of John's protegé could never be erased from her mind, nor from Howard's.

She got up and blundered towards the door, afraid she would vomit on the floor.

John called after her but she couldn't answer. White and shaking, she reached the sanctuary of her chamber. Without knowing why she did so, she slid the bolt and dropped limply on the bed.

'Karran?' John knocked loudly. 'Don't shut me out. I know it's lies. You needn't fear what I think.'

'I saw your face. Just for a moment, you believed. I know you did.'

'Karran —' He did not repudiate her assertion.

'Leave me, please. For a little while.' How cowardly she was being. But she valued Howard's good opinion and it was obvious that his faith in her had failed some crucial test. A less honest woman could have brazened it out, but her own honesty was an unwelcome stumbling-block on this occasion at least. Emily would have believed it. Emily had always sensed her fundamental weakness.

I must be strong, Karran thought. For Bart. Now that John has rejected me, I have only my son. Abel's friendship has come too late and I'm not in a position to accept Clive's without making matters untenable.

John's footsteps diminished. He'd loved her that evening at the theatre. She'd known it and backed away from the realisation. Now, in a curious way, she regretted that she was diminished in his regard. For the first time she wondered how old he was. Fifty? He looked much younger than Barney Kerruish but that was probably because he was an entirely different type. They were, she felt, both good men but John also had the bonus of pleasant looks and a fine physique. Why was her mind running on John's assets? Especially now that it was too late?

Footsteps crunched on the gravel below her window. She had a sudden desire to see John pass and went swiftly to the window, but it was only Abel letting himself out of the back gate. He looked very attractive, smiling, the pale hair bright as guineas. Yet she drew back so that he would not see her.

Abel was in a good humour as he watched his mount made

169

ready, then slid into the saddle and was off down the green tunnel of the drive. All seemed to be going well at Ravensdowne and he was looking forward to his assignation this afternoon. Everything was budding and the early warmth had brought on the clumps of primroses and drifts of wild flowers that softened the high hedges.

The sounds of the birds went by unnoticed. He was thinking about Charlotte Kerruish and the promise of greater involvement. The beauties of the day would not go unnoticed by a young, impressionable girl. Would she answer his note by her presence at Poyllvaaish Bay? He'd bribed a hungry urchin to place it in no one else's hand but the shipmaster's younger daughter's, and described Charlotte so that there would be no mistake.

As far as Howard was concerned, Abel was in search of painting materials. He had purposely run out of Chinese white so that there was some immediacy about his projected journey. Not that John would have minded his pursuit of the Kerruish girl but Abel wanted to say nothing until he was certain of his ground. Howard could welcome a liaison that might improve relations between Karran and her estranged relatives, though he'd been furious with Elizabeth for her recent treatment of his ward.

The Black Rocks drowned themselves in the greenish water. Cormorants preened sooty feathers. Bracken uncurled tender fronds. Whistling, Abel went on his way, and now Charlotte was banished from his mind. There was a farm set back from Poyllvaaish cove and Farmer Stark's eldest girl was dark and ripe as a black cherry. She was also completely uninhibited as Abel had good reason to know, having more than once shared the hayloft with Kate.

Kate Stark was out in the paddock, driving back the geese. It was work of a few minutes to tether the mount and make his way between the hedges to the barn where the girl now waited.

'Where you'm goin'?' she asked and sprawled in the straw.

'To Castletown,' he lied.

'Whatever for wi' all them men servants at the big house?'

'Because it pleases me.'

'And you mun always have what you wants.'

'Invariably. Always,' he amended, seeing that she did not comprehend. But there was something that she did understand. The way she arranged her body in the hay was an open invitation. It made one forget her low origins and the slightly acrid scent of her skin.

'You'd best hurry,' she whispered, letting him do what he would; almost as though she were one of her father's cows. Abel had decided to forego the pleasures of Kate's company now that he had far better fish to fry, but the sight of her figure and the welcome in her eyes as he saw her from the road had overcome his scruples.

'Why must I hurry?'

' 'Cos my dad's seen you. Last time. Said he'd skin me if he saw you again and send some buckshot after you.'

'And where is he just now?'

'Gone to market. But he'll be back soon.'

'You didn't tell him anything about me? Where to find me, for instance?'

'How could I? You never did say,' she pretended, wide-eyed.

'Neither I did.' He laughed softly and resumed his inter-rupted pleasure. At least she had been discreet. It was odd how women like Kate had always interested him far more than girls like Charlotte. There was that suggestion of Mother Earth, of harvests and fruitfulness. Generosity. People like Karran always reminded him of his own parsimonious begin-nings, his parents' chilly, hand-to-mouth pretensions. She'd seemed to know that there was nothing of warmth or normal-ity behind the facade of elegant breeding that always fooled people like Howard. Cold parents never bred warm children. He'd hated Karran's perception.

He heard the farmer's return and the clatter of hooves mingled with the rumble of cart-wheels. The lethargic after-math of coupling was ruined.

'Damnation!'

Kate clung to him, a soft, amorous leech. There were shouts and the sounds of running feet in the yard outside.

Abel became rigid.

'Don't worry,' Kate whispered and wound her legs around him.

He was suddenly repulsed by the constriction and pushed her away. 'Will he come in here?'

'Not unless he's looking for me. But he can't have noticed yet that I'm not in the house.'

'I should go.'

'You can't. Not till he goes out of the yard. So, why not — ? Just a cuddle —'

'Don't be a fool, Kate.' His voice had become curt. 'You

said Stark was after my hide not half an hour ago. Why should I welcome his displeasure?'

'What long words you do use,' Kate said, hoisting herself up on one elbow and favouring him with an unhindered view of the deep, dark valley between her breasts. But he was satiated for today and most probably for ever. Charlotte and Barney would never tolerate distractions like the woman who lay beside him.

Abel fastened his garments and went to the small window just in time to see Kate's father stump inside the farmhouse. Temporarily, the yard was empty.

'I must go.'

'When'll you be back?' Languorously, Kate buttoned her bodice.

'I'm not sure. I must work for the next week or two. Work hard.'

'I wish —'

'Wish what?'

'That you wasn't a gentleman. T'would be easier to keep you —'

He smiled perfunctorily, one eye on the sunlit cobbles, then he began, quietly, to descend the rickety ladder. There was straw on his clothing. Kate's father need only glimpse him to know what he'd been up to. And Charlotte would be waiting. What a fool he'd been to allow himself to be distracted by a bucolic strumpet when Kerruish's only daughter — only child — could be just half a mile away.

He emerged warily into the shadowy side of the square. The farmhouse door was open and he could hear the murmur of voices and a loud bellow of laughter. Swiftly, he turned round the corner of the barn and began to run towards the hedge. Someone was shouting and his stomach muscles clenched. He stuck, briefly, in the gap, then raced down the slope towards the brake where his horse was tethered. His hat blew off and he tried to retrieve it before it was gone for good. The breeze flicked at his blonde hair. His spine prickled. Outstretched fingers touched the edge of the brim.

The shot rang out with startling suddenness and he was conscious of a burning pain in his right hand and in his thigh. He almost screamed with the hot agony. Looking down, there seemed nothing but blood. Runnels and gouts of it, spurting and spreading between his fingers and down his breeches. The triumphant shout behind him was almost lost in a gigantic fear. Sickly, he clawed his way into the saddle and kicked the horse in the direction of Poyllvaaish. The muzziness was dissipating and he bit his lip against the crucifying agony. Why couldn't the shot have attained merely its original objective? He'd rather have been unable to sit for a month than have his precious, irreplaceable hand injured. God, he was whispering, dear, dear God, let it be as it was before. Then, like a thunderclap, he knew that nothing could ever be the same.

The moor gave way to sea grass and dancing pinks. The sand and stones spread out, shining in the light that hurt his eyes.

She was there. A little dim and wavering, but there —

Charlotte had been at the bay for at least an hour, wearing a new habit in ageing black — she wanted to look at least twenty-five. Sophisticated and intriguing, that was the proper image for Abel Costain with his contained fastidiousness and lustrous looks. It would be idiocy not to realise that her own attractions were limited and must continually be emphasised. Her mother had instructed her recently in the discreet use of beauty aids to improve her skin and eyes, and rouge to redden her lips. Her efforts had seemed to bear fruit at the theatre. She could see him still, smiling enigmatically, his gaze almost constantly on herself when Elizabeth was a hundred times more beautiful. Odd how she could admit that fact at last without bitterness.

She'd been returning from shopping when the boy had thrust the note into her hand behind Erin's back. Charlotte would never forget the way the child's expression had changed as she, equally swiftly, had put a coin into his grubby hand. She had known instinctively whose writing it was, so beautifully copperplate, so elegant.

Her nerves had cried out in frustration until she reached the sanctuary of her own room. He wanted to see her, to meet where Elizabeth would not descend like an avenging fury and spoil what had been so innocent. He respected her far too much to risk compromising her. At Poyllvaaish they would see no one likely to carry tales. Would she trust him? He longed to see her again.

Cheeks flaming, Charlotte had flung herself onto her bed, staring up at the tester with incredulous eyes. There was only one reason for Costain to write to her so secretly. He had held her in his mind all these weeks and months and had not found her wanting. Father would think cynically that her money was all that would attract most men but Costain did not require to hunt fortunes, not with his comfortable berth at Howard's estate. Everyone gossiped about Howard's liking and necessity for the young painter.

Charlotte was not so stupid as not to recognise her own value. It was plain that her father had little love left for his stepchildren. One by one, they had repudiated his initial attempts to become a father to them. And Erin had hurt him in some irrevocable way so that they'd become strangers. Charlotte was the one person who'd benefit from Barney Kerruish's propensity for money-making and now she was unashamedly glad for she did have something tangible to offer this young god who seemed to have everything.

It was then that she'd insisted on buying the new habit as she meant to take more advanced riding instruction and had approached a riding-school just far enough out of Castletown to be comparatively inaccessible as far as her parents were concerned. One or two missed lessons would be unlikely to arouse any comment.

She'd left this noon, ostensibly to report to Chapman's stables, but in reality to be here in plenty of time for the afternoon's rendezvous. Her father had seen her off on his way to the shipyard and had pointed out the Russian shebek at anchor in the harbour.

The sails looked smaller than those of the Kerruish and Quayle ships, but they were graceful enough vessels and there clung around them an aura of romance, for so little was known of Russia. Charlotte possessed a bone model frigate made by a French prisoner of the Seven Years War and prized it greatly. It seemed that Barney's love of the sea and its travellers had been bred into herself. The open freshness of the ocean had appealed so much more than the claustrophobic confines of the mine-shafts. Charlotte had always hoped that there would be a resurgence of the shipping trade. In the first quarter of the nineteenth century, the mines certainly paid better.

She stopped for a time at the Silverdale burn and allowed her mare to drink at its edge while she plucked a small nosegay of wild flowers to put in her buttonhole. The severity of the habit had begun to oppress her and she wanted to alleviate its darkness.

Sunlight striking on the marble rocks contrasted with the wet sand of the bay. The sky seemed to go on forever, filled with white galleons of cloud and split by the flashing arcs of gulls. Their sharp, stabbing cries pierced her but she welcomed the disturbance that matched her inner turmoil. It was as if every bird knew the reason for her unaccustomed appearance and tried to warn her. Go away, go away! they seemed to scream and she was in half a mind to heed their alarm bells.

It was in that first moment of doubt that she saw the tiny shape of a horse and rider approaching. Some trick of the sun made the distant forms shiver in a band of heat, so that she could make out nothing but the inexorable approach of a wavering shadow she secretly feared. All of her cleverness and will-power drained from her as the fluctuating figures drew nearer. Then she noticed the slumped position of the horseman and the splashes of red on the mount's flank, and her dreamy acceptance was douched with an icy awareness of danger.

'Mr Costain? Abel!'

She rushed forward then halted in her tracks, frozen with horror and disbelief. His snuff-coloured sleeve was spattered with darkened stains and his hand — Charlotte cried out and went close, staring into the white, shocked face.

'Abel!'

'Help me — down. Some — fool — has shot me.'

Mutely, she braced herself to take his weight and watched him slide to the sand, his eyes closed against the hurt. There were little wounds down his thigh.

She knelt by his inert body, then forced herself to lift up the stained fingers. Costain cried out and fainted. The pale lashes lay on his cheek. He was like a sleeping angel except that his lips were so white.

Charlotte was suddenly afraid. His hand, or what she could see of it under the encrusted mess, looked pitted with black holes out of which had poured so much of his blood. The leg injuries seemed comparatively minor.

Some memory of what she had once been told made her let go of the pitiful remains of Costain's fingers and pull up her black skirt to reveal her best petticoat. Unheeding, she set about tearing the white linen into strips, not at all an easy task for the seams were so strong, and she panted with frustration long before the snowy pieces lay before her. She tied the largest around his arm to lessen the flow of blood, then wrapped his mutilated hand as best she could with the rest.

Who could have done such a thing? Was there a madman in the neighbourhood who would do the same to herself? She was suddenly aware of the isolation.

Charlotte stared around the bay and saw a small cottage

some distance away. A thin trail of blue smoke spoke of occupancy. Even as she watched, a stocky, grey-haired figure emerged as if to go to the back of the dwelling.

'Help!' she shouted. 'Please, help!' And waved her arms.

The man stopped, then began to hurry towards them. With every step he took, Charlotte thought of Costain's hand as it was at the theatre. He had lifted it in acknowledgement and the lacy cuff had fallen over his wrist, delightfully graceful. Her senses were torn with pity and regret. She thought of that same hand painting — And now!

The fisherman came closer, hurrying as he saw the stains on the white bandages. 'What's amiss?'

'I don't know. I saw him coming. Hurt —'

'He needs the surgeon, miss.' Shocked eyes assessed the extent of the injury.

'I know.'

'Could you help me carry him as far as the house? He could stay there till you ride for the doctor. I'd be with him,' the man suggested, concerned.

'I can try. Who — who shall I say he's with?'

'Ben Cross, miss. Never fear, I'll watch out for whoever comes.'

Between them, they hoisted the unconscious man and carried him, toes trailing in the damp sand. Abel's fair head slumped against her thin shoulder. Blood seeped onto her skirt. His helplessness touched deep wells of strength within her. He'd need someone once his hand was healed, and Charlotte intended that bulwark would be herself.

The wall bed was too short for Abel but at least he was as comfortable as possible. There being nothing more she could do, Charlotte fetched her mare while Cross tethered Abel's mount and returned to sit with the injured man.

All the way back to Castletown she prayed that Doctor Gresham would be at home. He attended the Kerruish family and through him she could find out how Costain fared, should her parents prove difficult.

Dr Gresham was at tea but he listened to Charlotte's tale of having encountered a wounded Abel while coming from the stables, though he looked obviously puzzled when he discovered where the injured man now was.

'Please hurry,' Charlotte urged to distract him from further questioning. 'He's lost a great deal of blood. And I would like to know how he is should you have time.'

She felt restless and miserable as soon as the doctor left with his bag of surgical instruments. It was almost as though she felt those sharp scalpels in her own fingers. The thought of Abel unable to paint was like a wound that hurt her as much as it would him. Her whole body suffered.

Erin hardly noticed her lateness. She was brooding over Elizabeth's defection and Barney's ill-humour, caused by Nat's subsequent return to Liverpool. But Dr Gresham would surely call about Costain, and Charlotte must give some account of her part in finding Abel in such a state, so she told her mother much the same story.

'But what were you doing so near the beach?' Erin's green eyes had sharpened. 'And alone.'

'It was such a beautiful day. Mama, were you never young?'

'Aye, I was and I know of all the pitfalls.'

'I had the mare.'

'You know I don't like you to have friendships with *them*.'

'You make them sound monsters.'

'That's enough, Charlotte.'

'Even you wouldn't have ridden away from a wounded man.'

'How did it happen, I wonder?' Curiosity drove out disapproval.

'Poachers, I expect. They must have seen A — Mr Costain — and thought he represented trouble for them. Mistook him for a factor. Or an exciseman, perhaps, out of uniform! Why else should anyone fire at him? There are still folks smuggling. I heard Captain Jayce say so just the other day when I passed him in the street.'

'What's that mark on you?' Erin asked suddenly.

'Oh! His hand must have touched me as we took him to Ben Cross's cottage.'

'Have Elspeth clean it off at once. Your new habit!'

'Is a skirt more important than a man's life?'

Erin's eyes hardened. Charlotte had never been her favourite person, yet lately the girl had asked her advice on certain matters mainly connected with her personal appearance. To please Barney, Erin had been as helpful as possible, not that her new gentleness had brought her what she so wanted, his former affection, only a grudging approval. And now the chit was on her high horse, pointing out her own mother's lack of charity and flashing her mud-coloured eyes with indignation so that Erin was tempted to strike her. No. She mustn't do that. Elizabeth had caused sufficient trouble with her lack of discretion over the Kinrade strumpet. Barney had been very angry. Damn Elizabeth and damn Barney for the principles that had destroyed their marriage! But it had been her own fault and how she regretted it. Her life was so empty —

'I did not say that, Charlotte.'

'But you thought it!'

'How can you possibly read another's mind, clever as you think yourself.' Erin kept her voice annoyingly calm and reasonable. 'Blood is a difficult stain to remove and the sooner it's dealt with the better. And your father has yet to settle the account for the habit. It's the first time you've worn it. Remember?'

'Yes. Yes, of course.' Charlotte hated herself for the ignominious surrender, but she must keep the way open for a possible relationship with Abel. If she antagonised Erin completely she might dash her own hopes. Father might still be swayed by Mama if he doubted Costain sufficiently, and Mama could make herself look so beautiful when she wished. None of the doubts and agonies of Charlotte's childhood had really been exorcised, in spite of her parent's present coldness.

She went obediently to hand over the skirt, inwardly raging at her own necessity to lick adult boots. How splendid it would be to be one's own mistress. To make one's own decisions. And mistakes!

But, as she changed into a gown she suddenly hated for its colourlessness, she knew that she would resist any attempts to prevent her from becoming on more intimate terms with Abel. However he had come by his catastrophic wound, she could not forget its consequences. His hand must lose those essential skills that earned him such a pleasant livelihood. Talents that fulfilled the creative side of his nature. Life could seem a desert to someone like him unless something as satisfactory was put in his way. Not that it could ever compensate.

The house was quiet without Boyce and Sebastian. They had gone yesterday and that was probably the reason for Erin's sharpness. Boyce was so special since he'd turned into such a presentable young officer with those unexpected hints of breeding. Where had they come from with an Irish slut for a mother and a Manx smuggler for sire? Erin had changed the conversation very ably when she'd mentioned the excise, Charlotte thought.

The evening loomed ahead, empty and sterile. Charlotte kept seeing Abel Costain, white and lifeless. The marks on his snuff-coloured sleeve. Reddened linen —

'Even if he *is* a pompous old ass, Gresham knows what to

do,' Charlotte said aloud. He had a reputation for being able to stitch people up so that they were almost as good as new. But he wasn't a miracle-worker. She couldn't forget that shattered hand.

To her immense astonishment Charlotte found herself crying. She could never remember having cried before. Please let it be all right. Please! Please —

It was then that she recalled that Howard had completely slipped her mind. He could not possibly know what had befallen his protegé. Mama would never agree to her going to Ravensdowne. That 'sink of iniquity' she'd called it after the *Macbeth* evening. Papa wouldn't necessarily feel the same? He was too good a man for spite.

She heard the sound of the carriage wheels on the cobbles, the lonely cry of the gulls around the waterfront. Charlotte felt as if her heart would burst with sadness.

Running downstairs, her handkerchief wet with tears, she was in the hall just as Barney put his key in the door. Weeping, she ran to him and was engulfed in his arms.

'Charlotte?' he whispered, distressed, aware of Erin's silent figure by the drawing-room door. 'Child? You don't cry easy, my pet, so I know there's something that matters. Come into the study, my dear, and we'll see if it can't be put right. There, my darling. There, my dearest, calm yourself, do. It can't be so bad. Can it?'

In the leather-scented, cigar-haunted confines of Barney's holy-of-holies, Charlotte told her tale a second time, stressing the full horror of Costain's probable frame of mind when he was told the extent of his mutilation. 'He was so kind to me once. A long time ago, on the Douglas sands. He didn't condescend or look at me as if I were the plainest female on earth, as everyone else does. He didn't even know who I was, Papa. He was kind and genuinely interested. And at the theatre he seemed to find me attractive —'

'And you never stopped thinking about him, eh?'

'I did — remember —' Charlotte hiccupped distressfully.

'And now he's badly hurt and you — feel for him.' Damn the upstart!

'Yes. And I see now that no one could have told Mr Howard. He'd never think of going to Ben Cross's. And I do so want to know if Abel's as bad as I fear —'

'Abel, eh?' Barney concealed his shock admirably. Those riding lessons. He'd always had his doubts. Charlotte was secretly afraid of horses. But he believed she hadn't seen

179

Costain, of whom he had but a fleeting memory, until *Macbeth*. He'd have known if she'd been gallivanting abroad and she certainly hadn't had the opportunity. Perhaps this young man was more discerning than most and had recognised the jewel in their midst. His daughter was a sweet, intelligent girl, worth thrice that of Elizabeth Clive and four times better than those boys of Erin's.

He thought of Erin with the same frustrated pain he managed to conceal most of the time. As if the thought of her body didn't drive him mad. But the lies! He couldn't forget those if he lived to be a hundred. How hungry a man could get —

'We should tell Mr Howard,' Charlotte was insisting, her eyes swollen and strange. He'd never seen her tearful, not even as a baby. The effect was shattering.

'You're — you're especially fond of the young man, is that it?'

'I do like him. Yes.' Like! She meant — love. He hated Costain violently.

'And you were afraid we wouldn't understand. Eh?' He lit up a cigar with shaking fingers.

'Yes, Papa.'

'And those riding lessons were — a sham?' Her entire future depended on the answer.

'I'm sorry, Papa. I misled you. Not for any bad reasons —'

'At least you didn't lie to me. I couldn't have forgiven you that.'

'I didn't like doing it. Agreeing to meet him secretly. And then —' She began to cry again, silently and unnervingly. She's got it bad, Barney thought, bereft. I think she does love him, whoever and whatever he is. Well, she had to grow out of me. I wouldn't want to stop her from marrying if it makes her happy. Heaven knows *I* wanted marriage. His imagination stopped at the barrier of Erin's perfidy.

'I'll order the carriage, shall I? Drive to Ravensdowne? We can, at least, put an end to Howard's anxiety. It's only human, after all.'

'I knew you'd understand.' Gratefully, Charlotte kissed him, more than a little damply.

She's quivering like a young colt, Barney told himself. I've never seen her like this. What's to do if I find he's a wastrel? How in God's name do I keep her regard?

'You don't think you should sup first, my dear?'

'I couldn't eat. Truly, I couldn't.'

Barney thrust away the vision of pigeon pie and beef. Syllabubs. He adored sweets. Perhaps Howard would feed them. He could, of course, be in too much of a hurry to find Costain. Charlotte only imagined herself in love with him, naturally. She'd led such a safe, dull life. Damn Howard *and* his painter.

'Stay there, then, my darling.'

Barney went to order the carriage, then told Erin he and Charlotte could be quite late and not to stay up on their account. He kept his voice deliberately impersonal, a difficult matter when she could look so stricken. Sometimes he didn't know how he kept his hands from her. It was the thought of the way she'd deceived him that destroyed those softer impulses. Years and years of lies and no real sign of contrition.

He banged his way out of the house, his heart as sore as Charlotte's. It seemed that the Kerruishes were made to be hurt while Erin and her brood remained untouched by the havoc they caused. Nat Gelling had at least the grace to write him an apology for leaving the firm. Personal reasons. Hah! He'd be regretting it already. If Elizabeth was as cold as Clive made out, she wasn't going to change for a rather shy, simple man who was far too good for the likes of her. He missed Nat badly.

Charlotte climbed into the carriage beside her father, tearless now and very white and silent. Barney groaned inwardly. Whatever he did now was sure to be wrong. But he mustn't lose her. There wasn't anyone else who mattered.

Karran had just gone to bed when the Kerruishes arrived with their astonishing story. John, still smarting from Elizabeth's cruel attack on the girl he loved, was understandably cool at the beginning. And then he saw Charlotte's integrity and Barney's likeableness and knew that their concern was genuine. His mind spun like a wheel over Costain's disaster.

'*Where* did it happen? Why?' The handsome, distinguished face distorted. John never gave a thought to the new setback to the precious book; his only concern was Abel's reaction to what seemed the deliberate destruction of his artistic skill. Perhaps the same person who had sent an obscene letter to Karran had attacked Abel. Next time it could be Karran's child.

'He — didn't know,' Charlotte said, swallowing. 'He only said — some fool. As if it were a stranger.'

'I should go to him,' John decided, then thought of the ease with which so evil a creature could infiltrate the house. The letter had been delivered at the precise time none of the servants were there. Almost as if — one of the servants! Only inside knowledge could have served to determine the right moment.

'Doctor Gresham is reliable and the fisherman swore to stay with him. It would be better to wait until tomorrow.'

'Probably. And what of yourselves? I could have rooms prepared.'

'I told my wife we'd be back, however late,' Barney answered. 'She'd worry if we changed our plans.'

'Perhaps —' Charlotte began, her normal self-discipline absent. 'Maybe, I — ?'

'You!' Barney said sharply.

'I should like to go with Mr Howard in the morning. I told you, Papa, that Abel and I arranged to meet. That we wished to become better acquainted. Nothing has changed. The fact that Abel may never paint again makes no difference to my feelings, except to accentuate the need to boost his opinion of himself when he finds out the worst. I shouldn't care to think what he might contemplate — without support.'

'Miss Kerruish is right,' John agreed, heavy-hearted. She was the only one who had seen the extent of the gunshot wounds. He must visit Captain Jayce tomorrow, tell him the whole unsavoury tale. And send Karran to a place of safety. There was that aunt's cottage at Peel — He'd keep her destination secret.

'I could take Charlotte in the morning,' Barney suggested.

'No, Papa. You said you had an urgent meeting at St John's. Over the replacement overseer.'

'So I did.'

'And it's much too late to defer it. I shall be all right here for the night. And once my mind is at rest, I'll go home again.'

'But Mr Howard's servants are abed —'

'It's not that late,' John protested. He felt shocked and ill and not too happy about Miss Charlotte's insistence on remaining. But he had offered hospitality. 'Have some brandy before you go, Kerruish, and I'll see the housekeeper.'

He poured the liqueur into a glass and left his guests to their own devices.

'Must you stay?' Barney asked, downing the brandy. 'It's obviously inconvenient.'

'Haven't you accepted the fact, Papa, that I'd swim rivers and hack my way through jungles for Abel? You're going to say that I scarely know him but did you know Mama any better? I seem to recall you telling us once, years ago, that you

182

saw her one moment and were in love with her the next. All through her first marriage —'

'All right, Charlotte.' Barney was pale and sweating with remembrance. 'If I said that, I obviously meant it. Then. But what happens to you if Costain lies to you in the way your mother did to me? If you're as much like me as you make out, what then?'

'I don't care, Papa. That's where we must differ. We can't all be peering into the future for disasters that might or might not happen. It was before he lost his ability to paint that he showed his interest. Always think back on it.'

'Yes. I know that. All I mind about is your happiness. You're sure he's hurt as bad as you say?'

'Certain, Papa. The only reason I kept this meeting secret was that I wanted to be sure of my feelings before I told you. Now, I am. There's nothing more to hide. I take it you expected me to marry sometime? It's not that you're against the idea?'

'I — I hadn't thought to meet that problem so soon. You seem such a child —'

'Well, I'm not. And you couldn't call me exactly scapegrace. I'm usually taken to task for dullness and never having my head out of a book.'

'Not by me!'

'You must all learn to think of me in another way,' Charlotte continued as if he hadn't spoken, her dark little face set in stubborn lines.

'And what if this — this accident makes a difference? Costain could change his mind as a result.'

'Then I must make him change it back again.'

'You're *that* set on him?'

'Yes. I'm prepared to fight for him and to keep him, though it may not be easy.'

'Marriage seldom is, my dear.' Barney laughed bitterly.

'Shouldn't you and Mama — forget your differences?'

'D'you think I haven't said it to myself a thousand times? Some stiff-necked awkwardness in me whispers that behind every smile and promise lies something entirely different.' Barney looked longingly at the decanter. 'I wonder if he'd mind —'

'I shouldn't suppose so.'

'No. Best not help myself. It's not done.'

'Sometimes I think Mama's sorry. For whatever it was.' The admission was drawn out of Charlotte like a bad tooth.

But the last hours had changed her, shown her that nothing was ever black or white. She was in a strange no-man's land where all her preconceived notions took on other forms.

'Charlotte —'

'Perhaps I want to think of you being happy again when I'm no longer with you.'

Barney stared. 'You talk as if you were going tomorrow!'

'I would if that's what he wanted.'

No sign now of all that trembling and tearfulness, Barney thought. Charlotte had reverted to being herself, whatever that was. No one had ever quite known. She'd probably never speak so freely again as she had under the strain of the shock she'd received. For a moment or two he'd known her completely, then she'd ducked inside that shell she lived in and was gone, perhaps for good.

She had never liked her mother. All the more reason for him to believe what she hinted at. With Charlotte gone he and Erin would be thrown together in inescapable intimacy. No more conversations through his daughter or the servants.

'I'm sorry I had to leave you for so long,' John apologised, coming towards them. 'More brandy? Just to help you back.' He'd never thought of food at this hour.

Barney accepted the generous measure gratefully. Howard was not the ogre he was painted in gossip. He was charming and cultured, extremely personable in the dark blue coat that accentuated the colour of his eyes. Stockings and breeches were impeccably neat and there was no excess flesh under the silver-threaded waistcoat. Late though it was, his stock was as fresh as it must have been this morning and his firm skin showed scarcely a line. If rumours about his relationship with his ward had any foundation, it was not really surprising.

They said he'd always condoned Karran's loose conduct. Some whispered that the child was his and the dead man a convenient peg on which to hang the blame. Not that Barney had ever really believed any of the tales that circulated in the clubs. He'd rather hear the best of people. Slander offended him and he was quick to brush off would-be prattlers.

'Your room will be ready soon,' John Howard told Charlotte. 'Karran says she'll get up —'

'Oh, please, no!'

'She wasn't sleeping and heard your arrival. She wishes to put you at your ease.'

'Well, I must be off, then.' Barney had had enough for one day. It had been all alarms and disturbances and he had the sick feeling that Charlotte had already left him in mind, and couldn't wait to remove her physical presence. When she'd been born, and all through her growing up, he had never visualised the dreadful emptiness that suddenly filled him.

Howard had moved away and it was as though Charlotte sensed Barney's desolation. She took hold of his pudgy hands and smiled at him. It was not quite her old smile, but it helped to bridge the gap between the past and this unfamiliar being who seemed so adult and sure of herself and her future.

'It's all right,' she whispered. 'It's not as if I want to cut myself off completely. I just want you to — to let go and look on me as a separate person. Able to conduct my own life. Isn't that what all parents must learn? And I'm sorry if it hurts. I truly am.'

Speechless, Barney turned and hurried away while he could still control his feelings. He could not have spoken to Charlotte, but he managed to mumble some sort of thanks and farewell to Howard before he was shown out.

Let go, his daughter had pleaded and he knew she was right. But did it hurt like this for everyone? Had it given Erin the same pain when he'd shipped off her sons? True, they came back but there were ramparts between them now that even he could see. They were strangers. Old frames around new pictures.

He tried to recall Charlotte's face when she was two, five, ten, but the images refused to come. There were only the cool, dark features that belonged to some other woman eternally out of reach.

Karran, in a blue-green houserobe, looked lovely even with her thick hair tousled. Charlotte had braced herself to meet the daughter of her mother's enemy. Costain's wretchedness and Barney's emotional departure had drained her of energy and it seemed almost too much effort to prolong her polite intrusion.

Howard seemed determined that she be introduced to the Kinrade girl. The first thing that attracted Charlotte was Karran's voice, which was warm and low-pitched. It was right with her appearance and colouring. So often voices were wrong. And Karran's smile was welcoming without being effusive.

'You must long for bed after such a trying day.'

'Yes, I am tired. Yet I feel I may not sleep,' Charlotte replied.

Karran's movement as she pushed the hair from her shoulders was pure sensuousness. Why hadn't Abel pursued this magnetic girl? Was it possible that he really did care for herself? The answer seemed to lie in the quite besotted look that Howard gave Karran. There was at least love in that quarter. They seemed a couple.

'I've ordered some spiced wine,' Karran said, seating herself with effortless grace. 'It always seems to work with me.' She drew the gown over a glimpse of white linen yet there was nothing coy about the unconscious courtesy. Her face was full of character. One knew instinctively that here was a person who had lived and suffered, yet would not be destroyed.

I could like her, Charlotte decided, but I might never know her. She had the sudden dizzying sensation of walking a narrow track on a high precipice. She had broken away from home and planned to make a new life with a handsome stranger. Charlotte recognised her total presumption. A fine fool she'd look if Abel Costain rejected her. But he wouldn't! She couldn't allow that.

Conversation proved to be difficult. Surface politenesses were so wearying, but it was far too late at night to bring out into the open all the festering wounds of the past.

Karran, understanding, spoke at first only of Abel and the morning's journey, and John Howard excused himself and withdrew.

'How kind he is,' Charlotte said, sipping at the wine which had by this time arrived.

'John? Oh, yes. Far too kind to be so misunderstood.'

'Misunderstood?'

'Oh come,' Karran laughed with just a hint of sharpness. 'Do you imagine any of us blind and deaf? Didn't you hear those comments at the theatre?'

Charlotte flushed. 'Not really. I was thinking of other things.'

'Abel, you mean. I did notice your mutual interest.'

'Mutual? So I wasn't building dreams.' Tiredness fled briefly.

'Oh, he was undoubtedly charming you.'

'Does he charm every girl he knows?'

'Surprisingly, no. He's very secretive about his liaisons. If any.'

'You've never —'

'Seen him with another woman? No. Puzzling, isn't it, when he looks as he does. You're the first girl I've seen him

186

show any interest in. But he's a strange man. Deep. Not altogether comfortable —'

Charlotte was contemptuous. 'Who wants comfort? That's for old people, surely. Predictability. Don't tell me that's what you aspire to?'

'No. I was in love and it was anything but that. Do you realise what you are doing? Attempting to bring together two sides of a family separated by mutual dislike and mistrust.'

'That has nothing to do with Abel and me.'

'Inevitably, it must result in contact between your parents and Howard. And myself.'

'I suppose so.' Charlotte's eyes were suddenly too heavy to remain open. 'Does it matter? Is any of it of consequence?'

'Not at the moment, I expect,' Karran said compassionately. 'Let me take your glass, Charlotte. I may call you that?'

'Why not? It's my name. Papa has no affectations and I'm supposed to be like him.'

'He's kind, I've heard. There's not one of his employees who wouldn't work their fingers to the bone for him. So they say.'

'That was true while Nat was with him.'

'But now he's gone.'

'Much to Papa's chagrin. I may as well be frank. It's the talk of the island. Well, Castletown and Douglas. You must know that my sister Elizabeth and he have run off to Liverpool.'

'I — found it difficult to believe that she — a mother of such small infants —'

'Oh, she found it quite easy. She disliked them intensely.'

'Her own babies!'

'And Clive's. Poor things, they committed the cardinal sin of resembling their father.'

'Did she — hate him so much?'

'More. Much more than I can convey.'

'I imagined Gelling to have more integrity —'

'Nat?' Charlotte laughed discordantly. The spiced wine had gone to her head in a not unpleasant way and her stomach was empty. 'He had no chance. Poor fly! And she the spider.' Her tone corroded like acid.

'Perhaps — bed?' Karran suggested tactfully, not relishing further indiscretion. Charlotte was obviously not herself. It was unfair to encourage her.

'Oh, yes, please.' Barney's daughter was softer now and quite grateful. It must, after all, have been a traumatic day and she was in the stronghold of the enemy. It was only fair to present her with a bolt-hole.

'Come, then,' Karran said gently and lifted a candlestick. Together they went along the darkened passageway.

Charlotte's body seemed to melt into the goosefeather mattress. The night became one dark dream of Abel riding a blood-stained horse that shimmered against a background of sand and a sky in which gulls mourned incessantly.

She moaned in her sleep and tried to send the birds away but they stayed just on the edge of vision, a barrier between her and the man she loved.

Barney was exhausted by the time the carriage returned to Castletown. Howard had imagined them to have had supper, and he was light-headed with the effect of the two large brandies, plus the cigars he'd smoked in order to alleviate the griping pangs of hunger.

The front of the house was in darkness as the coachman deposited him on the wide steps. He let himself in quietly, arousing none of the servants for so trivial a matter.

Famished and disturbed by Charlotte's obvious intention of directing her own far too young life, he made his way towards the kitchen. There would be something in the pantry, some cooked fowl and ham or a cold pie. A syllabub, perhaps, left over from a previous meal.

He struck a strike light and lit the huge candle on the table. There were cold chops and a chicken leg. A portion of gooseberry tart and the heel of a loaf. The chair squeaked across the newly-washed flagstones.

Immersed in his fleshly pleasures, Barney did not hear a sound until Erin stood beside him, a sea-green robe pulled around her and exuding a faint scent of lavender.

'Well?'

'I heard you come back. I was anxious.'

'About me?' He laughed shortly, appetite gone.

'I kept a fire going in the drawing-room. And a glass of sack ready.' There seemed little point in staying in the chill, and the thought of wine was not unpleasant.

'Thanks. There'll be no need to trouble yourself further.' He averted his gaze from the red hair outlined with candlelight. In the dimness her face was so young. Barney was aware that his pulses raced in a way he'd almost forgotten.

188

There was a story in one of Charlotte's books about a woman who enchanted a boat-load of sailors and turned them into swine. She must have looked like Erin. And was equally deceitful.

'I'll come with you. It's no trouble.' Erin's plump white hand had released the neck of the robe, and Barney had a swift glimpse of pearly skin and a dark valley where he would have liked to rest his head under happier circumstances. But there had been all those years of falseness — How to exorcise the memory?

The well-tended fingers pulled the gleaming ribbons together. Barney rose from the table, the food queasy in his stomach and his feelings raw.

'I didn't hear Charlotte go upstairs,' Erin said, following.

'She didn't. Howard asked her to stay —'

'And you let her?'

'He asked us both. She was tired, so I agreed. But that's not all.' They had reached the drawing-room, as Erin referred to it, though sitting-room had been good enough for the Kerruishes. Barney could almost see Mama now, sitting under that woodland painting, in a grey dress and a frilly white cap. Mama would never have said anything that was not true. But neither had she been shapely and fascinating, her speech mixed with little bubbles of laughter, and teeth white as milk. It was odd he'd never taken to Erin's children when they were her counterparts. Then he knew that jealousy estranged him. They were all fathered by another man.

'What do you mean, that's not all?' Her voice had risen.

Barney threw himself into his favourite chair. 'You'd best become used to the notion that Charlotte's — gone.' The pain was rushing back and his hasty supper heavy as lead.

'How can she be gone?'

'Like Elizabeth, she fancies herself in the grip of an undying passion. But we — we know there's no such thing, don't we, Erin.'

She flinched from his bitterness.

'But don't,' Barney said roughly, 'pretend you're in any way distressed. I know how you feel about Charlotte. You've always despised her as you have me.'

'That's not true!' Erin had turned paper-white. 'I admit I didn't love you when we first married, but you knew that. You said it would come —'

'That was my first mistake.'

'But it wasn't.' Her voice was so low that only the night

silence allowed him to hear it. 'You — weren't wrong. I tried to tell you — It did come.'

'How could I judge what was true and what lies?'

'I know you were disappointed, about another child. But you see, Barney, I wasn't quite the girl I made out. I was afraid to have another. Me mother died of her fifth at just the same age as meself. And we Irish are superstitious.' Erin lapsed into her childhood dialect and twisted her pale hands distressfully. 'I couldn't risk it.'

'Why didn't you say so?'

'I was ashamed of me cowardice. I didn't want the lovely life you'd given me to come to an end. I'd two boys and two girls who might be left motherless. I knew how that felt. I hate meself now for putting me own safety before your own wishes. Somehow, it seemed to me you'd rather have me and no son, than neither of us. All women fear childbearing, Barney, deep in the heart of them, though few ever express it. I'd been lucky four times already but luck has to run out sometime — I had this feeling —'

'You still should have told me. Was I such an ogre?' His palms were suddenly moist and his heart torn by conflicting emotions. Had he wasted those last, precious years? Erin's eyes glittered with unshed tears and he'd swear she meant every word. But she'd looked so before. How did one come to terms with disillusion? He did not know where to start.

She was crying, not the noisy tempestuous grief he knew instinctively she rather enjoyed, but a silent stillness with the tears falling heavily onto her breast and drenching the ribbons and the soft green material. The wet, white coldness of her face made her a statue in the rain.

He had never seen Erin like this. Weeping, yes, seducing him even as she deceived. But never so bruised and defeated. And all over himself, a middle-aged, plain little man running to fat and not even sure if he could make love to her if that was what she wanted. It was up to him to make the first move. If that was what he wished. What did they all matter now, the lies and disappointments? They were getting old and life was still precious. Without Charlotte and estranged from his wife, he'd be a beaten man. Empty.

'Come here,' he ordered, his throat tight with an almost angry passion.

'No,' she said dully. 'You'll never forgive. I don't want you making up tonight and sick to the soul tomorrow with regrets. I'd rather it was all finished — now and forever. I was wicked

190

to Jesse and this is me punishment. To be cut off from your love which I never doubted for a minute until the day you found out about Mrs Payne. If you knew how palsied I was with fear. How I wanted to jump off Spanish Head or cut me wrists. But the same cowardly feelings that kept me from letting you get another child wouldn't let me destroy meself. You deserved better than the likes of me. And now that Charlotte's bent on going with that Costain, you haven't got much left, have you, since you set little store by money and fripperies. Not like me. And look where it's got me! Grovelling for a husband I lost by my own selfishness, like I lost the first. Well, I don't care to think of the future without you, Barney, so it's best if I make an end of it all so you can put matters right afore it's too late.'

'Too late?'

'To find a proper wife to care for you.'

'Do I understand — that you mean to go away? Divorce me?'

'Who said anything about divorce? I don't want to live unless you still care a little for me. Don't worry. It won't hurt, whatever I choose to do.'

He stared in disbelief. The old Erin would have made such a threat under a barrage of histrionics. But there was no firework display, only this alien passivity and eerie calmness.

'D'you think I'd let you!' The anger pushed through the distress and she heard it.

'You mean you *don't* want to be rid of me?'

'Oh, Erin. You've convinced me you do care. Don't ask me how or why. We'd best make what we can of what's left to us. I won't pretend it's not a relief. Will you come to me now?'

She came to the big comfortable chair very slowly, almost as though she were afraid to believe that he meant what he said.

'Here. Sit on my lap as you used to,' he said gruffly and pulled her towards him. Her body was stiff and defensive, as if the boot were now on the other foot and it was she who could not allow herself to be convinced.

He kissed the side of her neck and the curve of her shoulder. Tentatively, he attempted past intimacies. It seemed he was once more the immature bridegroom who had undressed behind a screen, approaching Jesse Kinrade's widow with a violent longing that was tempered by an unwelcome nervousness and fear of failure.

His fingers slid over the generous globe of her breast and

Erin shivered and clung to him fiercely. Her face was at last upraised for his kiss.

'You swear,' he whispered, 'that there was no other reason for denying me a son?'

All of Erin's life seemed to flash past in a string of brilliant tableaux. How could she say that it was Charlotte who had put her off bearing Barney's future children? Charlotte who was so much her father? It seemed ridiculous now that she could have objected to such a child. The truth would hurt too much.

'I swear on my sacred soul.'

God would forgive her, she was sure. Well, almost sure.

8

Abel had returned to consciousness when the big grey-haired man began to probe at the numerous buckshot wounds. A fowling-piece was such a primitive weapon. Lamplight showed him the man's heavy features dripping sweat and another, older face peering over the burly shoulder, mouth agape. It was purest nightmare.

He screamed.

'You'd best drink some of this,' the probing man said and took a bottle of brandy from a capacious leather bag. A scalpel clattered to the flagstones.

'You were lucky,' the big man said, 'that you didn't get the major part of the shot in your body. I don't understand how your hand —'

'It was outstretched,' Abel muttered. 'My hat blew off and I remember putting out my hand to catch it but he fired.'

'Who fired?'

Abel thought of Kate's father with a flood of hatred. He should denounce him, but to do that would be to alienate Charlotte and quite possibly destroy Howard's regard for him. The whole thing looked perilously close to French farce when in reality it was Greek tragedy.

'I never saw more than a vague silhouette beyond the bushes.'

'Which bushes?'

'I don't remember.' Abel swallowed and spluttered. 'I was thinking of Charl — of Miss Kerruish. We were to ride together. She was to meet me on her way from the stables and I intended to accompany her as far as the town. We did — meet later.'

The brandy ringed his brain with fire. Kate became included in the necessity for revenge. She shouldn't have been out driving the geese where he could see her in passing. He hadn't meant to stop. It was Kate's fault. Women were always at the root of trouble. But Stark, her father, should receive some special treatment when he was well again.

'No one would fire for no reason.'

'I might have disturbed some nefarious plan,' Abel said, his voice slurring. 'It's a lonely beach —' He had to invent some explanation or everything was lost.

'Cross? What d'you think?' Doctor Gresham asked softly. Another slug of brandy and his patient would be sufficiently fortified to submit to further attention. 'Smuggling? Was that what he interrupted?'

'Wasn't no boat anywhere,' Cross whispered. 'There would 'a been.'

'What are you whispering for, damn you!' Abel shouted, his eyes feverish.

'Now, now,' Gresham soothed, 'you'll do yourself no good. We are merely trying to find out who harmed you. Must have been a poacher thinking you were about to hand him over to the authorities. Or some enemy. D'you have anyone who wishes you ill?'

'I can — think — of no one — with such a grudge.'

No? Gresham thought and picked up the instrument. Young ladies don't usually make assignations in a place like Poyllvaaish Bay with their parents' good will. Barney Kerruish was known to be a firm, though devoted, father while Costain was a stranger with a reputation that did not bear overmuch scrutiny. Mrs Gresham had heard all of the rumours connected with Ravensdowne and imparted them gleefully over supper. She loved a good scandal. But if Barney had got wind of the proposed meeting, he'd hardly have left his daughter behind. Karran Kinrade perhaps, jealous of a rival? She'd already been involved in tragedy of the most unsavoury kind and they did live under the same roof. They said she was self-willed.

He dug into Costain's thumb and felt his body jerk and fall back limply. It was better this way. The boy's hand was a mess. Cross would help him turn the lad over while he attended to the thigh wounds. Lucky he hadn't had his kidneys punctured. If his hand healed, he'd have got off comparatively easily. He had the other hand unimpaired.

Gresham swabbed the bleeding punctures and set the shattered finger-bones.

'I'll look by tomorrow,' he told Ben Cross who was beginning to look greenish. 'If he wakes and is in pain give him some of this.' He took out a brown bottle and told Ben not to exceed the prescribed dose, measuring out the exact amount in a horn cup so that the fisherman could make no mistake. Then he rode off.

Costain moaned in his sleep and roused, crying out. Ben supported his head and gave him the opiate. It was not long before the injured man became quiet and Cross was able to settle down to sleep as best he could in a chair.

He was awake early. Costain was groaning again and railing against fate, or it sounded like fate. Ben gave him a little drink of water, then another dose of Gresham's potion. It would be poppy juice. Staring down at the pale, unshaven face and rumpled hair, he pondered about the business of the unseen assailant. Abel had come from the direction of Stark's land but why should the farmer attack a young gentleman? There was Kate, of course, who was no better than she should be. But this young Costain was on his way to meet the boat-builder's daughter, and Cross knew that Miss Kerruish was the epitome of respectability. Hadn't he talked to her, helped her, and she crazed with shock? No. T'was a mystery it seemed no one would ever solve.

The visitors from Ravensdowne arrived in the middle of the morning as Abel was emerging from his second laudanum-induced coma. His hand hurt damnably and he tried to persuade the oafish fisherman to give him more of the opiate.

'The doctor said only so much and you'd be best to save it for through the night,' Ben maintained obstinately, yet still in awe of his unexpected guest.

'Nonsense, man!' Abel said roughly. 'I demand that you let me have it.'

'The doctor was most partickeler —'

'Blast the doctor! Can't you see I'm in pain.' Do I have to get up and take it for myself?' The blue eyes were red-rimmed yet still handsome.

'You'd best not, young sir. T'would kill you to take over-much.'

'Do you imagine I care?'

'T' is not so bad, sir. You might 'a lost your hand altogether. Doctor says t'will only be stiff once the bones heal.'

'Only!' Abel was consumed with a furious panic. His head was filled with images of doom. He began to struggle from the crude bed but had only got one leg over the side when dizziness overtook him.

There were voices in the room, a cool hand on his forehead.

'Oh, God!' he half-sobbed. 'He should have killed me. Why didn't he finish the job?'

Ben Cross was explaining why Abel was so incensed and John Howard was telling him that Abel was not responsible for his actions. As soon as possible, the sick man would be transferred to a more suitable place and in the meantime someone would be remaining to look after him.

'There ain't much room, sir,' Ben pointed out doubtfully, 'for no one else.'

'Could you — would it be possible for you to stay with a relative for a few days?' John suggested,' and I will pay for the use of the cottage?' He mentioned a handsome figure that made Cross quiver with excitement. A season's fishing wouldn't produce as much. He could afford a new net and a Sunday suit. Some bottles of rum.

'My sister's in Castletown, Fish Street, back o' Rushen Castle. She'd have me.'

'Good.' John took out a money-purse and counted out the coins. 'Take it now and I'll have you informed when Abel is fit to be moved. Now, tell me about this medicine.'

Abel lay more quietly now that Charlotte sat beside him, holding a damp cloth to his brow. Karran was in the room. He saw her shadow weave against the whitewashed wall. He wondered by she had bothered to come, then remembered that he'd made overtures of belated friendship. His lips twisted into a travesty of a smile Charlotte imagined was meant for her.

'I suppose,' Abel whispered, 'it was you who fetched that butchering surgeon?'

He watched her lips turn white. Charlotte nodded.

'He's very good. I mean he usually succeeds. If it's humanly possible —'

'It was hell.' Somehow, though he had intended the description for effect, the words rang out raw and unforgiving. The hot blue gaze transfixed her.

'It must have been. Did he say anything? About later?' Her mouth quivered.

'Not to me. I was foolish enough to lose my senses. But he told Cross that my hand would be useless. Well, not in so many words. Stiff, he said, but useless was what he meant. Not that it came as any surprise. Oh, God! God —'

'I'm sorry.'

'It's not your fault,' Abel said in a way that tore at Charlotte's heart-strings as much as his pallor and the golden

196

stubble on his face. There was fever in his eyes and even his uninjured hand was hot. He bit his lips against the pain.

'I wish now I had replied to your letter. Said I couldn't come. Then you wouldn't have been hurt.'

'Didn't you want to come?' As if he didn't know the answer! It was there in her spaniel gaze.

'Of course I did.'

'I'd have been disappointed if you'd done that.' She'd expect some such declaration —

'But you wouldn't have been in that particular place at that particular time.'

'Only I was. Talking about it doesn't help.' Abel was conscious of a renewed need to hurt someone and Charlotte had quite suddenly begun to irritate him. 'Don't let's pretend we can change anything!'

'I expect you'd like some water to wash in,' she said quickly.

'Yes. Yes. I feel dirty.' He'd be rid of her for a little. But he mustn't antagonise her altogether. He needed Charlotte more than ever. Yesterdy he still had a choice. Today, realising the extent of his new disability, he needed the security she represented. He must apologise when she came back. Beg her forgiveness. He grimaced.

Karran was staring down at him, concerned. He lay there, hating her. She looked cool and austerely beautiful in the black habit and white blouse, her hair almost invisible under the hard hat. Howard would never give her up. He knew that now. Abel imagined he could still smell Kate on his flesh. Karran must too. Her eyes were unreadable but he divined the knowledge that lay behind them. She could see all his smallness, the aridity of his nature, as plainly as he himself did.

'How are you, Abel?' Karran thought he looked like Lucifer, half wanting, half afraid of Hell.

'What can I say?'

'It was a stupid question. I never know how to approach —'

'Invalids? Is that what I am?'

She bent down and touched his brow. 'I should imagine so. You are bound to have a severe reaction and you are much too hot.'

He watched her hands as she pulled down the blanket. Beautiful strong hands. Supple and oddly sensuous. He wanted to strike at them until they were like his. Listen to her screams.

Karran drew back. Surely she had imagined that burning

hostility? They had parted on excellent terms. He was ill and in torment. There could be nothing personal in his present despairing dislike. Abel had repented of his discordant feelings. So he'd said.

'Well,' John said, falsely cheerful. 'You look better than I expected, Abel, and the Kerruish child says Gresham knows his business. He'll have you right as a trivet.'

'Is that his name? He's better fitted for a smithy.'

'Abel! Anyone would of necessity have hurt you. But those pellets had to be removed. You could have lost your arm.'

'What difference could it have made?'

'You mustn't become depressed.'

'How do you expect me to feel?'

'As you do, I suppose. I'll speak to Gresham when he returns. I'll be staying here in the meantime. Someone must and I'm the one whose presence will provoke least gossip. I can't guarantee there will be *no* conjecture. We seem to live in a district where minds are like cesspools. In any case, Karran and Bart are going to Peel, for a holiday. She's been putting off visiting Deborah's cottage for too long. A pity it wasn't big enough to accommodate Mrs Quinn as well, but there it is.'

'I don't know if I want to go, just at this moment —' Karran began.

'But you *are* going. Tomorrow,' John said sharply. 'We needn't go into all the reasons here and now. It's best.' His tone warned her to keep silent.

'You — make it sound as if Karran is in — some danger,' Abel muttered weakly, his mind diverted from his own troubles.

'Danger? That's nonsense.'

'But — if there was, perhaps that could have something to do with what befell me?'

There was a long silence in which John and Karran stared at each other in a horrified complicity.

'You *shall* go,' Howard told her in a voice that brooked no argument, 'and Brand will go with you every inch of the way.'

'What is wrong?' Abel questioned.

'Nothing that need worry you at present. Ah, Miss Charlotte.' John stepped aside as the girl appeared with a brimming bowl of well-water and one of the clean towels brought with them from Ravensdowne. 'Come, Karran. There are last-minute matters to discuss.' He drew her outside the door so that Abel heard only an indistinguishable murmur of voices and saw their shadows, slanting across the stone-flagged floor.

Charlotte pushed back the matted hair gently, disturbed by the febrile touch of his skin. Whatever happened, he was hers for these few minutes at least.

Abel submitted to her ministrations almost thankfully. The touch of the cool water was pleasant. He closed his eyes and she slid the shirt from his shoulders to wipe the wet cloth over the shining smoothness of his chest. He felt the undisciplined trembling of her fingers and was conscious of a triumph that was, briefly, stronger than his wretchedness.

He had what he'd wanted, the undying devotion of an heiress he'd be able to twist around his finger. But at what a price!

He wished now that they would all go away. Somehow, he'd crawl down to the sea and walk in until the water closed over his head. Never to hold a brush again, or to stand back and look upon something that wouldn't have existed but for the flame of creation inside him and the bone, muscle and tendon that was so perfectly in tune with his eye and his brain. Had been! Had been —

'Don't think of it,' Charlotte whispered, correctly interpreting his expression.

'Go away! I want you to go.' Damn necessity and blast plain, intense females!

She got up, gasping, and hurried to join the shadows beyond the door.

For a moment, Abel was aware of a dark abyss that surrounded him. He should call her back. But even as he opened his mouth he knew that there was no need. She'd always return.

The combination of that cruel letter so secretly delivered and Abel's present state had frightened Howard, although he was no coward. He imagined Karran waylaid and fired at, her lovely face and body marred. Or dead.

He sent Ben in his boat to Perwick Bay to summon Brand and the baby and some baggage to come by road where Karran would be met, and to go straight to Peel with his precious charges. Mrs Quinn could come as far as Castletown and return to her sister's unitl such time as Karran again had need of her services. Howard would pay her a retaining fee.

He himself would stay with Abel until he could safely be moved. The boy was distinctly feverish and would require nursing. Charlotte was to come each day. There was no question of acceding to her request to remain, however fond she appeared to be of him. There had been enough gossip and malicious slander.

'How long am I to stay at Peel?' Karran had asked, unwilling to go.

'Until Jayce finds out the truth of the matter.' John had sent a message to the Captain before he set out.

'He may never unravel the tangle.' She frowned.

'Would that matter to you?'

Her expression told him that separation did matter. But hadn't she made it plain that her love for him was of a different nature from his own? She'd not forgotten Richards. He could not expect her to put her child's father from her mind simply because that was what *he* wanted. Karran did nothing lightly. The fact that she and Bart would be safe must outweigh the emptiness there would be at Ravensdowne when he returned.

Brand duly appeared to say that child, nurse and baggage awaited at Mrs Quinn's sister, Nessie's, house and Karran had gone rather wretchedly, aware of Howard's reluctance to see her depart. She had looked at her benefactor with new eyes, seeing not her most faithful friend but a tall, lean, attractive stranger, his face only slightly etched with lines of mingled pain and humour. There was nothing about him that was not stamped with the mark of generosity. He looked years younger since Emily's odd death, but there were still those moments when Karran surprised the shadow of doubt at the back of his eyes.

She had kissed him especially warmly, realising how she'd miss him, and he had seemed to withdraw himself from her embrace. Perhaps he didn't care to display too much feeling in front of others but she was obscurely hurt.

Once away from him and reunited with a sleepy Bart, she stared out of the carriage window, aware that some change had taken place in both herself and Howard. That bitter, vitriolic letter had altered his regard for her. Could Elizabeth have written it and bribed some urchin to deliver it just before she went off with Nat Gelling? Karran did not think it would be Erin. Or was it the work of some crank who had enjoyed the spectacle of watching a woman burnt to death and another humiliated and whipped? But why attack Abel when she was accused of seducing both him and Howard? Surely they thought him the innocent party, sought after both by her and John? Why ruin Abel's life? Would John be safe?

She fought against the coldness engendered by her thoughts and watched the moor and the hills slowly darken and merge with the evening sky. The rumble of wheels over the rutted track became a boisterous lullaby.

Karran awoke with a stiff neck and heavy eyelids. Bart was stirring and tugging at her hair and the lights of Peel were before them.

Brand left them in the small carriage and took the parcels and bags along the path to the cottage, then escorted Karran and the baby. The little place smelt damp and the candle flickered as though there were gaps in the roof or window. John had organised everything so carefully but had forgotten that a disused dwelling needed airing. But so had she!

However, the factor lit a huge fire and put the mattress close beside it, then, in his taciturn way, boiled water for tea and took food out of a hamper Karran had not noticed. Throwing a white cloth over the table, he set out the boiled ham and fowl and one of the cook's special loaves, with a round of butter stamped with the Ravensdowne mark of a bird and wrapped in leaves. There was a plum cake, dark and deliciously damp.

Bart ate hungrily and drank his milk from Wheatley Clive's mug. Sleepy with the intense heat, Karran drowsed over her late supper and watched Brand turn the mattress to the roaring inferno. There was that suggestion of Deborah about the room, a quicksilver rustling that Karran discovered was emanating from the big jar of honesty, twisting in the unaccustomed heat. Dried herbs spun and twirled in the air currents. It was almost as if Deborah were there, making her unseen presence known, whispering, 'Don't be afraid. I'll take care of you.'

The mattress toasted to Brand's liking, he made up the bed in spite of Karran's protests and prepared to leave.

'I'll be at the Viking Inn, Miss Karran, with the carriage, if you should want me. When I'm not around the waterside keeping an eye on things, that is.'

She thanked him awkwardly. She'd never been sure of Brand's opinion of her and he wouldn't care to be away from his own home and family because some deranged person threatened John's household. His father had been factor before him and had attended Erin's wedding to Jesse Kinrade. They both had. People said that Brand was made impotent by her own grandmother, Karran recalled. She found herself wondering if it were still true, then took herself sharply to task. She was as bad as the person who had written that abominable letter. And then she caught Brand watching her with the strangest expression and her heart gave a little skip of panic. What if the writer had been Brand? Impotence must lead to unnatural frustrations and unhappiness. She could not wait for him to go and barred the door immediately he'd done so. How terrible to doubt everybody, even the man sent to protect her. But he must hate Johanne.

Gently, she put Bart to the back of the bed which felt perfectly dry and was haunted by the scent of the herbs Deborah must once have stuffed inside mattress and pillow. Then she lay down beside him, the whispering voice of the fire lulling her back to a more comfortable sleep.

Brand returned next day. He pretended to be a holidaying fisherman and hung about the stream's bank with a hand-made rod and a creel, but he did bring her two trout for their supper.

She still did not quite trust him, but there was plenty for her to do in the cottage for the first few days so she was not able to brood over what could be unnecessary fears. Remembering what had happened at Laurence's tholtan, she became claustrophobic once the place was as clean and neat as she could make it. The overhanging trees oppressed her and she longed for space.

'I wish to ride,' she told Brand, when next he came with fish. 'Mr Howard wouldn't object if I took one of the horses up the road to St John's or Patrick. There's no one knows I'm here. Bart can sit in front. He'd love an excursion.'

'I'd have to go,' Brand said stolidly.

'Must you? I'm sure it would be perfectly safe.'

'It'd be as much as my job is worth, Miss Karran.' His dark eyes would not meet hers.

Karran wished that she were as sure of his loyalty as she was of Howard's. Away from John she no longer felt secure. He had always been her protector, no matter how she had disappointed him. She missed him more than she'd expected, yet she had more than once planned to leave him!

'Do you never feel that it would be better for us just to go back?'

'Oh, no, miss!' The words were jerked out of Brand like chestnuts out of a fire. 'We can't! It's — not time.'

She felt it was not what he'd originally intended to say. But now his tough face was impassive and he had made his body into a whipcorded barrier, blocking her way. It was as if he were her jailer.

'I was told to wait until either Mr Howard came himself or sent a letter to the inn.'

'Very well.' She was breathless with an agitation she strove to hide.

'We'll walk along together, then.' She had obviously disturbed the man with her restlessness and unwelcome suggestions. Or was she right and Brand the enemy?

'Come, my darling,' she said to Bart who could not wait to go outside. He might prove a handful on a horse, she reflected belatedly, but the feel of the breeze on her face and neck was an exquisite bonus. Her son was laughing and showing his white teeth. How very black and white he was. She could never love anyone else as much as she adored her child.

For some reason, once the horses were saddled, Bart wanted to ride with Brand who seemed pleased by the turn of events. 'Aye, little one. Of course you can.'

'Bart?' Karran was disquieted by the unexpected whim.

'Leave him be, miss,' Brand advised, swinging up the child and sliding a strong arm around him. This turn of events was not at all to her liking.

He could let go of her child, Karran thought, and pretend it was an accident. But Bart smiled devilishly as if he divined her unease and enjoyed it.

'We'll go to Patrick,' she said. 'There's a track towards Foxdale. I've a fancy for the moor today after being so cooped up.'

Sunlight filtered through the leaves and cast green-gold shadows over them. The track was dry and the busy hooves threw up a powder of brown dust. Karran would have liked to linger at the hamlet, but Brand affected not to hear her when she asked him not to hurry past the low, thatched dwellings with flowery gardens. No one marked their passing.

They climbed higher between the steep hedges and the breeze became a wind that caught at her hair. The trees were gone and the great shallow folds of the heights showed her racing cloud patches and the slow, circling shadows of sparrow-hawks.

Brand seemed to be drawing away from her and she called out in alarm. 'Brand? Wait —'

And then there was a rider in the distance and the factor was slackening his pace so that she could catch him up and lean towards the little boy. 'Will you come to me now, my pet?'

Bart shook his head. Perhaps he enjoyed the security of Brand's arm. A horse could seem dizzily high to a child. He might fear being passed from one to another.

The horseman came closer and Karran was, at last, sure of his identity. It was not the first time Clive had appeared at an opportune moment. She remembered Jem Boswell with a shudder of distaste. Over Clive's shoulder she saw the wheel of the Donaghue black against the sky and the smoke drifting from the windows of the miners' rows in the distance.

Now that he was almost upon them, Karran noticed how tired he looked and how neglected was his appearance. He was greatly changed from the rather arrogant young dandy of a few years ago. What was there about Elizabeth and Erin that destroyed their men? Light glittered on the slits of his eyes. They had not changed.

'Karran.' He reined in, obviously pleased to be with her.

'How are you?'

'All the better for seeing you. And this is the boy?'

'Yes. That's Bart.'

'He'll break hearts. Like his mother.'

Karran, very aware of Brand, seated like a judge with scowling brows, made light of the remark, but she remembered Clive's insistence that, if the occasion arose, she must ask for his help. She introduced the factor who remained surly, and said, 'We must be close to your house.' Seeing the trickle of blue above the plantain of firs and birches on the left, she pointed it out. 'Is that it?'

'Mingay? It is still mine. Just —'

'You speak as if it will not be for long. Could we — is there time to talk about it? It would be pleasant to rest and take tea. We came further than I meant.'

'Miss Karran —' Brand started to say but she would not be diverted.

'It is perfectly all right. Mr Clive is a friend.'

Brand looked at her as if to ask, with all that gossip about a certain evening in Douglas not so long ago? Mr Howard won't like any of this.

'Please give me the child, Brand. He looks sleepy.'

The factor passed Bart to his mother with the greatest reluctance while Karran and Clive rode a little way ahead, just out of earshot. Quietly Karran explained what she was doing here.

Clive's face turned ugly when she mentioned the letter that had caused her banishment, but he was intrigued to hear of Charlotte's involvement with Abel.

'I'm sure he's not good for her, but she seems absolutely

resolved to pursue him. I admit I'm sorry for her if she persists.' Karran sighed.

'Everyone thinks you are closer to him than is respectable, yet you seem chary of the fellow?'

'We've never been anything but tolerant of one another. It's lucky you and I haven't passed anyone else today or the next letter could be far worse.'

'You think there will be another letter?'

'Anyone wicked enough to send one must surely want to repeat the experience? There must be some twisted satisfaction to be gained. Do you know,' she glanced over her shoulder to check if Brand was out of earshot, 'I'm not even sure if it isn't him. My grandmother was reputed to put a spell on him, years ago, and he could bear me a grudge since she's now beyond his reach.'

'What sort of spell?'

'It was before your time,' she hedged, warm-faced. 'It's not the kind of disability a woman can talk of too readily to a man. Certainly not an unmarried woman.'

Clive laughed unkindly. 'No need to be more explicit. It's the sort of affliction that could cause more than rancour. Howard was cunning in his choice of bodyguard.'

'Oh, I'm sure he never thought —'

'I say he did. Not that I blame him.'

'I wonder,' Karran murmured, not liking the turn the conversation was taking, 'if there is really sufficient time to stop?'

'Of course there is.' Clive laid a hand on her bridle. 'I shan't let you escape. It's been lonely of late at Mingay, and the future is not — not so settled as I could want.'

'I'm sorry.' She wished that she didn't feel as much Clive's prisoner as Brand's. But she did feel sorry for Elizabeth's husband. There was something pathetic in his shabbiness.

'And I promise not to embarrass you with unseemly topics.'

'It's ridiculous, really, when I am obviously not so innocent as I make myself appear —'

'My dear Karran. I won't hear of you running yourself down in this way.'

'I have not even the excuse that Laurence was a mistake. I've never thought of him in that light.'

'But he's dead, my dear, and you must go on living. There has to be some other man. Once one has known —'

'Please. Shall we change the subject? I suppose this is the drive to your home.'

The pleasant grounds had not seen the ministrations of a

gardener for some time. Clive, seeing her perplexity, said, 'I have not had the money.'

'I did not mean to pry,' she replied quickly.

'I intend to tell you the whole story.'

The house came into view, still attractive, for there had not been time yet for that to run to seed in the same way as its precincts.

'Perhaps you'd like to take tea in the housekeeper's sitting-room?' Clive told Brand. 'I shall not let Miss Kinrade out of my sight and the child will be chaperoned in case you are worried.' He smile thinly.

Brand remained poker-faced but went off in the direction Clive indicated.

'There *is* something about his manner,' Clive agreed, frowning after him. 'Go in there, my dear, and make yourselves at home while I order your tea.'

The green velvet and oyster-coloured drapes reminded Karran of Elizabeth. She found herself wondering what Clive's wife and Nat Gelling were doing at this moment. Gelling had not seemed in the least Elizabeth's type. And how such a principled-seeming person could run off with a mother of small children, she would never fathom.

Karran, uncomfortably aware for the first time that Bart would almost certainly dominate the next twenty years of her life, hugged his sleeping body to her and laid him gently on one of the sofas, then went to the dusky mirror to tidy the loose ends of her hair.

Clive's face materialised beside her own.

'You startled me!'

'The carpet's so thick. Well, it should fetch a good price.'

'You are selling up? You've decided?'

He turned away. 'I've told no one yet. But the Donaghue's in a bad way. Every week the lode narrows and though I've spent hours every day searching the old shafts and tunnels, had countless samples sifted, there's nothing. It's like a cow running dry or the earth turning to desert. And a stupid venture didn't help.'

Clive told Karran about the ill-fated *Helen*. 'I had to show everyone how dynamic and progressive I was. All that expensive equipment will lie idle. Kerruish won't need it, for he has the same on the other side of the moor *and* two good mines to my ailing one.

'All I had left was Mingay but even that's mortgaged now. I'd take out another lease only I can't afford to buy it. All I can do is to go down again and again and make little blasts with gunpowder. But when the dust settles, it's all as it was before. And I've drunk and gambled and paid whores good guineas for what my wife would not give me.'

He turned back and looked at her through shining cracks that held her still and silent. 'You've always wondered what was wrong between us. Elizabeth wanted — admiration and pretty baubles and someone to kiss her hand when she felt inclined. I've always wanted and needed passion and to take the initiative. I did not have a wife and I resented the fact. Elizabeth made me cruel, made me doubt myself, roused the worst in me.

'And all this was doubly galling because I married her on the rebound of a great disappointment. The death of any hope that you'd ever look at me. For I did love you. But I couldn't allow myself to be seen as a spurned suitor and Elizabeth was a catch. Or so I imagined —' He shrugged, his smile cynical.

'I'm sorry,' Karran said mechanically. It was hardly her own fault.

'I'm a failure,' Clive whispered and his features twisted. 'I can see no blue sky. Nothing but clouds. I am — oppressed.'

She felt an overpowering urge to comfort him. But the sort of comfort he required was not in her power to give. Her throat ached with futility.

He came towards her, his face wild, and she was afraid, but the tea-things arrived at that moment and she was reprieved for a time at least.

She sat down beside the small table and poured tea, but Clive walked over to the glass-fronted cupboard and helped himself liberally to brandy which she refused.

'Couldn't Kerruish help?' she said in order to break the stormy silence.

'Don't you think I've lost enough face in that direction?' He tossed off the brandy as though it were water and poured another glass.

'Face! What does face matter? You took a perfectly legitimate gamble. Admit it.'

'I need a partner. A partner with money —'

'But who's to say matters will be any different? Unless you could interest someone with limitless resources who could stand the loss if the gamble didn't pay, you'd be beggaring another man. Where's the sense in that?'

'How very practical you can be.' Clive's distorted grin disturbed her. She had invited herself because she'd imagined

207

herself to be in danger, without any shred of evidence, and here she was in a worse situation.

'You make it sound a crime,' she parried with false lightness, glad of the restorative qualities of the excellent brew. 'Shouldn't you cut your losses now while there is still something left? You can't have mortgaged the entire house.'

'Half.'

'Well, sell the house, as you seem already to have planned. Pay off your men with what you have left over from your debts and hope they'll find other work. You'll not be able to pay them yourself shortly. Then you'd still have the machinery to sell and the ponies. They'd fetch something. You could then start again —'

'What! Start some tinpot business here after having been what I am?'

'Were,' Karran corrected. 'You are so concerned with your image! Aren't your children more important? Their future?'

'The children won't suffer. Elizabeth's mother said she'd care for them until I have sorted out my affairs. Not that she knows how bad they are.'

'I wondered why the house was so quiet.'

'None of this would have happened if you had been free when I first met you. I feel it. You have such commonsense and physically we might have been — very good for one another.' Clive was watching her intently.

'That's something we are unlikely to determine,' Karran told him and picked up her cup which was almost empty, but a camouflage of sorts. A man would not try to take hold of a woman clutching a vessel of hot tea. 'And as for commonsense, I didn't behave all that wisely. I followed my impulses —'

'Couldn't you follow them again? Pehaps all my problems could take a vastly differing turn if I had you.'

'You are married to someone else,' she reminded him stiffly.

'I'll divorce her, of course.'

'Think of the cost of such a proceeding.'

'It would be straightforward enough. Elizabeth is patently guilty.'

'Perhaps, if you'd given her more time —'

'She wouldn't have changed. But what she could see in a great, dour, unsophisticated lump like Gelling — !' He laughed, humourlessly. 'I'll never understand.'

'He seemed very kind.'

'Oh, God, Karran! Sometimes I feel I am going mad! I dream I'm in one of the lower levels of the mine and I'm lying looking up at the candlelit roof and I fix my eye on a peculiarly-shaped blemish. And although I never take my eyes off it, the blemish becomes imperceptibly larger and larger until I realise that the roof is coming lower, closer to me. Then I find I can't move — not a muscle.'

'You shouldn't keep driving yourself so hard. You must do as I've suggested,' Karran said, more disturbed than ever on Clive's behalf. She set down the cup and rose from the velvet-covered chair. The brandy had already affected him.

Clive looked greyer and even more strange. 'I need you,' he said hoarsely.

'You're young and clever. You could do it all again if only you'd forget your pride. I can't help you any further.' She must be firm. Insist on going —

'Ask Howard if he wants to speculate — He'd listen to you.'

'Leave him out of this! He's had a bad time —'

'Cushioned no doubt by his money. And you to — comfort him?' Clive's meaning was unmistakable.

'I never thought you'd stoop so low. I always imagined you had a certain integrity but now I know better. Perhaps you'd be good enough to send for Brand.'

'By God, I won't! Not till I feel like it. I'm not finished with you yet.'

Purposefully, Karran stepped towards the elegant velvet bell-pull but Clive was faster. He pinioned her arms and stared down at her out of shining fissures. There was something so devilish in his regard that she was afraid.

'Let me go.'

'No.'

'I'll scream.'

'And Brand and my housekeeper will come running. I'l see that they have plenty of fuel for goosip! One tug at that coat and blouse and there'd not be a button left.'

'To think that only minutes ago I felt kindly towards you.'

'Let me have you. Only once. Perhaps once wouldn't be enough for you —'

'No!'

'Very well. It seems I must help myself. No one will hear. The kitchen's miles away and I was obliged to dismiss all but the maid whom I was forced to keep on to satisfy the house-keeper. They won't come unless I ring. Be kind to me. Please?

You seem to have no trouble in being kind to the rest of humanity. Why not me?'

'You were my friend, or so I believed. I think you still could be, only you've had too much to drink. Let me go and we'll forget all this.'

'And never set eyes on you again?'

'How could we avoid contact? The island is not so large. We'd surely meet —'

'Always in the company of others.'

'It would be better that way. There's no future for us. Surely you can see that? Why saddle yourself with a second failure? For that's what it would be.'

His arms tightened around her. The brandy taken on an empty stomach had control of him. Clive was dangerous and Karran could not see how she was to deal with him in this reckless, self-pitying mood.

'I — I have some money you could have.'

The pale slits widened. 'Did Richards have money to leave?'

'Never mind where it came from. I have money invested. When I was a child I was given five hundred pounds. It's grown into nearly twice that amount now.' It would be worth the loss to divert his mind from his obvious intention.

'And you'd lend me such a sum? Knowing it could be good money after bad?'

'Yes. If you —'

'Conditions, eh?' He gave a bark of quite crazy laughter and blew brandy fumes into her face.

She tried to pull herself away from him but he was too strong for her.

'You'll let me have it — if I let you go now. Is that it?'

'Yes.'

'How do I know you wouldn't renege?'

'I'm perfectly willing to write a letter —'

'No, Karran.' His mouth was on her neck, his lips slid to the hollow at the base of her throat where a pulse jerked strongly. He lifted his head and she saw that he was pale, the slanted eyes sensuous. 'Don't make it hard for me. I intend to take what you refuse me. As I should have done that day we rode to Bradda. I'm no longer so gentlemanly or so scrupulous. Why not make up your mind to enjoy it? What have you to lose? Or I!'

She kicked out suddenly and sent the tray flying with the cups and saucers. The tinkling clatter was dulled by the heaviness of the carpet.

Clive swung her off her feet and took her, still struggling, to the large sofa near the hearth. The riding hat fell off and rolled across the floor.

'I beg you,' she whispered vehemently, remembering Bart, 'don't do it.'

'I can't help myself.'

Desperately, she pushed at his chest which felt strong as a hooped cask. If she screamed it would upset Bart dreadfully to open his eyes onto this humiliating struggle. Children remembered such nightmare episodes.

'I recall once that you saved me from a similar attack,' she cried out.

'And all the time wished myself in Boswell's place. As I am now.'

She couldn't allow this. Even if Bart were scarred as a result. Karran screamed and grabbed at Clive's hair. Gasping with pain and balked fury, he struck her across the face and tore at the neck of her blouse.

'I shouldn't do that again, sir, if I were you.'

For a moment both Karran and Clive were still. She turned her head and saw Brand standing at the open doorway.

'I came here to wait for you when I finished my tea, Miss Karran. Couldn't help hearing you call out. Do you want to leave now?'

Clive got up. His face worked angrily. 'How dare you —' His entire body trembled.

'Shouldn't I be saying that, sir?' Brand asked stolidly as Karran scrambled to her feet and bent to retrieve the lost hat. She repressed the urge to scream again. For days she had made Brand into a monster and here he was, a Sir Galahad. What a fool she had been! She could not look at Clive.

'Get out!' Clive said. 'Get out. And take your bastard with you.'

Brand looked murderous.

'He's not quite himself,' Karran told the man. 'Too much brandy.'

Clive turned his back on them and stared out of the window.

Now that Karran was safe, she could almost be sorry for him. She picked up her child and followed Brand from the room. She was close to tears, her former respect for Clive reduced to ashes in her mind. There was only one person in the universe who had complete integrity and she had never wanted or needed him so badly. Not in a physical way. Clive had sickened her of that. But as the shield and comforter he'd always been and surely would continue to be.

John, she thought. Let me come back.

John sat by Abel's bedside. He had burned with a fever for several days and talked ceaselessly in delirium. It had been like eavesdropping listening to Costain's secrets.

It was plain that he'd disliked his parents for he railed at them for their meanness. The father had apparently been a schoolmaster and the mother a governess. They had died of the same epidemic, unmourned by their son.

He spoke of women and it was never kindly. Howard was shocked at first over the explicit conversations with Abel's 'ghosts', and had gone outside to stare over the blinding cleanliness of the bay. But everyone occasionally had unclean thoughts. He himself —

Fascinated and repelled, he had returned to bathe Abel's forehead and to try to ignore the involuntary confidences that spilled from the boy's lips. This was not the young man he thought he knew. How convincing Costain had been with his veneer of shyness and hero-worship.

Abel had disliked Karran and despised Howard. The fever acted like some kind of truth machine, transforming former impressions to a falseness John would find hard to forgive. If it were not for the boy's terrible loss — One must retain pity —

Kate. Who was she? The name reminded John of Emily's penchant for the pretty maid who had run off from their London home with the footman. He could see his wife now, devouring the girl with a gaze he refused resolutely to identify too closely. John was on the path to Spanish Head and Emily was sliding towards the edge. His arm was moving but was it hindering or helping that dreadful descent? John groaned and got up to pace the small, stuffy room. He'd owed Emily that much loyalty, hadn't he? But she had been a barrier between himself and the girl he loved. Now she was not. She had become merely a starfish bleeding over the rocks that had killed her, then a mound in the graveyard. He *had* tried to save her. He was sure of it now and a weight seemed to roll away from him.

Howard stopped abruptly.

'The letter,' Abel said. 'The letter was — a great success. I paid her out for her — dislike of me. And her bastard with his claws into Howard. He spoiled my work, the miserable brat. How John could — indulge — such creatures. But — the letter

212

— was inspired —' He laughed softly and eerily.

In spite of the unwelcome warmth of the sick chamber, Howard was cold. All this time, he had feared the appearance of a second sheet of similar filth. An unknown assassin. And Abel had written that disgusting tract out of jealousy and vindictiveness. He could never have him back.

'Stark!' Abel raved. 'I'll kill Stark as he has already killed me. And all over that loose, cow-like bitch!' His laughter was terrible. 'Kate —'

'What is he saying?' Charlotte asked from the doorway.

'Nothing that makes any sense,' John replied, shivering. Stark. The remainder of the jigsaw fell into place. He knew Stark — and his daughter.

'You shouldn't stay, my dear. You might contact a fever yourself —'

'But I want to.' She went to Abel and laid her thin, cool hand on his brow and it was as if the touch soothed him. He lay quiet, his tongue stilled.

'See?' Charlotte burst out excitedly. 'There's sweat on his brow and his face! The fever's broken. Oh, thank God. It might have been too late.'

It *is* too late, John thought wearily. Disappointment, anger and a sour regret fought in him for supremacy. He'd nursed a viper and it would be a pity if the pitch that defiled Costain were allowed to touch Kerruish's girl.

'Charlotte?' He was not sure what he meant to say.

She raised a face that mirrored the shining fragments of relief and love. Even if he were to tell her what Abel had done, she'd never believe it. Everyone must make their own mistakes. Perhaps it would be better to warn her father when next they met. He'd voice his convictions to Barney and let him sort out the matter as he thought fit.

'What is it?' Charlotte asked, her gaze returning to Abel's wasted face.

'I forgot.' Howard wished it were true. He could never forget. But there was one outcome that filled him with a tired pleasure. Karran could come back even if he must pretend to be a father-figure for the rest of his days. She would be there at Ravensdowne and there would be Bart's laughter and mischievousness.

He stumbled from the cottage and began to walk along the beach with hurrying steps, displacing stones and dislodging seabirds, wanting only to put as much distance between himself and Costain as possible, for the time Charlotte remained.

He must wash himself of disgust and censure before he could face Abel in his right senses. Before the resumption of falseness. Weakness. The subtle demands for what John could never again give.

Peace was long in coming.

Clive had scarcely moved. His body was inexpressibly tired but his brain wide awake, relentlessly pursuing the images of love lost and ambition shattered. Once the effects of the brandy had worn off, he saw the enormity of his actions. Karran could never again trust him and even if she did not divulge the details of this afternoon's disaster, Brand had no reason to hold his tongue.

The maid had looked at him fearfully when she came to clean up the mess of china and spilt dregs, scurrying away like a rat once she had piled the tray.

Too weary to rise, Clive had sat at the window, staring at nothing, the sky dimming until finally it was dark and the bats came out, squeaking weirdly, and tiny pricks of stars as if even the sky was reluctant to favour him with more than a glimmer of comfort.

It became too cold to sit any longer and he rang for the maid to re-light the fire, then, when she'd gone, pulled open the lid of the bureau and took out the sheaf of papers. Bills from the butcher and fishmonger. He still had not paid Paul Kelly for the last consignment of ale from Douglas, and the casks he'd ordered from Dobree of Laxey, who could not yet know of his inability to pay, had not yet arrived.

There were bills still outstanding for the smelt mill. He'd already spent in the region of £500 but he owed amounts for timber, coal bricks and Poyllvaaish stones. Cigar bills, wine bills, the account for Elizabeth's pelisse, the one she'd forced him to order before the ill-fated night at the theatre and still unpaid.

He opened the Donaghue ledgers at the last pages. How many men would he be putting out of work? The black letters and figures stared back at him without meaning.

Clive forced himself to concentrate. The foreman. The Master of lead ore washers. The lead ore washers themselves. There were seventeen, including the woman, big Bessie, with her eight children. One of the nine had died of a fever last week. Thirty-five labourers and two apprentices. Five enginemen, three engineers, one book-keeper. Three joiners, seventy-eight miners. A total of one hundred and forty-four.

And that was only the mine. He hadn't yet glanced at the smelter figures.

Of the miners, five could go back to farms, and five to roadmaking. Three were craftsmen and might be taken on elsewhere. What would happen to the rest? They'd starve after they'd spent their last pay packets.

He grasped the pages and crumpled them with unheeding fingers. Rising, he fetched the brandy and a glass and poured a generous measure. Would matters have been different if he'd taken a partner? Remembering the fiasco of the *Helen*, he grimaced. A partner could not have conjured up ore where there was none, and, in any case, Clive liked to be cock on his own dungheap, deferring to no one.

The reflection of the flames in the window-pane reminded him of Elizabeth. He seemed to see her pale image in the glass, smiling at his downfall. He flung the empty goblet into the corner, then walked, less than steadily, to fetch another.

He felt stronger now, more able to cope with the renewed clarity of his mind. Clive had decided what he meant to do. He tossed off his second glass and put away the bottle. More, and he'd not be able to carry out his resolve.

Clive seated himself at the desk and wrote for a few minutes, then locked away what he had written. A curious, fatalistic mood had settled over his spirits. He was warm again and reasonably collected.

Leaving the room, he hesitated at the top of the stair that led to the back of the house and the stables. A candle flickered, casting hobgoblin shadows on the wall. He lurched down the wide steps.

Outside, it was cold and the sound of the pumping engine beat over the moor like a faithful heart. Soon its supply of life-giving blood would fail and the heart would stop. He wished, rather perfunctorily, that he'd seen Timothy yesterday, but he'd been disinclined to go to Castletown. Failure and self-neglect did not make for happy visits, and Kerruish's smugness would have galled him. Erin would have asked awkward questions and she was persistent when one hedged.

The brandy had hold of him now. As he saddled and mounted, Clive felt omnipotent. The drum of hoofbeats on the track was soporific.

A greenish moon emerged from behind cloud, showing him the black wheel of his mine and the glow of the furnace in the smelt.

Davis was in the engine-house when Clive entered.

'Are you going down again, sir?'

'I feel lucky,' Clive said and took a lantern from a hook. 'I want powder and fuses. Rod. A strikelight. Hammer. Tapers. You know. It's not the first time.'

Davis looked at him oddly. 'You're not taking anyone with you?'

'Not this time.' He picked up the hard felt hat and lighted the candle on its brim.

There was a dustcoat on a peg and Clive put it on. Davis had placed the articles he'd specified into a canvas bag to sling over his shoulder.

'I'll be in the mid-level this time. The left branch, I think.'

'How long will you be, sir?'

Clive shrugged. 'Some time. There's no reason to hurry.' The sense of predestination was strong. All the way down, only the grotesque shadows for company, he felt he had completed something important. It was not at all how he had expected to feel. Even the recollection of Karran had paled before this greater anticipation, but there was something of her in the pitchy blacknesses against the pale stone, the suggestion of eye-sockets and hollowed cheekbones, the opening of a tunnel that was a mouth to swallow him.

It was cold in the tunnel and he shivered in spite of the dustcoat and the lingering heat of the brandy in his stomach. The ceiling was descending like the one in his nightmare and he had to crouch to reach the next stretch. It was vaulted and worn like beach stones where water had dripped for centuries then found its way to the lower level. The chinks of shifted pebbles had a hollow sound like uncoordinated bells.

The place was icy now and he could see his own breath forming in front of his face, taking on strange, ephemeral shapes. Pale horses, white manes, smoke drifting. It was more tranquil than anywhere he'd ever been. The sound of the pump was faint and far away. The mechanical rhythm was no longer suggestive of life and heartbeats, more like slow hammer-blows, the hammer shrouded in veil after veil of cheesecloth. A spectral piston —

Clive had never come so far. The low, claustrophobic caverns swallowed up most of the light but ahead of him the tunnel went on like a rabbit warren, indented and buttressed, here and there a shrouded candle-stump on a ledge.

He stumbled over a pile of boulders that half-blocked the way. There were now no traces of previous infiltration, no candles, no props, no chipping at the rock. A turn in the passage all but shut off the muffled throb. The cold womb of the earth held him in this backwater of eternity from which it appeared that nothing could emerge.

Clive stared around him. He had pushed, crawled, jack-knifed and come out into welcome stretches where he could travel without too much constriction, only to end up in a low, fig-shaped cave which seemed to lead nowhere.

The candle-flame wavered, sending shadows scudding over the bland outward-curving walls. The air was cold as death. He shuddered and rubbed at his hands. Eons had elapsed and he was curiously disorientated, like an acolyte in a temple where he hoped to find God.

It seemed suddenly funny that the cave was damnably like one of the domes of the Regent's folly at Brighton. Clive laughed and the sound echoed and rebounded, growing smaller and finally dying away in a ghostly chuckle.

He set the bag on the ground and took out the hammer. There was a long, shallow scar on a level with his face and he began to chip away at one end of it with small finicky taps. Slowly, the tiny shards of rock fell around his feet. He pushed the metal rod into the ensuing depression, then began to strike the end of the rod with all of his strength. Slowly the rod sank into the resulting cavity. Clive sweated.

When the rod was halfway in, he withdrew it and felt in the bag for the gunpowder charge and the trailing stuff of the long fuse. When his preparations were finished, he stood for a long time moving not a muscle. He was as much stone as the hollow bulb of the cave. Then he picked up the bag and walked away slowly, paying out the fuse as he went. Once he almost tripped over it and thought he had pulled it away. He gritted his teeth against the tingling shock. But it remained firm. He had become disembodied, his thoughts stalking, frozen, in bone-white forests.

There was something he had to do. The end of the fuse dropped from his fingers and he knelt, scrabbling in the bag for the strikelight and taper. It was an age before it came alight and he held the thin waxen taper to the flame.

That impression of being a novice at God's altar came back at the sight of the pale wand and the shivering flame. He set it awkwardly to the end of the fuse and watched the stuff blacken, then blow out suddenly into a little fan of fire.

The flame retreated, swallowing the fuse like a black death.

He should get up and run. His body told him so but his mind fettered him in stone-cold clamps. Why run? What was there to run to? Had he ever intended to leave this place he'd chosen?

The dancing light slipped round the buttress that hid the hole in the rock. Run, his body insisted and he rose sluggishly but his feet were ton weights holding him where he was. He tried to break the deadly trance but could not.

The candle on his hat brim wavered and the light and shadow formed Karran's face as it was that first evening at the Bascombes' party.

He fancied she was smiling. The smile was still there when the gunpowder charge exploded and the Ali Baba cave shuddered and fell to pieces around him.

'I don't believe it,' Erin said and clutched at the mantel for support.

'It's true,' Norton assured her. 'The whole of Foxdale rocked.'

'The children,' she whispered helplessly.

'Will be all right,' Barney told her forcefully. He had a liking for little Timothy, who in some strange way was not unlike Charlotte. Virginia was what he called a peenging child but there must be ways of stopping her tendency to whine. And weren't they both orphans? 'Now don't fret, my dear. Sit you down and drink that. And I'll join you. There you are, Norton.'

They sipped their brandy, all trying to assimilate the shock of Clive's death. It would be some time before his body could be reached, but the extent of the fall could have only one outcome.

'You're sure he couldn't — ?'

'No, sir,' Norton denied strenuously. 'I've been over there myself. I thought it best in view of the fact that the Erin and Charlotte mines might be affected. Not that we can know until all the levels are properly inspected. Davis has the men moving away the rubble in shifts. But it's necessarily slow work, since the site of the explosion occurs in natural passageways reached by early tunnelling. And some of the entrances are low and the stuff must be passed by hand, for it wouldn't be possible to blast them any longer without the roof caving in. I doubt if any man ever went so far.'

'It makes me wonder why. We must try to find the answer at Mingay. I'd best go over there, my dear. You must stay with the twins. No. Don't argue. The poor creatures must be made to retain a sense of security and you rushing off here, there and everywhere, becoming emotional, won't help.'

'I suppose not. But take care, Barney.' She took his hand in a gesture of affection.

'I never take risks,' he whispered.

'You did. When you took me on,' she said as quietly. ' You don't — regret it?'

'Surely you know?'

'I like you to say it after all that time, eating my heart out and things wrong between us.' Her eyes glistened.

Norton was becoming restive and it was rude to exclude him.

'Must go, my dear. Expect me in a day or two.' Barney bustled out of the room and shouted for his coat and for the horses to be brought round.

Left alone, Erin found herself shaking. She had never seen a great deal of her son-in-law, but she had recognised the gradual descent from arrogance to worry and last of all a quiet desperation. Had it been an unfortunate accident or something more sinister? That day the twins were born, he'd admitted there were financial difficulties that could become worse. She'd tried to ask him later if his worst fears had been justified, but he'd become evasive. But he'd grown very parsimonious, Elizabeth had claimed. Elizabeth! She must be told. Erin reached for paper and quill and wondered if her daughter would set about regularising her union with Nat Gelling. Or had she encountered the same difficulties as had arisen in her relationship with Wheatley Clive? Erin didn't understand frigidity. It was lucky that Elizabeth had had the aforesight to send her mother a forwarding address.

Erin sat chewing the end of the quill thinking how best to word the letter, but there was only one way to say that a man had died violently.

Elizabeth did not understand her own reception of the news. Part of her had turned cold. Another experienced little flickers of what seemed like shame. She was angry for being saddled with guilt, however tentative. Hard on the heels of shock came the unwelcome thought of her children.

She tried to summon up their faces, but all that emerged was Clive's slitted stare and an echo of his voice. 'That wasn't so bad, was it?' Followed by that regardless turning onto his side to sleep, leaving her awake and trembling.

Elizabeth put the letter down, unable to read the rest. The wild, bleak panorama of Foxdale filled her mind. Chimneys, smoke, the red glow of furnaces. The glum children hanging around their mother's skirts. Clive becoming more and more bound up in the Donaghue, leaving her to her own devices. And to Nat —

It wasn't my fault, she thought with a sudden, hot panic. It wasn't! But there was her persistent coolness, the obvious boredom. Unnatural, he'd called her, both in her attitude towards him and her children. She crossed her arms over her breast.

The sounds of the city were wafted into the room. The rumble of wheels, shouts, children running. It had taken her some time to become used to that after the silence of Mingay.

None of the expensive grandeur of Clive's house had any place here. This room was simply furnished, a hotchpotch of differing colours and styles of furniture, but the wood surfaces were polished and the flowers Nat had given her were reflected in the black table-top.

Still with her arms pressed around her body, she wandered into the small bedroom. The faded hangings had once been a vigorous blue. The counterpane was crocheted lace over a lilac base, the dressing-table bare of the extravagances she had once enjoyed.

She wished that the bed had more meaning. Nat had been firm in his intention to be patient until she welcomed the natural culmination of their love. In spite of her very real feelings towards him, she still experienced restraint.

The first time she and Nat had lain together she had tried to give herself, but the deadly inadequacy had returned and Nat couldn't help but be aware of it. 'I'll wait,' he whispered and held her in his arms as though it didn't matter.

He'd fall in love with a real woman one day, Elizabeth thought with a nagging fear. No matter how much he protested that he'd rather hold her closely, only kissing and stroking her, the more she realised that their relationship was threatened.

'I love you. Take me,' she had insisted, but he wouldn't.

'I'll wait. It's worth waiting for. I won't behave like him.'

She could be dried-up and old before the barrier was pushed away. And he would have left her long before that. Any man would.

Sobbing without really being aware of the fact, she went into the kitchen which was dark and poky. It was a very small suite of rooms, but Nat's job at the dock was not as well paid as that of a mine manager.

220

'I'll be that again one of these days,' he'd told her, apologising for the skimpiness of her allowance. But he always kept something back, not to spend on himself but to buy her some treat. Flowers, a peach, chocolates, gloves. Ribbon to match her eyes. Papa used to do that for Erin. Elizabeth could no more remember Jesse's face than she could the twins'. Only Clive's burning stare.

She did not hear Nat come in. Her agonised crying had given her hiccups and she had already dropped a favourite pie-dish. The thought of Elizabeth Kerruish becoming unduly fond of a pie-dish had set her off laughing in a weak hysteria.

She drew a long, shuddering breath as Nat's arms came round her and his hands locked over her stomach. His chin dug into her shoulder. 'What is it? What's wrong?'

'Its — Clive.' Her voice rose in a wail she despised.

'What about him? Has he come here? Has he browbeaten you? Struck you again?'

She shook her head and the red mass of her hair covered his face for a moment, then swung away impatiently, like a twitched curtain.

'What, then?'

'He's dead. Blew himself up looking for a fresh lode.'

'Dear God.' Nat, visibly shaken, released her.

'Mama wrote.'

'You're white as a ghost. Come and sit down.'

'I can't. I feel as if there are so many things I haven't done. Must do —'

'My dear Elizabeth! There's nothing for you to do. You ran off with me. Clive will doubtless be in his grave by this time. Barney would show you the door. Even your children don't belong to you any more. You gave them up, remember?'

She stared, distraught. 'You're cruel!'

'It's better that you realise now. Now. Before you start putting yourself into false positions.'

'How hard you can be.'

'No. Only sensible. I wouldn't want you insulted. Turned away —'

'Mama —'

'Knows which side her bread's buttered. And you said you'd never been close.'

'I've never been close to anyone but Boyce and you.'

'Not Sebastian?'

'Not so much. But I love Boyce.'

'Not too much, I hope.'

'What's too much? A great deal.'

'Boyce has his own life to lead.'

'I fear he'll not be as happy as he could wish.'

'Why not?'

'He wants wars. Wants campaigns. But he was too late for the ones that interested him and there may not be others. No one wants more.'

'He'll have to face up to life without them, then, won't he.'

'You're jealous of him!' She was distracted from thoughts of Clive and death.

'Only because he's your brother and a permanent figure in your life. Not like a lover you might tire of and send away.'

'I'd *never*!'

'You can't know. How many years lie ahead of you? Forty? Fifty? It's a long time for someone like me to keep hold of you and your affections. Brothers don't have to try too hard. They're your flesh and blood.' He looked quiet and sad and she wanted to start to cry again, only her tears seemed to have dried into a hot soreness.

'I love you far more than Boyce. Girls will chase him and he'll have affairs with some of them, only that predatory Nina will get him in the end. And he'll never be sure of her —'

'Elizabeth! How can you possibly tell?' He laughed shakily.

'I just know.'

He put his arm round her narrow, green-bound waist. 'And what do you predict for Sebastian?'

She shivered. 'I wish you hadn't asked me. Nothing very pleasant.'

'No star-struck girls? No raging affairs?'

'Don't let's think of him. I haven't got the food ready. I was upset. Broke the dish. And now I couldn't eat.'

'Neither could I. I brought home some wine. Could you manage some of that?'

'Yes. You wont't leave me, will you?'

'Why should I want to do that?'

Her eyes blazed with unshed tears. 'Because the world must be full of women who are kind and good. And who could give themselves to you.'

'You will. When you're ready.'

He fetched the wine and poured out two glasses full. He gave one to Elizabeth and she held hers out and clinked it against his.

'This is much better than food,' Nat said and pulled her

against him. We're free now, he though. But she might want to leave matters as they were and he could hardly propose to her with Clive barely cold in his coffin.

They finished their wine and Nat continued to hold her. They just stood there, doing and saying nothing. But gradually he became aware of little pulses beating in the warmth of the body so close to his own, and the strong throb of the nerve at the base of her throat. The movement of her lashes against his cheek and the smell of the soap in her hair. Her beautiful hair —

He lifted his hand and stroked the red strands. There was so much life in them. Elizabeth pressed herself closer.

'It's funny,' she said, 'but knowing that Clive — realising that he's no longer between us — I feel free. More than free. I can't quite explain. But it's never seemed so right to be where I am. Do you think me — shameless?'

His heart thudded hurtfully. 'No.'

'It's as if I never was married. Never had children. As though we'd met years ago and this was the beginning of my life. It's — wicked of me, isn't it.'

Nat shook his head. 'Not wicked. Just — honest.'

'It was Mama who wanted it, not really me. She contrived a meeting with Wheatley. I knew later it wasn't the accident it seemed.'

'But you must have been attracted.' How demeaning jealousy was.

For the first time Elizabeth was entirely truthful. 'He was what everyone wanted and I had to have him. I can tell you. It was wrong and stupid and I deserved to be despised as he despised me. I wish I'd never done it. You are going to marry me, aren't you, Nat? You don't feel trapped now that it's possible to wed me?'

'How can you ask that?' He was angry and would have put her from him but she refused to let him go.

'I had to know for sure. Don't you understand?'

'You must learn to trust me better.'

'I'm not so good and principled as you are and never will be. Promise you won't mind? I'll try —'

'Elizabeth.' He wanted her quite badly but his conscience remembered Clive, dying in that stone tomb. Shattered bones. Wasted life —

'I find that I can't bear the thought of you setting me aside. Not tonight.'

223

It was ironic that on the one day Nat entertained reservations about coming too close to another man's widow, the chains that had bound her were struck away. She offered herself and he couldn't refuse.

'You *are* sure?'

She nodded.

He was committed. It was not how he'd imagined this moment, with a ghost between them. Nat could have fought Clive living. Yet how much better to have the matter resolved and no more lying awake unsatisfied.

Not for the first time Nat told himself that he was a fool, and lifted her against him.

Boyce sat up, listening. It *was* someone knocking at the door of his rooms. But, in the middle of the night! He rose from bed first annoyed, then curious.

In the light of his candle he saw Sebastian, greenish and exhausted.

'My God! You look like something the cat brought in.'

Sebastian stumbled inside, his shoulders hunched. 'It's — all right, is it?'

'What d'you mean, all right?' Boyce banged the door shut.

'There's no one here?'

'Oh. You thought I might have had some girl in my bed, eh?'

'Well.' Sebastian shrugged and looked very young. And frightened to death.

'Lucky you didn't come last night.' Boyce poured him a finger of brandy. 'Now, what's it all about?'

Sebastian emptied the glass and looked at him helplessly.

Boyce's irritation returned. He'd never been able to fathom his brother. And there'd been his damnable snivelling in the past. But Sebastian wasn't tearful now. He was cold as alabaster and stiff as a rock. Stunned —

'Come on,' Boyce barked. 'You get me out of bed at some impossible hour and it can't have been for nothing.'

'I — don't know where to start.'

'May I suggest the beginning?'

Sebastian set his jaw. 'It's — Richard.'

'Bailey, you mean?'

'Yes.'

'What about him?' Boyce picked up a cheroot and lit it, inhaling pleasurably. The tobacco smoke was reassuring. Sebastian refused to meet his gaze.

'You know that I — more or less — have to obey him.'

Boyce's eyes narrowed. 'Yes,' he replied slowly, recognising the nature of Sebastian's trouble. The young fool had always been the kind to fall prey to a certain type of man. The army had its share of predators as well as the navy.

'He had a friend. Giles Jordan. When Giles left he changed towards me. He wanted things from me. I couldn't refuse. Can I have some more of that stuff?'

Boyce gave him another brandy. 'I can follow the story so far.' Best not to be too sympathetic until he knew the rest. 'Lucky for you Mama and Kerruish have no idea.'

'That's the trouble! He says he's going to write to them.'

'Why, if he's getting what he wants!'

'I told him I couldn't do it any more.'

'Well! You do surprise me. But couldn't he just find someone else? Someone more willing?'

'He needs money. Said Kerruish obviously has plenty and that I must try to get some out of him. I tried to explain that was impossible in view of Barney's attitude towards us, and he became nasty and said he was going to let him and Mama know what sort of son they had. Spite, I suppose, for standing up to him. I couldn't stay there, knowing he'd have done it by now and that I'd have to answer for it. Oh, God, Boyce, what shall I do?'

Boyce whistled. 'You *have* messed things up, you young idiot. But it's not as if you'd committed murder.'

'Kerruish'll think it's worse! You know how strait-laced he can be.'

'You could deny it.'

'He'll believe it and that would only make things worse. I can't look Mama in the face. I know that. Can I — stay here, Boyce?'

'No, you can't. I've only these two rooms and I can't have you here like an albatross around my neck, Bastian. Sorry. It just wouldn't work.'

'A day or two, then.'

'What about Elizabeth? She might have you. Until you find your feet.'

'I'm out of funds.'

'I'll give you your coach fare to Liverpool and a little bit over.' Anything to get the young devil out of his hair.

'Thanks, Boyce.'

'You'd better share the bed.'

Sebastian flushed. 'No, I won't do that. The sofa'll do, and a blanket.'

'You're sure? *I* won't make any advances.'

'I wasn't thinking of you.'

Boyce fetched the bedclothes and threw them onto a chair. 'Help yourself. I don't have to get up early.'

'Good night, Boyce.'

'Good night, Bastian.'

The bedroom door closed. A wedge of moon glimmered through the pane. Sebastian turned and twisted on the couch. wondering how he was going to explain matters to his sister with Gelling about the place. Trying to visualise the arrival of Bailey's blackmailing letter to Kerruish. He'd demand money from Barney to keep his knowledge to himself. Say he'd let the news leak out so that Mama would never raise her head again in Castletown.

Oh, Christ!

The wedge of moon was like a pale, hideous smile.

John had gone to fetch Karran. He'd chosen his clothes with care, regretting the grey in his temples and the little lines around his eyes. If he looked tired, that last talk with Abel was to blame. He had let him know he knew all about the Stark affair and the business of the letter.

He would never forget Abel's eyes and the vicious, sneering rage, the accusations of sanctimoniousness.

'What about all my work?' Abel had demanded finally.

'I'll pay you for that regardless of whether the book is ever published. I'm not likely to find a third illustrator and the thing is not complete. But you are entitled to what you might have received had it come to completion. That's simply fair. Only you will never come to my house again, nor communicate with me or mine. Is that clear?'

'Very.' The handsome face was overlaid with malice and an unmistakable satisfaction that he was not to be dismissed without recompense.

John had to go out of the room to prevent himself from attacking Abel. Violence was so alien to his nature until recently. He went to his study and wrote a letter of credit in Abel's favour to be presented at the bank. The thought of Charlotte troubled him. It wasn't in his nature to interfere but she ought to know what Abel was capable of, and before he had too great a hold over her emotions.

Returning to Abel's room he handed over the credit note. 'I hope that is satisfactory?'

'Quite.'

'I'll see the authorities if there's any recurrence of past unpleasantnesses. I do mean that.'

'There will be none.'

'Get out, then,' John said, unable to bear Abel's smile.

'You haven't asked where I'm going.'

'I don't care. I hope I never see you again.'

'I suppose you'll be anxious to have your doxy back again, though.'

John raised his arm involuntarily.

'What! Would you strike a cripple?' Abel mocked. He had taken to wearing a black glove over his mutilated hand and displayed it ostentatiously.

'Get out of my sight,' Howard whispered.

Still smiling, Abel withdrew and a little later John heard him clatter off across the cobbled yard.

Howard returned to the room overlooking the bay. The cormorants squabbled and flew around Shag Rock and two gulls sailed past the window. He remembered Karran when she had first come here. He'd carried her to this same window-pane, wrapped in his houserobe. How excited she had been with her mane of dark hair and eyes like bits of jet. And then Richards had stolen her away. But she couldn't spend all her life regretting a dead lover? She must turn to him eventually.

He wondered how she had taken the news of Wheatley Clive's death. There wouldn't be a homestead on the island that hadn't heard of the accident in the Donaghue.

It was then that he knew he could no longer spend another day without her.

The journey seemed stranger than any he had taken. He saw the sea and the little town of Port St Mary where many of Barney Kerruish's small boats bobbed at anchor, yet nothing was real. The hoofbeats seemed to drum out her name perpetually so that Karran's features were superimposed on the track, the trees, the prune-black stretches of Barrule. Endlessly, he sat in the saddle, straight-backed and tireless, through Dalby and Glen Maye, by Ballchrink and Gordon, Knockaloe Moor, Corrins Hill and Thistle Head.

By the time Howard reached Peel, he could remember nothing but his urgency and a hunger that had grown on him since he glimpsed the smoking roofs and the dark garnet of the castle in shadow.

With the departure of Costain he was aware of a freedom from restraint. It would be better without Abel. His affections had been divided. Now they were whole again and able to be

227

centred on Karran. He dwelt on her with a passionate pleasure that might be strong enough to communicate itself to her where his words might fail.

The sight of the cottage made his heart beat so hard that it hurt. He tried to calm himself but could not. And he had imagined himself past such feelings!

She must have heard him approach because she flung open the door and hesitated for a moment in the gap. Then she began to run towards him, her hair flying, her face transformed by a delight that moved him unbearably.

Howard slid from the horse and waited.

It was Erin who opened the letter. The sunlight bounced off the silver coffee-pot and tray. She had enjoyed her breakfast and Barney had slapped her on the bottom as he left for his periodic look round the boatyard.

'I'll be back in an hour, my love.'

She was forgiven. Taken back into haven like one of his vessels after a storm. The twins were out for their morning perambulation and she could relax in her new houserobe until Barney returned.

She handled the letter curiously, not recognising the writing. It was addressed to them both. For a moment she was tempted to leave it. It was such a beautiful day and she felt happy again after the shock of Wheatley's cruel end. They'd reached his body eventually and the funeral had taken place. She'd been surprised by the number of people who'd attended, even if some of them might only have been hoping to be paid!

Elizabeth had written, and from the tone of her letter she was on a proper footing with Nat Gelling and hoping to wed him as quickly as was suitable. Sebastian had seemed more confident in his last epistle, and her darling Boyce was having a good time with several different girls instead of becoming too involved with that Nina person. Erin had been aware of alarm bells sounding in that quarter a few months ago.

She might as well find out what was in the letter she still held. It could be some exciting invitation. Erin broke the seal and unfolded the stiff, crackling paper. Half of her mind was on Muriel Bascombe's rout next week. They always enjoyed Muriel's suppers and she wasn't likely to ask anyone Erin actively disliked, not since that evening the Howards were there.

With a sudden sick horror, Erin forgot the Bascombes,

forgot everything except the neat, strong handwriting and the message it imparted. She could not stop reading. Again and again the terrible words imprinted themselves on her mind.

Nausea and dizziness rose up in her. The room shifted and swayed, the shapes and colours dimmed, whirling like fragments in a pool. She slid from the chair to lie still on the snuff-coloured carpet.

Barney came in unsuspecting. His heart thumped. She — wasn't dead? She couldn't be! She mustn't be. He couldn't visualise his life without her. Running blindly, he upset small tables and stools in his blundering haste.

Lifting her head he saw that her face was the colour of skimmed milk. But she was breathing. He bawled for someone to bring feathers and tapers and the disagreeable smell soon brought Erin to her senses. A window was opened.

Her huge eyes dilated as he assisted her to the sofa. Something was on the carpet where she had lain.

'Please — give it to me, Barney. It's nothing —'

'Nothing? How can it be nothing?' He picked up the letter and smoothed out the crumpled folds.

'Don't read it. I beg you —'

He hesitated in the face of her distress then said, 'If it's trouble we must share it. Isn't that what we agreed? What are you waiting for, Mary? Take that mess back to the kitchen and be quick about it. '

When the door closed behind the woman, he again lifted the sheet of paper and stared at it, first curiously, then becoming red-faced with anger and revulsion.

'Don't work yourself up,' Erin whispered. 'There's some mistake. That boy's lying.'

'No, he's not,' Barney said and now he was grey. 'That filthy young swine. It's going to look good, isn't it, spread about our friends. And enemies.'

'You've no enemies, Barney.'

'Every businessman has enemies. We'll be lucky ever to hold up our heads again.'

'But we can afford to pay, can't we?' Erin had started to tremble.

'Aye. But can I do it time and time again?'

'But this once! Make it plain you'll go to Bow Street next time. Only pay him off, Barney. For my sake. It was bad enough after Jesse. I didn't say much then because I was younger and I was sure of your love enduring.'

'Haven't I made it plain it still does?'

'You're older too and it can hurt to be condemned. You've had to suffer for all of us. Me. Elizabeth and now Sebastian. It's a rotten old family you've tied yourself to. A liar, an adulteress and —'

'A pederast.' Barney did not refute Erin's summing up.

'It wouldn't be Sebastian! That boy led him astray.' And wouldn't he have to be a man to be what Barney called him?

'He didn't seem to be unwilling, according to this.' Barney tapped the rustling paper.

'That boy would have to say that. Make it sound worse than it is —'

'Could it be any worse?' he asked wearily.

Erin looked away. 'No.'

'I suppose Bailey must be paid.'

'And — Sebastian?'

'Will leave that sink of iniquity.'

'You sent him there, Barney.'

After a minute he said, 'I did. But from the best of motives. Now I want him as far away from us as possible.'

'What does that mean?' she asked in a small voice.

'My cousin Frank.'

Erin half-rose, then subsided again. 'But Frank lives —' Her voice died away.

'Yes, my dear. Australia. It's a hard land. He'll not be encouraged to disport himself over there. I could kill him with my bare hands for distressing you so! It'll be for the best. You'll see.' He patted her shoulder with rough kindness.

She did not move or speak. Erin saw Sebastian lying on the cottage floor, his arms held out to her. Sebastian toddling, his hands forever clutching at her skirts. He had loved her to distraction. And now he loved men. She felt sick and there was a heavy load on her heart. Too heavy to shift. How had she come to have such children? What had she done that was so wrong? Her mother always maintained there was nothing wrong with a modicum of healthy neglect. Erin experienced a pang of homesickness that was almost a physical pain for her childhood home in Ireland.

'Erin?'

She shook off Barney's hand. 'Just leave me alone. You seem to have decided for yourself. You don't need me to agree or disagree. But he is my son. Maybe if he'd stayed in Castletown — ?'

'He'd only have fouled your doorstep. There's nothing that would have changed.'

'We can't know.'

Barney, seeing that nothing would at present rouse Erin from her unhappy state, rang for Mary to fetch her mistress some tea. He then went off to the bank to arrange the transfer of the money demanded by Richard Bailey and to tie up the loose ends of his business. He'd have to fetch that young satyr himself, not that his gorge didn't rise at the prospect. How Erin could have produced someone like Sebastian it was impossible to envisage.

The Kinrades were a strange lot and so were the Clives. All the way to the bank Barney thought of the letter he'd found in Wheatley's desk. A letter sealed and addressed to Karran Kinrade. He'd had it delivered to that cottage in Peel. Not that he wouldn't have given a deal to have known what was in it.

It made one wonder if it had been an accident or if Wheatley had arranged his own death. Ironic really, when the blast had opened up a new and rich lode of ore. Timothy Clive was going to be the wealthiest child on the island. They were already digging the new shaft above the site of the explosion.

Barney remembered Charlotte just as he reached his destination. He was going to have to reach some decision over his daughter and Costain. Who'd have thought Charlotte would turn out to be so strong? But to wed a man with virtually one arm. His only child! He cursed silently and pushed open the door.

'Well?' Abel said. He and Charlotte were walking on the shore. His arm hung stifly. He tried to move the black-gloved fingers but they did not respond. There was only the gnawing pain that seemed likely to attend him for the rest of his life. Someone must pay for that. 'What did your father say?'

'That we must wait. That there's no hurry.'

The blood pounded in his head. He couldn't lose Charlotte now to her father's caution. Howard's generous payment wouldn't keep him for ever and he was useless without that one talent. He must be cushioned in the long future ahead of him. But Charlotte could turn against him in one of his black moods. She still did not understand why he had left Howard's to return to Port St Mary. The rather lame story of Karran's jealousy of him and of the girl's trouble-making had had a quiet reception. He was afraid that his irritation would become more difficult to contain as time went on. And if there were any rumours later about the real reason for his break with Howard, he'd prefer Charlotte totally in thrall. Even her patience and understanding were not limitless. There had to be a bond that could not be broken.

'But there is!' Abel insisted softly. 'And I do have means.'

'Papa says he'll think about it again when he comes back.'

'Comes back?' His voice sharpened.

'Yes. From fetching Bastian from Elizabeth's. He ran away from school. Mama says he'd got into bad company. And he was bullied. Bastian would hate that.'

'Yes, he would. How long is your father going to be away?'

'It could take some time. He says he'all attend to some business while he's over in Liverpool.'

Abel experienced stirrings of triumph. 'And your mama?'

'She hasn't been well. Papa thought she should stay at home and rest.'

'Rest?'

'Stay in bed in the mornings and be cosseted by the servants. Retire early.'

'It doesn't sound like your mama.'

Charlotte frowned. 'No. I thought she could be pretending. Trying to wheedle somthing out of Papa. But she doesn't seem interested in anything he tried to tempt her with, not even an escritoire she wanted violently only a matter of a month ago. I didn't think she cared enough for any of us to react in the way she has.'

'Mother love is incalculable.'

'I suppose so.' Charlotte looked at him consideringly. 'Speaking of calculations —'

'Were we?' He gave her the full benefit of his studiedly brave, and attractive, smile.

'You know what I mean. How are you, mathematics wise?'

'Reasonable. My father kept me up to the mark.'

'I'm not supposed to tell anyone this, but the Donaghue will be needing a new manager. Just before he was killed, Wheatley told the previous man he'd best look for another post as he'd not be staying open much longer. Then, after they cleared the mess away, there was a far better seam exposed than exists in any of Foxdale mines. It·seems awful that Wheatley had to die in order to uncover it. They said he'd misjudged the gunpowder charge. Seems funny when he'd done it several times before but he could have been tired and careless. You — can still write, I suppose?'

'Yes. I've always been ambidextrous.'

'You mean, you'll be able to paint as well?'

232

She had touched the raw nerve.

'No, I *don't* mean that.'

'Sorry.' She was hurt.

'Now there's no need to bite that pretty lip. It's my fault for being so snappish. '

'You have every right to moments of rebellion.'

'How loyal of you. But how could you cope with those moments if we're always together?'

'Always?'

'Married. You already know I want to marry you. We've talked of little else recently.'

'I'm sure Papa won't make me wait too long —'

'Why must he make you wait at all? When I want, and need, you so much?'

For Charlotte the day became almost too bright to bear. the sunlight struck back from the flat, pale sand so that she had to close her eyes. That timbre of his voice with its passionate regret. Her body was flooded with delicious warmth. She'd make him forget his shattered hand. Fill his life with interest. If they were wed, Papa would have to make him mine manager. Give him back self-respect.

A gull shrieked and broke the bubble of peace.

'I — need you just as much,' she admitted.

'When we both feel the same and I am so desirous of marrying you, would it be so dreadful if — ?'

'If — what?'

'If we — anticipated the ceremony?' Again that gallant, beautiful smile. 'Who's to know? I might die tonight and never have known you.'

They had reached the dunes and there was not a soul in sight. The sea rushed up as though it would engulf them.

Charlotte could not speak for breathlessness.

'No one would know. How could they? We are alone, Charlotte. I've been here a dozen times of late and never seen a soul. And it's fitting it should be here. Didn't we meet on a beach? We could meet every morning that your mama is recuperating and your papa is in Liverpool.

'Stay here with me now and make me the happiest man in the world. I'd rather have you with the ring on your finger but since he refuses to consent, that's not possible. What do you say, my darling? Charlotte?'

She had never understood the full meaning of the story of the Garden of Eden until this moment. It would hurt to deceive Barney but it would hurt much more to disappoint

Abel. It was a miracle that he felt as she did.

The age-old struggle between what Charlotte had been taught and what her new woman's mind and body desired went on for agonised minutes, while they both looked out to sea as if nothing concerned them but the shattering arcs of the green waves.

Charlotte sighed.

Abel's heart plummeted. How could he get the girl pregnant without her co-operation? It was the one trump card that would move her father. He said stiffly, 'I see that I misjudged the depth of your feelings. I suppose it was too much to hope for.'

She turned on him a gaze that was almost the green of the waves and filled with an intensity that made him want to laugh. Not that he could! His role was that of the agonised suitor. The man who had suffered and now needed the healing ministrations of the woman he loved. A doubt assailed him of his ability to pleasure Charlotte when he disliked both her face and body. He must make himself overcome the distaste. Remember Kerruish and his comfortable fortunes. Think well upon Charlotte's position as his sole heir. It was common knowledge that he found his wife's offspring sadly lacking, particularly of late. Abel had made it his business to find out everything possible about the family he meant to infiltrate like some unholy cuckoo.

'You didn't,' Charlotte said in a stifled voice.

'Didn't what?' He evinced convincing surprise.

'Misjudge.' The colour ran unbecomingly into the dark-skinned cheeks.

Oh God, he thought, I feel tired already, but it must be done. If it's not perfect she'll imagine it to be her fault. I'll tell her it gets better. He smiled as if overcome. Gratefully. Transported —

'Charlotte!' A husky whisper. A glimpse of the black-gloved hand to flick at her sympathies. The grasp of his whole hand and a purposeful step towards the windblown dunes. It would be the only purposeful thing about the entire proceeding. 'My darling.'

Mutely, she allowed him to take her where he would.

John Howard had forgotten Charlotte Kerruish and his good intentions. He had given thought to none of the family. The first time he'd recall the word he'd meant for Barney would be when he heard of the somewhat hasty wedding.

Howard was too bound up in his own affairs. The new lightness of the atmosphere at Ravensdowne was as heady as a good wine and he could not waste a moment of it. He had perhaps twenty years left and Emily had eaten up so much of his youth. Karran's white witch of an aunt had freed him to embark upon a similar space of happiness. It seemed like Fate.

Looking from the window, he saw Karran in a white dress, walking on the pebbly shore with Bart. They were both laughing, immersed in each other's company. How handsome Bart was. Howard tried to picture him in twenty years' time when he himself was ready for death and saw only — Karran.

Disturbed, he opened the window and leaned out calling to her. They both looked up, simultaneously, their faces echoes of one another. Echoes of yesterday. Yesterday —

THE END

ECHOING YESTERDAY
by Alexandra Manners

Clemence was a child of the Island . . . fair, wild, with an ethereal beauty, she seemed at one with the moors, the wind and the surging seas. It was inevitable that the near-pagan Luke Karran would be fascinated by her – drawn to her beauty – wanting to take her silvery fragile fairness and crush it as he would a butterfly . . .

As the people of the island – the farmers, the fishermen, the miners, who were her people also – watched the unfolding of their passionate courtship, a whole new saga was born – a story as tempestuous as the elements that raged around THE ISLAND . . .

0 552 12084 7   £1.50

ZEMINDAR
by Valerie Fitzgerald

To Laura Hewitt, India was an exciting challenge – an India of extravagant princes, of the British Raj, of the first rumblings of disquiet and tension smouldering silently from state to state.

Laura had travelled there as the companion of her indulged newly-wed cousin Emily – trying, on the journey to suppress both her love for Charles, and her resentment of Emily who had stolen Charles from her.

Their destination was the kingdom of Oudh, to the vast zemindar estate of Charles's unknown brother, Oliver Erskine. And even before Laura had set foot on land she heard tales, rumours, conjecture about Oliver Erskine, the ZEMINDAR.

0 552 99019 1   £2.50

A WOMAN OF TWO CONTINENTS
by Pixie Burger

The superbly dramatic story of a passionate woman pursuing her destiny in two worlds . . .

From the elegance of the London Season, to the plains and mountains of Argentina . . . from a luxurious villa on the riviera, to an estancia in South America . . .

She was an Anglo-Argentine – clinging fiercely to the old life-style – to a world of Edwardian garden parties and formal elegance, a woman in a land dominated by men . . .

0 552 12142 8   £1.95

TILLY TROTTER
by Catherine Cookson

'CATHERINE COOKSON is a major storyteller: her gift for narrative and for characterization convinces and intrigues' SHE magazine

Set amidst the bustling Tyneside towns of County Durham during the reign of young Queen Victoria, TILLY TROTTER is the compelling story of a young girl living happily with her grandparents on the edge of the Sopwith estate.

But hard times lie ahead for beautiful, slim Matilda. Envied by the women for her unusual beauty, lusted after by the men, Tilly is accused of witchcraft, experiences the cruel drudgery of working in the local coal-mines, and knows the heartache of a passionate love that is not returned. Yet Tilly emerges as a courageous young girl with a strong instinct for survival . . .

0 552 11737 4 £1.95

CHASING RAINBOWS
by Esther Sager

A DAZZLING STORY OF LOVE, ENDURING COURAGE AND SOARING TRIUMPH!

As small girls, the two sisters had been inseparable. Warm-hearted Libby, adored by her silver-blonde younger sister, Winna. Then a childhood accident changed her life forever . . .

But as she grew into a beautiful young woman, Libby taught herself to overcome the physical disadvantages of her handicap. Then she met Adam – cynical, disillusioned and heir to the Bainbridge millions. Just as Libby was beginning to accept his love, Winna walked back into their lives . . . And Libby found that searching for love was just like CHASING RAINBOWS . . .

0 552 11981 4 £1.50

THE MARIGOLD FIELD
by Diane Pearson

THE MARIGOLD FIELD is a story of poor, proud, high-spirited people . . . people whose roots were in the farming country of southern England . . . in the bawdy and exuberant streets of the East End.

Jonathan Whitman, his cousin Myra, Anne-Louise Pritchard and the enormous Pritchard clan to which she belonged, saw the changing era and incredible events of a passing age – an age of great poverty and great wealth, of straw boaters, feather boas, and the Music Hall . . .

And above all THE MARIGOLD FIELD is a story of one woman's consuming love . . . of a jealous obsession that threatened to destroy the very man she adored . . .

'An exceptionally good read. One of those *comfortable* books you can live in for a while with pleasure.' – *McCalls Magazine*

'When Maxie takes Anne-Louise home on Sunday, when his relations assemble loudly at the meal-table . . . there is an instant of the finest, broadest comedy . . .' – *Sunday Times*

If you have enjoyed this book, you can follow the continuing of the Whitman family in SARAH WHITMAN, the superb sequel by Diane Pearson.

0 552 10271 7   £1.75

SARAH WHITMAN
by Diane Pearson

A 'God is an Englishman' kind of novel – about a very human kind of Englishwoman, a woman who fought her way up from domestic service to schoolmistress and whose life was touched by three men, one who taught her what it was to love and be loved, another who waited for her in vain, and a third – the strange tormented man who was to be her destiny.

Rich in adventure, history and human passions, this is a novel of astonishing breadth . . . and enthralling panorama of life and love between the wars . . .

'The very stuff of reality . . . SARAH is superb.' Norah Lofts

0 552 10414 0   £1.75

A SELECTED LIST OF FINE NOVELS AVAILABLE IN CORGI PAPERBACK

While every effort is made to keep prices low, it is sometimes necessary to increase prices at short notice. Corgi Books reserve the right to show new retail prices on covers which may differ from those previously advertised in the text or elsewhere.

The prices shown below were correct at the time of going to press.

ORDER FORM

All these books are available at your book shop or newsagent, or can be ordered direct from the publisher. Just tick the titles you want and fill in the form below.

CORGI BOOKS, Cash Sales Department, P.O. Box 11, Falmouth, Cornwall.

Please send cheque or postal order, no currency.

Please allow cost of book(s) plus the following for postage and packing:

U.K. Customers—Allow 45p for the first book, 20p for the second book and 14p for each additional book ordered, to a maximum charge of £1.63.

B.F.P.O. and Eire—Allow 45p for the first book, 20p for the second book plus 14p per copy for the next seven books, thereafter 8p per book.

Overseas Customers—Allow 75p for the first book and 21p per copy for each additional book.

NAME (Block Letters) ....

ADDRESS ....

....